Dead Woman's Curse

K.M. Martinez

ISBN-979-8-9871186-0-3
Ebook ISBN-979-8-9871186-1-0

For my family who supported me through the crazy times.

Chapter One

The atrium was cool, a sharp contrast to the scorching weather outside. The skylight overhead spanned the entire ceiling, its glass a cataclysm of color—red, green, blue, and orange—and gave way to a proud golden sun that winked merrily down on the sole occupant below. It was there that Melanie Mendez of Clan Kale stood. She stared up, not admiring the glass but instead looking through the window as if it wasn't there at all. She was looking past it, into the world beyond the pretty shield of color.

Mel liked to think she wasn't a fool, but as she stood ramrod straight, warring with reason and reluctance, she had to wonder: *Maybe I'm not the smartest person in the world.* It was a difficult decision she was set to make in a few moments—a decision that would irrevocably change the course of her life—but she had little choice. There was no going back. There was only one way to go: forward.

And yet questions plagued her.

Can I do this? Will it do any good? Will they listen?

Before she could come to a decision, *Sapienti* Mari Mendez, Mel's grandmother and Elder to Clan Kale, walked through the massive wooden doors. Robed resplendently in Kale gold, she sat languidly on one of the many benches that lined the room. Her compact body hardly took up any space on the bench.

"So?" the older woman prompted, adjusting her black sash so it didn't touch the floor. She leveled dark brown eyes at Mel. The tight bun that held her grey hair made her tanned, weathered face look severe.

"I have reservations," Mel said after a long moment, her weariness bleeding through. She ran a tired hand through her long, disheveled brown hair. That morning, when she'd looked in the mirror, her normally tanned complexion had looked peaky, and her brown eyes were bloodshot. She was exhausted. Mel was starting to think her time in the land between Hell and the living was having an effect. Since she and Core O'Shea of Clan Ferus had returned from *Inter Spatium Abyssus* three days before, she'd gotten almost no sleep, which had led to this creeping weariness in her bones.

"I'd be surprised if you didn't," *Sapienti* Mendez responded, raising a hand. "But a tribunal will clear the air. It's exactly what's needed to get the other clans aligned."

Something needled Mel in the back of her skull. She rubbed a hand down the back of her neck.

The night before, while she had sat tiredly at the kitchen table, poking at her dinner, her grandmother had asked her if she'd be willing to speak at a tribunal and give testimony about the traitors, the Eighth Clan, and their actions at this year's Agora. Atrocities, led by Anton Morel of Clan Janso and *Sapienti* Wershall of Clan Ivor, had led to the death of many clanspeople. The deaths had enraged everyone, including clans Mayme and Tam, which were normally the most even-tempered of all the clans.

Yet Mel was feeling torn about the request, and not quite sure why. Only days ago, she had been wanting to tell her story. *What's wrong with me?* she thought.

She looked at her grandmother, steeling her resolve.

"I don't think this is the way," she finally said, and the ache in her head eased.

Sapienti Mendez made a frustrated noise. "Then what, Mel? What else are we to do? They want your head right now. If you speak of the events, then we can at least circumvent *some* of the violence. Some clanspeople will believe you."

Some, not all, Mel thought, and her grandmother knew that as well. Not everyone would accept her testimony.

Again that cold needle slid down, its edge ragged and ripping.

"No," she said.

"No?" Low, menacing. *How dare you* was unspoken but clearly implied. "You refuse?"

"We can't fight a battle with the other clans as well as the Eighth," Mel replied. "That's what we would be doing. Even with Clan Ferus on our side, it's too much. Clan Moors is ready to explode now that *Sapienti* Messer has died."

"Mel—"

"The problem is *me*," Mel continued with a rush, pacing the floor. "They don't trust me. We need to dampen their ire, and my testimony at a tribunal will only stoke it. Too many of their brothers and sisters were traitors, and my revealing that will merely hasten the divide. They will balk at the thought of their own clanspeople betraying our ways."

"Do you have another solution?" *Sapienti* Mendez asked.

"They're not ready to face…"

Mel trailed off. That needle stuck sharply in the base of her skull, and something slipped loose from around her chest.

There's only one path. You know this. You have to walk it…

****

A slap on the table stirred her out of her chair. She jumped to her feet, heart stuttering, ready to fight. But it was just Gabe. Mel's younger brother looked down on her surprised face and laughed. His brown hair was a mess, his face unshaved, but his spirits were high, his smile bright, and his brown eyes shining. He was just happy she was here with him, alive, and batted her hands down playfully when she halfheartedly tried to slap the small mustache off his face.

"Come on, lunch is ready. Better get some before Victor finishes it all." He leaned over the table, interested. "What's this? Are you doing spells? No wonder you dozed off. That's boring stuff."

A book, *Purging With Fire,* was open on the table where she was sitting, and various glyphs and symbols in *Old Tongue* were scratched into her notebook. *Seek,* one line revealed. *Destroy,* said another, and in the middle was a wretched-looking skull with a spiral spinning out of its grotesque mouth.

Gabe pulled her along as she blinked blearily, wondering how she'd ended up in the library. *Wasn't I just in the atrium?*

It was a sign of how tired she was that she let him lead her by the hand like a child. She *felt* like a child. She wished she had the *responsibilities* of a child. All she'd have to do was wake up and go to school. But no.

"I hear Grandma's not forcing you to testify at the tribunal," Gabe said as they walked the halls.

"What?" she said, confused. "Really?"

"Really. The new plan is *so* much better. Thrash said a lot of clanspeople have already cooled since the announcement. Can you believe it? They're being conciliatory toward *us.*"

Mel was too tired to think about what Gabe's words meant. "Well… that's great," she said.

Am I dead or am I dreaming? she wondered, squeezing Gabe's hand so tight he squawked. *Is this real life?*

When she tried to leave the house for some fresh air before lunch, Drew Wiley cut her off with his tall body, blocking her and gently directing her back to the table. So did Tío Jorge when she tried the front door, so she bemusedly gave in, falling into a chair with a shake of her head.

When she finally had enough sense to question her predicament, Gabe gave her a quizzical look over his plate of arroz con pollo and related that it was her own doing—that she needed to stay out of sight.

"No going back! No backsies!" he said, shaking his fork at her.

Dread filled her then—because she didn't know what he was talking about. But before she could ask, he took off in search of Siva Reddy. And after that, the dread didn't last long. In fact, it floated away like dandelion seeds in the wind.

Time kept blending as it does when one has declined into punch-drunk exhaustion. Yet Mel kept going. She had nowhere to be and no one to see, but she paced the house like an animal. She was already regretting the decision not to speak at the tribunal. She just knew it was the reason she was stuck in this house. *I should've just done the damn testimony.* It would've meant freedom. It would've meant war with the clans, too, but still… *freedom.* Now she was stuck in the house, out of sight of everyone but a trusted few. The cage made her skin clammy.

After a while, she looked for a bed to fall into. But her room was too close to her cousin Charlotte's—even though they were at opposite ends of the house. Everywhere was too close. Her cousin was lying pale and unconscious, and Tía Alice wailed like a siren whenever she went in there. It was awful. Just thinking about Charlotte made a heavy guilt settle on Mel. She should've known Wershall's dark stone was dangerous. She should've never left it alone for Charlotte to grab. Now her cousin was barely alive.

Mel's grandmother had tried everything to revive her—and failed. The First Healer had now taken over her care, but still there was no change. And for this, Mel felt a deep sadness in her soul. She wept when she dwelled too much on it.

So she tried not to.

Instead, she stalked around the house in the dead of night, feet creaking on floorboards. Victor woke and watched her with his steely brown eyes but said nothing. He just sat his massive body on the stairs, and every time she rounded the corner, there he was, shaved head gleaming in the falling light, massive hands resting on his knees.

When she finally grew too tired to stand, she gave up—and ended up on the floor. She dreamt of blood and sinew ripped from torn bodies. Bones splintered and cracking. All of it echoing in her ears as men and women screamed. As Death screamed.

Her sleep was fitful, and she yearned to wake from it, but it kept her trapped in its clutches. The more she tried to stir, the deeper she burrowed into its snare.

A woman appeared. Her glowing gold eyes shimmered in the darkness, watching with keen interest. She said nothing. Just watched with a countenance drawn in disappointment…

Hours passed, but it felt like only minutes before warm hands found Mel's face. She opened her eyes to find shrewd green ones looking down at her.

The First Healer, Isis Trevino.

"I thought you were Cori," Mel said, dazed.

"Sorry," the First Healer responded. Her gold wire-rimmed glasses hung by a thin chain around her neck. Her skin had a sallow look, but otherwise she looked sprightly and well-rested. She frowned. "You're not well."

No shit, Mel thought. Then closed her eyes and fell once more into a light slumber that provided no rest.

****

"I have a confession," she announced the next afternoon. She was among a small gathering of Kales in the atrium. "I don't know what you all are talking about."

"We're talking about *you*," her grandmother said.

Mel blinked slowly and stared at her grandmother for way too long. Long enough that her grandmother furrowed her brow.

"Someone needs to guard you," *Sapienti* Mendez explained.

"What?" Mel asked.

"You're the heir, Mel," said the First Healer. "You need someone to lead your guard. Especially since you're…" Her words died off. She gave Mel's grandmother a concerned look before turning her eyes to Mel again.

"I know you feel you don't need one," her grandmother added, "but this is non-negotiable."

Mel felt anger stir in her gut. She would *not* have a guard. Was it not enough that she was cooped up in the house? Now she needed someone to *watch* her? No. That was where she drew the line. She drew air into her lungs and prepared for the fight to come.

"Thomas."

That was *not* what she had meant to say. *Sapienti* Mendez and the First Healer looked as confused as Mel felt. She cleared her throat and took a short breath, ready to correct herself. She didn't need a babysitter. That was what she had meant to say. And she would say it. Right now.

"Thomas Thorn will lead my guard."

"Thorn is a good choice," her grandmother said. "Recall him. I want him here as soon as possible—before the services begin. We have Kales attending from all over. Then there are the other clans who have yet to vacate the property…"

Her grandmother's voice faded out as Mel looked at the skylight. *What is happening to me? Why am I feeling so goddamn adrift?*

Feeling eyes on her, she turned. The First Healer was staring at her. Isis pointed at her own wrist—the healer's way of reminding Mel of her appointment. Mel decided she'd ask her some questions then.

7

Isis would know. And if she didn't, Mel would root out the answer.

Mel leaned her head back again, looking at the colors above. *Where is Cori?* She hadn't seen the Ferus in… well, she didn't know how long it had been. But she would really like to see her. She missed her voice and her hair and her eyes and her smile…

"Come on, Mel," a quiet voice said. Thrash. His soft brown eyes looked hollow. His chin-length hair fell into his face. "Come on, you need sleep." He grabbed her hand, pulling her out of the atrium. Mel was thankful for his short stature as she threw an arm over his shoulder. "Real sleep," he continued. "Not that shit you been doing on the floor in the living room. What are you, an animal? Get a real bed, loser."

They walked up the stairs to her room. Mel looked toward the opposite side of the hall, where Charlotte's room was, but it was quiet. No siren-wail this time. Only a silent guard standing up against the wall.

Mel let go of Thrash, pushed through her bedroom door, slipped her pants off, and slid under the covers.

Sleep came with a warm amber light behind her eyelids. Comfortable, she sank deep into the calm, her breath even and slow. Her heart pushing and pulling. Pushing and pulling…

****

What a wonder two days' rest can do for you. Mel woke feeling so much more like herself. She washed up and sat down for a quick breakfast of sausage and eggs that Victor had made. Hunger had finally made an appearance after several days of queasiness, and she scarfed everything down with gusto. Her gaze moved to the kitchen window when she heard the flurry of activity outside. Kales were walking off into the forest toward the Kale memorials, preparing to attend the first day of the Death Rites. Nineteen clanspeople had died the night *Sapienti* Wershall opened the gate in the pit, and now the rest of the clan would start the process of putting their dead to rest.

Mel bit her lip as she watched them walk in the early-morning gloom.

"Don't even think about it," Victor said, pushing more eggs onto her plate.

Mel raised her brows at her older brother. He was dressed in his finest tunic, the one he used for special occasions.

"You're thinking about joining us, but you can't," he said. "No one can see you, Mel."

"And *why* can't they see me?" she asked, remembering how just about everyone had kept her inside the house.

"You know why," Victor said, after draining a whole glass of orange juice.

"Actually I don't. Remind me."

An eyebrow climbed up Victor's forehead as he studied his sister. "You're serious? You don't remember?"

Just then Gabe, their younger brother, came in. "Victor!" he said. "Come on. Grandma's waiting." He quickly piled egg and sausage on a slice of toast before folding it in half, then stuffed the entire thing in his mouth at once.

Victor got up from his seat and put his dishes in the sink. "We'll talk more about this when I get back," he said to her. "But no bullshit. Don't leave this fucking house. I'm not fucking around, Mel."

"You ain't the boss of me. You ain't my daddy, neither," she sassed him, following her brothers into the sitting room where her grandmother stood waiting.

Sapienti Mendez turned as they walked in, but Mel's attention was on the double doors leading outside, where a figure in white and beige was approaching.

"Is that Siva coming by?" she asked Gabe.

Gabe looked out the doors. "Hell no, that ain't Siva!" He grabbed Mel by the arm and pulled her back into the kitchen out of view.

"This is just how I wanted my morning to start," Mel grumbled. "Ordered by one sibling to stay in the house, and manhandled by the other like some wayward kid."

"Shut up," Gabe said.

They heard the door open, then their grandmother spoke.

"Cleo Newberry," she said. "What can I do for you?"

"I've come to announce my presence and inform you that I am acting as representative for Clan Mayme," answered the rich voice of Cleo Newberry. "As you know, Clan Mayme is in the midst of choosing an Elder, so I will be envoy while we are guests in your territory."

"I see," *Sapienti* Mendez said. "And have any other Maymes arrived?"

"I brought three in my retinue," Newberry answered. "But they, as well as the rest of my clan, will stay out of your way. We do not wish to inconvenience you any more than we must."

"It's no inconvenience," *Sapienti* Mendez replied. "Thank you for announcing yourself. And please, let my son Luce know if there's anything that can be done to make your stay more comfortable."

"Actually, *Sapienti*," Newberry replied, not acknowledging the dismissal, "I wish to express my sympathies. I hope your granddaughter is at rest."

Charlotte isn't dead yet, Mel thought angrily. *Must everyone act like she is?*

"I also wanted to speak to you about a matter that has been brought to my attention," Newberry continued. "I've noticed there has been some activity around your home…"

Mel peeked her head around the corner. She wanted a look at this

Mayme that saw fit to bring Kale business to her grandmother's doorstep moments before the Death Rites. Cleo Newberry was a tall African-American woman in her mid-forties. She had short-cropped copper hair, and hazel eyes that kept looking everywhere but at *Sapienti* Mendez.

Gabe hurriedly pulled Mel back behind the wall before those flinty hazel eyes could catch sight of her.

"Some of my clansmen saw your First Healer with a bone knife chanting while carving glyphs on the entrances and windows," Newberry finished.

"Yes, our First Healer is known for such things," *Sapienti* Mendez replied lightly. She didn't elaborate further.

"Most clanspeople would think of such things as overzealous," replied Newberry. "But I think we both know it's a sign of the times ahead."

"I agree," *Sapienti* Mendez said. Mel heard the doors swinging open. "Now, if you please—we have rites to attend this morning."

Mel and Gabe stepped out only after the doors had closed behind the Mayme. Victor and *Sapienti* Mendez were watching Newberry walk back to the tents.

"Drew Wiley reported that *twelve* Maymes arrived with her two days ago," Victor said.

"A Parliament?" Mel asked.

"Not just any Parliament," said *Sapienti* Mendez. "Cleo Newberry and her cohorts were involved in serious crimes against their fellow clanspeople. Janice never told me the specifics, but she did imply that many Maymes died as a result of the woman's actions. Newberry was banished as a result. This is the first time I've seen her in over twenty years."

Gabe leaned casually against the wall. "Siva says she's not one to mess with. Newberry is the best and worst of Clan Mayme.

Intelligent but also a *true* bird of prey."

"Are the Maymes following her?" Mel asked. "I would think since she was responsible for the deaths of so many that there would be dissension among them."

"At first there was," Gabe replied with a shrug. "But now they've all fallen in line."

Mel pondered this. Clan Mayme was always the peaceful sort, but they weren't weak, and they would never follow Cleo Newberry if the woman was making a grab for power. It made no sense for Clan Mayme to bring someone of Newberry's repute back into the clan, much less send her as their envoy. It was so unlike every experience she'd ever had with the clan… and made Mel wonder what the hell was going on with Clan Mayme.

****

After everyone else left for the Rites, the house felt large and abandoned. Mel retreated to her room with a sigh. But as she got to the landing, on an impulse she decided instead to go to Charlotte's room for a quick visit.

But she stopped when she heard soft muttering from within.

She looked at the guard still posted at her cousin's door. "How long has my aunt been inside?" she asked quietly.

The guard, Justine Wiley, looked at Mel with serious eyes. Mel's clanswoman was not one to be trifled with. With a smart mouth and even smarter hands, the short blond was a formidable fighter. But even she would not want to be in Mel's shoes at the moment. Tía Alice had made it very clear she blamed Mel for Charlotte's condition.

"Only about five minutes," Justine said.

Mel contemplated going back to her room until her aunt left. But judging from past experience, she knew her aunt might well stay with

Charlotte late into the night. Besides, Mel had been intending to talk to her aunt—whenever she calmed down.

I've waited long enough, she thought as she reached for the knob.

"Let me accompany you," Justine said, stepping from the wall.

Mel stepped through the door and felt a hollow ache in her chest at the sight of her cousin. Charlotte lay on her back, eyes shut, as if she were slumbering peacefully—but her normally tanned skin was pale, and her usually lustrous light-brown hair was listless and greasy.

Tía Alice was holding Charlotte's hand and singing a lullaby. She didn't stop or even look up as Mel entered the room, just kept her eyes on Charlotte's face. Mel's aunt looked as bad as Charlotte did. Her brown hair was frizzy, there were bruises under her eyes from lack of sleep, and her pale, drawn face made it clear that she'd been crying.

Mel sat gingerly on the bed, close to the footboard. She didn't push for conversation. She just needed to see her cousin and make sure Charlotte was still holding on to life. She placed a hand on Charlotte's ankle and rubbed it soothingly through the blanket. If Charlotte still possessed any awareness at all, Mel hoped she knew she was there with her.

Tía Alice's singing broke off. "You shouldn't be here."

Mel's breath hitched. She kept her eyes on Charlotte's face, not daring to look at her aunt. Not wanting to see the anger there.

Justine moved closer, but said nothing. She merely watched the two, looking for any sign of impending violence.

"Tia, I'm sorry," Mel said. *I tried to get her home safe.* "Please, I ju—"

"*Go*," her aunt said. Her voice was terrible. Like gravel. Fraught with pain.

Mel sighed in disappointment. She moved to get up… but not quickly enough.

"I said *go*! *Go!*" her aunt screamed. *"Get out of here! Get out! Get out! Get OUT!"*

Tía Alice leapt to her feet, moving furiously toward Mel.

Justine quickly stepped between them. "Okay, calm down," she said, holding the older woman's arms gently. "Please."

"*Don't* tell me to calm down! This is her fault. It's *all her fault!*" She called Mel every curse word in the book, and punctuated it by spitting on Mel's shirt.

Mel felt her face growing red with embarrassment. With one last look at Charlotte, she departed, anger and resentment in every step. Fuming, she fled to her room and slammed the door behind her. She grabbed the chair from her desk and heaved it across the room. It crashed into the wall and fell to the floor.

Belatedly, she remembered the room she was in used to be her mother's—and so had the desk and the chair. With remorse, she picked the chair off the floor, set it down gently, and sat in it. Her gaze found the picture of her parents on the nightstand. It was a wedding photo, with both dressed in their finest. Her dad—who Victor was the spitting image of—was wearing a nice black suit with no clan colors. He had a wide body, short-cropped hair, and a clean-shaven face. His brown eyes sparkled as he looked at Mel's mother, who wore a fine gold dress and a wide smile. Mel's appearance favored her mother; they shared the same brown eyes, dark wavy hair, and bronze skin.

"Sorry, Mom," she said, wiping away angry tears. "Sorry."

She gave herself one whole minute to feel sorry for herself, then she got up, locked her door, and threw her closet open. She changed into a gold tunic and pants, finely made for special occasions. The tunic was sleeveless, with black stitching up and down the edges. Then she put on her sash, a black one that had belonged to her mother, wrapping it around her waist.

She made to grab her wristbands that were on the bedside table…
but they were gone. *Goddamn it, Victor!* The wristbands had secret
blades hidden within, and she knew her brother had been eyeing
them. He must've taken them without her knowing.

She was slipping on her boots when a knock sounded on her door.

"Mel!" It was Thomas. The grizzled, black-and-grey-haired man
had arrived the night before and was staying in the next room. "Are
you okay in there? I heard a crash."

"I'm fine, Thomas," she called, tying up her laces. "Just a little
temper tantrum. I'm over it now."

She hurriedly strapped her gold swords to her back, then grabbed
the rope she had stashed, tied it securely to the wooden bed, and
pulled her window open.

"Can you open the door?" Thomas said.

"I'm good," she said, throwing the rope over and tossing one leg
over the sill. "Just a little tired. Drama makes me sleepy; I think I'm
going back to bed."

"Quit messing around, Mel, and open the door," he said gruffly.
"Your grandmother wants eyes on you at all times. Don't make this
harder than it already is."

Mel didn't respond as she slipped down the rope. She knew the
lock wouldn't hold Thomas for long, so when her feet met solid
ground, she ran swiftly from the house.

****

It was still dark out and would be for another half hour. Soon the sun
would come up and the heat would fall onto the land in waves. At the
moment, though, the temperature was bearable, which meant Mel could
be outside and not immediately start sweating through her tunic.

She felt a tinge of guilt over her antics with Thomas, but he was
strict, and she knew he would never let her attend the Death Rites.

You chose him, she reminded herself. *You hardly remember it because you were half out of your mind with sleep deprivation, but still, you chose him.* In the back of her mind, she knew she'd chosen *too* well. She would not get one over on Thomas again.

She had been walking for a few minutes when she realized she was being followed. At first, she thought it was Thomas, but he wouldn't sneak up on her, he would've just yelled out at her by now. The footsteps crunched on the dry grass, trying to quietly toe the ground as they crept up behind her. They weren't doing a very good job of it, but still, Mel paused in concern. How should she proceed?

She wanted to get to the services before they started so she could find a place out of the way where she could blend in, unrecognized— and not be hassled about sneaking out. But in her hurry out of the house, she'd foolishly left her veil behind. So much for blending in with the rest of the clan.

And now she had this follower to deal with.

She knelt, assuming a defensive position, and pulled her gold swords from their scabbards.

Three figures broke through the trees about a hundred yards back. Even in the darkness, she could see them turning their heads every which way, looking for her. Mel frowned. She had thought the men were a lot closer.

"I think they went this way," she heard one whisper, pointing in Mel's direction.

That was definitely a whisper. And yet Mel had heard it clearly from a hundred yards away. It was then she realized with a start that the three *were* trying to be quiet. Her hearing... it was just... sharper.

Well, they're too far away to catch me, she thought, preparing to move on. But before she could so much as rise to her feet, a figure in a gold tunic and breeches fell from a tree some distance away, directly between Mel and the three men.

He faced Mel's pursuers. "What are you three doing here?"

Mel couldn't see her clansman's face—he was turned away, and wearing a gold veil— but she sure did recognize his voice. Drew Wiley stood tall and broad and completely at ease.

"None of your business, Kale," said one of the three.

Drew was undeterred. "You're on Kale territory, and the area you're trying to enter is sacred."

"Bullshit," said the man. "Clan Kale is hiding something, and we're going to find out what it is." He stepped forward.

"This is a sacred area," Drew said again, his voice low. "You cannot pass."

"You going to stop us?"

In reply, Drew pulled out two long gold knives. Mel heard the sliding of metal and knew the three men were pulling out weapons as well.

She ran swiftly to Drew, but was too late to participate in a remarkably brief engagement. All three men were down by the time she was at Drew's side.

She knelt beside one of the bodies and felt for a pulse. "He's still alive," she said, surprised.

"*Sapienti* ordered no killing," Drew said. He sounded disappointed.

Mel nodded. There had been enough death already, and Mel's grandmother was trying to mend the bridges between the clans.

"You're not supposed to be out," Drew said, sheathing his knives. "At least take this."

He took off his veil and pressed it into Mel's hand. Mel rolled her eyes, but put it on without complaint.

Drew blew two shrill whistles and waited. A few minutes later, ten Kales arrived and dragged the three men to their feet. Only then did Mel recognize the men as Jansos. The Kales escorted them back to camp, no doubt to deliver them to *Sapienti* Reddy. Mel hoped they would be punished, but knew they probably wouldn't be. For all she knew, the men had been working on *Sapienti* Reddy's orders. Sandeep Reddy, unlike his brother, the late Hermanth Reddy, was a man who held suspicion and distrust for all. He would want confirmation that Mel's clan was actually attending the Rites and not meeting for another reason.

War, for instance.

She resumed her trek, and Drew fell in silently at her side.

Soon the trees opened into a grand, well-tended garden. Mel walked carefully along the bluebonnets and bluebells, trying not to trample them. Among the flowers, many stone monuments rose from the ground, each listing many names—some with too many to count. They ranged in height from five feet tall to ten, but one stood larger than any other—the newest monument, currently surrounded by the rest of Clan Kale.

Her clanspeople were clad in gold and wearing veils. Mothers held their children's hands, and fathers stood protectively over their families. One little girl, no more than six, knocked into Drew's legs, and Drew reached out to steady her before kneeling down to look in her eyes.

"Are you okay?" he asked.

"I can't—I can't find my dad," said the girl, on the verge of tears. "Everyone looks the same, and I can't take off my veil because it's disrespectful."

"Don't worry about that," Drew said. He pulled the cloth from the girl's face. "He's around here somewhere. We'll find him."

The three of them walked among the crowd, waiting for someone to recognize their missing daughter. It didn't take long. A man with an older girl and boy grabbed her and swept her into his arms.

"Chloe," he said, "what did I tell you about running off?"

"I got scared," she said, hugging him about the shoulders. "*Sapienti—*"

"Chloe, I already told you, there's no reason to be scared of *Sapienti*," her father said.

"Jody and Dan told me she was going to bury me in a hole!"

The father looked down at his two other kids.

"That is *not* what we said," said the girl. Both she and her brother were doing their best to look innocent.

"Then what *did* you say?" their father asked.

The two siblings shared a look, then looked sheepishly at their father. The boy answered this time.

"We *might* have said that *Sapienti* was going to choose a little girl to throw on the pyre during the Burning Rites. But we didn't say anything about a hole!"

Mel snorted behind her hand while the father looked at his older children with disapproval.

"What did I tell you about telling stories to your little sister?" he said sternly.

"We were just playing," said the girl, apologetically. "We didn't think she'd believe us."

The father shook his head. "You two ought to be showing some respect. You know *Sapienti* has lost so much the last few days."

With a nod of thanks to Drew, the man ushered his kids out of the way so others could pay their respects.

Mel took the opportunity to approach the monument, raising her fingers to touch the names etched there. Bradley Ignacio Alvarez. Stephanie Louis Bradley. Maria De Le Rosa. Franco Hernandez. The names went on and on…

And then Mel stopped short. Etched right there on the stone were words she had never expected to see:

Melanie R. Mendez
She gave her life for her clan.
We shall remember her forever in our hearts.

Mel's anger was instant, filling her belly with heat. She looked at Drew for an explanation.

He put a hand on her shoulder. "Are you all right?"

Before she could answer, a single whistle sounded from the woods, so shrill that it made Mel's ears ring. In an instant she was off and running toward the sound, along with most of her clan.

Drew outpaced her, and Mel fell in behind him, knowing his larger frame would cut through the crowd of runners easily. They pushed forward into the woods, and then Drew stopped so suddenly that Mel crashed into his back.

"Oh, shit. Sorry," he said.

They were trapped in a crowd of her clanspeople, all them crushed together, shoulder to shoulder.

"Get back!" a frantic voice screamed ahead of them. "Don't fucking come near! Back up! Now!"

Mel tried to push forward through the wall of bodies.

"I said move *back!*"

The crowd moved an inch backward, but no more.

Mel thought about leaving and finding out from her brothers later what the trouble had been about, but just then the wind shifted and the scent that reached her nostrils woke memories and nightmares of a hot, dead land and decayed flesh.

Death.

Drew looked at her with alarm. He opened his mouth as if to warn her—to call her by name…

… but Mel already knew. Knew she was about to present herself openly, and could do nothing to stop it.

Already her clanspeople were parting, the dense wall of bodies falling away. Mel walked through them easily, ignoring them as they clutched fists to hearts and bowed their heads.

On the ground before them was a man in Kale gold, lying spread-eagle on his back. His eye sockets were bloody holes in his head, his mouth a gory cavern of broken teeth. His tongue was half severed and hung by a thread over bruised, bloody lips.

At Mel's approach, a large black bloodied worm stirred abruptly on the Kale's chest, its ends brushing the ground and smoking as if on fire. Mel quickly realized it couldn't touch the earth without burning itself alive. *Interesting.*

Kneeling beside the Kale, Mel wrinkled her nose as that foul scent flooded her senses again. She watched, detached, as the creature squirmed. Then she snatched it up and raised it to her face. It snaked itself around her arm and *squeezed,* and she smiled grimly at its open, hissing mouth. The small red teeth snapped at her, and its white, beady eyes sparked with a hate Mel knew all too well.

"*Malum,*" *Sapienti* Mendez said from behind her.

Mel rose, sensing the unease from the older woman and the growing apprehension in the rest of her clan.

Seek.

She carelessly tossed the creature on the ground in front of all. It caught fire instantly. The worm rolled in fervor, but after a few moments it stilled and calmed, reduced to ash.

Destroy.

Chapter Two

The Kales stood in small groups buzzing with nervous energy as the dead man was wrapped in cotton and prepared for transport. *Tío* Luce, looking bedraggled and exhausted, oversaw the whole thing, while *Sapienti* Mendez did her best to assure everyone that the death would be investigated.

It was decided that today's Death Rites would be postponed due to the incident, so when Tío Luce, Thrash, and Tío Jorge left with the body, the clanspeople followed them back to camp.

"At least we know your protections are working," *Sapienti* Mendez said to the First Healer.

Isis looked up from the burnt remains of the *Malum*, snorting in disgust. "Not well enough."

"Cut yourself some slack," *Sapienti* Mendez said. "The damn thing is dead."

"It shouldn't have been able to step onto the property *at all*," Isis replied. She held up a hand. "And I'm not being hard on myself. I'm being realistic. The wards need to be stronger. They *should* be stronger—strong enough to keep the evil out."

"I'm sure we'll figure it out, First Healer," Mel said, and received a heated look for her comment.

"You," the older woman said. "So much for staying out of sight.

And worse yet, presenting here out in the open. I'm glad Thomas was able to keep the majority of the clan away and only a small handful witnessed your little exposure. Do you have any idea how brightly you glow when you... *do* that? We might as well put a star on your head."

Mel bit her lip and wondered why she'd bothered speaking in the first place.

The First Healer shook her head in frustration. "Why didn't you follow the plan we agreed on? Why can't you follow directions?"

"*Whose* directions?" Mel asked, letting her frustration spill over. "Because I don't remember giving my consent to put my name on that monument!"

The First Healer frowned in confusion. "What do you—"

"That's enough," *Sapienti* Mendez said. "This is not the time. We have other matters to discuss."

Mel tried to let her anger go. She breathed deeply and knelt down on her haunches, watching her grandmother. *Sapienti* Mendez was troubled and was trying hard to hide it. The *Malum* had obviously shaken her.

Sapienti Mendez turned her attention to the three men sitting on the ground a few yards away. These men were the only witnesses to her clansman's death. Mel had heard Tío Luce telling them to stay where they were and await instruction, and so they had—with pale faces, holding their arms, hugging themselves. Mel could smell their sweat and fear, and it rankled her. Their trembling bodies, their uneven breaths, it all annoyed her for some reason she couldn't explain. Her insides roiled as concern edged into her chest. Questions arose as well. Where had her clansman encountered a *Malum?* Were there more?

Jesus, did someone open a gate?

She looked at the small group of Kales standing guard. They shot a lot of glances her way, but none of them had made a big deal of her presenting or showed any interest in seeing her face. Her clan seemed to roll with the punches. It surely didn't hurt that Mel's grandmother had given them stern instructions to mind their tongues.

These thoughts were still running through her mind when Gabe joined her. "Look at you, breaking the rules," he said jovially. "You're supposed to stay in the house."

He wasn't taking any of this seriously, of course. And why would he? He'd missed the whole thing doing God knows what.

"You don't say?" Mel snapped.

Gabe sat down beside her. "What's wrong with you?"

Mel pointed in the direction of the monument. "Why didn't you tell me?"

Gabe looked confused. "Why didn't I tell you what?"

"Don't play stupid with me, Gabe. You should've told me last night. Both you and Victor should've said something."

"Mel, I have no idea what you're talking about."

Mel spoke quietly so as not to be overheard. "I'm *talking* about the fact that my name is on that goddamn monument."

"Of course your name is on there," Gabe said, now looking thoroughly confused. "That's how you wanted it."

Mel's head snapped up. "What? What the hell are you talking about?"

"What the hell are *you* talking about?"

Mel wanted nothing more than to get to the bottom of this, but just then one of the sweaty, scared witnesses had started to speak to *Sapienti* Mendez.

"I found him unconscious," the man said. "He woke and told me something had attacked him just outside our border, but before he could tell me what, he bent over in pain. I called Reynolds and Santos for help, and the three of us helped him back toward camp, but the whole way he complained about his stomach. Then his eyes started to get bloodshot, and his skin turned pale and waxy. He collapsed halfway, grabbing his stomach, and started vomiting blood. We picked him up and carried him, all three of us, going as fast as we could and calling for help. We were almost to the camp when he started shaking so hard we couldn't hold on to him. Then his eyes... burst. And out of his mouth... oh, God..."

"That's fucking gross," Gabe muttered to Mel. He elbowed her side. "You ever see anything like that before?"

Mel nodded. Yes, she had. Plenty of that in *Inter Spatium Abyssus*.

"Did he say he'd encountered anyone—or anything?" asked *Sapienti* Mendez. She had her hand on the man's shoulder, and her voice was gentle and calm.

"No."

"Where was he keeping watch?" the older woman asked.

"Northwest quadrant."

Sapienti Mendez looked in the direction they'd come. Then looked at Mel.

"We have a problem," she said.

Mel nodded and opened her mouth to speak, but it came then: the irresistible exhaustion that came with the Kale beast. She tried to keep it at bay, taking steady breaths, but it was no use. Her eyes fell shut and her body slumped to the ground.

She was out.

****

When Mel woke up for the second time that day, it was because someone was in her room. From the comfort of her bed, she could hear heavy-booted feet thumping on the floor. Then she heard a whispered conversation that seemed to be escalating into an argument.

"Hey, man—she's asleep, we shouldn't be in here," someone whispered.

"I gotta check her," said the other. "You didn't have to come with me. You coulda stayed at the door."

"No way, man. Thomas told me I had to keep an eye out," said the first. "On her and on anyone that comes in."

There was a *shink* as metal slid out of a scabbard.

"Hey! I'm just taking out my med kit—put up your sword."

"I'll put it up when I'm good and ready."

The door creaked open. "Shut up, the both of you," Victor said, no-nonsense. "Quinten, do what you came to do, and be quick about it."

"I was told I needed to stay with—"

"Fine. Stay then. And *you*—"

"I have a name."

"I don't care what your name is. You're a guard. *Her* guard. Don't fuck it up. Don't either of you fuck up, 'cause if you do, you'll be hearing from me."

The door shut, leaving an awkward silence.

"What an asshole."

A shaky sigh, then: "He's pissed off 'cause he has to search the woods for signs of *Malum* and was charged with telling the other clans about it as well."

Mel snorted, then sat up. "He's actually like that most of the time," she said.

Two stunned Journeymen stood at the foot of her bed.

"What's going on?" she asked, testing her limbs. They were a little achy, but most of the fatigue had passed. She was still clothed in her tunic and breeches, but someone had taken off her boots, and her mother's sash was neatly folded on the nightstand.

One of them cleared his throat. "First Healer sent me to check your vitals," he said.

"You must be Quinten, then," Mel said. She squinted at his face. "I've seen you before."

Quinten Reed was a healer, and not a very good one, if his reputation was to be believed. He was a bit too small in big situations. Mel had heard that he'd fainted quite a few times at the sight of blood, which was a problem when you're trying to be a medical professional—much less a healer for a clan where most of its members got bloody at one time or another.

"Quint, actually," said the young man. He had messy brown hair, fair skin, and a very wrinkled healer's gown. His gray eyes roamed Mel's face. "You're supposed to be dead."

"Hey, man," said the other Kale, in a slow drawl. This one was also young. He had on a gold tunic and breeches and had black hair and shiny blue eyes. Several golden ornamental throwing knives decorated his tunic. "You're not supposed to say that to her face. Just go with the flow, you know?" He looked at Mel. "I'm Keven."

Thomas's nephew, Mel remembered. *A little slow with his words, but an excellent swordsman.*

"You can put up your sword," Mel said with humor. "I hardly think Quint is going to attack me."

Keven sheathed his sword, then stood sharply, putting his hands behind his back.

Oh, brother, Mel thought, watching him go rigid at attention. *Is this what I have to look forward to?*

"So, Thomas sent you to watch me?" she asked Keven. He nodded without looking at her.

She turned to Quint. "And Isis sent you to check on me?"

Quint nodded. "But she didn't tell me who you were. Just said there was someone up here that needed monitoring."

Apparently, Thomas wasn't going to take any more chances. The thought made Mel a little frustrated, but she couldn't blame him after she had already snuck out of the house once. And now, with the current situation as it was… well, she couldn't go traipsing around alone.

Gotta keep the secret a secret. Gotta stay dead.

"All right, Quint. Go on. I'm ready."

Quint placed his hands behind her head just as the First Healer had done many times before. Mel stayed quiet as he worked, watching the young healer squinting in concentration. His chanting was more mumbled than the First Healer's.

When Mel felt a heat spread through her head and halfway down her neck, she said with some astonishment, "You're using *Spiritus.*"

Spiritus was used to heal both physical and mental attacks. It could be used in combination with spells and other artifacts that could pull a person from near death. Mel knew this from her *Hae* teachings. The histories of the clans had extensive information about *Spiritus,* but she'd never seen it work. Like all the *Hae* stories, it was just a legend. *Until a couple days ago.*

Quint removed his hands, and a small grin curved his lips. "You can feel it? Really?"

"Yeah, I can feel it," Mel said, looking at his hands.

That's strange, she thought. *How many times have Isis and Grandma done the same, yet I never detected a thing?*

"That's so weird," Quint exclaimed, echoing her thoughts. "I wasn't sure if I had the gift."

"Man, you've never healed anyone?" asked Keven from his place at the foot of Mel's bed.

"I've never done anything like this before," Quint replied. "Well, there was one time the First Healer had me assist with some kid. Little dude was nuts, talking in tongues and stuff, but afterward she shuffled me outta there before I could see if the healing worked."

Quint still had a look of disbelief in his eyes, but Mel was starting to realize why the First Healer had chosen him to treat her. There weren't many people who tested high in *Spiritus*, and apparently this shabby-looking young man was one.

Quint put his hands back on her neck, and the warmth spread across her skin again. "Mel, you have a lot of newly healed wounds here," he said, pulling down her tunic. "Was *Spiritus* used to heal these?"

"No," Mel said. "Those healed naturally."

"Naturally, huh?" He felt her shoulder and collarbone. "That's some scar. Looks like something bit you."

"Cool, man," said Keven, leaning in for a look.

"Whoa," Quint said, in surprise. "Would you look at that."

He motioned to Mel's right side, where the marks had been burned into her skin to represent the trials she had passed. The descendants of Lasade Kale were expected to pass the trials every year. The first time Mel underwent them was when she ascended from an Advanced to a Journeyman—a seasoned, well-trained Kale who was loyal to the clan and *The Ways,* the beliefs and way of life that all the descendants adhered to.

"Looks like you tested well for *Spiritus*, too," Quint said with a smile.

"Well, I am my grandmother's... granddaughter," Mel said, closing her tunic. "I haven't trained in a while though. Decided to focus on actual medicine when I decided to be a nurse practitioner."

"Hmm," Quint said thoughtfully.

"What?" Mel asked.

"Nothing," he said innocently. "I think that should do it. I mean, you seem pretty healthy. I didn't sense any illness."

"You can sense illness?"

"Well... yeah. I think so," Quint said, his ears growing red.

"Thank you, Healer Quint. I appreciate your honesty. It calms the nerves."

Quint spread his hands. "If you think you can do better…"

"I *can* do better," Mel said, accepting the challenge. But at Quint's smirk, she had a sense she'd been tricked.

"You're lucky I'm stuck here until the First Healer arrives," he said, but his smile was contagious, and Mel couldn't help but grin with him. "She's known to take her time. That'll give us plenty of time to practice."

So that was how Mel ended up spending the afternoon discussing *Spiritus.*

Quint reviewed with her the two ways to heal. One was through the chanting of spells, while the other was more intuitive, the healer using their senses—but both required *Spiritus.* It was difficult to master because there was a level of virtue required: an intention not to do harm, but to fix and cleanse. Some people just didn't have it—or couldn't find a way to harness their spirit in a way that would provide comfort and healing to another individual.

Mel recalled the cleansing spells her grandmother had taught her when she was younger. There were many, all dedicated to healing the three pillars: *Corporus, Mentis,* and *Spiritus.* Each of those pillars could be attacked at any time, and a good cleansing spell targeted to the right pillar could even keep a person from death. It was these spells that Mel had failed to remember when Charlotte fell victim to Wershall's stone.

She was determined not to make that same mistake again. So she eagerly chanted the spells in *Old Tongue* several times with Quint, taking care with the pronunciation, knowing that emphasizing the wrong word at the wrong moment could affect the spell.

Keven mostly remained silent, but eventually grew bored. "Hey man," he said, "can't y'all do a cool one? Something I can actually *see* you heal?"

He pulled a knife from his tunic, handed it to Mel, then held out his hand.

It took Mel a moment to realize his intent. But it was Quint who objected.

"I don't—aren't you supposed to be keeping watch?" he said.

"Aw, come on," the young Kale replied. "I'm bored of all this chanting."

"Tell you what," Mel said to Keven. "You chant with us for this last one, and we'll try a curative spell."

"I didn't test well with *Spiritus*," said Keven doubtfully.

"Everyone's got a soul," Mel said. "And everyone can use it."

Keven shook his head. "I'm serious, Mel. When I tested for *Spiritus*, First Healer basically shooed me out of the room." He frowned as if remembering a bad time. "My oaths had barely left my lips before she was kicking me out."

"She shoos everyone out of the room. You take your test, and she stares at you like she wants to fight you while you repeat your oath to the clan. Then you get the boot," Mel said, laughing. "Don't you think with the way things have been going, it might come in handy to know a spell?"

Keven scratched his chin and squinted at a spot over Mel's shoulder. "Well, I guess so."

"That's the spirit," Mel said, patting the bed next to her. "We'll chant this spell a few more times, and then I'll use that knife of yours."

"Mel, I don't—" Quint began.

"Quint, you gotta get past your fear of blood," Mel said. "You're a Journeyman healer. Time to act like it."

****

It was only with great effort that *Sapienti* Mendez managed to tear Mel away from the impromptu *Spiritus* training. She stepped into Mel's room, took one look at the three of them, and proceeded to warn Mel about expending too much energy. She wasn't supposed to be using her gift, she needed to rest.

But her grandmother's warnings couldn't stop Mel from cutting into Keven's hand. Quint held his breath and closed his eyes, but after some prompting from the others, he opened them and watched wide-eyed as Mel healed the cut, a curative spell from her lips causing the edges to close cleanly as if there had never been a wound there at all.

Only when they were done would Mel speak to her grandmother—which she did eagerly, because she wanted some answers. What was going on with her health? What was with her fatigue? Why couldn't she remember the decision to fake her death? And most importantly, was that really her idea?

"Yes, it was," *Sapienti* Mendez said quietly, her eyes serious. Mel could sense her grandmother's apprehension, though the woman was trying not to show it. "You stood in the atrium and looked me dead in the eye and told me to do this, Mel. I argued, because I knew the consequences, but you were very convincing. You don't remember this?"

Mel shook her head, a coldness sliding into her chest. She looked away, trying to push the fear down. "I want to know what's happening to me. I want to stop it. This back and forth of fatigue and pain, remembering and not remembering… it's throwing me off. And with this self-imposed confinement, it's getting hard to breathe, Grandma. Plus, now we may have *Malum* somewhere. How am I supposed to help when I'm so…" Mel trailed off, her frustration rising.

Her grandmother covered Mel's hand with her own. She waited until Mel's eyes met hers before speaking.

"I'll ask Isis to give you a full workup as soon as possible. I'd have her do it now, but she's seeing to Charlotte. We'll get to the bottom of this. Just stay positive."

Mel nodded, and the two made their way downstairs. They were met with great fanfare, as the rest of the family had already gathered at the table for a late lunch. Mel did her best to mask her mood as she tucked into the chicken enchiladas with rice and beans, but every forkful tasted unpleasant in her mouth. She gave up after a few bites. She instead focused on Gabe and Thrash's conversation. Something about the difficulty between the clans that still inhabited the campsite. There seemed to be a growing discord and an uptick in violence and threats.

"Three Journeymen from Clan Moors were messing with a couple of kids from Clan Tam," Gabe was saying. "They were bullying them, pushing 'em around, even hit one of them, saying it was in the spirit of training. So we made an executive decision and threw the assholes out." He grinned, then eyed Mel's plate. "You gonna eat that?"

Mel shook her head and pushed the plate over to him. "How did Clan Moors react?"

"They weren't happy," said Thrash from behind his cups, slurring his words. "But what can they do? There were witnesses all around. We weren't the only ones that took exception."

"I, for one, don't give a fu—I mean, *care* what they think," Gabe said through a mouthful of Mel's food. "The Agora is over. They shoulda all left."

Everyone looked at *Sapienti* Mendez and Tío Jorge.

"We're working on it," Mel's grandmother said. "But until the council is restored and an action is agreed upon, I don't believe we'll be getting rid of our unwanted guests anytime soon."

Mel sighed, rubbing her face. Why did things have to be so complicated?

When lunch was over, the family questioned *Sapienti* Mendez about the Kale that had died earlier in the morning. Mel's grandmother told them what she knew: that he had been identified as David Cortez, a Journeyman in his mid-twenties who had attended the Agora with his wife and brother-in-law, both of whom were Maymes. Victor would have to alert the family of Cortez's death.

"But what *happened?*" asked Gabe.

Sapienti Mendez shrugged. "Your brother and Luce are searching the area where he was stationed. I believe he had to be close to the border when he was exposed."

"And the other clans?" Mel asked, trying not to stare at Thrash, who had poured himself yet another cup of wine. "How did they react to the news?"

Sapienti Mendez sighed. "Clan Ferus agreed to help, as did Clan Mayme. Clan Janso offered one clansperson, and the others said it was *our* problem."

Mel frowned and shook her head. "That's just great. If the situation were reversed, we would help."

"Yes, we would," her grandmother agreed. "But this is what happens when a clan doesn't have a strong leader. They flounder."

"I don't see it as floundering," Mel said disapprovingly. "More like a dereliction of duty."

Sapienti Mendez made a grunt of agreement.

"I wanna help with the investigation," Thrash said, sounding a lot more sober than Mel wanted to give him credit for, "seeing as Dad is heading it up, and I think he could use all the help he can get at the moment."

Mel recalled her few conversations with Tío Luce. He always seemed distracted and out of sorts. The situation with Tía Alice probably had him feeling guilty, and Charlotte's condition certainly wasn't making him feel any better. She eyed Thrash. Her normally lively cousin wasn't looking great either—his brown eyes looked tired, his skin a little pale.

"No, Thrash," *Sapienti* Mendez said firmly. "I want you all to take turns keeping Mel company."

"Grandma—" Mel began, but was cut off by one heated glare from the older woman.

"Enough," she said. "Now tell the family about the gap in your memory. The family needs to know."

"A gap in your memory?" Gabe asked, looking from Mel to *Sapienti* Mendez.

The others looked on in similar confusion.

Mel sighed and tilted her gaze toward the ceiling. "I can't remember discussing the plan to include me in the memorial."

"*That's* why you were acting weird this morning," Gabe said. "What else don't you remember?"

"How am I supposed to know?" Mel snapped. "I can't know what I don't know until someone tells me."

"Hey, don't bite my head off," Gabe shot back.

Sapienti Mendez intervened. "This is part of why I don't want her alone."

"I'll stay with her first," said Gabe. "I've got plans tonight, though, so someone else needs to take over around seven."

Mel knew he must be spending time with Siva of Clan Mayme, his sort-of girlfriend. She was glad he'd found a girl who could not only hold his attention but keep up with him as well. She just hoped that Siva's father, *Sapienti* Reddy, didn't have a problem with it.

"All right," said a reluctant Thrash. "I'll take the night shift."

As the rest of the family coordinated their own times, Mel sat quietly. She was annoyed and embarrassed at needing to be babysat... but also grateful to have a family so willing to make sacrifices for her.

****

"I appreciate this, Gabe, but if you want to head out a little early, it's fine with me."

Mel and Gabe were in the library, where Mel was reading some books her grandmother had provided about *Spiritus* and the Kale beast. Mel could spend hours at a time reading, but she knew books didn't have the same appeal to her younger brother.

"No can do," said Gabe, shadow-boxing amid the stacks. "I said I'd watch you, and that's what I'm gonna do."

"I'm already being watched by Thomas and Keven," Mel said, motioning to the door, behind which Keven stood guard. "You know, I can't believe I assigned him as my guard. I hardly remember that either. That discussion is a goddamn blur."

Gabe pulled out a small notebook and pencil from his pocket. "Does not remember demanding Thomas be in charge of her security."

Mel felt redness spreading on her face. "Jesus. I really can't believe this."

"Yeah, I can't either," said Gabe, putting the pad and pencil away. "First thing Thomas did was chew us out for not calling him when the Eighth broke into your house."

Mel grimaced, remembering the night before the Agora. A man had broken into her home, attempting to steal her gateway stone. The stones were rare, and at the time, the Eighth needed one to fulfill their plot to access *Inter Spatium Abyssus*. But Mel's brothers had accompanied her home that night and prevented the Eighth from stealing the stone.

"There wasn't much he could've done," Mel said. "He's not a cop, and we don't have many Kales in law enforcement in the city anyway. Besides, the ones we do have are too young to have any influence."

"Tell that to Thomas," said Gabe, then spoke in a voice imitating the older man: "*I'm of the Gold Guard. I am the day, I light the way.*"

He chuckled. "You'd think the sun shines out of his ass."

Mel laughed too. "Almost *everyone* is of the Gold Guard."

"I know!" Gabe exclaimed. "*I'm* the Gold Guard, *you're* the Gold Guard, *Victor's* the Gold Guard. Show me someone in the Black Guard—I'd like to shake their hand."

The finest warriors of Clan Kale were divided into two sects: the Gold Guard and the Black Guard. The Gold Guard were much larger in numbers; almost everyone who passed the trials and became a Journeyman was assigned to the Gold Guard. But every now and then, someone was assigned to the Black Guard—the small sect of spies and assassins. Only the *Sapienti* and a few other trusted clanspeople knew who they were.

"Hey, have you heard from Nico?" Gabe asked, changing the subject.

Nico Solis was Mel's good friend and confidant. Mel had been trying to reach him for days and had finally gotten a response back.

"Yeah," Mel said. "He said he'd be here sometime in the next few days."

Just then, a wave of dizziness came over Mel, like she was on a carousel spinning out of control. She felt as though if she jumped off, she'd get obliterated, but if she stayed on, she'd miss her opportunity to act. And there was just so much to *do*. But how could she prepare for everything when there was a possibility she'd forgotten something? What else was she missing? What conversations? What decisions?

"Try not to stress so much," said Gabe, an uncharacteristically serious look in his eyes. It looked so alien on him that it made Mel pause, but before she could mention it, he shook his head and his face cleared. "All this stuff you don't remember happened just a few days after you got back. You hadn't slept in a week."

"I guess," Mel said, grudgingly. "Those days are a blur."

"I'm sure you remember Cori being all doting with you though," Gabe said, waggling his eyebrows suggestively. "*That's* not a blur, right?"

Mel rolled her eyes. The red-headed Irish woman from Clan Ferus *had* been very attentive with Mel when they'd gotten back home.

"We're just friends," Mel said with a wave of her hand.

"*Sure* you are," said Gabe. "You guys sounded like you were doing friendly things to each other in your room the other night."

Mel opened her mouth to object, then snapped it shut. Could she have slept with Cori and forgotten about it? They *had* confessed their feelings to each other—sort of. Maybe the near-death experience pushed them into bed a lot sooner than she would've normally been comfortable with.

She looked at her brother, who had a mischievous look in his eye. "You're fucking with me, Gabe."

"*Am* I?" said Gabe. "Are you *sure*?"

Mel smacked him on the arm. "You're an asshole!"

Gabe laughed. "You're too easy," he said, falling into a chair beside her.

"It's just like you to make fun of me when I'm going through a crisis."

"Well, we can laugh or we can cry. I'd rather laugh," her brother replied. "Plus, it's not like you're dying or anything."

Mel shook her head and went back to her book. "You know, Gabe," she said, "it wouldn't hurt for *you* to learn some of these *Spiritus* spells."

"Uhh, no," Gabe said, getting up from his seat. "I'm good, thanks."

"No, really," Mel said, pointing at a passage. "Come on, I can help you. We can start with this one. It's an easy one, you just gotta—"

"You know what I miss?" Gabe interrupted, jumping into one of his fighting stances. "That fine-ass staff. You know the one?" He mimicked throwing a staff.

Mel looked at him through narrowed eyes. He was, of course, referring to how he'd saved Mel's life when she was in *Inter Spatium Abyssus*. The Lost Soul, Aza, had had Mel in his sights and was just about to behead her with his cursed red blade. If it wasn't for Gabe throwing his staff through an open gate into *Inter Spatium Abyssus* and spearing Aza in the chest, Mel would've died. But this was at least the eighteenth time Gabe had reminded Mel of the incident, and she suspected he would continue to remind her for the rest of their lives.

"Fine. Loser."

It was infuriating to have a brother like Gabe. Infuriating and gratifying all at the same time.

Chapter Three

"Hey man, I don't think we should be doing this," said Keven. Surely he knew he was fighting a losing battle; there was no way Mel and Gabe were turning back toward the library. Probably he just felt compelled to note his objection.

Even Mel had gotten tired of books. What was that saying? When you're forced to do the things you love, the joy goes out of it? That was exactly how Mel felt at the moment. So when Gabe had said, "I wanna see the dead guy," well, Mel had closed the book she was reading, *The Blood and the Burning,* and agreed.

Gabe and Keven had followed her through the house before Mel realized she didn't know where she was going. That was when Gabe took over.

Cortez's body, he said, was being held in the building that contained both an apothecary and infirmary; over the years, the Kales had used this building to teach triage and first aid. Now it had become a temporary morgue.

Mel, of course, wasn't supposed to be outside—hence Keven's objection. But Mel didn't care. *Self-confinement be damned,* she thought. *It just makes me want to go all the more.* Still, she did ask for the veil hanging around Keven's shoulders. *I really ought to start carrying my own,* she thought as she wrapped the fabric around her head.

"Don't worry, sis," Gabe said with a wide smile. "If you have a case of the vapors, I'll carry you back like I did this morning."

Mel shoved him playfully on the shoulder. "Just lead the way."

The three hurried down the stone path, hoping not to encounter anyone. The sun was still out, as it was late afternoon, generating a dry and stifling heat. In minutes they were all sweating through their tunics.

As they were nearing the infirmary Mel heard voices ahead of them on the path. Voices she recognized.

"Hide," she whispered, pulling Keven and Gabe with her into the thick brush.

Keven knew enough to shut up, but Gabe was a different story. "What the fuck, Mel? There's thorns here. I'm getting pricked!"

"Shhhh!"

"I don't even hear—"

"Shut your mouth, Gabe, and watch," she whispered, pointing down the path.

There, just a little farther along the path, stood Sandeep Reddy, a tall, lean man with a turban and full beard, *Sapienti* to Clan Janso. Sandeep Reddy was dressed in a fine purple tunic, accompanied by some of his clansmen. They were facing *Sapienti* Mendez, the First Healer, Tío Jorge, and Thrash.

The Janso Elder seemed to be in the middle of an intense discussion with Mel's grandmother.

"He claimed there was a Kale among you with golden eyes. Every Kale in the vicinity bowed in submission."

"In submission?" *Sapienti* Mendez scoffed. "We're hardly a people to submit to anyone. Are you sure of what your clansman witnessed?"

"I trust my people. I trust what they saw. Will you not cooperate and share what you know? Who is this person? What are you hiding from us?"

"Hiding?" *Sapienti* Mendez repeated lightly. "I'm going to pretend you didn't just accuse me of something of which you have no proof."

"So you *are* hiding something," *Sapienti* Reddy said, stepping closer as if to intimidate.

But Mel's grandmother would not be bullied. "Even if there *was* anything, it'd be clan business. I trust you understand, as I know without a doubt that you would not share your clan's secrets with us."

"I would if it affected you," replied *Sapienti* Reddy doggedly. He was standing so close to *Sapienti* Mendez now that he was staring almost directly down at her.

Sapienti Mendez smiled up at him coldly. "As I would if it affected you. Our Burning Rites, however, do not. I'm surprised you would approach me about this, Sandeep. Your man should not have been at our ceremony. He broke Kale law. You know that our Death Rites are sacred. You know that only those within the deceased's clan may attend unless invited. You're lucky I don't demand you turn him over to us for punishment. And I assure you, this will be the *only* time I excuse this behavior. Next time, there will be consequences."

"Consequences? You speak of *consequences?*" Sandeep Reddy made a frustrated noise. "Mari, I'm telling you this as your peer. There are many in my clan who want war with Clan Kale. There are whispers that you handled the Eighth Clan situation horribly—that many clansmen died as the result of *your* failure. You failed to protect us in your own territory. And now there may be *Malum* on the loose. It's enough to make any reasonable person question your leadership."

"And what does the newly ascended *Sapienti* of Clan Janso believe?" *Sapienti* Mendez asked.

Sandeep Reddy opened his mouth but then closed it quickly. He stared at *Sapienti* Mendez and the Kales for a long moment. "One granddaughter in critical condition, the other dead," he finally replied. "It's plain to see that you have paid dearly this Agora. If it were my family, I'd have only myself to blame."

Even from where Mel stood, she could feel the anger that emanated from *Sapienti* Mendez in waves. "Blame? No, no, Sandeep. I don't blame myself for things that are out of my control. No, you see—I *prepared* my granddaughters, both of them, the best I could, and they both did me proud when they went up against the Eighth."

"Ah, so you see it as an acceptable sacrifice—"

"*And*," *Sapienti* Mendez continued, speaking over the Janso, "I did my best to communicate to everyone my concerns about the Eighth Clan, but *Sapienti* Kelser did not believe, and so did not educate Clan Moors. It's no wonder now, with the way Wershall had his ear. And with Anton Morel and his ilk spreading disunity— preying on the weak of mind and body, stroking the prejudices of clanspeople who think they have a monopoly on honor—well, pride is a sin too, Sandeep. And I'm *not* responsible for the prideful acts of those outside of my clan."

"I will not argue this any longer," *Sapienti* Reddy said coldly. "But I do believe you know where my clansman Anton Morel is. I would like him back."

"As I've said before," *Sapienti* Mendez replied, "Anton Morel has been lost to us since the day he provided his witnessing. I haven't seen him since."

That, at least, was true. Mel knew her grandmother had neither seen nor spoken to Anton Morel since the day he stood up to the clans and gave his interpretation of what happened during *Ambulant Laboriosam*. Mel's brothers had told her how Anton had blamed everything on Mel—even though it was Anton himself who had killed Hermanth Reddy, Sandeep Reddy's brother, and had stolen his gateway stone. All to tear a hole into *Inter Spatium Abyssus*. It was *all* Anton Morel.

Sapienti Reddy did not reply. He just watched *Sapienti* Mendez with narrowed eyes before finally bowing and walking away, his retinue following.

"Way to go, Grandma," Gabe said, and Mel shushed him. More Kales were arriving, running from the direction of the main house.

"*Sapienti*, we have visitors from the south," one said, stopping before the Elder.

"Who?" *Sapienti* Mendez asked.

"Viola Nunez and her husband, Blas Nunez."

Mel sensed Gabe's excitement at this news. The Peruvian Kales had been silent for years. All Mel knew was that her grandmother and her sister, Viola, had had some sort of falling out and hadn't spoken since.

Maybe they can put the past behind them, Mel thought.

But Gabe was holding his fist in his hand. He was undoubtedly thinking about new blood to spar with. Mel's brother was nothing if not predictable.

"I'll be up in a moment," her grandmother replied, dismissing the messengers.

As soon as the messengers had left, the First Healer spoke. "This is the last thing we need."

Sapienti Mendez nodded. "I don't have time to toil with them. She either challenges me or leaves."

At her grandmother's words, an alarm pulsed through Mel. *A challenge?* Challenges were dangerous.

The First Healer seemed to have similar misgivings. "You're going to force a challenge?" she said. "Now?"

"Like I said," *Sapienti* Mendez replied, shifting her long robe, "We don't have time for this."

Mel decided it was time to step out of hiding. After all, now that Reddy and the others had departed, only her trusted clanspeople were around.

She emerged onto the path and strode directly toward her grandmother, prepared to question the woman's foolish decision. But she'd barely taken three steps before her vision blurred and a ring inside her slid out of place, slipping from its holding... and fell.

She saw recognition in her grandmother's eyes, flaring in her irises, and then Mel was falling, down, down, down into a pit of flames.

****

If there was one thing that put Victor in a bad mood, it was being a Kale *liaison*. It was widely known that he was a man of little patience. *Well* known. So being assigned to help "coordinate" the Cortez investigation... well, it was decidedly not what he wanted to be doing at the moment.

What he *wanted* to be doing was talking to his wife, Liz, and the kids. But all of his calls had gone unanswered, and now he was afraid to call again. Last night, he'd decided to put it off—*I'll call later,* he told himself—but then later came, and he still didn't call. And this morning he chickened out again. *I'll try again later,* he told himself once more. *Liz is just mad. Women get mad when men do things they don't want them to do. Yeah, that's all it is. Besides, maybe it was all for the best with everything that's going on. Maybe this is safer.*

Ah, who am I kidding, he thought. *Of course this is safer.*

He rubbed his head, the small stubble of growth scratching his palm, and wondered again how he was going to get through the day. His temper was pushing to the surface, and he'd been short with more than one person already. *Hopefully this shit is over with quickly,* he thought as Justine and Drew Wiley arrived, veiled, eyes smartly roaming the area.

"Drew, see if you can find the trail," Victor said.

Drew nodded and moved away with his sister, unsheathing a long knife as he went.

Victor looked over at Tío Luce, who was talking to Cleo Newberry and six other Maymes. The older woman kept glancing in Victor's direction, her hazel eyes assessing everything the Kales were doing. Victor didn't like it.

"Hey," Calvin Smith said from his perch, where he stood alone fiddling with his sword. Smith, who also went by Smitty or Smeogol depending on who was addressing him, had been the lone man from Clan Janso assigned to assist. He'd shown up half an hour ago but had done nothing but mill about, lacking direction from someone in his own clan. "Thrash isn't here?"

"No," Victor answered.

"Is he joining? I haven't seen him in a few days."

Victor looked at the blue-eyed young man and wondered once again if he was there to help, to spy, or to try to spend some quality time with Victor's cousin. *Probably all the above.*

Just then three Maymes broke off and started walking east. "Follow them," Victor ordered. "Take a sat phone and keep in touch. Let us know if y'all need help."

Smitty sighed and got to his feet. "I guess that's a no."

Victor ignored him. He called out to another Kale to follow the Maymes and Smitty before moving his attention to the Wileys.

Victor was frustrated. The one thing his clan needed was time: time to repair its reputation, to get a handle on things, to prepare for things to come. What they *didn't* need was another incident so close to the events of the Agora. And this Cortez thing was going to cause all kinds of questions. Questions they didn't have the answers to. Even now, he could feel Newberry's judgmental eyes on his back, and he wished, for once, another clan would feel the effects of the Eighth Clan and their demon allies.

"Well, *you're* looking perfectly pleased to be here," said Cori O'Shea. She appeared from the brush, leading a small group of Ferus armed with swords. Killian O'Shea was among them, and he gave Victor a small nod. Both Cori and Killian had red hair, blue eyes, and a touch of the wild in them, making them look almost like twins, though Cori was a few years older.

They stopped short of Victor and looked over the proceedings. "We hear there was another attack," Killian said, watching the Maymes with interest, "but didn't get all the details."

Victor quietly reported the morning's events, trying not to let on to the discomfort he felt.

"Could you all have missed any that came through the gate?" Cori asked, and Victor knew she was referring to that awful night when Wershall opened a gate in the pit.

"No," he said. "Clan Kale fought them in the arena while Clans Ferus and Mayme killed any that tried to flee."

Cori looked at her brother in question, but Killian nodded in agreement.

"We kept the line," he said. "None got past."

"Are you *sure* about that, Ferus?" Cleo Newberry asked. She and her retinue had walked over to join Victor and the O'Sheas.

"I'm sure," Killian said mildly. "But if you don't trust me, you can ask your clansmen who were there."

"My clans*people*, you mean? All right, I'll make sure to do that." She nodded to one of her fellow Maymes, and the man turned back toward camp.

Sure has a lot of pull, Victor thought, watching the older woman. She was impressive in her own way, standing confident in her white-and-beige tunic, a sword at her waist. She didn't look like most of the Maymes that Victor had had experience with. No, Newberry seemed... harder.

"You seem to be in charge of the investigation," Newberry said, turning to Victor. "What are your plans?"

"My uncle is in charge of the investigation," Victor corrected her.

"Please," Newberry responded with a wave of her hand. "Your uncle has no answers to any of my questions. He's also demonstrated very little interest in calls to action. You, on the other hand, are actually leading your clanspeople."

Victor looked toward his uncle. Tío Luce was leaning against a tree looking back toward camp. It was easy to see his heart wasn't in this.

"I have a clansman searching for a trail," Victor responded. "I plan to follow it to ascertain where Cortez was attacked. From there we'll see if we can track where the *Malum* came from."

"Sounds practical," Newberry responded. "But… what about the impractical?"

Victor frowned. "I don't know what you mean."

"She means what about the outliers," Cori said. "The things you can't plan for. Things that are outside the paradigm of certainty."

Newberry made a noise of agreement.

Paradigm of certainty? Victor thought. *Sounds like Mayme shit.*

He studied Newberry. He could tell the older woman was testing him. But there was no need. Victor would always do what was best for his clan, even if it meant a blow to his ego from not managing the investigation solely on his own. Working with the Maymes, as well as the Ferus, and even the sole member of Clan Janso, would only encourage good working relations.

"What do you suggest?" he asked the Mayme.

Approval touched Newberry's eyes. "How many miles is your border?"

Victor pressed his lips together, but spoke in spite of himself. "The northwest quadrant is about eighty miles."

"That's loads of ground to cover," said Killian. "We only have— how many? Twenty clansmen?"

"We have more than that," Victor said. "We have Rangers stationed every few miles. They've been alerted and are instructed to report any activity."

"Did any of your Rangers report anything the past three days?" Newberry asked.

"Yes," Victor said. "But it's unrelated."

"How do you know that?"

Victor sighed, feeling his very limited patience had already been thoroughly spent. "Because it was over by the house. We'd noticed two people coming down the road on foot." He remembered the man and woman standing at the door, wringing their hands, looking cautiously into the house. They seemed harmless, if a little nervous. "It turned out they were religious folks. I suppose they noticed all the tents and cars and assumed we were having services."

Cori laughed, loud and free. "Oh, that's rich. You should've invited them in, shown them around. I'd have liked to meet them. I love talking to Godly people."

"You love *arguing* with Godly people," Killian said, grinning.

But Newberry was having none of their humor. "Any other reports?" she asked.

Victor shook his head. "Other than that, everything has been quiet. We're searching this area because it falls within the territory where the four Rangers were stationed. Cortez and Norton were assigned this sector. Reynolds and Santos were assigned the next."

"And none of the clansmen involved can accompany us?" the Mayme asked.

"No. They're being checked out by healers. Since they had first-hand exposure, we'd like to make sure they're not infected."

Newberry scrutinized Victor with an intensity he was rarely subject to. It was as if she knew that he was keeping some information to himself. Which he was. She didn't need to be aware of everything.

She didn't need to know that the three Rangers were fine, or that Mel had handled the *Malum* with aplomb.

"I recommend a search of a forty-mile radius," the Mayme said at last. "The assigned sectors of the involved Rangers and those sectors that border theirs. We'll have to trust that the Rangers assigned to the other sectors will be extra vigilant."

"We can trust them," Tío Luce said, to everyone's surprise. Apparently he had joined the group without being noticed. "Victor, make sure there is a Kale clansperson to act as a guide for each Ferus and Mayme group."

****

Victor and Tío Luce accompanied the Wileys, who had identified a trail. Newberry chose to join them as well, as did the O'Sheas. Victor couldn't show his frustration at having Newberry's critical eye over his shoulder, but he had no qualms about letting the O'Sheas know of his displeasure. He lobbed barbs toward them every chance he got, but neither Cori nor Killian took the hint. They just smirked and kept walking several yards parallel with a third Ferus who watched the Wileys with quiet intensity.

"Quite an eventful few days you've had," Cleo Newberry said. "An attack at the Agora. A cousin in a coma… the death of your sister."

"Yeah." Victor spared a glance at the older woman. "Thank you for your condolences by the way."

"You have them," she replied readily. "For all the good it does. It hardly seems like something you'd be interested in."

Victor frowned in confusion. "I'm not sure what you mean."

"My clanspeople say you've barely shed a tear. And although everyone grieves differently… *you* seem to not be grieving at all."

Victor turned toward her, drawing up all the anger, all the

frustration, confusion, and hurt he'd felt while Mel and Charlotte were in *Inter Spatium Abyssus*. The sickness, the hollow ache of not knowing whether they were alive or dead.

But he did not deign to reply to the Mayme.

The older woman looked taken aback. Her hazel eyes softened before the hardness returned. She opened her mouth to speak, but was cut off by Cori.

"My condolences for your loss, Victor," Cori said. Her tone was not *quite* sarcastic… but close. Either way, Victor could tell she was being disingenuous. "It happened so suddenly. I'm sure you were taken aback. I know I was. She seemed so healthy last I saw her. A little tired, but still healthy. It's such a shame."

Victor gave the Ferus a hard look. *Quit your shit!* But it was no use. The Ferus continued, wickedness in her eyes.

"But that's the thing when you're of weak body and mind. Death slips inside in the cover of darkness and takes you in your sleep. Steals your soul out of you like a thief. And Mel was always too sweet for this world. Too, too sweet. I know I speak for the entirety of Clan Ferus when I say we will miss her."

Victor wasn't sure if the Ferus was trying to keep her *I hate Mel* persona going, but she was certainly doing a good job of it if she was. That, or she was angry with Mel for not sharing her plans, which was very likely, as it was just like Cori to take personally something that had absolutely nothing to do with her.

"I see the reports of your antagonistic relationship with Melanie Mendez are true," Newberry said to Cori. "Hate her even in death, O'Shea?"

"Oh, I do not hate her," Cori responded easily, her hardness abating for a second. "The woman saved my life when I was a girl. I have nothing but fond thoughts of her."

Newberry snorted, clearly not believing the Ferus. She opened her mouth to reply, but Victor intervened before the conversation could get any more macabre.

"I'm happy she's at peace," he said with such lack of emotion that Cori had to cover her laughter with a coughing fit. Even Killian had to bite his lip to keep the smile off his face.

Luckily Newberry's attention was on Victor, and it gave both O'Sheas time to get themselves under control.

"That may be," the Mayme replied. "But it's unfortunate that the one person who could put to rest many questions is no longer among us."

"You do have a very viable witness right there," Victor replied, motioning to Cori.

"Hear that, Killian? I'm a viable witness," Cori said. "I survive a mass murder, then survive *Inter Spatium Abyssus,* but no one outside of our clan seems to remember that."

"We remember," Victor said. "But you're right, we seem to be the only ones who do."

"As far as I understand," Newberry said to Cori, "you didn't witness the entirety of the events. Fell through the gate, didn't you?"

"Not before I saw fucking Anton Morel stick a knife in *Sapienti* Reddy," Cori said. Then she added, her voice cold as a glacier, "Nor did I miss Tabitha Bartley stabbing *Sapienti* Bartley in the fucking throat."

Newberry stopped short, her mouth open. "No."

"Yes," Cori said, unyielding. "Her own niece. *Sapienti* Bartley never stood a fucking chance."

Victor kept his eye on the Mayme. *You won't stand a chance either—unless you work with us.* He didn't voice his thoughts, though; he was too unsure of who the Mayme was and where she stood. Her past was a question. What had she done to deserve banishment from her own clan? And why was she recalled? What did it all mean?

And does it matter?

Victor tightened his grip around his axe. For a moment he thought about killing the woman. She was vulnerable, still reeling from what Cori had said. He could cut her down, and he knew instinctively that the others of his clan would take care of the other Maymes. Within seconds, what was left of Newberry's retinue would be killed—and that would be one less thing to worry about, as far as Victor was concerned.

But then he'd have to worry about the Ferus as well, and although Cori was no stranger herself to being vicious, he wasn't sure if she would stand for such behavior. And Killian wouldn't for sure. To him such an act would lack honor. And he'd be right.

So Victor loosened his grip, turned away, and strode off after the Wileys, leaving the Mayme to hurry after.

****

"So what am I looking at?" Victor asked, standing amid knee-high brush, thankful he was wearing sturdy gaiters. More than once he'd been bit by snakes in dense areas similar to this one.

Drew Wiley answered in his low, careful voice. "Right there," he said, pointing just left of Victor, "was a struggle."

Victor observed the area. It looked to be slightly disturbed, perhaps, but that was all. "Where's the blood?" he asked.

"The *puke* is over there," Drew said. He pointed to where Tío Luce and the O'Sheas were standing, just a few meters away. The third Ferus was kneeling and sniffing the air. "This is definitely where Cortez collapsed," Drew continued, his brown eyes flitting around the area. "If we continue to follow the trail, we'll find where he was attacked, no question."

"I concur," said Newberry. It was the first thing she'd said in hours. "We should keep moving." Abruptly she turned and disappeared through the brush.

Victor was just about to follow when Cori slammed into him,

knocking him onto his back in the tall grass, as she tore past him, sprinting back the way they'd come. Killian and the other Ferus were quickly on her heels, yelling at her frantically to stop.

"What the fuck?" Victor said, getting to his feet and looking at Tío Luce, but his uncle was just as confused as he.

"Victor," Drew said. The tall Kale had a look of concern on his face. "We have to go back."

"What?" said Justine. "We have our orders, Drew. We need to keep going."

"No. Don't you feel it?" Drew said.

Victor frowned. He didn't feel a thing. "I don't know what you're talking about, Drew. Justine is right. We have a job to do, and I don't care what the fuck is going on with the Ferus or anyone else. We're going to follow this trail and find out what happened to Cortez."

Drew grabbed his shoulder. "Victor—"

Victor pushed at him, trying to put him on the ground, but the tall Kale would not be moved.

"Victor, stop. Please. Can't you *feel* it?"

That was when Victor noticed Drew's eyes. He had only seen shimmering gold like that in the eyes of one other person. But whereas Mel's eyes looked animalistic and dangerous, Drew's eyes featured only a soft glow in his irises.

"Victor," he said. "It's loose."

****

The third time Mel woke that day, it was in the arms of Cori O'Shea. At first, she was pleasantly surprised, wanting to move closer to the woman, to breathe in the aroma of her hair and fair skin—a scent of flowers and clean soap. But then she saw the look on Cori's face, the apprehension in her blue eyes, the rigidness in her body.

"Mel."

Calm. Too calm. Like Mel's grandmother's voice this morning, right before she dropped the bottom from under Mel's feet.

"It's me… it's me," the Ferus said.

"Okay," Mel said, looking into those wide blue eyes. "Cori, what's wrong?"

Cori relaxed, her body softening. Slowly she guided Mel, leading her into the woods.

"What's wrong?" Mel asked again. "Where are you taking me?"

Then she smelled it. The tangy, metallic scent of blood. Following the scent, she looked down. It was on her. All over her hands and clothes. So dark it looked maroon on her breeches.

"What the—?" She tore herself from Cori, spun around, and ran back to the spot where she'd awoken.

"Mel, wait!"

Mel didn't listen. She needed to see. Needed to *know*.

There were two other Ferus there. One she didn't recognize, and that one wouldn't keep his eyes off her while he held his sword at the ready. The other was Cori's brother, Killian O'Shea, who stood uneasy, holding his own sword and rubbing his short buzz-cut head.

But she barely saw either of them. Her gaze was drawn to the five dead bodies on the forest floor.

Two were disemboweled. One had a large, claw-like wound on its neck. The other two had cavernous holes in their chests. Pools of blood had seeped into the grass and stained the foliage.

Mel felt sick. She scrambled away and leaned against a tree, breathing deeply, trying to hold on to the contents of her stomach.

Cori stood next to her, quietly. Minutes passed. Mel didn't turn. Didn't look again at the scene.

In time, a small group of Kales arrived, and Mel heard her brothers among them. Still, she didn't move, wanting only to be alone and away from the dead.

"I killed them," she whispered, dazed. "I slaughtered them like animals."

"They were Eighth," Cori replied, with that reasonable tone that Mel was learning to hate. The tone everyone took when they tried to convince her that what she had done was *right*. "You knew they meant to do harm to your clan."

"But I don't *remember* it, Cori," Mel snapped, her anxiety clear in her voice. "I don't remember a *thing*. It's just an empty hole in my head. A black space."

She explained what was happening with the memory gaps. Explained that the last thing she remembered was approaching her grandmother—and then waking up here in the middle of the woods.

"It has to be the Kale beast," Cori said, holding Mel by the shoulders. "It has to be."

"How can you know that?" Mel said. "Are you experiencing aftereffects from being in *Inter Spatium Abyssus*?"

"No, but—"

Another voice shouted from nearby. "Mel!"

It was Thomas. His grizzled face pushed into view through the brush. "Jesus, we were looking for you all over. Come on, we gotta get back."

"What about the bodies?"

"Don't worry about it, kid. Your uncle and brothers are going to take care of it."

Mel hated leaving this mess for her family to clean up. After all, it was *her* mess. But she already felt that overbearing fatigue creeping under her skin.

"Come on," Cori said, putting an arm around Mel's shoulders. "I'll go with you."

Thomas looked like he wanted to argue, but one look from Mel had him turning and leading the way.

Mel took a deep breath, steeled herself, and looked back one last time at the grisly scene. Her clan was already at work. Her brothers were stacking the bodies carelessly in a pile. Drew and Justine Wiley were digging a hole with small shovels.

Tío Jorge and Thrash were speaking with Killian. And the other Ferus, the one Mel didn't know, pulled a blade from his belt, cut into his palm, and let the blood spill down his arm. His eyes followed the blood, then he lifted his head and turned those eyes on her.

Mel turned away, not liking the weight in them.

****

By the time they got back to the house, Mel was in a state. The exhaustion had swept through her body like a flood, bringing her to her knees when they were only halfway back to the house. Cori and Thomas had helped her along, making comments along the way about how they were lucky she weighed no more than a feather.

"Good thing you're not Victor," Thomas had joked.

But to Mel, nothing about this was a joke. She couldn't throw off the overwhelming feeling of helplessness. She heard her grandmother's voice in her head: *Don't ever put yourself in a bad situation.* She was being stupid and careless. She needed to be *better.*

As they approached the side entrance, *Sapienti* Mendez and the First Healer were waiting for them with Keven, who took over for Cori. The two women quickly ushered the small group into the house and toward the library.

"Grandma—" Mel began.

"No," her grandmother said. "Don't speak. Not yet."

Her grandmother hurriedly opened the secret door that led to the bowels of the house. The basement to Mel's ancestral home hid not only a dungeon, but secret rooms of all sorts, including the Sun Room, which was used to contain the Kale beast within Mel. Just the thought of having to go down the stairs to that room filled Mel with dread.

"No!"

"Shush, Mel! Someone will hear you," *Sapienti* Mendez said. "Viola and her husband are staying in the house, and they already know something is amiss. Please, just trust me."

"No! No! No!"

Mel's fatigue disappeared, and heat flared in her chest. She found the strength to pull free of Thomas and Keven.

"I will not! I will not be caged! I will not be imprisoned!" The words came out of her mouth, her tongue burning.

"Jesus!" the First Healer said, putting out a cautionary hand. "Stay back, Thomas!"

Mel saw red all around her. She needed to run—to get away. Before anyone could cage her and dump her into a hole of darkness. She would never see the light again if that happened.

A voice broke through the haze. Firm and calm.

She turned and looked into golden eyes. The voice spoke again, closer. It reached out to her, flaring, calming… soothing.

The fire in Mel's chest burned itself out. The gold eyes before her turned back to blue, and Mel found herself looking at Cori's concerned expression, very much herself again.

"It's the Kale beast," her grandmother said softly. "I saw it in your eyes before you ran off. It probably wants out now that it's had a taste. I know it's not what you want, but you *need* the Sun Room."

Mel felt empty and bereft. Lost. She still had blood on her hands and clothes, and now a war was taking place inside her body. A war she didn't think she could win.

Cori took her hand. "You've got this, Mel." The Ferus smiled, confident. "Come on. Let's show the monster who's boss."

Mel let the Ferus lead her down the stairs and into the darkness.

****

Mel sat on the bed in wet hair and fresh clothes. Her grandmother had worked quickly while she was out hunting the Eighth. The older woman had done her best to make the Sun Room as hospitable as possible, adding more light, a desk, a couch, and of course, more books. But as Mel looked at the tomes, she knew she wasn't going to read a single one of them. Not one.

Cori was stretched out beside her, and had no issues reading the secret books of Mel's clan. She actually seemed to be enjoying herself, humming along as she read, thumbing the pages with interest.

Keven was on the couch, twirling a sheathed sword between his legs. Mostly he was watching Mel's grandmother and the First Healer—who were busily discussing Mel as if she wasn't even there—but every now and then his watchful eyes would slide toward the Ferus and the book in her hand. Mel half expected him to storm over and slap the book away.

She half wanted him to, if only to distract her from the conversation at hand.

"She needs to reconcile herself with the Kale beast," Mel's grandmother was saying. "There must be a part of her that's still repressing it. Perhaps there's a part of her that doesn't want it."

"Come on now, Mari," said the First Healer. "The Kale beast is not a person with feelings. It's an eternal entity that lives within the heir. When the heir dies, it passes to another."

"I don't believe that," *Sapienti* Mendez said. "I don't believe the beast that is inside Mel is the same as the one that was inside Lasade Kale. It doesn't make sense that Kale and every heir down her line shared the same beast."

"Why not?"

"Mel's beast is her own," *Sapienti* Mendez replied. "It's her, it's in her eyes, it's in her blood."

"It's a manifestation of her id," Cori chimed in, flipping a page.

Both women looked annoyed at the interruption.

"What do you know of it, Ferus?" asked the First Healer.

"I've had more exposure to the Kale beast than the two of you combined," Cori said. "And when it manifests, it's still Mel. It smells like her, it feels like her...plus, it's in this book."

"I've read that book a million times," said *Sapienti* Mendez. "That's not what it says."

"It's not what it says *directly*, but it's the gist." Cori put the book aside and looked at Mel. "What do you think?"

"I think it's a curse," Mel responded.

"Well, tell us how you really feel," said Cori.

"It *is*," Mel said. "It's always been there. Always. Just under my skin... waiting. And I—I've always fought for control. Every second of every day, I fought to keep it under. And I'd gotten good at it. *Really* good. Just keeping everything calm. Just keeping everything at bay."

"But you kept every*one* at bay, too," said *Sapienti* Mendez. "You walked through life like you were wrapped in plastic. And that's no way to live. I'd rather you feel every emotion, as terrifying as they may be, than have you live half a life in such a meaningless way."

"You say that because you *need* me," Mel said heatedly. "You need me to be this person that you want me to be. To lead the clan and walk *The Ways*. But how can I do that when I can't even control myself, I can't even remember things, I can't... I mean *fuck*, people don't even know I'm alive! And *I* did that! I did it! I made that call! And I don't even remember it!"

She looked around and saw looks of concern on everyone's faces. That only made her angrier.

"Well, say something! Don't just give me those pitiful looks like I'm all on my own here. Someone say something to make me feel better. Tell me it's going to be all right."

"It's going to be all right," Cori said, taking Mel's hand in her own.

"But you need to calm down, because your eyes are turning," the First Healer added.

"And you are *not* alone," *Sapienti* Mendez said, sitting down next to Mel. "You may feel like it, but I'm here right with you. So is the rest of the family. We're here for you. You just have to let us be."

"It just feels like I'm regressing," Mel said, discouraged. "I thought that this stuff would get easier, not harder."

"I know it doesn't feel like it, but it's actually much better," Cori said, squeezing Mel's hand. "The first time I saw you manifest the Kale beast you were on death's door—out for weeks."

Mel was confused. "What do you mean?"

The First Healer narrowed her eyes. "Way to let the cat out of the bag, Ferus."

"What?" Cori replied with a shrug. "There's no need to keep secrets now—not with all that's happened."

"What are you two talking about?" Mel asked.

Cori looked at *Sapienti* Mendez, raising an eyebrow.

"Cori witnessed the first time your beast manifested," said *Sapienti* Mendez.

"When?" Mel asked. She couldn't recall any time before the last few days when she'd manifested the Kale beast.

Mel looked at the Ferus, but it was her grandmother who answered.

"It was more than ten years ago," she said. "We were guests of Clan Ferus for the winter."

Mel recalled those days. She was twelve, and her family had gone to train with Clan Ferus in the winter months after Ireland had received snow for the first time in a long time. They were there for about four weeks. But... nothing about the beast.

"I remember being sick," Mel said. She gave her grandmother an accusing look. "You told me I had the flu."

"Well... you *did* have flu-like symptoms," her grandmother said. She was completely unapologetic.

Mel could do nothing but laugh. "I'll give you this, Grandma: you're never sorry for anything."

"Should I be sorry for protecting my granddaughter from knowledge she's not ready to comprehend?"

"No," Mel said, smiling. "No, I suppose not." She turned to Cori. "What exactly happened?"

Cori's eyes grew distant as she thought back to the incident. "There was a man," she said. "His name was Ewan Daniels."

Daniels. Something stirred in Mel's memory. "Wershall wanted Anton to take Hermanth Reddy's stone to someone named Daniels."

Cori nodded. "He and his family were descendants of Clan Ferus, but they didn't hold well to *The Ways*. My father had tried to get him and his kin to fall in line, but nothing would shake Daniels's resolve; he wanted power. He felt the gateway stones in Clan Ferus's possession would grant it."

Cori's voice was growing more and more rote as she spoke. Mel could tell that she was speaking about something that was rarely spoken about. A dark time—a time fraught with confusion and pain.

"One night, he staged a coup while my father was out on a training exercise. He and his family attacked and killed many of my clan. They killed all who stood in their way—even children. I hid Killian, but in so doing I left myself exposed. Ewan Daniels's brother, Warren, found me—and my mother.

"They knew about me somehow. They collared me with a strange silver ring so I couldn't feel my wolf. Then they dragged me and my mother to the vaults. Once there, Ewan threatened to kill my mother if I didn't open the vault that held the stones. I told him I would do so if he took the ring off, but he didn't. It's as if he *knew* I would shift, and what would happen to him if I did.

"He had a gun to mother's head, Mel. A fucking gun. And I—I couldn't betray my father or my clan. I couldn't let Daniels take what was in the vault. But just when he was going to pull the trigger... you came."

The Ferus looked at Mel then. Her blue eyes bright, the look on her face soft and open.

"She didn't know it was you at the time," Mel's grandmother cut in. "You were in and out of that vault like the wind. Nico found you and got you back to your rooms when you fell ill."

"Nico?" Mel said.

"Yes," her grandmother replied. "You and Nico had avoided the trainings that day—to my great disapproval. Both of you had stolen away for some reason or another when Daniels and his kin attacked. Two of his men found you. The things Nico said they tried to do to you... well, it was enough to manifest the Kale beast. You felled the two men and moved on toward the vaults where Cori and her mother were."

Mel tried to recall any of this, but nothing surfaced. It was just a blank space in her head. Why couldn't she remember? Was it just a symptom of her condition? Was the Kale beast an illness she would have to deal with the rest of her life?

"How did you know it was Mel who saved you and your mother?" the First Healer asked Cori.

The Ferus looked up, that openness disappearing swiftly. "Well, *Healer*, there's this thing with scents—I'm pretty good at identifying them, actually. Placing them. Linking them to people they belong to, you know? So it was just a matter of matching the scent to its owner."

Mel rolled her eyes. She could tell the relationship between these two women was going to be an antagonistic one. Under other circumstances she might have found the situation amusing. But nothing about these circumstances was amusing.

"I was a murderer at the age of twelve," Mel said darkly.

"You saved my mother," Cori replied firmly. "I had another six years with her because of you. Don't feel sorry for Daniels and his family. *They* made the choice to betray our ways."

Mel tried to believe her, tried to set aside the guilt she felt for the killing, but couldn't quite get it done. So she changed the subject.

"I'm guessing Warren Daniels survived?"

"Scurried away like the bug he is," Cori said. "My father tried to hunt him down, but the man is a ghost."

Something in the back of Mel's mind started to turn over and over. Warren Daniels was a major player for the Eighth. He had helped Wershall with the Agora plot. He was responsible for many deaths, and... he'd also hurt Cori.

She looked at the Ferus, wondering what would have happened had she not manifested her beast that day. *She might've died,* Mel thought. *We wouldn't be here together...*

"I think that's enough talk for now," Mel's grandmother said. "You need food. Keven?"

The young Kale snapped to his feet. Mel had forgotten he was there, he'd been so quiet.

"Could you go upstairs and grab something for Mel? Cori too. And see if Thomas is back with Thrash."

Keven nodded and quickly left.

"So what's the plan?" Cori asked the older women. "What does Mel need to do to get better?"

Mel looked expectantly at her grandmother and the First Healer, but neither responded.

"I guess I'll just stay here until the answer to my problem magically appears," Mel said, falling on her pillow in a heap. "God, I feel so helpless."

Her grandmother finally stirred. "I don't have the answers for you, Mel. I don't think anyone in the world knows what you're going through. But maybe there is someone in another who does." She reached into her pocket, pulled out a brown-and-gold stone, and handed it to Mel.

Mel closed her fist around it, running her thumb across the glyph of a triangle inside a circle inside a square. As she looked up at her grandmother, she felt the first glimmer of hope.

Yes, it was time to talk to someone who knew about these things. It was time to talk to Lasade Kale.

Chapter Four

Very little was said as the Kales worked to dispose of the dead Eighth clansmen. They had little time to complete the job, as the sun was already setting and the night creatures had begun to make themselves known. Crickets were singing their tune by the time they finished digging a grave large enough for all the stacked bodies.

What an ugly fucking mess, Victor thought, staring at the scene. It wasn't easy to bear witness to the results of the violence Mel had unleashed on these people. It wasn't just that she'd killed them, it was the brutal manner in which she'd done so.

And yet it was plain to see that the men had been up to no good. They were armed with short, deadly knives, and their packs contained a variety of suspicious items: tunics in various clan colors, a phone, a long-lensed digital camera, laptops, some trinkets and oils, and a strange black necklace that Victor had handled loosely before shoving it back in the bag with the other items and handing it over to his uncle. Best case, the Eighth had been preparing to spy on the camp and its descendants; worst case, they had been preparing to do harm with the oils and trinkets. *Poison? A curse?* Victor thought. It could've been anything.

As he pulled a severed arm from under a bush, wincing at the sickening squelch and feel of lukewarm flesh, he noticed a tattoo on the skin—a bird depicted in faded blue ink. It reminded him of the tattoo on the Eighth clansman who broke into Mel's house all those days ago.

"Hey brotha, whatcha doing with that arm? Nothing weird I hope," Gabe said, kicking one of the bodies into the grave. "Why don't you drop that in with the rest?"

"I ain't you, brotha," Victor said. He tossed the arm in the grave then helped Gabe pick up the last body. "These Eighth clansmen like their tattoos of fucking birds."

"Fucking *carrion* birds," said Gabe. "Don't you listen to anything Grandma says?"

They dropped the body into the grave with the others. "As if I could forget," Victor said, wiping his head with his forearm. "Though honestly, I wish I *could* forget some of the things I've seen and heard the last week."

"Ignorance is bliss," Gabe agreed with a nod.

The days had been difficult in the aftermath of the Agora. Many of the clans had decided to stick around, which didn't help the situation, especially seeing as only two of those clans had an Elder to lead them. The other four were in limbo until a *Sapienti* was selected. "*Too many capitans and not enough marineros,*" Gabe had said earlier in the day. Victor had to agree. There were so many people who thought they were leadership material but were in actuality play-actors behaving arrogantly, reaching for what little influence they could grasp—and in the process making everything worse. Many were demanding answers to questions Victor didn't think anyone had the answers to. *Who among us is Eighth Clan? How did they infiltrate the clans? Who is their leader?*

Did they really expect those questions to be answered? No one knew who held the strings. There was even debate over who was responsible for the events of the Agora. The Ivors, for one, were in denial about their *Sapienti* being a traitor.

"Any luck with the Cortez investigation?" Gabe said, drawing Victor out of his thoughts.

"We found where Cortez was attacked," Victor replied, then gave Gabe a quick update.

"What a fucking mess," Gabe said. "And now this." He gestured around them.

Victor nodded. "It could've been worse…"

"Yeah, coulda been more of *ours* dead. Looks like Mel's got *some* control."

"Or some instincts," Victor said.

He turned to Drew, who was sitting on his haunches with his shovel resting between his legs. "Need help burying them?"

"No, me and Justine got it," Drew said. "Jorge wants us to burn them before we bury them." He gestured to Justine, who was throwing dried brush into the grave.

Victor looked over to his uncle and Thrash, who stood with Killian O'Shea and his Ferus clansmen—Owen something or other. Victor's uncle had a serious expression on his face as Killian spoke about what had brought the Ferus out to this area of the Kale property. After some discussion, the Ferus left back toward camp, and Tío Jorge and Thrash rejoined the other Kales.

"Do we gotta worry about them?" Victor asked, his eyes following the Ferus as they disappeared into the woods. "They both look… disturbed."

"*I'm* disturbed," said Gabe, wiping his hands on his breeches. "This is not how I planned to spend my night."

"They've both had blood oaths," Thrash said.

"What does that matter?" asked Victor. "They make a promise with a little blood, but what's to keep them from spilling their guts when they get back to camp?"

"Seeing shadows everywhere, brotha?" said Gabe.

Gabe had an affiliation with Killian, and Victor knew his brother saw the Ferus as a good, honorable man, but Victor found trust difficult under the best of circumstances, much less in these trying times.

"You know it, brotha," Victor replied evenly. "The less people that know Mel's alive, the better."

"Killian always knew Mel was alive," Thrash responded. "And what are you saying? It's not like we can kill everyone who stumbles onto the truth."

Oh, I don't know about that, Victor thought.

"We don't need to worry about the Ferus," said Tío Jorge. "They're our allies, and Cori has a strong bond with Mel. They won't betray their own clanswoman."

"Fine by me," said Gabe. He looked around at everyone. "Now, who's got a light? The quicker we get this done, the quicker we can get back to camp." Clearly, he was thinking of getting back to see Siva Reddy.

"And we left Tío Luce alone," Victor added. "We need to catch up with him."

"You're going to have to cancel your plans, Gabe," said Tío Jorge, "and Luce will handle the investigation by himself for now, Victor. You two are coming with me. We're going on a hunt."

Victor lifted an eyebrow. *Did you let a few get away, Mel?* "How many?"

"Two," Thrash said, grabbing some wood for kindling. He lit it and let it burn halfway before throwing it into the grave.

Within minutes the fire was blazing, making the night's heat almost unbearable, but not as unbearable as the stench of burning flesh that filled the air.

Victor grabbed his axe. He didn't see any sense in waiting here for the fire to finish its work. "Which way?" he asked his uncle.

Tío Jorge pointed west. "Thrash, you need to head back to the house."

"What? Why me?"

"Because Thomas has plans for you. And so does your *Sapienti*."

"I don't want to be a babysitter," Thrash said. "Mel is fine! She's got like three people watching her, and two fucking healers, including the *First* Healer."

"Hey, cuz, no need to cuss at Tío Jorge," Gabe said under his breath.

But Tío Jorge spoke over him. "And how many people do you think she'll need to watch her when the Kale beast makes a reappearance? To protect her from herself? From others? Or better yet, when she has a moment of weakness and can't protect herself at all?"

"Send Gabe or Victor then," Thrash argued, pointing at his cousins. "I have a special interest in finding the Eighth Clan. More so than anyone here."

"Thrash—" Gabe started.

"No," Thrash snapped angrily. "My sister is in a coma because of them. I've been patient for *fucking* days. I want to go on the hunt. I have the right. The *only* right."

Tío Jorge put his hands on Thrash's shoulders. "I understand how you feel. *Exactly* how you feel. There was a time, when my wife and son were taken from me, where I wanted revenge too. I won't let you make the same mistakes I made. You can't come with us. You're too emotional. It'll only put you at a disadvantage. Worse, it'll put *all* of us at a disadvantage."

More of a disadvantage, Victor thought. He was emotional too. He couldn't pretend he didn't take what the Eighth had done to his cousin personally. But if Victor was on the edge, then Thrash was over the cliff.

The anger slowly left Thrash's eyes until only the pain was left behind. They all knew what had happened to Tío Jorge's wife and son, though it wasn't spoken of often as it still caused Victor's uncle great pain.

"What am I supposed to do, Tío?" said Thrash. "I can't just do nothing."

"You're not going to do nothing," Tío Jorge replied, looking Thrash in the eyes. "You are the finest swordsman in all of the clan, and our *Sapienti* is back at the house with Viola and her husband. You know what that means."

Thrash blew out a frustrated breath.

"Yeah, cuz," said Gabe. "We haven't seen them in what? Ten years? Who knows what that beady-eyed Blas has been plotting. So come on, just take one for the team, go hang out with Mel and Grandma, and make sure everything is copacetic. And if it's not, you got my permission to stick 'em." Gabe mimed stabbing someone with his staff.

Thrash crossed his arms, glaring daggers at him.

"Well, Thrash?" Victor said.

"Fine. I'll stay," Thrash said coldly. "Now get the fuck out of here before I change my mind."

****

Victor, Gabe, and Tío Jorge left Thrash alone with the Wileys, who were going to wait until the fire was out, then fill the grave, before following. As they walked along in the darkness, Victor's uncle took the lead, his flashlight panning from side to side as he walked. Victor could tell when his uncle had found the trail; his pace quickened and the flashlight grew steadier, shining direct like a spotlight.

"How come someone didn't raise the alarm?" Gabe asked in a whisper. "Shouldn't there have been a clansperson at watch?"

"I was wondering the same thing," Tío Jorge said. "Someone had to have seen seven people cross onto our land—especially after what happened this morning. Everyone is on alert."

This made Victor's heart rate pick up. He hoped the Kales assigned to ranging had made a mistake, because the other possibilities were even worse. Either they betrayed the clan, or they were attacked on duty.

"We should hurry it up, Tío Jorge," Victor said, "If the rangers were attacked, they could still be alive."

"I know. We'll come up toward the border soon. Keep your eyes open."

Victor nodded, gripping his axe tightly.

But when they reached the border, there was no sign of the Kale rangers, nor was there any evidence of foul play.

Tío Jorge paused as if to get the lay of the land before giving a call. Ten minutes later four Kales appeared, out of breath and bending at the waist. One of them was Alec Paul, a tall, heavyset man with dark hair and blue eyes.

"Where's York and Brown?" Paul said, looking around as if hoping the two Kales were hiding behind a tree.

"That's what we're wondering," Tío Jorge replied. "You haven't seen them?"

"No."

"No call of distress?" Gabe asked.

"No," Paul said again. "There's not been a peep."

The other three rangers nodded and said the same.

Tío Jorge told them how the Eighth had made it into their land, and how they'd all been dealt with but two.

"Damn it," Paul said. "First David and now this."

"You knew Cortez?" Victor asked.

"Yeah, we went through the trials together. He was supposed to be on watch today in this sector. Brown took his shift."

Victor expressed his sympathies, but Tío Jorge was all business. "The trail is leading into Larson's property," he said.

Most of the Mendez property shared a border with a national park, but a small area jutted up against the property of Gordie Larson, a rancher who knew nothing about the clans or their purpose. Larson's business was on the far side of his acreage, miles away from the Mendez property, and he kept to himself.

"Then we need to follow it onto his property," Victor said.

His uncle frowned. "Larson wouldn't want that. He's a private man. We stay out of his business, and he stays out of ours."

Victor heard his sister's voice in his head: *It's all our business.* One of the few times she would get her ire up was when she was arguing how far Clan Kale should step in when dealing with issues. Mel was of the mind that if anything in their world touched someone on the outside, then a clansperson had no choice: they had to engage.

"But we're going anyway, right?" Victor said. "Regardless of how Larson feels."

Tío Jorge nodded.

"Yeah," Gabe said, turning to Victor. "If Larson is waiting for us with a shotgun, just toss your axe at him."

Victor gripped his axe so tight his knuckles grew white. "My axe doesn't leave these hands."

Gabe snorted. "I forgot it's your first love. Do you sleep with it too?"

"Like you don't sleep with your staff."

"Guilty," Gabe said with a laugh.

They left the four rangers behind. Paul wanted to accompany them, but Tío Jorge insisted that the rangers couldn't spare even one man. As it was, the four already needed to cover their own quadrant as well as York's and Brown's.

Gabe was the first to cross into Larson's land. "Fuck!" he shouted, dropping his weapon and shaking his hands. "Goddamn static electricity."

Victor laughed. "That's what you ge—*mother fuck!*" He too dropped his weapon as he stepped across the border and felt a sharp pain crawling along his skin. "What the fuck was that?"

Tío Jorge drew up next to them, looking at his nephews in confusion. He had crossed into Larson's property without issue. "Quit messing around," he said. "We got work to do."

As he moved on, Gabe and Victor looked at each other, equally confused. Then Gabe shrugged and followed after Tío Jorge.

What can you do? Victor thought as he, too, followed.

****

They were silent the rest of the way. Tío Jorge had turned off the flashlight, not wanting to draw any unwanted attention. Now they huddled together, walking at a slower pace, watching for shadows in the night. Victor kept squinting through the darkness, trying to focus beyond what he was capable of—like he was using a microscope and rotating the lens, trying to get a clearer look, but to no avail.

"Tío Jorge," Gabe whispered through the darkness. "Over here."

Gabe moved to the left, leading them toward an area where the land smoothed out a bit. Tío Jorge turned on the flashlight to get a better look. They were in the middle of a campsite. A pile of ash lay in the center where a fire once had been. The grass around it was trampled, and a bedroll sat abandoned nearby.

"Must've made camp here last night," Tío Jorge said. "But no one has been here all day. Come on, let's keep going."

They resumed, picking up the pace a little.

The heat of the night was upon them now, the sweat dripping beneath their tunics and breeches. Victor felt it beading on his brow and falling into his eyes. He tried to blink the stinging salt away while wiping his face with his forearm.

It was then that he heard steps coming up behind him. He turned quickly, raising his axe. Beside him, Gabe and Tío Jorge held their weapons at the ready as well.

The footsteps slowed and ceased. For a long moment there was nothing but the quiet of the night. Even the bugs and creatures didn't make a sound.

Until something did.

A shrill whistle pierced the air, and Victor relaxed. He returned the call, and moments later the Wileys came into view.

"Sorry," Justine whispered. "Didn't mean to come up on y'all like that."

Drew moved to the front, taking over as tracker. Tío Jorge allowed it, holding his small sword aloft as he moved to follow.

Drew set a fast pace, his gold knives in his hands gleaming slightly in the night. The other four pushed on behind him, heedless of the darkness.

The five walked for another hour before they encountered another sign of their quarry. As they reached a road, they found fresh tire tracks digging into the earth. *Large vehicles, then*, Victor thought. *Looks like they dropped the Eighth off then turned around.*

Without a word, the group turned up the road in the direction the tire tracks led—following a path that Victor knew led to Larson's home.

****

Drew and Justine Wiley took the lead, then came Tío Jorge and Victor. Gabe brought up the rear, staff in hand. The walk had given him time to think—but not about what would happen once they reached Larson's house. He was too busy thinking about Siva Reddy, the lovely woman from Clan Mayme that seemed to have captured his heart.

What an unlikely couple they were. Siva, so smart and sophisticated, and Gabe, well… Gabe less so. A *lot* less so, if he was honest. He was one for blood and guts and fighting, whereas Siva didn't like violence. She believed there were times when violence was called for, but it was never a decision that should be taken lightly.

And yet Siva had chosen to pursue Gabe. Or was it Gabe who had pursued her? However it started, now they were fully entangled, and Gabe couldn't see a reason to disengage. He would prefer to be wrapped in the Mayme's arm right this minute. He'd had little time over the last few days to see her, so busy was he with clan business and the aftereffects of what Mel was going through. And Siva was busy as well. Clan Mayme was in disarray with the death of their *Sapienti,* Janice Bartley. And there was always the matter of Siva's father, who was unlikely to be happy when he learned of Gabe's relationship with his daughter. They had escaped his notice so far, but Gabe knew it was only a matter of time.

"Brotha," Victor said, gesturing with his axe. "Look."

Up ahead, Drew had stopped. The tall man was peering into the woods, his knives out at the ready. Tío Jorge turned on the light and panned it across the trees. It touched a branch just as it swung noisily, but there was nothing there. Just emptiness.

But Gabe's senses picked up something beyond the darkness. He held his staff at the ready.

"Justine! On your left!" Drew warned, but his sister was already swinging her arm, her short sword moving fluidly.

The thing—whatever it was—moved quickly out of range.

"I can't get it!" Justine yelled. "It's too fucking fast! Watch it, Drew!"

Drew's knives moved quickly, spinning and thrusting, but

finding no purchase. "It's staying out of range! Goddamnit!"

The thing retreated again, and the Kales stood at the ready, listening for movement. Gabe heard a sound to his left and turned quickly, swinging his staff instinctively. The blade cut through the mass, and a guttural sound came from the creature as it fell to the ground. Just as Gabe was about to cut into the creature again, Victor's axe came down in a devastating arc, landing with an ugly wet sound. Fluid squirted out in thick ribbons and spattered Victor's breeches.

The creature fell silent and still. Tío Jorge directed the light onto it, and Gabe got his first good look.

It was a woman. Her hair was disheveled and dirty, and her skin was slick with a pinkish coagulant. In every orifice, she looked to be leaking the ugly fluid—her nose, her mouth, even her cold, dead eyes. The ugly gut wound where Victor had struck her down was quivering.

"We need to burn the body," Tío Jorge said with urgency. "Now!"

Drew pulled a book of matches from his pocket and threw them to Tío Jorge. Gabe's uncle lit one and tossed it onto the woman's body. She went up like dry kindling just as her carcass burst open and spewed out... something.

"Gabe!"

But Gabe was already stabbing his staff into the *something*, which resembled a giant black worm. It squealed like a kitten as Gabe twisted the blade. *Nothing that ugly and grotesque should sound like something so cute,* he thought.

The thing stopped moving, an ugly deep maroon oozing out of it.

"Burn it, Gabe," Tío Jorge ordered.

Gabe picked the ugly thing up, still skewered on his blade, and threw it into the fire. He watched as the dark creature burned, yearning for it to turn to ash. What was it Mel had said about the Eighth Clan? *They are consorting with demons and Lost Souls.* And as he watched, a smoldering fire took hold in his chest. It filled him with purpose and strength.

It filled him with fury.

Chapter Five

In the windowless Sun Room, Mel couldn't tell if it was late evening or early morning. She had attempted to activate her stone to visit Lasade Kale in *Inter Spatium Caelum*, but she didn't have the strength. Even as she held the stone with purpose, fatigue set in, robbing her of both reason and purpose. So instead she'd spent the majority of her time here dozing off, completely unable to keep her eyes open for more than a few minutes.

Cori had left her at some point along the way, saying she needed to get back to the Ferus tents, but Quint was with her now—passed out on the floor on his back, snoring lightly—along with Thomas, who was sitting on a chair quietly at watch. The man hadn't moved since he had arrived to relieve Keven.

Mel tossed the covers aside, rose from her bed, and took a seat across from the older Journeyman. The lines in his skin were pronounced in the low light, his grizzled beard covered half his face, and shaggy grey and black hair fell about his forehead and ears. But his blue eyes shined with sharp intellect.

"Where'd you get that?" Mel asked, pointing to Thomas's weapon.

Resting on his legs was an aged war club with a serrated edge of the same gold material as Mel's swords. Just looking at the weapon made Mel felt uneasy; she sensed a viciousness there.

"Just a tool," Thomas replied as if reading her mind. "A means to an end."

"I prefer a sword. Less messy."

"That it is," Thomas said, picking up his club. He rotated it casually and ran his finger along the gold edge. "But it's a messy job we have ahead of us. It needs a messy instrument."

The man had a point. War was coming. Mel could feel it in her bones. The world had been disturbed and turned on its end, and it was all due to the Eighth Clan. Their presence brought a blight to all that was pure and good. And worse, they had opened the door to that which was truly evil. How could they ever be forgiven?

And a more personal question: How would Mel ever accept the dark parts of herself? It seemed like a catch-22 to be blessed with such power—the power that came with being the heir of Lasade Kale—and yet still have to deal with the illness that came from letting it flow through her freely.

"I'm sorry about this morning," she said. "I just really wanted to go to the Rites."

Thomas barked a harsh laugh. "It's fine. But you don't need to sneak around. I would've gone with you if you'd asked."

Mel sighed in frustration. Not at Thomas, but at herself. She really had been making things difficult for herself recently. She should quit with the antics and trust the people around her. Act like an adult.

"I'd like to go to the Rites," Mel replied, levelly. "I want to pay my respects and be there when we send our clanspeople off. I can't do that from this room. I need to be with the rest of the clan."

Thomas nodded. "I don't see why we can't take a walk outside in our veils and tunics. If we end up near the memorials at the same time as the Rites, well…"

Mel smiled. "Thanks, Thomas." Then another thought occurred

to her. "Will you make sure to tell me anything I might not remember?" She dreaded the possibility of having another gap in her memory. "I mean, since you and Keven will be my shadows. Can I trust you to do that?"

"Absolutely." Thomas leaned back in his seat and placed the club to the side. "Choosing me as head guard was a very wise decision."

"Because you're Gold Guard?" Mel asked. "Everyone's Gold Guard."

"But not everyone can be trusted to handle the responsibility of being in *your* guard. Not just to protect you, but to keep you grounded—to keep you in control. Aside from a life-mate, those who are in your personal guard are your most trusted, most skilled, and most loyal."

Mel studied the older man. She could do much worse than Thomas Thorn. He had always been a good clansman. Always completed the trials every year like clockwork, making it a point to be in one of the first groups. This year after completing his final test, he had been battered, bruised, and bleeding, yet still had the energy to look over to the group awaiting their turn and say, "Are you clan or man?"

The guts he had. The gall. It was immeasurable.

"How many?" Mel asked.

Thomas smirked, knowing he'd won the battle. Mel would not fight him on having a personal guard. "Three so far."

"You, Keven, and who else?"

"Thrash," Thomas replied.

Mel frowned disapprovingly. "Thomas… He's my cousin."

"So am I."

"No you're not."

"We're all cousins."

"No, sir, we are not," Mel said firmly. "Some of us got some fresh blood in our family line."

"You keep telling yourself that, kid," Thomas said, a twinkle in his eye. "Anyway, Thrash is the best swordsman in the clan."

"He's also got a lot on his mind with Charlotte. He's not focused. You know that."

"I know he's hellbent on making the Eighth pay. Mel, I know more than you do of his struggles. But he's got to be here with you. For now, at least until he comes into his own."

"What do you mean by that?" Mel asked. "Come on, Thomas, don't you be keeping secrets from me now."

"I'm not keeping secrets. I just have a hunch."

Mel opened her mouth to ask another question, but then remembered: she had given Thrash her gateway stone to hold for a bit, and her cousin had had a reaction to it. In fact, he'd unintentionally activated it. And although his experience was negative, he wouldn't have been able to activate the stone at all if he didn't have a bit of the gift himself.

"Fine," Mel said, then, hopefully: "Maybe he'll train with me."

She'd had so little physical activity the last few days; a little light training would do her good. She wasn't made to be idle. She needed motion. Needed purpose. Like the war club that now stood leaning up against the side of Thomas's chair. An instrument waiting to be called on, to be needed.

"Are you going to try the stone again?" Thomas asked, pulling Mel out of her thoughts.

"Not until tonight," Mel replied. "I think I blew too much steam yesterday training in *Spiritus*."

Thomas nodded. "If I remember correctly, the two are linked: *Spiritus* and *Inter Spatium Calium*."

Mel agreed. After all, when one died, it was their spirit and *only* their spirit that crossed into *Inter Spatium Calium*.

"And if I also remember… food helps charge the batteries,"

Thomas said, getting up from his seat. He walked to the corner of the room where Mel's grandmother had set up a table and a red cooler. "You didn't eat nothing yesterday before passing out."

Mel took a seat at the table as Thomas set out bread, cold cuts, and vegetables. She made herself a sandwich of turkey, ham, and lettuce with thick slices of tomato. Thomas helped himself as well, and they both talked as they ate, mostly about Mel's time in *Inter Spatium Calium* and *Inter Spatium Abyssus*. Then Mel asked Thomas for his advice on the logistics of being perceived as a dead woman, and how that was supposed to work in the long run.

"Don't worry about that," Thomas said. "When the time is right, you'll be able to live in the open again. It's just not now."

Then they discussed various clanspeople that they felt were good candidates to be in her guard.

"What about the Wileys?" Thomas suggested.

"Then who would watch Victor's and Gabe's backs?" Mel replied. "Plus, the Wileys are best out in the field, especially Drew. A personal guard needs to be okay with the static-ness of the job, don't you think?"

Thomas nodded. "True. What about Alec Paul? I *think* he knows you're not really dead, so it would save me having that conversation with him, and he was running with your brothers before you got back."

"Too green," Mel said. Paul had just completed the trials for the first time that summer, and although he seemed decent enough, experience mattered. She already had one green guardsman in Keven, and Thrash was young as well, despite his gifts with a sword. She felt she needed to add a veteran.

"What about Roy?" she said.

"Coudrou?" Thomas frowned. "His hand-to-hand is exemplary, but his swordsmanship is lacking."

"It's not atrocious," Mel said. "He was chosen last year to represent the clan and a couple years before that too. He just has a weakness that everyone knows about. Some quality time training with Thrash might solve that."

"He should've solved his issues with *Rain in High Wind* a long time ago. We can't afford to choose someone with a weakness, Mel." His voice was firm. No Roy Coudrou.

"Okay, then who?" Mel asked.

"I'm thinking Gerald Cade," Thomas said.

"Cade?" Mel almost sneered.

"I know he's not one of your favorite people, but he's not as bad as you think."

"I know he's not *bad*, but he's *annoying*. He challenges everything I say."

Thomas laughed. "It can be good to have someone like that around you. They push you to grow, force you to think unconventionally."

Mel raised an eyebrow. "I think I'm already handling as much growing as I can take."

Thomas didn't roll his eyes, but there was something in his face that made Mel think he wanted to. "Very well."

"Good," Mel said. "No Cade."

"We don't have to decide on someone right now," Thomas said. "Think about it. But I also want to talk about you. You mentioned wanting to train with Thrash, and that's a good idea, but I have a better one."

"What's that?" Mel asked

Instead of answering, Thomas rose to his feet. He walked over to Quint, shoved the young healer awake, then walked out of the Sun Room.

Mel looked at Quint in confusion. The healer, disheveled and half asleep, shuffled his feet after the older clansman. Mel waited all of two seconds before following in their wake.

****

"When you said you had an idea for training, I thought you meant sparring," Mel said, out of breath, sweat dripping off her face and hair.

After leaving the Sun Room, Thomas had led her down a corridor and through a locked door into another secret room, this one wide and spacious, with a soft black material on the floor that felt gauzy and spongy under her bare feet. The walls were inscribed with glyphs that could have been mistaken for mere decorations if not for their dampening and suppressing properties, and on the ceiling was the Kale sun, gold and bright.

"You should save your breath," Thomas replied. He stood along one wall, arms crossed, watching Mel severely. "Again."

"Maybe you should do it with me," Mel said, wiping her face with her arm.

"Are you kidding? I don't have the dexterity for this."

Mel gave him a side-eyed look, but knelt at the ready without complaint and started the warrior dance again.

Warrior dances were somewhat similar to a kata. Each dance was a series of movements designed to bring about the stretching of mind and body, using the pillars within a descendant. This particular dance focused on *Corporus* and *Mentis.*

Mel ran through the sequence again: a series of flips and rolls, punches and kicks, ceasing all movement to stand on one leg, spinning slowly on the toes of her left foot. Then a jump, two rotations staying as horizontal as she could, landing on one foot, and twisting her feet to meet an invisible opponent, followed by another series of punches and kicks.

When she finally reached the end of the dance, out of breath and drenched in sweat, a slow clap reached her ears. She turned to see Cori leaning against the wall next to Quint.

"Not bad," the Ferus said, her eyes bright, a wide grin stretching across her lips. "But how will you do against an opponent?"

The Irish woman's challenge had a touch of condescension to it, which made Mel's ire rise. It reminded her of when she and Cori were at each other's throats. But she could see the glimmer in the Ferus's eyes that spoke of affectionate jesting.

"Come over here and we'll see," Mel replied with a wave of her hand.

Cori lazily pushed herself away from the wall and began to take off her boots and socks. She and Quint exchanged a few words, the clan competitiveness rising between the two. *It's always there,* Mel thought, *just beneath the surface.* Cori and Quint parted with good humor, and the Ferus walked up to Mel, rolling her shoulders in anticipation.

"I've been waiting for this," she said, stretching her arms above her head. "For years."

"No *Spiritus,*" Thomas instructed.

"The old-fashioned way then?" Cori said, readying herself.

"Whichever way you want," Mel said, crouching into the ready position. "You're the guest."

The Ferus moved to the ready as well, and Mel attacked with a burst of speed.

Cori was instantly on her heels and could do nothing but throw up a series of blocks before she managed to roll out of the way and go on the offensive, throwing her own punches and kicks. Two of them slipped past Mel's guard, striking her heavily on the sternum and face.

That hurts, Mel thought as she avoided an uppercut.

Cori threw a right cross and Mel caught it with her left hand, then dove for Cori's right leg with her free arm, which she wrapped around the Ferus's thigh. Mel pulled her hard over her shoulders before rolling; Cori's back hit the ground, and Mel let the momentum carry her over the Ferus. Cori let out a loud grunt when Mel's shoulder hit her sternum.

Mel quickly moved into side control, squeezing a tight hold on the redhead's upper body. Cori tried to push out from under, but the space was tight, and Mel made herself as heavy as she could. Mel used a savage wrist lock to trap Cori's hand between Mel's chin and shoulder, then held Cori's elbow with both hands as she turned her shoulder into Cori's hand, aiming for a ninety-degree angle for both the arm and Cori's hand—which bent backward, fingers toward the mat.

With great effort and flexibility, Cori threw her legs up toward Mel's head. She caught one under Mel's neck, and the other over. Then she crossed her ankles and squeezed.

Mel knew she was in trouble as she felt the pressure on her windpipe. She let go of Cori's arm and pushed roughly at Cori's legs, dislodging the choke. Mel threw her body on top of the Ferus again, wrapping an arm around the woman's neck and trying to push the advantage. But the Ferus quickly scrambled away, rising to her feet.

Mel also leapt to her feet, not wanting to be caught on the ground.

The two continued clashing, both giving as good as they got. As several long minutes passed, Mel felt the drain of endurance making her sluggish, but she pushed further, pulling deep from her well. She knew that it was only when one was completely exhausted that one found what they were truly made of. Only then could one truly learn their limits.

Limits that are made to be broken.

Every day you push a little more, and a little more, never

accepting the line. You *pushed* that line, further and further. The day Mel stopped pushing that line… well, that was a day she didn't want to contemplate.

Cori was tiring, as well, but managed to take the upper hand by tackling Mel to the ground. Mel had to dodge punches and elbows, and the few that she couldn't avoid smarted unpleasantly on Mel's face and torso.

Pushing for distance, Mel set the balls of her feet on the Ferus's hips, kicking her away. She twisted to her side, attempting to push to standing. But the Ferus grabbed the back of Mel's breeches and pulled her down. Mel landed with her back to Cori's chest.

Oh, no! Mel thought as she fought to keep Cori's arms from circling her throat.

Mel was in a bad spot and knew it. *Never put yourself in such a position.* Her grandmother's voice. *Your opponent has control over your life. Do you want someone other than yourself to have that control?*

Mel hurriedly put her hands up over her neck and attempted to block. But the Ferus was persistent and wrestled Mel's hands away. Then Cori's arms were around her neck, and the squeeze began.

Mel felt something burst in her chest, red hot. It stretched all the way to her fingertips. Air she didn't know she had hissed past her lips, through her teeth…

"Enough," Thomas said, pulling at Cori's arms.

The Ferus let go and pushed herself into a sitting position.

"All right, Mel?" Thomas asked.

Mel nodded.

"Your eyes shifted," Thomas said. "Relax. Breathe. Let it run itself out."

He made sure she was okay, then he went over to Quint and the two got into a serious discussion about the sun serpent—*again.*

Mel remained on her back, letting her body quiet. She felt the heat leaving her blood and muscles little by little.

"What happened?" Cori asked. "Can't even have a friendly spar?"

Mel shrugged. "If I could control it, I wouldn't be in this mess."

Cori lay down beside her. "Well. You're lucky I like a woman with a bit of fire."

Mel snorted. "Do you like sad, weak ones who don't know what the hell is happening to them?"

Cori turned her head to look at Mel. "You're not weak. This road is not easy, being what we are."

Mel didn't look at Cori, but could feel her gaze. "Still, I'm... not my best."

"And you think I've been *my* best these last few years?" Cori said. She raised herself on an elbow. "Always *implying* that you were weak or a coward even though I knew you weren't. All to get a rise out of you." She shook her head. "You know, I always made it point never to cross the line, but I *knew* that if I did it over and over that you would see it as me believing that you were..."

"Unworthy?" Mel finished. "Yeah, I did."

"I'm sorry for that."

"You've already apologized, and I've forgiven you."

"Just like that?" Cori said.

Mel laughed, long and loud. "I think going through hell and back will put things in perspective," she said, finally looking at the Ferus. "But I also don't want you to feel indebted to me because of what we went through in *Inter Spatium Abyssus*. I don't want you to feel like you have to be here for me while I go through this. This is..."

"Real," Cori said, seriously. "It's real, Mel. It's not me acting like a fool and you trying to pretend my acting like a fool doesn't affect you. This is what I *want*. This is what I've *always* wanted. But if you don't want me to be here, I'll understand. You just have to say so."

Mel looked away and took a deep breath. She knew what Cori

wanted—but what did *Mel* want? A friendship? A relationship? It seemed the wrong time to even discuss a relationship, with everything going on. But if she was honest with herself... there was definitely a part of her that yearned to be in Cori's presence.

"I think you're lucky I have plenty of fire in me," Mel finally said, making her voice light. "I've got maybe too much of that, to be honest. Wouldn't mind giving some of it away. Would you like some?"

The Ferus smiled, then looked bemused. "Have you tried? Giving some away?"

Mel knew immediately what the Ferus was talking about. One of Lasade Kale's many gifts was acting as a conduit. She had been able to pass on the gift to others. Was Mel able to do the same?

"I haven't tried," she said. "I'll have to ask when I see her."

The questions were stacking up. The stone sat heavy in Mel's pocket as she stared up into the gold sun. It glowed slightly in the dim light.

Soon.

Chapter Six

Gordie Larson's home was situated in an unkept field of dead grass and grimy debris. Tires littered the driveway next to several empty pickups, and a child's bike lay on its side with broken training wheels. A green watering can, filled to the rim with murky water, sat next to the bike, and Victor kicked it, spilling its contents, wanting to rid himself of the sight.

But what he really wanted to rid himself of was the vision of the house that stood before him. White paint was peeling off its sides. The rotting beams on the decrepit, wrap-around porch were half-fallen in, obscuring a large picture window on the front of the house. The lights were off and it seemed like no one was home, but Victor walked up the broken stairs and paused at the doorway anyway, trying to sense movement inside.

The door was shut, but there were gaping holes in it. At some point someone had pushed their way in. Someone or some*thing*.

Victor gripped his axe tightly. He could feel Gabe at his back, breathing down his neck.

"Ready, brotha?" Gabe whispered.

With a sharp nod, Victor turned the knob and pushed the door open. The darkness that beckoned was a stark contrast to the early-morning light that fell softly over his shoulder.

The smell of musk and wet rot met their noses, but nothing stirred. Victor stepped through, knowing Tío Jorge and the Wileys were doing the same at the back door. He put his back to the wall and inched forward slowly. Gabe followed.

The first room was a living room, featuring shabby couches on a tan carpet, a huge fireplace, and a television on an entertainment center that had seen better days. *Where's Larson? Where's his family?* Victor thought. Larson lived on this property with his wife, kids, and grandkids, but there was no sign of anyone.

The next room was the dining room. A long table was surrounded by chairs that looked hardly used. Still no sign of inhabitants. Through the doorway, Victor saw the Wileys and his uncle in the kitchen.

"Brotha," said Gabe. "Smell that?"

Gabe was motioning up the stairway to the second floor. There was indeed an unpleasant smell coming from upstairs. Together, they started up.

The second floor had several bedrooms, and Victor and Gabe checked them one by one. They looked lived in, but all were empty.

Gabe grabbed Victor's shoulder and pointed to a suitcase in one corner. "Ain't that Mel's?"

Victor picked it up, set it on the bed, and opened it. It was full of clothes.

"This her stuff?" he asked Gabe.

"Yeah. That's all hers." He swore. "Brotha, someone took this bag from Mel's tent. You know what that means."

Victor nodded. Someone in Clan Kale was working with the Eighth. Was *in* the Eighth. Victor gritted his teeth, his anger rising so suddenly it nearly left him breathless. *A traitor inside the clan,* he thought. *Sonofabitch.*

"You think Larson was working with them?" Gabe asked.

Victor shrugged. "I don't know. But let's keep moving."

There was only one room left, at the end of the hallway, and it appeared to be the source of the rank smell. The door was wide open. The brothers looked at each other, gripped their weapons tightly, and rushed in.

But this bedroom was no different from the others. An unmade bed, a dingy chair… but there was no one here. Nothing out of the ordinary. And no sign of what was generating that awful odor.

"What the fuck is that smell?" Gabe said, covering his nose.

"Shut up," Victor said. He'd heard a slight buzzing. *Flies.* He followed the sound to a door in the wall. He thought it was a closet, then realized by its size that it must be a dumbwaiter.

Victor placed his hand on the knob. He turned back to look at his brother.

Gabe held his staff like a javelin, his eyes on the small door, and nodded.

Victor yanked the door open swiftly.

It was like opening a submarine hatch underwater. The flies poured out in a wave, and the smell was suddenly everywhere and overwhelming. Victor threw a hand over his mouth and nose, trying to shield himself from the disgusting foulness.

Inside the dumbwaiter was a mess of rancid gore.

"Jesus!" said Gabe. "Looks like something threw up, gave birth, then died by eruption. What the fuck did that?"

"I don't think I want to know," Victor replied, grimacing. "But this damn thing can only go one way: down. Come on."

They went back downstairs and met up with Tío Jorge and the Wileys, who had uncovered some unpleasantness of their own. In the kitchen was the body of a Kale ranger, half his face and neck burned off, along with a deep burn erupting from his heart. The man's tongue was shriveled to ash, and one of his eyes a waxy congealed socket.

Victor's uncle was pouring oil over the body, chanting a cleansing spell, but Victor found he had to look away. This was no way to die.

"Browning," Justine said. "Didn't stand a chance."

"They burned him?" Gabe asked, his voice hollow.

Drew was crouched down to inspect the body. He ran his hands down Browning's arms and torso. "Whatever they did to him, it looks like he burned from the inside out."

"He spontaneously combusted?" Victor said.

Drew rose to his feet, nodding.

"Those fucking Eighth," Justine said. "They fucking cursed him. Goddamn it, where'd they get the skill and power to do that?"

"We'll need to have someone research this," Drew said. He pulled out his phone and took a few pictures. "It might've been something they had in their possession—an object or trinket. They might've not even known what they had." He looked around him. "I wouldn't be surprised if whatever happened here was an accident. It feels... strange here."

Victor looked at Drew, then the others. *What could've done this? The Eighth Clan? Or something else?*

"We don't have time to move him," Tío Jorge said. As he put the oil back in his tunic, Victor got a glimpse of something between the folds of the garment: a crystal that looked like flames. But that couldn't be. "We have to move on," Tío Jorge continued. "York may still be alive."

"You mean move *down*," Gabe said. He'd found the kitchen door to the dumbwaiter and had opened it, revealing only a rope descending into darkness. "Victor and I found a dumbwaiter of horrors upstairs. Looks like it goes down another level."

"Great," Justine said, pulling out her knives. "I suspect it's about to get *Resident Evil* up in here."

"Is there any other way down?" asked Victor. "I'd rather not slide down that rope."

Instant regret. The others looked at him with raised eyebrows.

"*Sugah!*"

"Don't want to get blood on that tunic, Victor?"

"Afraid of the smell?"

"He can't hold his axe *and* the rope."

"Shut up," Victor grumbled.

"My name is *Victor*," Gabe said, "and I don't like to slide down rope. I prefer pipe."

"Fuck you, Gabe."

Tío Jorge shushed them and led them to the basement door. The man's eyes were dark and cold, and his demeanor sobered the others, who immediately dropped the silliness.

"Ready yourselves," he said. "Whatever's down there, it doesn't leave this house alive. Understood?"

The other four nodded.

Tío Jorge put his hand on the knob, but Gabe put a hand on his shoulder.

"I'll go first," Gabe said.

When Tío Jorge opened the door, Gabe stepped forward, leading the way. Tío Jorge went next, then Victor, with the Wileys bringing up the rear. As they moved swiftly down the stairs, Victor sensed something hostile—a dangerous energy that made him want to turn and flee back in the direction from which they'd come. He couldn't—he *knew* he couldn't—but the fear grew in his chest, spreading like ice water into his hands and feet, planting him firmly on the steps like a stone statue that existed only to be struck, to crumble into dust. To be forgotten in the fragments of failure.

You are weak. You will see. The thoughts came unbidden. *You will die. You are a man. A weak man...*

His uncle and Gabe had pressed forward, seemingly unaffected by whatever had struck Victor with paralysis. That was when Victor felt a warm presence at his back. Justine was right behind him, her gold sword in one hand, and she pressed the other on Victor's shoulder. He looked back and saw that Drew had done the same to her. Almost immediately, the darkness that had been pressing on him abated, and he found he was free to walk forward once more.

"We are clan," Drew said quietly, eyes blazing.

And Victor remembered. He was not a man. He was a Kale.

He continued his descent, the two behind him a reservoir of strength. They caught up to his uncle, pressing ever closer to the malicious presence that yearned to destroy them.

****

The walls were alive, thrumming with dark electricity and adorned with unfamiliar glyphs written in blood. On the floor were bones, cracked and broken, their spongy marrow mixed with dirt and crud. Bones and worse, fleshier things.

Gabe did his best to step carefully as he approached the door at the opposite end of the basement. *That's where it is,* he thought. Knew. Whatever it was, it was dark and malevolent. He could not let it out of this house alive. It would only bring about death and destruction.

On the door was a drawing of a skull. Cyclonic lines burst out of its eye sockets and mouth. *I know this,* Gabe thought. *I've seen it before.* But the skull's representation escaped him, like whispers in the dark just beyond his hearing.

He put his hand on the knob and opened the door wide.

And everything changed.

Time and space twisted and turned. The walls shuddered. The glyphs erupted in a red blaze, lighting the basement in fire. The Kales lost their footing and fell into the filth.

And movement came from behind them.

The bones and flesh and sinew were molding and forming, coming together into—

"Blood magic!" Tío Jorge screamed.

That was not what Gabe wanted to hear. Blood magic was disgusting, and explained what had happened to the Larsons. Killed and bled, but by who? Who had recited the spell?

But he didn't have time for questions, because the dark creature had re-formed, its body a putrid mass of blood and bone. It had no eyes, yet it seemed to be looking at the five of them with unmitigated hate.

Drew attacked without hesitation, his long knives moving in tandem, and Justine threw herself into the fight beside him. The two of them moved in sync, slicing the creature every which way, wounding it over and over, yet not slowing it in the least.

Victor and Gabe joined the fray. Gabe swung the blade-end of his staff at the creature's head, right where the eyes should be. His blade cut through, but seemed only to further enrage the beast, which glowed and shimmered. And still did not slow.

The four attacking Kales stood back to regroup. It was then that Gabe felt a pulling on his tunic. *The blood! It's using the blood on our clothes!* he thought.

The four of them went flying through the air, crashing into the walls, and Gabe lost his grip on his staff. *Son of a bitch!* He scrambled for it, but just as he was about to wrap his hands around its length he was flying again, and this time he tumbled right through the open doorway.

The door slammed shut behind him, cutting him off from his staff, the blood monster, and his clanspeople.

He was alone.

****

The room was quiet and well-lit. Sunlight streamed through windows that lined the wall just beneath the ceiling. But the light was the only thing clean or pure about this place.

Two circles were drawn on the floor. In one, a pile of bodies had been stacked atop one another other—seven souls, pale and bloodless, with a sword used to skewer them together. Its cheap bronze handle sprang forth from the top.

In the other circle was a table, and on top of it lay York, Gabe's clansman. His face was obscured by an opaque substance—no, an *organism*—that seemed to breathe whenever he did. His booted feet were marked with blood, as were his breeches. His tunic lay open, revealing symbols carved on his chest that Gabe had never seen before.

"Oh, fuck," said Gabe. All he could think about was that woman in the woods. The bursting in her chest as a worm exploded forth. "Oh fuck, York. Tell me you don't have a baby demon in you."

"No," said a voice.

Gabe spun around to face the speaker. A young man stood in the corner of the room, filthy and disheveled, as if infested. Chains were wrapped around his arms and neck, but they merely hung limply from his body, tethered to nothing.

"Jesus," Gabe said. "You need some help, guy? I know people that can help. Get you better. Not so… sick?"

"No," the man said, his voice a droning monotone. "We are alive. For the first time in our life, we see things. The way they are and the way they should be." He stepped toward the bodies and laid his hand close to the handle of the sword. "There's evil here, in this world. Did you know?"

Yeah, Gabe thought. *I'm looking right at it.* And then: *Who the fuck is us? And can I kill it? What did Grandma Mari say? Never touch anyone who has been touched by darkness. They can give you what they have. And my fucking staff is in the next room!*

He glanced back at the door. It was now covered with a seal, glowing angry and red.

He wants me here. But why?

"People tried to lock us in," the man continued. "They kept us in this room. They wanted to use us for their own purpose. But we are not theirs to use. We do not care for their petty squabbles about power they don't have. No. A power is growing, here, among us. Just across the way—into the woods—is a woman…"

Gabe's head shot up. "What did you say?" He looked straight into the man's eyes, which had a strange sheen, and a look Gabe couldn't place.

"There is a *woman*. She almost destroyed us. We chased her through the woods. We almost had her in our teeth. But then… she wounded us. *Deeply*." He put his hands on his stomach, as if over an invisible wound. "She cut us through our body, and our lifeblood was spilling. We were dying. Slowly, we were dying. Alone. In this strange land. Until another came across us…"

And then got possessed. Excellent, Gabe thought. What was he going to do? He wished Victor were here with his axe. His brother would chop this man's head off. And then later he could hunt Mel down and give her a firm talking to for letting a *Malum* live long enough to possess a man.

"But we've *seen* her," the man continued. "Even now we see her, fighting with the wolf, fighting her nature. Every day she grows stronger. So strong… and yet so vulnerable. I've seen her weakness. I've seen consciousness leave her. Leave her vulnerable and open."

The damn *Malum* had gifted this man with *the sight*. And now he'd seen Mel at her weakest. *Goddamnit! How much does he know?*

"What else do you know of this woman?" Gabe asked.

"I know she's marked. I know she brings the end of days." The man walked over to York and looked down at him with something like… devotion. "But when he comes, I will tell him everything. He will change things, to how they should be. And he will kill the woman."

The man faced Gabe once more. "I need you now. Your blood. A descendant unwilling."

Oh, I'm unwilling all right, Gabe thought, crouching at the ready. *Come on, you fucking demon. I may not be leaving alive, but you won't be either.*

The man attacked, uncoordinated and sloppy. Gabe quickly sidestepped, but somehow a blow struck his nose. Blood spurted out, the pain sharp and sudden.

Jesus, did he knock my nose clear off?

Sliding away, then diving back in, Gabe threw a quick three-punch combination. All three landed, but without effect. He kicked at the man's knees, and it felt like kicking a cement block.

Gabe narrowly avoided a bear hug, then rolled away before once again attacking with fury. But every punch, every kick, was met with indifference. And the man continued to stalk forward to end Gabe's life.

Gabe avoided the man's attacks as best he could, but he was tiring. And then finally the man grabbed him, wrapped his hands around Gabe's neck, and squeezed. Gabe felt his feet leave the ground as the man used unnatural strength to pull him into the air. The pressure on his windpipe crushing, and a ringing exploded in his ears as he struck the man's arms and hands—to no avail.

The man opened his mouth, and something scrambled hideously beyond his tongue. Gabe turned his face away, wanting no part of it. His strength was quickly fading, his limbs growing sluggish. Blood from his nose dripped into his mouth.

He was overcome with mania. An uncomfortable heat exploded in his chest, centered in his heart. He was exhilarated *and* afraid.

Afraid of the heat, yet he yearned to let it flow, let it stretch along his limbs, burning strength into his muscles.

That was when he remembered. He stretched his arms wide and pressed the mechanism along his wristbands—*Mel's* wristbands. The blades shot out, gold and gleaming, and Gabe swiftly stabbed the man—right through his neck and up toward his brain.

Those crazy eyes grew dull. The strength left the hands around Gabe's throat, and as he gasped for breath, he felt those fingers release him. He landed heavily on his knees, coughing for breath, the ringing still filling his ears.

The man had fallen too. Dead. Black blood poured from his wound, along with something else. A small, bug-like creature that crawled from the man's mouth.

Gabe scrambled over and stabbed it with his knives. The creature squealed and fell motionless. Only when Gabe was sure it was dead did he look again at the man, who lay still and silent.

"Fuck you, demon!" he screamed. "Fuck you to fucking hell!"

Then he let himself lean on the wall, rubbing his still-aching shoulder and neck. His face was on fire from the blow to his nose. He spit blood, then turned toward the seal on the door. How was he going to get out and get back to his brother and uncle. How were they faring against the blood monster?

The air around him began to hum, and Gabe felt electricity pulsing along his skin. Something was happening—something pernicious.

He turned his head when he caught movement. The bodies skewered one upon the other had begun to struggle—and he looked over to see they now had their eyes open, their mouths forming silent screams. Their arms and legs flailed grotesquely.

The two circles on the floor glowed an angry red.

And then York started to move as well. First his hands, spider-like fingers curling. Then his arms, pushing him up to a sitting position. He pulled the foul organism off his face—its sticky slickness gripping like tendrils to his skin—and threw the dark, oily thing to the floor, where it immediately dried and crumbled into dust.

York rose to his feet. His face was the face Gabe knew. Nothing out of the ordinary—except for one thing. His eyes were crimson.

York grabbed the handle of the sword and pulled it from the stack of bodies, revealing a blood-red blade. The flailing men and women went silent.

Then York moved his gaze to Gabe.

He looked Gabe in the eye, glanced down at the blades at his wrists. He smiled with hideous intent, red sword pointing at Gabe, taunting.

Well at least he knows nothing of Mel, Gabe thought. *At least I did that right.*

They met each other in a frenzy, Gabe dodging and sliding, avoiding the red blade by mere inches. But his knives were too short to meet their mark, and the entity within York was too skilled with the blade, too quick on his feet. Worse was the look of wicked glee in those crimson eyes. To York, or whatever he was now, this was all just a game. York was toying with him.

Gabe found himself on the defensive, backing toward the wall. He narrowly avoided a strike at his head, then rolled clear. As he stood, York turned once more toward him, again with that taunting smile on his face, grotesque and broken all at once.

And that was when Gabe knew he had no chance—there was no winning here.

Nothing left to lose.

He lifted his wrists, the knives forming an X in front of him. As he glared at York, he let the burning spark once more in his chest. And this time, Gabe let it come. Let it flow.

York hesitated, as if he could sense that something had changed. "Come on, demon," Gabe taunted with a smile. "I'm waiting."

"For death," the demon in York replied, then attacked Gabe with renewed fervor.

They meet in a clang of blades, orange sparks flying. Gabe still can't change the reach of his knives, but the fire in his veins makes him quicker, makes him hungry to see black blood spilling from the monster in front of him. Impulsively he punches his blades directly at York's head. The demon barely avoids the strike, shifting and turning, then brings his sword back up and swings it in a deadly arc. Gabe brings both knives up quickly, crosses them, and catches the red blade inches from his face.

York leans forward, his crimson eyes glowing as he uses all his strength to force Gabe to his knees. Then he turns his wrists, slides his sword out from Gabe's knives…

… and slices Gabe cleanly across the throat.

Gabe falls to one side, hands at his neck, trying to stem the flow, but the blood gushed out through his fingers, already forming a puddle on the floor. The ringing in his ears grows louder, constant, making his eyes burn.

The pain… so far away. His body is numb. His arms and legs limp. His breath heavy.

He barely has the strength to focus his eyes as York moves toward him with that broken smile. He raises his sword for a final blow.

Gabe closes his eyes. *Siva.* Her smile. Her face, her lovely eyes. He will see only her, here at the last.

But then an explosion. Splintering wood. Tío Jorge, holding fire in his hand, screaming in *Old Tongue*. Gold fire erupting across York, who runs screaming. And Victor is at Gabe's side, grabbing his throat.

"He's still alive! He's breathing!"

"Get him up! We've got to get out of here!"

Hands hauling him up. Gabe's eyes close, and when he opens them again, he sees Justine throwing a match onto the floor. The smells of gas and fire fill his nostrils.

He shuts his eyes again.

The next time he opens them he's in a truck, being jostled side to side. Victor is gripping him tightly.

"Hold on, brotha!" Victor yells. "Hold on!"

But all Gabe can see is smoke in the sky.

Chapter Seven

Mel briskly ascended the steps out of the sub-level, anxiety filling her with each step. Her training had been interrupted by Thrash, who had arrived with serious news: Viola and Blas Nunez knew she was alive; Tía Alice had told them everything. And by the wide-eyed look in Thrash's face, she knew it wasn't good. So she'd taken off swiftly, with Thomas, Cori, Quint, and Thrash following her.

"Mel," Thomas said, barely keeping up with her. "We don't know what they know. There may not be a need to confront them."

"You heard Thrash," Mel replied brusquely. "There's no point in hiding. If they're going to make a move for my grandmother's position and use my situation as an excuse, I need to be there."

She pushed open the door that led into the hallway. Two Journeymen stood guard outside the atrium door, both in black tunics and breeches. She didn't recognize them, which meant they must be with Viola and Blas.

As Mel approached, one blocked her way. "Private audience," he said. He was young with dusty brown hair.

"Move aside," Mel said firmly.

"We don't follow orders from you."

"DeLeon…" said the other, in a warning tone. He was older, maybe late thirties.

"Move," Mel growled. *This is* my *home.* "Before we move you."

Common sense seemed to prevail. Either that, or the young Journeyman didn't care to argue with her and the group at her back.

"Fine," DeLeon said, stepping aside. "We hear you do what you please anyway. Regardless of the consequence."

Mel stared hard at the young Journeyman. She opened her mouth to dress him down, but the other guard pulled his partner aside.

"Apologies, cousin," the older guard said to Mel. "You must excuse him; he is a newly ascended. Just passed the trials this summer." He looked past Mel at Cori. "Cori O'Shea, it's an honor to see you again."

"The honor is mine," Cori responded.

Mel eyed the Ferus curiously. *I'll have to ask her about that later.* Then she turned back to the older guard. Now she recognized his face. "Antonio Nunez. I haven't seen you in—"

"Since you were a kid, sneaking around and stealing my knives," Antonio said. His voice was pleasant, but his eyes were careful. "You've grown strong. My father will not be pleased to see you as such."

Mel cocked her head. "I always wondered if the Peruvian Kales carried with *The Ways* or if they'd broken apart completely."

Antonio shook his head. "We still follow *The Ways*. There are just some slight differences." The words seemed to pass his lips with great difficulty.

"I'd like to speak to you sometime, cousin. Get to know what those differences are. Get to know you as well," Mel said with a smile.

Antonio nodded. "One day, soon." He stepped aside. "But now, I think you have business to attend to."

Mel opened the door and walked in. The morning sun streamed through the skylight above, illuminating the scene. Mel's grandmother sat in a chair next to the First Healer, both with a look of annoyance on their faces. Next to them was Blas Nunez, short and thin, with dyed black hair and a narrow face. He was wearing a black robe and an ostentatious necklace of a sun. Beside him stood Viola Nunez, who looked like a younger version of *Sapienti* Mendez, but with fewer wrinkles and less grey in her hair. That, and her eyes reflected a timidness that would never grace her grandmother's face.

"So, she *is* alive," said Blas, rising to his feet. "Lying to the other clans, manipulating them so they stop the very well-deserved criticism you brought upon yourself for your mishandling of the Agora. This is grounds for you to be displaced, Mari."

"Is it?" Mel's grandmother replied coolly. "I hadn't realized. You hadn't said it once in the last five seconds or so."

So, it's going to be one of those conversations, Mel thought.

Blas Nunez rounded on *Sapienti* Mendez. "Clansmen are dead. On *your* property. It was *your* responsibility to keep them safe."

"Were you here, Blas? No. You weren't. Your family has deemed the Agora and other clan events irrelevant. You know nothing of what has been going on."

"Oh yes, I heard you before," he said. He made a sweeping, dramatic gesture. "The Eighth Clan is running rampant."

"You don't believe in the Eighth Clan?" Mel asked.

Blas Nunez gave her a measuring look. Mel stared right back into his beady eyes. *I will know if you're lying to me.*

"The Eighth Clan is nothing but farmers with pitchforks," Blas said. "They stand no chance against warriors."

"Farmers?" Mel scoffed. "They've infiltrated the clans. Descendants who were born and raised to the Great Seven have betrayed *The Ways*."

"I don't believe you." Blas turned to Mel's grandmother and the First Healer. "Or you two. You all stick together, don't you? Plotting the same story."

"It's not a story," Mel snapped. "Those farmers with pitchforks—

those small men and women who have so little skill and understanding—have succumbed to evil. They don't know what they're doing, and *that's* what makes them dangerous. They know just enough to bring about the end of days." She shook her head, disgusted and tired. "They *know* demons exist. They *know* Lost Souls exist. And they're arrogant enough to believe that they can bend these dark creatures to their will. But Lost Souls and *Malum* and all the other dark creatures serve their own dark masters. To work with something from Hell, *you* submit to *it*. And you," she said, pointing at Blas, "are exactly what they're hoping for: someone who underestimates them."

"They are chaos," the First Healer said. "Absolute and utter chaos."

Mel nodded. "When I questioned Wershall," she said, avoiding the gazes of Blas and Viola Nunez, not wanting to go into *how* she questioned Wershall, "I learned that Lost Souls seduce those from the Great Seven to switch allegiances, then task them to spread discord and disunity. I also learned there are many Eighth Clan cells, and some are more expendable than others."

"How many cells?" asked Viola. Her husband turned coldly toward her, but the woman kept her eyes on Mel.

Mel shrugged. "I know that not all were sent to *Inter Spatium Abyssus*, but I can't give you numbers. Wershall, for all his boasting, was not of the inner circle, nor was he well connected."

"The inner circle?" Blas Nunez scoffed. "There is no inner circle. No organization."

"There is," Mel said. "The upper echelon of the Eighth Clan. They give the orders, and they all answer only to themselves. Each is tasked with a territory. And they all have designs to expand."

"So they all fight amongst themselves," Viola said, ignoring her husband's glare.

Mel nodded. "Their utmost desire is power. The Agora plot may not have even been tasked by the circle member that is assigned this territory."

"*Our* territory," *Sapienti* Mendez said. Then to Blas and Viola Nunez, she said, "We are planning to retaliate, but we must be smart and methodical in our decision. We cannot be hasty. Patience is—"

"If they are as dangerous as you claim, why must we wait?" Blas interrupted. "Swift action should be called upon. Patience is for cowards."

"You really are a small, stupid boy," the First Healer mumbled to herself. Mel's keen ears caught what everyone else did not.

Sapienti Mendez was more diplomatic. "Patience is a virtue. I suggest you practice it."

Blas's face reddened. "I do not trust *you* to handle this issue effectively."

Mel's ire rose. She could tell that her grandmother was displeased as well.

"Blas, she is Elder of our clan," Viola said reasonably.

At her words, Blas looked as though he was about to explode in fury at her. Mel saw Viola begin to wilt, to protect herself through subservience to her husband.

"I hope you don't mean to strike your wife," Mel said firmly. "In our presence, or in private. That would upset me greatly."

The older man rolled his shoulders, putting on an air of unconcern. It was a slimy armor that she has seen before and had grown to detest. "I don't know what you're talking about. I love my wife and treat her accordingly."

Liar. Mel could sense the man's misogyny as he looked at the women in the room.

"What happened to you that broke you so, Blas Nunez?" *Sapienti* Mendez asked. "Your mother was a good woman. She followed *The*

Ways. She loved her family and her clan. How did she spawn a hateful little man like you? How do you take my sister's name away and force yours upon her when you know that is not our way? She is a Mendez."

"She is a *Nunez.* She is *my* wife. And none of it is your concern," Blas Nunez replied.

Sapienti Mendez rose from her seat, as if to take exception to the words, but before she could speak, he said: "I will say so again: you are unfit to lead this clan."

"You've been saying so for decades," responded the First Healer hotly. "But unless Viola plans to do something about it, there's nothing to be done."

"*I* will do something about it," responded Blas. "I challenge you, Mari Mendez, for *Sapienti* of Clan Kale."

"You are of the wrong *sex,*" Mel blurted, and then blinked, surprised the words had come out of her mouth and not her grandmother's. It must be the fire in her chest; it had to be.

"Are we still following archaic rules?" Blas Nunez argued. "Even the Maymes have moved on from their sexist attitudes."

"*You. Are. Of. The. Wrong. Sex,*" Mel bit off. Then clamped her mouth shut. The words had come out against her will.

"It's for your protection, Blas," the First Healer said. "Kale was a woman. Her gifts flow naturally through other women—"

"I refuse to believe in a world where a woman can do something a man cannot," Blas said. "You are the *fairer* sex, after all."

Weaker was very much implied.

"Is that why you've fashioned yourself as Chief of Clan Kale?" Mel asked, again feeling that heat under her skin, pushing up toward her collar and into her face. "Is that not why you wear the black? Why the Kales who accompany you wear the same?"

She could feel the First Healer and her grandmother shift

uncomfortably. Mel wasn't sure why the two were apprehensive. They *should* be angry—as angry as she was. It stirred in her belly, rising exponentially. She looked away from Blas Nunez, not wanting him to see it in her eyes. She was afraid of what she might do to him. *He disrespects me. He stands there and disrespects me with his words, his presence, and his actions. I should show him what we do to Kales who stray from the path...*

Only then did it dawn on her then that the First Healer and her grandmother were apprehensive of *her*. They were worried about her anger and what she might do.

Her eyes found Viola Nunez, who looked at her with newfound understanding. Mel quickly looked away, finding the woman's eyes too familiar, too much like her grandmother's.

"I wish you strength, Tía," Mel said, her voice devoid of heat. Careful, as if stepping on the thinnest film of ice. "For the nights to come. Remember your name and where you come from. Kale women are not made to be oppressed."

Then she turned and walked to the door.

Blas Nunez's voice sounded behind her. "She is exactly where she needs to be. You *all* will be once I'm done."

Mel stopped, her hand on the doorknob. For one terrible second, she felt as if her anger would run over everyone in the room and burn the whole goddamn place to the ground. But just as it filled to the brim, she caught herself. She let out a long, harsh breath that misted like heat in winter, floating up toward the ceiling.

Then she threw the door open and walked away hurriedly— before she did something she would regret.

****

"You should've nailed his fucking head to the wall," Cori spat.

The Ferus had heard the entire conversation from outside the atrium,

111

and had let the three other Kales know exactly what was going on. The two guards heard her too, and watched her with trepidation.

"I can't hurt everyone who I disagree with, Cori," Mel said tiredly.

They were sitting outside on the front steps. Mel had needed some fresh air; the argument with Blas Nunez had left her with all sorts of bad feelings. Thomas had tagged along dutifully, but Thrash had dragged his feet and now sat several feet away, refusing to speak. Quint was there as well, apparently feeling it was his duty to convince Mel to let the anger go.

"Yes, you can," Cori said. "You will find fewer people disagree with you if you let the Kale beast out."

"I'll find fewer people will tell me the truth, too," Mel said, rubbing her hands on her breeches. "I'd like open dialogue, not a bunch of people who blindly agree with me."

"Have it your way," the Ferus said. "But if that's how it's going to be, you better mind that temper."

Mel sighed in agreement. "I know."

She leaned back to look at the redhead, who was staring out toward the road. There was little to look at—no cars passed, as the road came to a dead end shortly after it passed the house—but every so often a descendant would walk by in clan colors.

"Someone's always watching the house," Mel said.

Cori nodded, but it was Thomas who answered.

"All the clans have eyes on the house. They all want to know what your grandmother is up to."

"Good luck with that," Mel responded. "*I* don't even know what she's up to."

"That's because you're it," Thomas said. "*You're* what she's up to. Keeping you safe. Letting you heal and adjust. When you're ready, you'll be presented to the clans. They'll fall in line or not. We will know then who is true."

Mel looked up at the older man. "You know I don't have that kind of power."

"You'll be surprised how much power you'll have," Thomas responded. "How much weight your words will carry. You'll see."

Another clansman walked by, this one wearing purple.

"Can they hear us?" Mel asked.

"No," Thomas said. "Even if they had Cori's hearing, there's a spell around the house. Keeps conversations private."

"Are you sure?"

"I tested it out myself, kid," Thomas replied archly.

Mel couldn't help it; she smiled under her veil. "So tell me something, Mr. Thorn. Did these spells always work, or did they just start within the last week?"

"Some always worked," Thomas replied, watching the Janso walk out of view. "Protective ones were hit or miss—I never put much stock in them. The suppressive ones always worked, though. That's how we successfully hid you."

Mel placed a hand on her chest and felt the little gold sun under her tunic. "I always wondered why she made me promise never to take it off."

Thomas smiled. "Thinking ahead, your grandmother. Anyway, the protective boundaries are especially strong. I suspect when we're all dead and gone, they'll still be holding."

Mel's eyes found the totems at the front of the house, just before the road began. She had always known they were there, but hadn't put much thought into them, assuming they were decorative.

"Offensive spells have lost their luster," Thomas continued. "But that's changing."

Changing? Mel thought. Was it her? Had she opened some door? No. It was the Eighth. It had to be. Anton Morel, Wershall, and their ilk. They'd opened the door to *something*, and Kale had matched it with her own. The balance. It was always there somehow.

It was then that Mel wondered if the world would ever be the same. Could they close the door on evil once and for all? Would that be possible? What would need to be done? She wasn't sure, but she knew that the Great Seven needed to work together to prevent the Eighth Clan from taking things too far. She knew without a doubt that there was a line, and that if that line was crossed, it would be nearly impossible to shut the door, much less shut it quietly without those outside of the clans knowing.

Mel looked at Cori. "You told me why you're here, but it's possible to have more than one reason to do a thing, so… are you *also* following orders? Keeping an eye on us for Clan Ferus?" Her words were accusing, but she kept her tone light.

Cori was quiet for a moment before speaking. "Yes."

Mel nodded. "Do you tell your father everything?"

"Only if it's pertinent." Cori met Mel's eye. "Everything else is mine."

"So our conversation with Blas…"

"That will be reported," Cori said apologetically. "But you can trust my father. He won't share what he's learned with the other clans. He respects your grandmother immensely."

Mel tried to decide how she felt about that. A part of her, that dark part that wanted to keep secrets behind a wall that stretched high toward the skies, was not pleased. But Lasade Kale had once told her to trust Cori, and that's what she needed to do. It was also what she *wanted* to do.

"All right then."

"Is it?" the Ferus asked.

As Cori looked at Mel, her blue eyes serious and warm, something light and airy touched Mel's chest. But for once the heat wasn't anger; it was pleasure and assurance.

"I can do worse than Cori O'Shea of Clan Ferus," Mel said. "A lot worse."

She was just falling into the delight in Cori's smile, the joy in her eyes, when that ring in her chest came loose again. It shifted and moved, making way for the fire.

"Oh shit," she heard Quint say.

But Mel was already swimming in the flames.

****

"Mel." The woman's voice was urgent. "Stay with it. Let it take you. Don't let it leave you behind."

The woman had her hands on Mel's shoulders. Mel tried to focus on that—on the woman's grip. The tight hold that was squeezing to the point of pain. But there was something else pulling her. A sense of… chaos. What was it? *Who* was it that was coming toward her with that scent of blood and darkness?

She stood and turned her gaze to the road. A man was walking by, dressed in the color of pale sand. When he saw her looking, he came to a stop—and when his eyes met hers, he froze, then turned to run.

But before he could go two steps, someone grabbed hold of him by the shoulders.

"Wrong place at the wrong time, kid. Shoulda stayed in camp."

Mel turned away, unconcerned, looking down the road, past the point where it went out of sight, obscured by the trees. Moments passed before she heard it. Something was roaring, coming toward her.

She broke off at a sprint, ignoring the yells behind her.

Then something wrapped around her legs, and she came crashing to the ground.

"Christ, cuz—I mean, shit! Stop!"

She pushed free and leapt to her feet. The thing was almost upon her. She smiled, readying for the impact. She was going to kill it. Flip it on its end…

But before it impacted her, the creature screeched to a halt. Mel jumped on it before it could strike, but when her feet landed on its flat surface, it didn't move, didn't even react. Why didn't it want to fight her?

And then she saw—it had eaten some of her people. Even now they were looking up at her from within its transparent skin.

She struck the creature, shattering it. There was yelling as her people escaped from within.

Again, someone grabbed her around the legs. "Damn it! Get down! It's a truck!"

"Help me!" shouted another voice. "Gabe's bleeding!"

She moved toward the voice and realized the creature wasn't a creature at all. It wasn't even alive. But the man lying being pulled from it was. Barely. She could smell his blood and fear. And when she saw him looking up at her, eyes clouded in pain, she realized… he'd been attacked by darkness. But where?

Her eyes searched the trees. It was out there somewhere. Scheming.

She watched as one of the men laid hands on the injured and started chanting. She recognized the words and the spirit in which they were said. He was trying to heal. To cleanse. But he didn't have his hands positioned correctly. They were both on the bleeding man's neck. She jumped down and knelt alongside the healer, grabbed a hand by the wrist, and placed it over the man's chest.

The healer started chanting again. And as he chanted, something shifted inside Mel, moving the ring back into place.

****

Mel's breath came heavy as she looked down at her brother. His tunic was stained with blood down the front, but as he looked around at everyone, his eyes showed a little bit of that familiar spark. The wound around his neck had healed, leaving a puckered scar of new, pink skin.

He swallowed a few times, then opened his mouth. "Thanks, man," he rasped to Quint.

The healer, looking green around the gills and shaking, patted Gabe's shoulder. "Let's get you inside."

Victor and Drew gently lifted Gabe up as everyone else backed away to make room. Gabe kept telling them he was fine to walk, but Quint and Justine shushed him, and he allowed himself to be carried to the infirmary, accompanied by all four of them.

The Mayme watched all of this without a word, until Thomas insisted he follow Thrash into the house. The Mayme looked at Mel one last time before he did as instructed—thankfully without a fight.

After the Mayme had gone, Thomas looked at Mel. "You need to get inside too, kid."

But Mel turned toward the trees once again, trying to push her senses, trying to see if there was anyone or anything out there watching them.

"Hey," Cori said. "What's the matter?"

"It's out there, Cori."

"What is?"

Tío Jorge came up behind them, looking exhausted and spent. "From the depths of Hell, it's come. To feast on the innocent and bring darkness to the lands."

As Cori looked out into the trees, her blue eyes canvassing the area, Mel felt a coldness in the pit of her stomach.

A Lost Soul walked the Earth.

And the world would never be the same.

Chapter Eight

The air in the atrium crackled with nervous energy. The sun was high in the sky, shining through the windows onto the heads of all the occupants, its heat almost offensive. Tempers were high. Victor and Tío Jorge had just finished their telling of the events at Larson's home. The First Healer and *Sapienti* Mendez looked at each other, holding a conversation without speaking, but their anger was plain to see. Disgusted by the fact that the Eighth Clan had operated right under their noses—for *weeks*.

"Are you sure it was a Lost Soul?" *Sapienti* Mendez asked.

Tío Jorge nodded. "It was called upon by its servant. There were bodies which were killed to create its weapon."

The First Healer hissed. "An abomination."

"And the dead?" *Sapienti* Mendez asked.

What she really meant was *the evidence*, Victor knew.

"Burned," he said. "All of them. As well as the house."

"And the Eighth?" Thomas asked. He stood alongside Mel and Thrash, who were both conspicuously silent. "Are they dead, too?"

Victor paused to look at Tío Jorge. "We can't be sure."

His words drew a sigh of disapproval. Victor was disappointed as well. He wished he knew. Wished he knew which of the numerous individuals killed at Larson's house had been Eighth and which had been Larson's family. It would make things so much easier.

"And the burned Kale," *Sapienti* Mendez said. "Obviously there is a connection with the Eighth, but is there one with Cortez?"

Victor nodded. "There was a woman who had been similarly infected," he replied. "It's too much of a coincidence. There has to be a connection."

"How similar?" *Sapienti* Mendez demanded.

"She was a host as well. But there were some notable differences," Tío Jorge said before Victor could reply. "Her body was more... corrupt."

The First Healer's eyes narrowed, then she leaned over to *Sapienti* Mendez and whispered in her ear.

"We need to tell the other clans," Tío Jorge said. "They need to know."

"They will see this as egregious," the First Healer said.

"We've done the best we can with the information we have," argued Tío Jorge. "But we are not omniscient. We can't know what the Eighth are doing at all times."

"Isis is right," *Sapienti* Mendez cut in. "They will see it as egregious on our part. Too much has happened. This *gross* oversight will push us further away from the other clans."

"Not *all*," Tío Jorge said. "Clan Mayme has always stood with us. And I believe Clan Ferus will as well. Clans Tam, Ivor, and Moors are in disarray, and they will be until their leadership is chosen."

"What makes you think Clan Mayme will be aligned with us?" the First Healer asked. "They have no leadership either."

"Because Clan Mayme can be reasoned with."

"Clan Mayme is already in the process of choosing a replacement," *Sapienti* Mendez said. "We won't know what direction they will lean until their *Sapienti* is chosen. I am hopeful, but for now that is all I am."

"That leaves one other, then," Tío Jorge said. "Clan Janso."

"No," said *Sapienti* Mendez.

"Mari—" Tío Jorge began, but *Sapienti* Mendez cut him off.

"Don't misunderstand me, Jorge. If we choose to tell the clans… I *will* try. I'll try to convince them that we are doing everything we can, but Sandeep Reddy is not his brother. He will see me as weak—our clan as well. You *know* this. He will push to maneuver himself into a position of strength. Of all the clans, Clan Janso was, and still is, the most expansive."

"He knows we won't give up our territory," the First Healer added, turning toward Thomas. "But that doesn't mean he won't *try*. First he'll attempt to convince the other clans that we aren't worthy protectors. Then he'll press to have our territory split up between the other six."

For a long moment, no one else spoke. An air of expectation built in the room. And Victor wondered what everyone was waiting for. To him, the answer was clear. To hell with the other clans. Let them fend for themselves, the bastards.

He was just about to give voice to his thoughts when a stern look from his uncle made him stay silent.

His sister stepped forward her place at Thomas's side. It was then that Victor realized it was she the First Healer had been speaking to, not Thomas.

"We need to tell the other clans of the Lost Soul," she said. "They need to know and prepare." She looked bone-tired.

"And if they press for advantage?" the First Healer asked.

"Then they will see just how weak we are," Mel responded. "The Lost Soul is formidable, but it is not immortal." She looked at her uncle. "I suspect you've wounded it badly, Tío. I ask you to finish what you started: hunt it down and kill it."

Victor, too, looked at his uncle, watching.

Tío Jorge nodded in acquiescence.

Mel turned to Thrash. "You, cousin, you've been wanting to hunt down the Eighth. Now you will have that chance. You and Thomas will find any that remain. And you will bring them back here. *Alive.* We have questions. And they have answers."

Thrash's eyes grew with a fire that Victor hadn't seen since before Charlotte and Mel returned from *Inter Spatium Abyssus*. Victor could tell that his cousin would test the "alive" part of his sister's request, and suspected that was why Thomas had been chosen to accompany him.

"I will go," the older man said. "If you agree not to go anywhere without Keven and Quint."

"I promise," Mel said with a careless wave of her hand.

"I'm not kidding, Mel," Thomas said.

"She's not either," said *Sapienti* Mendez, looking at her granddaughter. "Are you, Mel?"

"No," Mel replied soberly. "On my honor, I promise to stay put."

Thomas was appeased. His blue eyes turned inward. *On to the task at hand,* Victor thought. *On to hunting down traitors.*

"Do you not have any demands of me?" Victor asked his sister.

Mel frowned, her weary brown eyes finding Victor's. "Aren't you supposed to be helping Tío Luce investigate the Cortez death? How is that going?"

Victor grimaced. He had no idea. He really ought to get on the sat phone and see where his uncle was so he and the Wileys could join him.

At Victor's silence, Mel turned toward the massive doors.

"I hope you're going to bed," Victor said, irritated—in part at Mel and in part at himself.

"Don't worry, I am," she said without turning around. "The sun serpent gnaws at my bones. I'll be in the Sun Room if I'm needed."

She left, taking Thomas and Thrash with her.

Sapienti Mendez faced the First Healer, and without a word, they seemed to come to a mutual conclusion. "Alert the other clans, Jorge," said Victor's grandmother. "We'll tell them tonight."

****

As Victor left the atrium, he felt torn. The Lost Soul that had almost killed his brother was out there in the world, spreading its madness and doing what it pleased. Victor should be out there killing the damn thing. Instead he had to track a dead man's trail with Tío Luce.

I doubt I'll see anything but blue skies and green grass with Tío Luce, he thought. Then he rubbed his eyes. *But maybe that's not such a bad thing.* He had been awake for more than twenty-four hours and was starting to feel the effects.

Victor grabbed the sat phone, and the urge to call his wife was so strong he almost dialed her number. But in the end he ended up calling Tío Luce. He got an update, noted his uncle's location, then headed for the kitchen where he knew he'd find the Wileys. The two were sipping coffee when he walked in, but stood when they saw him.

"Are we leaving?" Justine asked, and at Victor's nod, both she and her brother slid their knives back into their sheaths. They each carried multiple knives, stashed in their tunics, boots, and breeches.

Victor led them out of the house with his axe stowed on his back and one of the long knives Drew favored at his hip. "They found the location where Cortez was attacked," he said. "It was just past the northern border. Apparently there was a… *host* a short distance away. My uncle said the host fared worse than Cortez."

"I didn't think that was physically possible," Justine said. "Fuck me! Cortez didn't look like he fared well *at all*. Can you imagine, Drew? The poor thing must've exploded."

Drew murmured in agreement.

"Apparently it wasn't a pretty sight," Victor said, loosening the veil around his neck. "My uncle spent most of the night cleaning up."

"Jesus," Justine muttered.

They all piled into Victor's truck and took a dirt road that cut right across the property, reducing a two-hour hike into a matter of minutes. When Drew spotted the small group of Kales and Maymes, Victor veered in their direction, parking the truck along a stream that was drying out. A sandbar stretched along its edge, soft sand mixed with dirt and teeth-sized pebbles.

It was only when Victor was standing in the sand that he noticed the pink residue of blood upon the bank. Where the sand butted up against dried grass was a pile of unrecognizable tissue and bone.

"Who was it?" he asked his uncle, trying not to gag at the smell. He could taste the ripeness of it in the back of his throat. He breathed slowly out of his mouth, hoping his breakfast wasn't going to come back and haunt him.

Tío Luce had been digging a shallow hole next to the ruined remains. He stabbed his shovel into the grass and leaned against it heavily while mopping his brow with a white kerchief that was sopping with sweat.

"Couldn't get an ID if we tried," he said, shaking his head. "Body was spread all along the bank. We raked it all night. One of the worst things I've ever seen in my life."

Justine had the eyes of a woman who was sorry she'd missed it, but Victor shared his uncle's disgust. Drew grabbed an extra shovel and quietly got to work.

Victor looked around. The other Kales, along with the participating Maymes, had formed a watchful perimeter in the tall grass, their alert eyes never in one place for long.

"The Maymes look to be cooperating," Victor said quietly, his gaze finding Cleo Newberry, who was kneeling a short distance away, her hand hovering inches above the ground, chanting in *Old Tongue.* "Is that a cleansing spell?"

Tío Luce nodded. "The protective spells only hold within our borders. Out here…" He blew a shaky breath as he looked out into the woods, then collected himself. "Don't let that Mayme fool you— all she wants is information. And she doesn't think much of my mother. It's taking me every diplomatic bone in my body not to lose my temper."

"That bad?" Victor said. Very few people insulted his grandmother. The woman was strong and held her clan together with a firm grip. Few had anything critical to say about her, but of course the events of the Agora had put his grandmother's leadership into question.

Tío Luce nodded. "When she's not subtly insulting our *Sapienti,* she's interrogating our clanspeople. You'd think we were in league with the Eighth the way she's carrying on." He blew out a frustrated breath. "How's Gabe?"

"Alive and kicking," Victor said, eyes still on Newberry. "What do you need me to do?"

His uncle looked around—at the remains, the creek, at everything. Finally he pushed the shovel at Victor's chest. "Right now, I just want you to dig."

So Victor dug—furiously. He let the exertion work his muscles, feeling the sweet pain that burned there. At times like this, a mundane task could take him out of life's complications so suddenly that he was amazed at its power to do so. He worked until his mouth was dry and sweat poured from his body. And then he kept working.

It was through this fog of concentration that he heard the call go up. He dumbly looked up as all around him his clanspeople and the Maymes sprang to heightened alertness. A Kale was running toward them through the brush, holding a sat phone.

He stopped in front of Tío Luce, who had been speaking to Cleo Newberry, and talked quietly to him. Victor caught a few words as he grew closer: *miles from here ... blood everywhere ... dead.*

"What's happened?" Victor asked as he reached the others.

"We've found something," Tío Luce said. "Take some clanspeople and check it out. I need to stay here until this is done. Do not move without me. Just investigate the scene."

He gathered the Wileys, and after a quick call to get a precise location, they set off through the wood. Their pace was quick, but not so intense as the night before. Four other Kales ran with them, along with a few Maymes, Cleo Newberry among them. They had been moving for a half hour before the woman sought him out.

"I suppose you're not going to tell me what had you running off so quickly yesterday," she said, falling into stride at his side.

Victor stepped widely to the left to avoid a tree, as if he hoped the change in path would create distance between him and the Mayme.

"It's best not to keep secrets, Victor," she said. "In these times, secrets will divide."

"You'll hear about it tonight," Victor grunted.

"Oh, is that what the *summons* was for?" she said. "I won't be attending your grandmother's little gathering. I'm not one to come when called, and she's not my *Sapienti*. I shouldn't have to drop everything for her."

Victor was not his uncle. He would not endure hours in this woman's presence while she insulted his grandmother. Stopping, he turned to face her fully. "You know what also causes divide? Snarky, disrespectful *clanswomen* who have up until now sat on the sidelines while *my* clan has taken major hits."

"Major hits?" she said, the condescension dripping off her words. "No—clan Mayme doesn't know about major hits, but we know *loss*. We've dealt with *many* lives lost on *your* territory."

Victor noticed that both Kales and Maymes had surrounded the two of them, and there was tension in the air. He handed his axe off to the nearest Kale and tore the veil from his face. He didn't want to give the impression that he was going to draw arms on the woman.

"I'm not talking about Clam Mayme," he said. "Clan Mayme has been supportive at every turn. I'm talking about *you*. You, who think you're so much better and smarter than everyone here, and yet you don't have the intelligence to not show my grandmother, my *Sapienti*, disrespect in my presence. She invited you into our home, invited you into our confidence, and you did what? Spat in her face because you interpreted it as a *summons*. We're allies, you and I. Clan and honor dictates that from us. But I won't stand here and let you twist something we're doing out of goodwill and friendship into some power play. That's not who we are."

"Oh, really? And what of all the things you don't speak of? If you think I'm dumb enough to believe your *Sapienti* will divulge every single detail—"

"She doesn't need to tell you every clan secret. Those are ours to keep, just as your clan secrets are yours. But what you need to do is trust us. Trust that we will tell you that which affects you. That's what tonight is about, Cleo. I just wish you'd pull your head out of your ass long enough to go back and see for yourself."

"Go back? Are you out of your mind? If you think I'm leaving your clan to manage this on its own, you're crazy. I'm staying—if only to clean up your mess."

With that, she turned and continued on her way, taking the Maymes with her. Victor almost yelled at her back that she didn't know where she was going, but that would've been childish. *Let her go, let them get lost,* he thought. If that was childish too, so be it.

"Damn, dude," Justine said. "She's wrong... but she's right, too, you know?"

Victor didn't know what she meant.

"You gotta give a person like that time, Vic," she continued. "She's all business, you know? She's all about this life, but she hasn't seen what we've seen. She thinks she knows, but she really doesn't, and she won't until it's right in front of her."

"She helped rake a dead body last night, Justine," Victor replied.

"That ain't the same and you know it. A lot of us can clean up dead bodies, compartmentalize it away, but until we're face to face with the thing that killed it… well, that's different. You know it and I know it."

Drew grunted as if unsure whether he agreed.

"Wait till she sees the *Malum*," Justine said. "Then she'll know. Preparation goes out the door. Training kicks in. If she's really smart like she thinks she is, she'll realize that."

"So what is she right about?" Victor asked.

Justine smiled. "She wants to fight alongside us—'cause she thinks we're idiots and don't know our asses from our elbows—but I can't hate a woman that wants to fight alongside us."

Victor was angered to hear that the woman thought so little of his clan, but he couldn't change the woman's mind. And he certainly couldn't make the woman go back to camp. If she didn't want to learn there was a Lost Soul loose, that was her problem. And in Victor's opinion, Cleo Newberry was not nearly as smart as she thought she was.

With bitterness in his mouth he proceeded, taking the lead from the Maymes with ease. The look he shared with Newberry as he passed her was one of mutual distaste. He didn't speak another word the entire way, and neither did she.

When they reached the site, they found two Ferus standing with three Kales and the Janso, Smitty. They all stood casually, hands loosely at their sides, looking as if they'd all just decided to take a light stroll through the waist-high grass—except for the fact that they were armed to the teeth. They were in a wide-open field with very few trees and a view of a highway several miles away. A much smaller, country road stretched through the middle of the field.

It was a beautiful, pastoral scene. And then the wind shifted, and the smell of death reached Victor's nostrils, pulling his gaze toward what had brought them all here. An entire herd of cows lay dead. What was left of their carcasses was already decomposing. Flies danced and flesh-colored maggots squirmed within the rot.

Victor pulled the sat phone from his waist and called his uncle.

"We're here," he told him. "It's bad. There's a road and a highway nearby."

"How quickly can you clean it up?" his uncle asked.

"I can start now," he replied, then looked at the highway in the distance. "But I can't do the real cleaning until dark."

"All right, I'm done here. I'll meet you there shortly."

"Tío," Victor said, before his uncle hung up. "There's more than one."

"I know," his uncle said. The disappointment in his voice was clear. "This is worse than we thought."

A lot worse, Victor thought. He did not look at Cleo Newbury. He did not want to see the accusation that he was sure he would find in her eyes. Instead he turned to the Wileys, and they got to work.

Chapter Nine

Gabe was trying to sleep when the First Healer walked in, but the small cot in the infirmary was not at all comfortable, and the air from the HVAC was set to blizzard, making him freeze under the thin blanket. As the older woman stopped at the foot of his bed, he gave up even trying to rest.

"Gabriel Mendez," the First Healer said, shaking her head. "What are we to do with you?"

"What'd I do now?"

The First Healer pushed her wire-framed glasses up her nose. "Fighting a Lost Soul by yourself? It makes one wonder if there is something wrong with your head. Did you hit it especially hard during the games?"

Gabe coughed a laugh. "Now, doc. What was I supposed to do? I was locked in that room all by myself. I had no choice."

"Well, I suppose you didn't," she said with a huff. She placed her hands on his shoulders, and Gabe felt a warmth spread under his skin. "Any pain?"

"No," Gabe said, trying not to balk at the *Spiritus* the healer was using. He'd never experienced it before. "But I'm so damn tired. I can barely keep my eyes open."

"That's normal. Your body has been through a traumatic

experience. The healing usually takes its toll as well."

"I should've died," Gabe said. He tried to sit up, but the fatigue was too much. It kept him pinned to the cot, not allowing him the strength to do anything but watch the healer.

"And a week ago you would have," said the First Healer, putting her hand on his chest to stop his stirring. "But I can sense you're growing stronger by the day."

Gabe was having trouble paying attention. That warmth under his skin felt nice and cozy, and he could feel himself getting pulled into the sleep realm. He wondered what the First Healer had done to him to make him so comfortable. But those thoughts were for another time. Sleep beckoned, and Gabe fell into it willingly.

The next time he woke up someone was holding his hand. He grinned without opening his eyes, picked the hand up, and placed a kiss on the knuckles.

"Very smooth," said Siva.

Gabe opened his eyes and took a good look at her. Caramel skin with dark hair and dark eyes—she was a beauty. *His* beauty.

"You're a sight for sore eyes," he said, letting his eyes roam her body.

"Am I? I wasn't sure if you'd miss me—since you stood me up last night." Her eyes were twinkling, and there was a smirk on her lips.

"I didn't mean to," Gabe said soberly. "There was some trouble."

Siva squeezed his hand. "I understand. What exactly happened? I'm sensing some serious energy on the grounds."

"What do you mean?"

"We've noticed the Kale property has a pretty strong boundary along its borders."

"When you say 'we'…"

"I mean most in my clan."

"Have they picked up on anything else?" Gabe asked.

"They've sensed all the suppression spells around the house and are wondering what that's about." Siva bit her lip in uncertainty. "And… there was a strange energy the past few days—twice it happened. Only Cleo and I were sensitive to it. I think she has some idea what it is, but she won't share. She means to keep it to herself until our *Sapienti* is chosen." She looked Gabe in the eye. "But *I'm* pretty sure it was your sister."

Gabe sighed. That was so not what he wanted to hear. Siva knew Mel was alive, but very few outside Clan Kale did. And if descendants were now able to sense Mel in some other way, it would ruin the whole point of faking Mel's death in the first place. Even if they didn't know it was Mel, they'd want to investigate.

"Why do you think it's Mel?" Gabe asked.

"Come on, Gabe, give me some credit. You don't survive *Inter Spatium Abyssus* without some help. Her and Cori have their gifts, don't they?"

Gabe didn't reply, but he could tell from Siva's expression that he had given himself away. "Are any of the other clans sensing anything?" he asked.

"I think it would be safe to assume that they have. I know Clan Janso has—I've seen them wandering the grounds trying to find the source of the energy." She frowned. "And my father certainly knows something's going on; he even approached Cleo. I wasn't privy to that conversation, but I'm sure he's trying to show himself an ally to Clan Mayme."

Gabe closed his eyes. *Great, just what we need.* Mel really needed to get a handle on her abilities. Exposing herself would bring attention, and attention would bring questions—questions that no one wanted to answer. And now clans were acting as though Clan Kale had nefarious intent.

"So," Siva said. "You going to tell me what happened last night? Or do I have to pull it from you telepathically?"

"You can do that?"

"No," she snorted. "If I could, I'd know more about what was going on around here."

Without going into specifics—he was not at liberty to tell her the who, where, or why—Gabe explained that he had been injured and nearly died. It was only Quint's smart thinking and gift with healing that had saved his life. Gabe could tell that Siva had questions, but thankfully she accepted his limited explanation and moved on to more important matters.

"We have a missing clansman," she said. "Would you know anything about that?"

Gabe bit his lip, recalling Thomas hauling off a Mayme. "Maybe."

"Gabe!"

"It's not what you think," he said hurriedly.

"Really? So my clansman didn't accidentally see something he shouldn't have and your lot spirited him away?"

"Okay, maybe it is what you think. But he's okay—we didn't hurt him."

"Oh, that makes me feel *loads* better."

"Fine," Gabe said, sitting up. The room spun a little, but he got to his feet—against Siva's protests. "Let's go find him. You can see for yourself."

He could tell she wasn't sure what to do. Would it be clan or Gabe? But after a moment she came to a conclusion, grabbed Gabe's arm, and pulled him out of the infirmary.

****

"I always wonder why the good Lord saw fit to bless me with stubborn grandchildren," *Sapienti* Mendez said ruefully. She sat in her office, tidying up the mounds of paperwork on her desk. "I give them love, safety, and time to heal, and all they want to do is run around at their weakest."

Gabe stood on the other side of her desk on unsteady legs. He felt as if he was going to pass out on his feet. The walk from the clinic to the house had been an exhausting one, even with Siva's help. He didn't like showing weakness to Siva, but he had to prove to her that his clan meant well and had done no harm to her clansman.

"I apologize, *Sapienti*," Siva said respectfully. "It's my fault."

"Oh, I doubt that, Siva," said *Sapienti* Mendez, looking at her grandson archly. "Gabe has a way of doing what he wants when he wants. Now, Gabe, what has pulled you out of bed when you so need your rest?"

Gabe cleared his throat. "I told Siva that we have her missing clansman."

Sapienti Mendez paused—then gave Gabe an unfathomable look. "Yes, we do," she said finally. "He witnessed a private matter and has refused to take a blood oath."

"May I see him, *Sapienti*?" Siva asked. "I can convince him to take the oath. It may be better, coming from me. And I have taken an oath myself where Mel is concerned." At *Sapienti* Mendez's piercing look, she added: "He did walk into something having to do with Mel, correct?"

Gabe's grandmother rose slowly and moved around the desk to stand in front of Siva. "Actually," she said, "I have decided to reach out to Cleo Newberry. Our clans have always worked well together; I feel that should continue."

Siva looked surprised. "I appreciate that, *Sapienti*."

"And I appreciate your willingness to be a friend of Kale. Now, if you wouldn't mind—I'd like a moment to speak with my grandson."

Siva nodded and left the two alone.

Gabe seized the opportunity to stumble to one of the chairs and collapse into it. With Siva gone, there was no need to maintain the pretense that he was anything less than completely spent. But when *Sapienti* Mendez moved toward the door—no doubt to call for a healer—he raised his voice to stop her.

"No," he said hurriedly. "I'm okay. I just need a moment."

"You need your bed, you stubborn boy," his grandmother said. She looked him over and ran her hands down his head, tutting. "After this, I want you to go back to the infirmary."

"I think I'll take one of the bedrooms instead," Gabe said, letting his head rest on the back of the chair.

"Fine. But first tell me why you saw fit to tell Siva Reddy about clan business."

Gabe looked up at his grandmother's face. He knew with certainty he was speaking to the *Sapienti*, the Elder of Clan Kale. Her eyes had hardened, and her face was inscrutable.

"I trust her," he said.

"You *love* her," his grandmother said. "And although I know you do not love nor trust easily, I must stress to you how important it is to *not* share our clan business."

"Siva has taken the oath," Gabe argued. He wished he could get to his feet, to really drive the point home. But he had to settle for a very, *very* displeased look.

"She has," his grandmother said with a nod. "She agreed to keep Mel's secret. And for that I am thankful to her. But just because she's given her oath doesn't mean she should be privy to everything—"

"Cori spends almost every *second* with Mel. She hears all sorts of things. And you don't have an issue with *her* knowing our business," Gabe said. It seemed unfair that his sister was able to share so much with Cori and yet here he was getting scolded for something Mel did *all the time*.

"The situation with your sister is different."

"Why?"

"It just is. There are things you don't know about and that I'm not at liberty to share."

"Well, that's convenient," Gabe replied. "I have to put up a wall for Siva and Mel gets to have full disclosure with Cori. That's hardly fair, Grandma."

"Fair?" his grandmother said. "I suppose it isn't—but that's the way of things at the moment. And I think we both know you'll manage. Won't you?"

Gabe stared angrily at the wall for a long moment before nodding.

"Now, did she share any of *her* clan business with *you*?" she asked.

Gabe looked at her incredulously. "Seriously?" He shook his head, but grudgingly related what Siva had said about the energy that had spread along the grounds and how Siva believed it was Mel.

"It seems my decision to bring in Newberry will be for the best," his grandmother said. "She already may be on to us more than I had believed. And her willingness to keep her knowledge to herself shows that she is aware that there are those among her own clan who can't be trusted. It also may waylay whatever designs *Sapienti* Reddy has in store."

"Newberry could be keeping her secrets for other reasons," Gabe said. "Nefarious reasons."

"Yes, she may. Either way, we will know soon. If she takes the oath, she can be trusted. If she doesn't… then we will not count her as our friend."

"Will we count her as our enemy?" Gabe asked.

His grandmother paused, looking out the window. The late afternoon sun lit her eyes and made them glitter like brown jewels. "I'd rather not pass judgment on someone so quickly without cause. If she refuses the oath, that alone is not reason to assume she is Eighth

Clan. She could very well have other reasons for staying neutral."

With effort, Gabe rose from his seat. His legs were a little steadier, but he was still exhausted, and wanted the comfort of a bed. "You know I trust you, Grandma, but there's still a part of me that wonders what is to keep a descendant's mouth shut even after they've taken the oath."

Sapienti Mendez smiled grimly. "I suppose nothing but their honor."

"And if they have none?" Gabe asked.

"I believe you know the answer to that," she replied.

Gabe did know. Usually when a descendant of the Great Seven broke their oath, they were exiled from their clan. But what was exile to a descendant who had already turned their back on *The Ways* to become Eighth? It wasn't as if they would feel any loyalty to the clan they were born into.

"Don't worry, Gabe," his grandmother said. "We will deal with whatever comes. *Our* way."

Gabe nodded. He didn't know much about the strength and bond of blood oaths, but dealing with events *their* way, the Kale way… that was something he could put his faith and trust in.

****

Ohanko Nash was a tall, dark Native American with long black hair that fell down his back. They found him in a dingy white tunic watching television in a stark room on the first floor, under the watchful eye of Keven Thorn. But when Siva walked in, he stood with a nonchalance that made Gabe pause. The Mayme showed no fear or distress. That demonstrated that he had been treated well, but still, Gabe would have expected at least *some* discomfort at his situation.

Siva told Nash to sit tight, that everything was being worked out.

He merely raised a careless hand and said, "Ohanko Nash does not have any place to be." Then he folded his tall frame back into his chair and resumed his watching.

After that uneventful encounter, they started upstairs, with Gabe intending to find a vacant bedroom where he could get some rest. But the fatigue was getting to him. Every step was achingly slow, and he was hung tightly to the rail, afraid he might lose his balance. He considered calling for a healer, but he didn't want to suffer the indignity. He was a Kale, damn it. He shouldn't need the constant care of a healer. He should be able to gut it out.

"You okay?" Siva asked, gazing up at him in concern. "You don't look so well."

Just then a dizzy spell hit him and he stumbled into the wall. Just as he was sliding toward the floor, another set of arms grabbed hold of him, the grip strong and sure.

"Well, aren't you a mess," said the melodious voice of Cori O'Shea. "You and your sister are a pair."

Gabe huffed in irritation. "Fuck you." He was still smarting from the conversation with his grandmother concerning the Ferus, and wanted nothing more than to wipe that smirk off her face.

But Cori didn't rise to the bait. Instead she laughed, full and loud. "More alike than you know," she said. "Come on, let's get you to bed."

"I don't need help."

"Yes, he does," Siva said, and shot him a look that told him he'd be in all kinds of trouble if he didn't behave. "Excuse his bad mood; he's pissed that he's weak from his wounds."

I am not weak! Gabe wanted to scream it until his voice was raw, but he didn't have the energy even for that. So he was left with the laughing Ferus pulling him up the stairs like a sack of potatoes, wondering how the hell she'd gotten so strong.

She led him to a bedroom, where Siva took over and gently guided him into bed.

"What are ya doing over here anyway, Ferus?" Gabe asked Cori. "Have a fight with my sister? She throw you out?"

Cori snorted as she looked down at him with bright blue eyes. "Not likely." She took a seat in one of the chairs that lined the wall. Her flaming hair was in a tight braid which she flipped casually over one shoulder. "I think your sister grows fonder of me by the day."

"Oh, I know exactly how fond she is of you," Gabe said, and smiled wickedly. "You liking the friendzone there, Ace?"

Cori snorted. "I won't be there for long."

"Ohhh, don't we think highly of ourselves?"

"And why not? She could do a lot worse than me."

Cori was way too pleased with herself. The happiness was practically seeping out of her. Gabe scowled but tried one more jab. "Mel's a fickle creature," he said. "If you're not on her twenty-four seven, she'll dump you and move on to the next."

Cori rolled her eyes and turned to Siva. "I don't know what you see in him."

"He has his moments," the Mayme said. Then she turned and gave Gabe a quick peck. "I need to head back and call Cleo with an update—I don't want her to worry about Nash. I'll be back in a bit." She turned to Cori once more. "Be nice, Cori. He's my fave."

"Your fave *what*?" the Ferus asked, but Siva was already out the door.

Cori turned to Gabe. "Fine. I'm just going to tack on whatever I like at the end of that sentence."

"Do it. But I'm her favorite in the whole world. The *whole* of it. You're not even a blip on the radar."

"I don't need to be," Cori said. Then the smile fell from her face, and her eyes grew serious and cold. "Nico is here."

Gabe sat up abruptly. "Where?"

"In the Sun Room with Mel."

Gabe rose from the bed.

"Lie back down. I didn't tell you so you'd go running off."

"But I need to—"

"You don't need to do anything. Nico and Mel are having a private conversation. Then he'll skitter off in the night like he usually does."

"You really don't like him, do you?" said Gabe, settling back down. "Why is that? Lord knows you've no reason to feel jealous."

"I'm not *jealous*," the Ferus snapped. "The man just irks me."

Gabe smiled tiredly, glad for Nico's presence. The man had done what Gabe had failed to do: put the Ferus off, at least for just a few moments. That helped drain the fire out of him, and at once he felt the need to rest. He felt his eyes slip shut as he wondered what Nico and Mel were talking about.

"I guess I'll shove off then," the Ferus said.

"Hey, can you get the door?" Gabe asked.

But as she departed, Cori left the bedroom door wide open.

"Thanks for that!" he yelled.

"You're welcome!" came the reply.

Gabe blew a frustrated breath through his teeth.

****

It must have been hours later when Gabe felt someone shaking him awake. They were gentle about it, but still he wanted to punch them in the face. All the more so when he opened his eyes and saw the Ferus, back once again.

"What are you doing, creeper?" he snapped.

Cori snorted from where she leaned against the wall.

"It wasn't her, it was me," said Mel, grabbing him by his collar. "Get up, hurry!"

His sister was moving way too quickly and talking way too fast for Gabe's sleep-addled brain. "Jesus," he said as she pulled him up. "What's gotten into you? Don't you know I almost died? I lost a like a million pints of blood, you loser. I'm not getting out of this bed."

"Gabe," Mel said urgently, "the clans are meeting in five minutes. You need to be there."

"Why?"

Mel didn't answer. She just stared at him intently.

After a few moments of this, Gabe sighed with annoyance. "Fine." He threw the blankets off his legs. "Whatcha want me to do?"

Ten minutes later he was stumbling inside the gathering that was taking place in the atrium, trying to at once be subtle and quiet and succeeding in neither. All conversation stopped when he walked in. The Maymes, Ferus, Tams, Moors, Jansos, and Ivors were standing in small clusters throughout the room. There were also a few Kales dressed in all black, and he found his grandmother holding court in the center of the room. Giving her a winning smile, he walked to a bench and parked himself next to Blas Nunez, who was clearly not happy to receive his company. Gabe's aunt, Viola, sat on the other side of Blas. She eyed Gabe with a curious look before giving him a small smile, which he returned.

"What'd I miss?" he whispered, but it must have been a lot louder than he thought judging by the glare he got from the older man, who didn't respond.

Rolling his eyes, Gabe focused on what his grandmother was saying.

"… the concerns of the clans have been escalated, and so we've agreed to an earlier time for this gathering. I realize you all have questions, and I will do my best to answer them, but first there must—"

"This dead Kale—Cortez?" This was from a Mayme, but not Cleo

Newberry. In her stead was a man with a hawk-like face and grey eyes. His voice was high-pitched and carried clearly through the low din of the room. "What have you discovered? Have you found those responsible?"

"You know as much as I do, Lovel," Gabe's grandmother replied. "It's why we asked you all to take part in the investigation."

"My clan believes you're keeping information from us," Lovel said.

"I've provided that which impacts all the clans," *Sapienti* Mendez replied.

"Sounds like a convenient excuse to keep us in the dark."

"I agree," said *Sapienti* Reddy. The Janso stood among four of his clansmen, and looked hard at Gabe's grandmother. He didn't say another word, but he'd said enough; the damage had been done. The floodgates opened, and the Moors party all spoke at once.

"We came here for answers, and you give us nothing!"

"Where is your honor? Honor dictates responsibility in the actions of your clan."

"Responsibility?" Gabe's grandmother replied. "What would Clan Moors like me to take responsibility for?"

"You *know* what we want you to take responsibility for," said one of the Moors. "Our *Sapienti* is dead! And it happened here! On your lands!"

Gabe heard a satisfied noise and looked at Blas Nunez. The beady-eyed Kale looked pleased at this turn of events.

"We're all sorry for the loss of Rudolph Kelser. He was well respected—"

"Oh, spare me your condolences. I've heard all about how well you respected him from his nephew, Horace Avery."

At this, Gabe felt his anger spark. He had history with Avery. Gabe opened his mouth to speak, but a look from his grandmother kept him quiet.

Sapienti O'Shea cut in. "Horace Avery is a traitor and a liar, and his word is of no importance to this meeting. If you wish to believe him, you're only falling into the hands of the Eighth."

"Horace Avery is a Moors," replied the Moors representative. "He's always conducted himself with honor."

"No, he has not," said *Sapienti* O'Shea. "As I'm sure those of your clan have explained to you, he and his cousin Damien Jenson, along with two other Moors, were involved in the abduction and torture of Gabriel Mendez. They were then challenged out of *Assugere* for the disrespect paid toward Clan Kale. That is how Jenson and your other two clansmen died, *not* in battling the *Malum*—as I've heard you've been telling all who are willing to hear."

Gabe raised an eyebrow when the Moors representative looked at him.

"We believe that to be an exaggeration," the Moors said smoothly. "Clansmen can get overly excited during the games, given their competitiveness."

"Then you are mistaken," said Lovel. "My clanspeople also witnessed the treachery by Horace Avery. I'm told he and his party were even wearing black, which we all know the Eighth is so fond of wearing."

The Moors looked at Lovel, then around the room to see if any would speak up on Horace's behalf. When none came forward, he stepped back and fell silent.

"It's easy to accuse from the safety of the heavens," said *Sapienti* O'Shea. "Easy to point fingers when half of you weren't here."

"The events that happened are not easy to stomach," *Sapienti* Mendez added. "Nor are they easy to accept. But we must not turn away from each other. We must work together. So now I ask you to please open your ears and hearts and *listen*."

Gabe heard Mel's voice in his head. *You are a witness,* she had told him as she rushed him out of his bedroom. *Make them believe.*

"I was here," said *Sapienti* Reddy. "I know what I saw. You speak of a lot of pretty words, Mari, but you still can't explain how the events of the Agora happened—or accounted for your negligent way of handling it. I know what I saw then, and I see it now." He turned to the other clans. "In the spirit of friendship and honor, I must speak of what I've witnessed. And that is ineptitude. Clear-cut ineptitude."

Protect the clan. Protect the clan. Protect the clan.

"What we see here is a clan that is incapable of keeping their own house in order," *Sapienti* Reddy continued. "Why should we work with them when they've demonstrated such an inability to protect their own? They can't even protect the *Sapienti*'s direct descendants! *Two* of her granddaughters have suffered the result of her failures— one is dead and the other dying. Is this who we want to be responsible for holding these lands? Should we not have someone more capable?"

If *Sapienti* Mendez was angered by *Sapienti* Reddy's accusations, she didn't show it. But there was something in her eyes, something keen and predatory. She sat on a bench with the First Healer, leaned back, and looked to Gabe with a gesture that seemed to say *go ahead.*

Gabe raised his eyebrows in surprise, but then grinned darkly.

"You see many things, *Sapienti* Reddy," he began. "But did you see that your clan brought the gateway stones into play?"

The entire room suddenly paused, and all eyes turned to the Elder of Clan Janso.

"Ah," said Gabe. "I see you neglected to mention that—in the spirit of *friendship and honor.*" He stood, grateful his legs were steady enough to keep him from wobbling. "I was there as a witness when *Sapienti* O'Shea entreated your brother to give up his stone, warning him of its danger. But your brother did not believe him, and refused."

"Is this true, *Sapienti* O'Shea?" the Ivors representative asked.

The Elder of Clan Ferus nodded.

Gabe smiled. "One could say this whole mess could've been avoided if only the man had seen reason." He paused to let them all chew on that for a few moments. Let it sink in so deep, the awareness bled out of their eyes.

"Then there was Anton Morel," Gabe went on, "who we *know* opened the gateway during *Ambulant Labiorosam*, killing our brothers and sisters."

"How do you know this?" asked the Tam representative.

"Yes, how can you possibly know that Anton is guilty?" *Sapienti* Reddy asked, going on the offensive. "Missing men do not speak."

"Cori O'Shea," Gabe responded. He gestured to *Sapienti* O'Shea, who again nodded.

"Why were we not told of these developments?" Lovel asked.

"Can you honestly stand there and say you were ready to listen?" Gabe said, looking from clansperson to clansperson. "He speaks of our clan's negligence," he went on, pointing to *Sapienti* Reddy, "but how much better would your clans fare—any of you—if there were so many variables working against you… most of them coming from the very clan that is making a play for your territory?" He gave *Sapienti* Reddy a look of contempt. "But please, continue on about our ineptitude when your own brother holds the crown, and your own clansman, Anton Morel—who is directly responsible for *all* the deaths—was an agent of the Eighth."

Sapienti Reddy gave Gabe a look of furious intensity that would've made a lesser man wilt. But Gabe just smiled, which only made the older man angrier.

Sapienti Mendez spoke calmly. "I didn't call this meeting to point fingers or to shame anyone, and certainly not to formally charge anyone—that can only be done through a Tribunal. So if we are done with this discussion, I'd like to move on to why I've asked you all here."

Gabe turned toward her, bowed deeply, and took his seat.

His grandmother stood and spoke. "A Lost Soul roams the Earth."

The room was silent but for the sudden intakes of breath. If the room had been tense before, now it was a pressure cooker.

"I'm sorry, what did you say?" said Lovel.

"You heard me," *Sapienti* Mendez replied.

"How?" asked the Moors.

It was Gabe who answered. "A *Malum* escaped when Anton Morel opened the gateway. It possessed a human, who completed the ritual that summoned the Lost Soul."

The questions flew fast and furious. Where did this happen? Who is the host? What has been done to contain it? *Sapienti* Mendez answered everything as directly as possible, keeping no secrets. When she told them that Gabe had fought the Lost Soul and barely survived the encounter, they all wanted a look at his wound. He opened the collar of his tunic, revealing the angry red scar of the Lost Soul's sword—a scar that he knew would never disappear no matter how much power grew within him.

"This is dark news," said the Tam representative. "I must leave and alert my clan." He walked quickly out the door, taking his retinue with him.

The others followed—*Sapienti* Reddy staring daggers at the Kales before departing—until only the Clan Mayme representatives were left.

Lovel looked at Gabe with concern. "A mark like that will always bring attention."

"It's fine," Gabe said. "I'll just cover it with my tunic."

Lovel snorted and looked to Gabe's grandmother.

"He means that it leaves a presence," *Sapienti* Mendez said. "One that can attract darkness. We're working on creating something to numb the presence."

"That's good," Lovel said, then to Gabe: "The closer you stand, the more I can sense it. And if I can, so can others." With that the older man left the atrium without a backwards glance.

"Cheerful guy," Gabe remarked.

"I doubt he wanted to be here, but Newberry gave him no choice," his grandmother replied. "But I believe we lived up to our reputation."

"Our reputation to make a difficult situation worse?" Gabe said.

The First Healer blew out a frustrated breath. "That's no doubt what they think of us."

"They all walked in here with intention," *Sapienti* Mendez said. "Whether it was to tear us down, take our lands—"

"Point their knobby little fingers at us—" the First Healer interjected.

"—or just witness what we had to say out of curiosity. The point is, due to what you said, Gabe, they're now a lot less sure about what they believe. And I'd rather they be in a state of confusion than misguided in their steadfastness that we're to blame for everything. Now we at least have them questioning. Now we have them on their heels."

"Just like we're on *our* heels," Gabe said.

"Exactly," his grandmother responded. "We're in this together."

"Do you really think so?" Blas Nunez said as he stood, his black robe falling heavily to the floor. "You think you've what? Saved us from their judgment?" He snorted contemptuously. "All you've done is provided the nail in your coffin. A Lost Soul walking the Earth! Why don't you just give up your mantle now? Give it up peacefully before I take it from you like the undeserved, weak woman you are—"

"Father!" cried one of the Kales in black, sounding both exasperated and embarrassed, but one heated look from Blas had him falling back to silence.

Blas Nunez turned back to Gabe's grandmother and opened his mouth to resume spitting his vitriol, but Gabe stepped right up to his frail body and looked down into his beady little eyes before the older man could mutter one more word.

"You're lucky you're an old man," Gabe said, feeling fire in his belly. "Otherwise, I'd throw you through that goddamn window."

"You and whose army, boy?" Blas retorted. "You think the Kales where I come from will follow this *woman*?"

"You go too far, Blas," said *Sapienti* Mendez. "You should leave."

"If you think me so weak as to take orders from you, you are mistaken. If you think I would follow you, you are mistaken. You— a *woman*—who stands by nothing but her own arrogance to see us through these trying times. Unlikely!"

"If you keep saying *woman* like that, I might think you have something against the fairer sex," said Gabe. "And I gotta tell ya, I'm not one to just stand back and let that shit happen."

"Nor am I," said a voice from the door.

Mel had arrived with Quint and Keven. One of the black-clad Kales moved to intercept them, arms outstretched to grab at Mel's arm, but Keven pushed him roughly away.

"Nor do *we*," said *Sapienti* Mendez, looking heatedly at Blas Nunez. "I'll say this one last time: *Go*. And pray for my leniency over such disrespect."

"I will pray for nothing but your *swift* removal!" Blas roared, then seemed to compose himself. "And I will have it, if it's the last thing I do. My clansmen will not stand for this. You will be removed for your weak leadership. Clan Kale needs strength and virility, both of which you lack."

Gabe would have knocked sense into the man had his knees not chosen that moment to wobble from fatigue. He had to satisfy himself with a heated glare.

Mel stood silently with her eyes shut tight, her jaw clenched, then turned her back on Blas and Viola Nunez. *Violence,* Gabe thought. *She's seconds from losing control.*

"Mel," he said, but there was no need.

A calmness overtook her. She turned toward him, her gold eyes lucid. Then she looked at the First Healer and *Sapienti* Mendez and spoke... in another language. It was lyrical and melodic.

Old Tongue, Gabe remembered. He'd heard it before in many of his teachings, but he'd never heard it spoken so fluently. And so *quickly.* Not even his grandmother or the First Healer spoke in such a manner. It was so fast he couldn't understand a word of it, but he could tell that her words were causing tension in his grandmother and the First Healer. Even Viola Nunez seemed affected, though her husband stood dumbly, looking at everyone suspiciously.

"We can't—" the First Healer began, but Mel spat out something more, short and brutal, before stalking out of the room, leaving Keven and Quint hurrying to catch up.

When the door had shut behind them, the First Healer turned to *Sapienti* Mendez. "Mari, the risk! And with everything going on, this is—"

"No," *Sapienti* Mendez interrupted. "She's right." She walked toward Blas Nunez, not even looking at the two black-clad Kales who had crept closer. "You want the opportunity to be *Sapienti* of Clan Kale? Very well. I will give you your opportunity."

Blas Nunez looked triumphant. "You just agreed to be led willingly to your death," he said. "You think you're so clever, but I came for a challenge, and now I have one. And I *will* win. Then Clan Kale will not have to suffer under your weak leadership any longer."

He turned to go, but *Sapienti* Mendez's voice stopped him short. "We will do the trial as it was done in the old days."

The older man turned quickly, eyeing her with uncertainty. "That hasn't been done in centuries. You don't have the *means*."

The First Healer walked to an iron cabinet that stood in one corner. She opened the doors and pulled out a candle that looked to be made of crystal. The wick was lit with a small, bright, gold flame that looked as if it might go out at any second. There was no draft in the room, but the flame flickered in and out as if there was.

Blas Nunez's face was unreadable. "May I...?" he said, motioning toward the candle. "To verify its authenticity?"

The First Healer handed it to him, and he waved his hand over the candle, daring not to touch the flame. Then he tried, unsuccessfully, to blow out the candle. After a moment he grabbed a pitcher of water that had not been touched during the gathering, and shoved the candle within it. The candle went out, flameless, and he gave the First Healer a snide smile. But when he removed the candle from the water, the wick caught again.

"Water cannot harm the flame," *Sapienti* Mendez said contemptuously. "So. Do you agree or not?"

Blas Nunez huddled with the male Kales in his retinue, and though their voices were low, it was clear that their discussion was heated, and one young male broke off and ran out of the room. Blas Nunez's son seemed to be attempting to talk his father out of his intentions. But finally the son stepped away, pain and anger on his face.

"Do you agree?" Gabe's grandmother asked again. "Or do we have to stand and watch as you try time and time again to put out the candle?"

The Kale who had run from the room came back and handed Blas Nunez a crystal about the size of his hand. And before anyone could react, Blas Nunez picked the candle up and brought it down on top of the crystal. The candle broke in half, one half falling to the floor. The flame flickered out and died.

Blas threw the other half of the candle on the floor and sneered. "Agreed." With that, he turned and walked out of the room.

The two black-clad Kales turned to follow. The son waited for Viola Nunez, who walked with effort toward him. As they departed together, Viola turned and looked at the candle with remorse.

"I'm sorry, Mari," she said. "This is my fault. Not just today, but all of it. I should have stood up to him." Her eyes were red, but no tears fell. It was as if she had spent them long ago. "But he made me feel small. So small I just… disappeared."

Her son held her arm, hugged her to him, and led her out the door.

"You should've come home," *Sapienti* Mendez said, so low Gabe could hardly hear. "I would've reminded you who you were."

Her voice was filled with longing for time to fix a mistake of long-felt regret.

Gabe watched as his grandmother picked up the broken candle. The wick caught once more, and now both halves had flames that danced and shifted in a breeze that didn't exist.

He was glad the candle wasn't destroyed—Kale fire was not something that he wanted to see diminished. But even so, he felt a hollowness as he made his way back to bed. Tired and exhausted, he fell heavily on the mattress.

To his surprise, the First Healer showed up only a minute later, pushing through the door with a leather bag that she had to carry with both hands. She set the bag on the bed, opened it, and began rummaging through it, pulling out items and tossing them on the bed.

"Hey!" Gabe said as an item smacked him on the leg. "Who pissed in your Cheerios?"

"Your sister did, Gabe! Your sister did!" she said, pulling out a jar containing some translucent substance. "Now we have to have a challenge in the midst of all this—this—*madness*!"

"Come on, it can't be that bad," Gabe said. "Grandma will put old Blas in his place and that'll be the end of it."

"Oh, really? That's what's going to happen, is it? Do you know what *happens* during a challenge for *Sapienti*? Do you know the danger involved? No! You don't! But I *do*. I don't give a piss about Blas Nunez, the little shit, but your grandmother—she's not as young as she used to be, and this trial will be *dangerous*. She could get seriously hurt. Hey, but what do I know? I'm just the First Healer! I've only spent my whole life studying the arts of healing the body and mind, and the best ways to avoid death. And on top of that, now your grandmother has ordered me to get you on your feet—by whatever means necessary."

Gabe frowned. "Wait, hold up. Go back to how dangerous the challenge is." His head was starting to hurt, and a knot formed in his stomach.

The First Healer motioned for Gabe to open his tunic. He did, and she smothered the translucent goo all over his neck, right over his scar. It was warm to the touch. Then she grabbed a charcoal and drew glyphs along his torso. The act seemed to calm her down, and after a few moments of quiet, she finally spoke.

"The challenge for who will lead the clan will be done in the old way. That means your grandmother and Blas Nunez will each be provided the candle to light a fire. Whichever one is able will be Elder."

Gabe was relieved. "That doesn't sound dangerous."

"The flame is *unstable*," she replied. "I just don't believe that we know enough. It's been too long since it's been utilized."

Gabe intended to ask more questions, but just then the older woman started chanting, causing a scorching pain to spread along his neck and chest—a pain like he had never felt in his life. He screamed as the agony tore through muscle and bone, carving and shifting, before blessedly the darkness took him.

****

When Gabe regained consciousness, he was sitting beside Roy Coudrou in the front seat of a beat-up truck. Coudrou's dark thinning hair was wild around his head, like a stringy halo, and bushy eyebrows hung over his green eyes. At the moment he was driving at breakneck speed while chewing a wad of gum, his forearm lying carelessly along the top of the steering wheel.

Coudrou took a hard left, and Gabe was flung sideways with the momentum before he settled back into place. He winced at a twinge in his neck, but realized with relief that the deep fatigue that had plagued him all day was gone.

"Fuck, Coudrou!" Gabe said, blinking against the sun in his eyes.

"Hey, you're up!" said Coudrou. He gave Gabe a toothless smile, then lost it as he gave Gabe a double-take.

"What?" Gabe said.

"Oh—nothing." The toothless smile was back. "I just thought your eyes—anyway I wasn't sure you'd be okay the way we had to drag you into the truck. But that's what I get for not believing the First Healer."

Gabe put a hand on the dash to keep steady as they hit a bump. "Where are we going?"

"Paul and I are taking you to your Uncle Jorge. We're meeting up with him to find that Lost Soul."

"Paul?" Gabe asked.

Coudrou knocked on the window behind him, and it opened to reveal Alec Paul's shaggy head. "Could you take those bumps any harder, Coudrou?" he whined. "I'm holding on for dear life back here."

"Shaddup!" Coudrou said before pressing harder on the gas.

The old truck sounded like it was pushed to its limits. The man drove like he had no care for himself or others. *He might as well be fucking drunk,* Gabe thought as he was thrown once more into the passenger-side door.

"How much longer?" Gabe asked, grasping the handle above and deciding to never let this man behind the wheel again.

"Just a few minutes," Coudrou replied, finally slowing down as he turned onto a two-lane road. The area here was less wild and more groomed. The few houses scattered about had acres of well-tended land between them.

"This ain't fucking good," Gabe said, looking at a couple of small kids playing in a sprinkler in front of one house.

"It sure as hell ain't," said Coudrou.

He drove a little while longer before they came upon a parked truck, which he stopped behind. Tío Jorge stepped out of the other truck with four Kales. Gabe recognized three of them, and knew them all to be quite capable.

Ana Flores was older than Gabe, with dark hair, bronze skin, and hazel eyes. Her face had the weathered look of someone who spent too much time in the sun. Reese Logan was honey-haired, with serious blue eyes that looked out of place on her childlike face. She was tall and lithe, and wore the long, pale gold robe of a healer. Hector Puma was a long-armed, wide-shouldered man with jet-black hair and grey eyes.

But the last Kale was one Gabe had never seen before—a Peruvian Kale. Her dark hair was speckled with grey—though she didn't look the worse for it—and her amber eyes looked sharp and alert. She wore a black tunic and breeches, and when she noticed him checking her out, she smiled.

Gabe's quickly turned his attention to the area around him. The lot nearby was clearly uninhabited; the house had fallen into disrepair, and the yard was unkept. *No wondering eyes here,* Gabe thought as he got out of the truck. *Perfect.*

"Clothes?" Tío Jorge barked.

"In the back," Coudrou replied.

Gabe followed his uncle as the older man opened the tailgate. Paul dropped down from the truck bed, his tall frame towering over Tío Jorge as he threw several duffel bags onto the ground. As he bent over to open them, the other Kales crowded around.

"Here," he said, revealing the clothes inside. "There's also short swords in the toolbox."

Gabe grabbed a black long-sleeved denim shirt and blue jeans, and quickly changed out of his tunic and breeches. Looking around, he saw that the others had also dressed in dark denims.

Tío Jorge pulled Gabe aside. "How are you feeling?" he asked quietly.

"I'm well," Gabe said. "I don't know what the First Healer did, but I feel great."

"Good," Tío Jorge said. "Let me know if that changes. The procedure can have its ill effects."

He then knelt beside a hard case that had seen better days, and opened it to reveal a variety of small vials full of powders and other substances.

"What's that?" Gabe asked, but just then Paul came over to hand him a short sword. Gabe forgot about the containers as he stowed the sword across his back, the hilt touching his hip. His hand circled the handle, testing to make sure it would unsheathe unencumbered. When he was satisfied, he put on a long jacket that hid the sword, grimacing at the heat. His staff was too big to hide as it was, so he pressed the mechanism that separated it in two, then placed it in its long case, which he slung over his shoulder.

"Don't forget those," said Coudrou, gesturing to the wristbands that lay along the bed of the truck. "Mel said you can have them, since you've helped yourself to them already."

Gabe smiled as he tied them on. "I mean, they were just sitting there going to waste." He unsheathed the golden blades and smiled. "I'll find a use for them."

"All right," Tío Jorge said, closing the hard case. Gabe thought he saw a white glyph glowing on the case before it faded away, but it happened so quickly he wasn't sure. "Follow me," his uncle said.

Tío Jorge led them into the cover of the nearest trees, which afforded them some relief from the heat. Gabe's uncle knelt down, pulled out a map of the area, and laid it on the ground. He poured a white powder all around the perimeter of the map, then located their current location on the map and poured a small amount of gunmetal grey powder there.

As Gabe was watching all this curiously, the unknown Kale stepped up alongside him. "I am Olga Micos," she said in Spanish. "I have come to kill death."

Gabe liked her immediately. "I have to come to kill death as well," he responded.

Tío Jorge was now closing up the vials and placing them in his pocket. Flores knelt beside him.

"What's this, *Seniorem*?" she asked, pointing at the dark powder. "And why did I want to swipe the vial out of your hand?"

Gabe could feel the same urge. One glance at the others told him they all did.

"We've attempted to track the Lost Soul from Larson's home without success," his uncle began. "The trail dried up as we reached this area. There's been no sign of it, which causes me great concern. If we don't act now, it may slip out of our grasp and onto another clan's territory."

He looked each Kale in the eye. They all knew the stakes. Mass destruction would follow if Clan Kale let the Lost Soul get away.

Tío Jorge pointed to the circle of powder. "The spell is simple. This powder makes up a boundary. If the Lost Soul is still within it, then it will not be free to leave. The powder is actually the ashes of a Kale. A loved one."

Gabe looked at his uncle's face, wondering whose ashes they were. His son's? His wife's? Either one was macabre and upsetting.

"The dark powder is the ground-up bones of a Lost Soul," Tío Jorge continued, looking at Flores. "That is the darkness you sense. We will use this powder to track its location."

Micos stepped forward. "You will need a catalyst now," she said. "We cannot complete the spell without a link to the Lost Soul."

"That is why Gabe is here," Tío Jorge replied. He pulled out a knife.

"Gonna sacrifice me to the gods?" Gabe asked. "After all the work the First Healer did to get me in tip-top shape?"

"Give me your hand," Tío Jorge said. "I need some of your blood. You've been wounded by the Lost Soul with his own weapon. You're our best chance of hunting it down."

Gabe let his uncle take his hand, then grimaced as the older man cut his palm. Gabe's blood spilled forth, so bright it glistened with electric intensity as it fell onto the grey powder.

Gabe felt his breath catch in his throat. His heart pounded in his chest.

"It's okay, Gabe," said Tío Jorge. "You're fine."

"It would be more alarming if you bled black," said Micos, this time speaking in English. "Red is the color of the living."

Gabe nodded distractedly as Tío Jorge continued with the spell, chanting in *Old Tongue* with his eyes closed.

Seek... Seek... Find... Seek... Seek... Bind...

What is Lost… Find… What is Lost… Bind…

Micos joined him, and the two of them continued chanting. Suddenly, as if acting on its own accord, the outer ring of powder started glowing and pulsing. Then the blood started to form a trail, winding and curving along the map. At last it stopped, pooling in a single location.

"That's not far from here," said Puma.

"No, it isn't," said Tío Jorge, folding up the map. "We must hurry though. It could move at any second."

They returned to the vehicles, but it took another twenty minutes to reach the location. The sun had started to sink below the horizon, and the sky was cut with violet and grey. The land stretched out in shadow before them.

From bad to worse, Gabe thought as he got out of the truck. The housing development here was inhabited, the hedges and trees well-kept, but at the moment it was quiet, its cookie-cutter houses shrouded in gloom.

"Here," Coudrou said, placing something on Gabe's shoulder.

Gabe grabbed it, then saw it was a face sleeve and mask. "This is going to scare the shit out anyone we come across," he said.

"God, I fucking hope so," said Coudrou, putting his on.

Gabe laughed. "You look like you're going to rob a goddamn bank."

"As conspicuous as that looks, we could've just worn our veils," Paul said.

"We could, but where's the fun in that?" asked Coudrou.

Then Tío Jorge spotted Coudrou, frowned, and motioned for him to take off the mask. "That won't be needed," he said impatiently as he passed out security camera jammers. "Now listen up. We're splitting up into four groups. I want you all to walk the streets. If you sense the Lost Soul, give us a call and we'll meet up."

"How will we know when we've sensed it?" asked Logan.

"You'll know," said Tío Jorge, and then he was gone, Puma at his side.

"It'll be like the spell with the bones," said Flores to Logan, as they headed in the opposite direction. "Come on."

"We'll take that street," said Paul, pointing down a well-lit avenue. "Come on, Coudrou. Don't mess about."

That left Gabe with Micos.

"I guess we're partners," she said.

Gabe looked at the older woman, the strength in her eyes, the calmness in her stature. "I guess so," he said. "We should hurry."

They headed away from the direction Paul and Coudrou had taken, scanning the box-like houses. Not a light was on, not a stir, not a life about.

"It's as if no one lives here," said Micos.

"I know. Too quiet," said Gabe. "And no lights?"

"Perhaps they're all dead."

"Wow, you're a downer."

Micos shrugged. "It happens."

"Hopefully not here. These folks are innocent."

They stopped at an intersection and looked left and right as if there was a possibility of a car passing, even though they hadn't seen a single car on the move since their arrival. Then they continued on.

Gabe didn't sense a thing. If the Lost Soul was here, perhaps he was hiding himself. Could it do that? Mask its presence? Or maybe it had already left while they were racing to reach it. Had it sensed the spell? Did it know it had been bound and tracked?

"How innocent can they be?" said Micos, her eyes still searching.

"What do you mean?"

"Lost Souls are attracted to fear, anger, and hate," said Micos. "This place festers with all three."

Gabe frowned. "It's just people living in their pretty homes with their children."

Micos stopped suddenly and pointed to a yard where flies buzzed noisily. Gabe nodded, and together they walked closer. Apart from the flies, the scene seemed peaceful, except for the sour stench that gradually increased in Gabe's nostrils.

And then he saw it. A man on his knees, his back to the two Kales, his hands at his face.

Apparently, the man heard them approaching, for at that moment he turned toward them, revealing a face bleeding from deep cuts. In one hand he held a kitchen knife, which he placed on his forehead and pulled slowly downward. His eyes were filled with helplessness, and his lips trembled.

Micos pushed in front of Gabe, wrenched the blade from the whimpering man, and put a hand on the man's shoulder as he sobbed quietly.

"Are you sure they are innocent, Gabriel Mendez?" she said. She raised the man's shaking hands so Gabe could see. In each palm a glyph was carved in the flesh, and blood dripped sluggishly down the man's arms.

Gabe felt a piercing, cold ache tearing down his throat, burrowing, ripping at the tethers that connected him to his own mind, slicing, slicing, *slicing...*

Chapter Ten

Mel sat alone at the makeshift table in the Sun Room, sharpening her sword with a whetstone while Quint and Keven sat talking quietly. She wasn't sure if this method worked to sharpen the golden blade, but years of sword maintenance had built a routine in her that was difficult to break. Plus, it was busy work that helped keep her mind off of the multitude of things going on that she had no control over. It was difficult, waiting for news. She hoped someone would come soon with something.

Placing the whetstone down, she eyed the blade critically and grabbed a folded cloth from her pocket. As she unraveled it, she was surprised when something hard fell, spinning and sliding, onto the table. She slapped her hand atop the object, catching a glimpse of it before doing so. *No*, she thought, feeling her heartbeat and breathing pick up. She sat there for a moment, before finally, finally, lifting her hand—revealing a small ebony pin of a dagger. *Oh no*, she thought closing her hand around the pin.

"Mel?" Quint called. "Are you okay?"

Mel didn't know if she wanted to cry or scream. She rose and walked toward the healer. "Was Nico here?"

Quint frowned, confused.

"Because this is his pin," Mel said, holding it up. "It was in my pocket. And he only ever leaves it with me when he's about to do something." She watched Quint, whose face fell with realization. "He was here, wasn't he? And I saw him."

An uneasiness spread through the Sun Room. Quint was agitated, wringing his hands, while Keven gripped his sword hilt as though he would unsheathe it at any second to attack a foe. But there was no foe—no one he could fight off with fist or sword. No, this adversary was invisible, and it displayed itself at unpredictable moments. So what were Quint and Keven to do when the moment came and went without them knowing? What were they to do when a conversation was mentioned so casually just to have it explode in their faces?

"I saw him, didn't I?" Mel asked again. "Tell me what happened. Because I don't remember."

The healer looked at Mel with concern in his eyes. "I—I don't know if..." He paused. "We don't want you to get upset," he said soothingly. "Let's just—"

"Tell me what happened!" Mel demanded, then ran a shaky hand over her face. "Sorry, just, please, tell me."

Quint looked like he'd rather be anywhere else, but finally he spoke. "Uh... okay. You had a private meeting with Nico."

"Okay..." Mel nodded, encouraging him to continue.

"And after that meeting... Nico visited with Anton Morel. And apparently... well, Anton is missing a finger now. I treated him though!" the healer added quickly. "He's fine! He's not in any pain, and it's healed. Well, as best it can be without the appendage."

Mel rubbed her face, wondering what she might have said to Nico that would have caused him to take Anton's finger. *Jesus Christ,* Mel thought, running a hand through her hair. *What did I say?*

Anton. She hadn't seen him since right after she got back from *Inter Spatium Abyssus.* Not since the encounter in his cell...

****

The darkness was ink black. Whether his eyes were closed or wide open, it made no difference to Anton Morel. He was one with the darkness, a part of its whole, sinking into nothingness. Had it really been only a few days since he'd been locked up? It felt like months. In his solitude, he had imagined himself as who he was weeks ago. Strong. Impenetrable. Powerful. Now, he sat forlorn and broken, chained to a chair, not even allowed to lay his head down to sleep, nothing but a cold metal table for company.

His clansmen weren't coming for him. He knew that now. He'd been abandoned. Thrown away like chattel. The Eighth Clan only prized those with strength. The weak were discarded. He'd seen it happen several times over the years, had even been a party to it, and yet it had never occurred to him that he would ever find himself in this position.

How wrong he was.

He had been promised the girl, Charlotte. Charlotte, who had burned so brightly—a ray of light that could take any man's breath away. Anton could still remember the first time he saw her, three years ago across the quad. She'd been out of her colors then, laughing with one of his clansmen. Thierry Lambert wasn't someone Anton would have ever thought to worry about, but as Lambert stood there clasping Charlotte's hand in his, gallantly kissing her knuckles and garnering laughter from the woman—well, Anton was given reason to reassess. So Anton walked over and introduced himself. The look in Charlotte's eyes as she gazed upon him said it all. She was struck. It took no time to distract her from Lambert.

He spent the afternoon talking to her, urging her to take a tour of the grounds with him. Janso territory was beautiful—not like the dry, unkept hell that was Kale territory. And in no time Charlotte was in his arms, sharing a kiss. It was short-lived, however, because she *showed up to call Charlotte away. To turn Charlotte against him.*

But Anton didn't want to think of her. *No, he wanted to think of the moments before. He wanted to think of that kiss.*

Ever since that day, Anton had been on fire. It was what the songbooks spoke of. Everything they spoke of. Everything.

Now, some other Eighth clansman would have Charlotte. Wed her. Bed her. Anger filled him, rushing up to the back of his teeth, filling him with the need to scream his frustration. Charlotte should've been his. She had *been his.*

He'd had so many plans. He was going to show her The Ways *as they were meant to be followed. He was going to show her his strength, and then with time, she would see that his way was right. She would be grateful. And then... then she would give him all he wanted.*

He would've been patient. Courting her, making her fall in love with him. Then he would have wedded her and put a child in her.

It was all planned. That was as it should've been.

If not for her.

Charlotte's horrid cousin.

Rage festered at the thought of the coward, the blight of Clan Kale, besting him. It shouldn't have been possible. Melanie Mendez was weak. Everyone knew that. And yet she had beaten him—and opened a gateway with her stone.

That should not have been possible.

Charlotte was the stronger one. Charlotte had to be the heir. It had been discussed ad nauseam by his clan, and they'd agreed—unanimously—that Charlotte was the one. She was the one with strength. The one who competed.

Melanie Mendez was a disgrace.

It didn't make any sense... but no bother. Melanie Mendez was dead now. There was no way a woman would survive Inter Spatium Abyssus *alone. Anton smirked at the thought, and a laugh burst from his throat.*

But heaviness fell over him once again. He was plagued by his continued absence of powers. The spell to break the Orb of Lasade should've taken place by now. But his clansmen must've failed at that, for he was still weak, unable to break from his bonds.

Nothing would've brought him more pleasure than to gain his powers and use them to kill the Mendez brothers, Victor and Gabriel. Oh, how he would've enjoyed watching the life leave their smug faces. But unfortunately, he was just a man. Trapped and waiting.

To die.

No. That was not who he was.

There was still a chance. He had to give the impression that he was submitting to The Ways *of these weak Kales. He needed to speak to their* Sapienti. *He had a right to demand it, a right to face his accuser… and they would give it to him. They would have to produce a witness to his crimes. And they could not.*

So they would have to let him go.

Just as these thoughts gave him hope, Anton heard footsteps. A clattering of metal and muffled voices followed, then a door slammed. The footsteps moved away, getting gradually quieter as they left, before Anton screamed for them to come back.

A moment later someone opened the door to his cell. Anton was unable to see their face—they bore a torch, and the light blinded him.

"Jesus Christ, Morel," muttered a woman. "Shut the fuck up."

"I need… I need…" His voice was so hoarse. He cleared his throat and tried again. "I need to speak to Sapienti *Mendez."*

"Ohhhh," said the woman. "You want to speak to our Elder?"

There was a mumbling from another, but Anton couldn't make out what was said.

"What's that?" the woman asked her companion.

As the other's mumbling resumed, Anton squinted through the harshness of the flame. He saw two figures, one taller and one shorter, standing just inside the door. The shorter was a woman of gold hair and fair skin. The taller was a man with dark hair and eyes. They had their heads bent together. It was the man who held the torch.

A moment passed, then the woman laughed, airy and light. "Oh yes, you're right," she said. Then to Anton: "We'll get you an audience with the next best thing." There was mischief in her voice. "You just stay put, Morel. We'll be right back."

Then the light was gone, and the door was closed.

Anton sat in his chair and stewed. The audacity of the girl to laugh at him. When he got out of this cell... he'd make her pay. He'd make all of them pay.

First, he'd go back to Clan Janso and tell them what Clan Kale had done to him. He would drive the wedge between the two clans even deeper. It would please the inner circle of the Eighth to no end to see the discord he'd spread among the Great Seven. Perhaps they would accept him into the inner circle even though his plan had failed. Perhaps there was still a chance he could have Charlotte. I can always hope, *he thought.*

Footsteps once more approached his cell. Anton drew himself up as best he could, preparing himself for Sapienti *Mendez. He hated her, but he knew she was a strict follower of* The Ways. *She would have no choice but to release him or to suffer a loss of honor.*

The door opened, and in stepped the man with the torch and the short blond woman. They stepped to the sides, and Anton deflated when he saw the imposing form of Victor Mendez step in behind them.

"I asked for your Sapienti," *Anton said, irritated. "Not you."*

"Oh, we heard," said another voice, and then Gabriel Mendez strutted in after his brother.

The younger Mendez had an insufferable smile on his face. Fury surged in Anton's stomach; he wanted nothing more than to punch the light out of the boy's eyes.

"Where is your Sapienti," *Anton bit out. "According to* The Ways *I have a right to see her. I have the right to face my accuser. Your grandmother must produce them. If not, then I must be let go."*

"Our Sapienti *is busy," responded Victor Mendez lazily.*

"I have the right!" Anton yelled. "I have the right to an audience. She cannot keep me locked up in this room when I have committed no crime."

"But you have *committed crimes, Anton," said a woman from the doorway. She had an accent—a brogue. Anton knew that voice, but couldn't place it. He squinted into the darkness behind the door. There were two more people there, just outside of the cell. "I witnessed you kill Sapienti Reddy," said the woman. "I saw you steal his stone from his body and open a gate into Inter Spatium Abyssus."*

"And who are you?" Anton said, trying to hide his nerves. Did someone survive the attack at the clearing? Surely not! He had witnessed all—those of the Great Seven and those in his own clan—die, killed by the Malum. This was just a ploy. To scare him. "Come out into the light!" he demanded. "I have a right to face my accuser. Let me see your face."

The accented voice spoke again, too quietly for Anton to hear. It was low, coaxing.

"Are you too afraid to face me?" Anton asked. "Too afraid to look into my face as you tell your lies?"

"We fear very little," answered the woman. "You would know that after what we've seen."

"And what have you seen?" asked Anton, pulling at his chains. "What magnificent lies do you have for me? I'll set the story straight. It's all a farce. All of it. That's why you can't look me in the eye as you spit out your fairy tales."

There was no answer this time. No reply—just silence. A silence that made everyone else in the room tense. Anton looked at the two Mendez brothers. They stood at the walls on either side of him. The older watched Anton with indifference, but the younger had an uncharacteristically serious look on his face as he watched the door.

There was movement at the door, and a figure stepped forward.

Melanie Mendez.

She was alive.

But she looked more animal than woman. Dried blood along her mouth and neck. Dark hair a mess. Tunic no longer gold, so full it was of black and red blood.

Anton sucked in a breath. She would've had to kill demons to get those black stains. Humans for the red.

Mel strode closer, bringing the smell of death with her.

Behind her, like a living, breathing shadow, was Cori O'Shea. The Ferus woman's clothes were just as bad, but her face was clean. She sniffed the air, then focused her feral eyes on him. She had her hand on a long, curved knife belted at her side, and she thumbed it impatiently.

"Hello, Anton," Melanie Mendez said. "Surprised to see me?"

She pulled a chair to the table and sat down. She waited for Anton to answer, but he merely fixed his cold gaze on her. How was she here?

She brought her hand to the table, rolling a stone in her fingers.

A black and red stone.

Master Wershall's stone.

That was when fear crept its way into Anton's bones. There was only one way she could have that stone. His master would never have given it to her while there was life still in him.

"You're scared now." There was something in her eyes now. Anton could see it, just beneath the brown of her irises. Stirring. "I can sense it," she continued. "The coldness spreading along your spine and up your neck."

She continued to roll the stone in her fingers, the red gleaming in the torchlight. Her eyes hidden as she watched the stone spin. Anton felt a strange relief when her gaze left him. He did not like what he saw stirring in those depths.

"I've been thinking about what I would say to you," she continued conversationally. "What I would do to you after what you've done."

Anton shifted as far back in his chair as he could. He suddenly did not want to be sitting here, so close.

"You killed Sapienti *Reddy in cold blood," Melanie Mendez said in a dead, emotionless voice. The stone spun a little faster, making a whistling sound on the metal table. "You opened the gate into* Inter Spatium Abyssus *and released a* Malum *on defenseless clanspeople. I care nothing of the Eighth who lost their lives, but there were also several good, loyal descendants who died because of you."*

She paused, her hand flat against the table. The stone continued to spin.

"I don't need to ask you why," she said. "I know why. I know everything about you. You were hated among your clan because of your conceitedness, your arrogance. Because you treated them as you treated everybody else: with disdain, as if you were better than them."

Anton desperately wanted to take his eyes away from her. But he couldn't.

"And Sapienti *Reddy," she said, her voice hardening at the name, "always there to correct you, always there to tell you to step back in line. To value your clanspeople as if they were your brothers and sisters. But you don't have family, and you saw none as such."*

Just then someone started screaming in the next room. No one reacted, and Anton didn't either. He was too caught up in what was happening in front of him to care for the person in the next room.

"So you treated your clanspeople like they were shit under your boot. And still you were surprised when they tried to teach you their lessons— heavy-handedly, I admit, but lessons nonetheless—and tried to impress upon you that your way was the wrong path."

How did she know these things about him? Who had told her all this? Anton felt cold fear creeping up his spine.

"I know how Sapienti *Wershall recruited you when you were just a boy. He played up to your vanity, and you fed off it like a parasite. To*

you, he was your savior, but to him, you were just a toy to play with. He didn't value you. It was only because you held a spark of your gift that he paid you any attention at all."

Anton didn't know what she was talking about. He had a spark of a gift? How could that be? And if so, how could Master Wershall have known? So many times, Anton had spoken with the man about what they would do once they were greater… but was Anton great all along? Did he have power inside him? Was that how he had been able to open the gate?

Wershall had said that Anton needed to be the one to open it. Many times, he'd said it needed to be so. But Anton always assumed that was because he was chosen. Not because he had…

He looked up at Melanie Mendez.

"Oh, he didn't tell you?" she asked quietly. "I'm not surprised—the Eighth with their secrets. They're not known for full disclosure." She shook her head and glared at the stone. *"You know… the road to get back here was not an easy one. The things Cori and I had to do…"* A distant look came over her, a slackness in her face. *"Well, it wasn't pretty. And what kept me going, in addition to my need to bring my cousin home…"*

Charlotte is here? She's not with my clansmen?

"… was my need for justice. To make sure you paid for your crimes. For all the traitors to pay for their crimes. But even these reasons wouldn't have gotten me home alive. Not even my training in Supervive could have done that. No. I used my gift."

She said this as if she herself was surprised. Like she was a non-believer brought into the light.

"I've realized these past few hours that there are those of us who still have a small spark of our gift within us. Kale must have left it there as a failsafe. Just in case."

Her hands were shaking now, but Anton knew it was not out of fear. He knew when people were afraid, and Melanie Mendez was not.

She was angry.

He could feel her anger, just as she could feel his fear. Why didn't I see this before? *he thought. And her anger was so… potent. An incensed heat that practically burned his skin. It causes his fear to transform into full-blown terror.*

"*A failsafe for the unexpected,*" she continued. "*A dark object left behind, perhaps. Or an idiot with a death wish who decides to summon a demon. We were that failsafe.*" Melanie Mendez looked him dead in the eye. "*You and me, and Cori, and all the others who have that little spark.*"

She snapped up the stone and put it in her pocket.

"*But it wasn't enough for you,*" she said, her voice cold. "*You wanted more. You were willing to kill to get it. To kill Charlotte to get it.*"

Anton froze. No, that's not how it is, *he wanted to say.* I love Charlotte.

"*You're a fool, Anton,*" Melanie Mendez said, her words laced with anger and disappointment. "*A goddamn fool. You nearly got my cousin killed. The Eighth Clan was going to bleed her dry so that they could have their goddamn powers back. But she's not the heir, Anton. It would've been all for nothing.*"

No! I didn't know!

The words were stuck in his throat.

Melanie Mendez stood, and his terror was debilitating now. Her eyes looked right into him. Gold and gleaming. She stood quietly for a long moment. Then her breathing changed. Something in her manner, her presence… was wrong.

"*Anton Morel,*" she said calmly. "*I didn't have the courage to do this before, but I do now.*"

The others in the room held their breath.

"*Unchain him and hold him to the wall,*" she said carelessly.

All was a blur as the table was moved and Anton with it. Hands pulled him roughly to his feet. He meekly tried to fight them off, but it was hopeless—he was too broken. They pushed him flat against the wall—Victor and Gabriel Mendez holding him tightly, keeping him from breaking free. Someone else ripped open his tunic.

"You're a member of the Eighth Clan," Melanie Mendez said, eyes blazing gold fire, as Cori O'Shea handed her the long, curved knife. "It's time you bore their mark."

Anton found his voice then, knowing what she intended to do. "No! No—don't! You can't do this to me!"

"I can," she replied firmly, so close to him. "You're in my territory, committing crimes against my blood and against my clan." She put a hand behind his neck and peered intently into his eyes. Instantly Anton felt a shift. The air, the ground, time and space…

He was on his knees, looking up at a woman with wild energy, golden eyes, and a darkness that spreads to her temples. As she looked at him, the flame inside her was a fury. In her eyes, blood and death. The sickly smell of burnt flesh reached his nostrils.

She knelt down to eye level, putting a heavy hand on his shoulder. Looking into him for a long moment.

Then she plunged her bare hand into his chest, twisting and pulling at something inside him. Something vital…

The vision ceased—and Anton was once more in the cold cell, broken and helpless, standing, though only the hands on his chest prevented him from falling to his knees as he was in the vision.

"I'm doing you a kindness," she said, and he wasn't sure which woman spoke—the one that stood now before him, or the one from the past. "If you were of my clan… well, you wouldn't survive the punishment."

The cold blade cut into Anton's skin. He screamed and screamed, knowing that no one would hear him.

****

Mel hadn't liked the anger that had filled her when she was in Anton's presence. And it had only gotten worse since then.

She shook her head. "And what else?" she asked Quint.

The healer hesitated, clearing his throat and swallowing audibly. "You—well—you ordered your grandmother to accept Blas Nunez's challenge for *Sapienti* of the clan."

Mel had absolutely no recollection of this. Of *any* of it.

How could I do something so dangerous?

She walked toward the table, set her hands upon its flat surface, and took several calming breaths. She wanted to upend the table. Throw the chairs across the room. Punch the wall with her fists. She wanted to scream in frustration and weep in anger.

Instead she pulled the gateway stone from her pocket. "I'll be traveling to *Inter Spatium Caelum.* I need to find answers. This can't wait any longer."

"Wait, Mel," Quint said. He almost stopped when her gaze landed on him, but he powered through. "Let me get the First Healer. We'll help you across. You shouldn't travel without our help, especially in your condition. It could cause you harm."

My condition? she thought bitterly. But she agreed. "Fine," she said. "But make it quick."

As Quint sprinted off, Keven spoke. "Would you like me to go get Cori? I'm sure she'd come back."

"No," Mel replied. Cori had gone to tend to clan duties, and although Mel was sure she would return right away if Mel asked, Cori had already spent the entire day with Mel, and Mel couldn't bring herself to monopolize any more of her time.

Quint arrived with the First Healer in tow. They both wore serious expressions as they prepared Mel to travel. Isis drew a glyph on Mel's forehead, then made a thick line in black paint down her chin to her throat.

"I can't talk you out of this?" the First Healer said as she worked. "It's not exactly the best time. The challenge is in a few hours."

"Just pull me out beforehand," Mel said. "I need to be there. I'm responsible for it, after all."

She took off her boots and lay in bed. The First Healer pulled the covers over her. Mel held the stone in her hand and closed her eyes, imagining the forest she had seen before. The stone pulsed warmly in her hand as the two healers started chanting.

****

The forest was dark and still. Stars winked brightly overhead as cicadas sang their song, loud and free. A light wind touched Mel's face as she stood atop a large tree stump in the center of a wide stone circle. Each stone had a carving—some had glyphs of protection, others with circular patterns. White wisps floated over her head, incandescent and weightless. Mel watched one land on the palm of her hand, pulsing weakly, warm and gentle—and soft as down. She raised her hand and let it drift lazily away. It floated higher and higher, into the treetops.

She hopped off the stump and began to pick her way through the forest.

The last time Mel was in Inter Spatium Caelum *was when she first met Lasade Kale—the Original who had fallen to Earth and founded Mel's clan. At the time, Mel hadn't known who the woman was or what her intentions were. She seemed like a dangerous entity in an idyllic dream world. So juxtaposed. So… powerful. Burning brighter than any star. Kale had been a vision so grand, Mel remembered little else of the experience.*

Now was different. As Mel walked, she noted the many strange sights. A field of irises, their petals soft and delicate. They glowed slightly in the moonlight, sweet-smelling and feeling like feathers on her fingertips. Nestled amongst the white flowers was a stone plaque with words in Old

Tongue: Wisdom is Power. Dignity is Grace.

She followed a dirt path lined with large stones, each one several feet high. It took a second before Mel realized the stones were chiseled into figures. There were statues of a fierce man and woman wearing strange feline masks and curved sabers. Another statue represented children laughing atop a large bear with vicious-looking claws and teeth. Many featured people under stars and moons and skies.

Mel passed a stream of crystal-blue water that held stones of scarlet and gold. Though she felt as though she were gazing down into the stream's depths, when she dipped her hands into the cool water she found it was no more than two inches deep.

Twice she heard singing, soft and mournful, but pleasing to her ears. The music echoed through the forest, and Mel followed it, hoping to find the singer. But just when she thought she'd find what she sought, the song stopped and resumed from a different direction, and from a different voice.

Abandoning the song, Mel selected a path of her own choosing. She followed her instincts until she emerged from the trees to find herself facing a pyramid of white stone, rising so high that she couldn't see the top. Steep stairs were carved into one side, going up and up.

She paused to look around. There was not another soul in sight.

She began to climb the stairs. Time seemed to stretch as she ascended, and her thoughts became a jumble in her head. She needed to speak to Kale, to ask about the loss of memory. The loss of time. She needed to know if the voice that spoke when she was lost was her own voice... or someone else's.

She needed to know if she was losing her mind.

And most of all, she needed to know whether the creature inside her— the one that saw out of her eyes and spoke with her lips—was the Kale beast.

If it was the Kale beast... well, she'd figure out what she needed to do to wrest back control. If it was something else…

Her breath was raw in her throat as she climbed the final step and fell to her hands and knees in exhaustion. After catching her breath, she rose on shaky legs, her sweaty tunic sticking to her body. She wiped her brow with dirty hands that stained her face with grime.

She was at the top of the pyramid. Braziers of smoke and flame guarded a wide entrance so dark Mel could see nothing within. She stepped forward, the wind in her ears and hair. White noise buzzed as she grew nearer.

But just as she was about to step over the threshold, she hesitated, drew a breath, and stepped back. Something she could not put a name to was telling her not to pass through.

She decided at once to withdraw.

Relief spread through her as she turned away, but that relief vanished at the sight before her.

Blocking the way back down stood a man, tall and broad. Long blond hair fell over his pale skin, straight nose, and rose lips. He would have been beautiful if not for the otherworldly blue, thunderous eyes that stared down at Mel. He drew breath through his nose, expanding his enormous chest. Mel observed his breathing closely, waiting for the forceful inhale that would precede an attack.

"You're not supposed to be here." The man spoke in Old Tongue, *his voice low and powerful. His eyes swept carelessly across her body. "Your kind doesn't belong."*

Mel noticed his fine purple tunic, the flutter of grey at his waist. "You're Consilio Janso."

"And you are a Kale." He stood rooted to the spot, looking severely down on her, his nose turned up, his lips curved in distaste. "I abhor Lasade Kale and her descendants."

Mel tensed at his words, her legs ready to leap should he attack.

"I know very well that her descendants cannot help who they were

born to," the man went on, "can't help the blood that runs through their veins. But you—you are not one of her many warriors. You are her heir—an abomination that should not exist."

Shit! *Mel thought, as Consilio Janso stepped toward her. She moved quickly out of his path and away from the dark entrance at her back, not wanting to give him the opportunity to toss her within.*

Janso lunged at her, and she moved again, his hands missing her by inches.

"You're quick, Kale, I'll give you that," Janso said. "But you will not survive this night. If you had any cleverness, you would not have set foot in this place. You signed your death warrant the moment you graced my presence. For I, Consilio Janso, know too much of Kale's power. The destructiveness. The devastation. I cannot give you the opportunity to grow into your own. It would mean madness for you. There would be no place safe from your anger. Men, women, children… they would all die. The world would burn because of you. And I, Consilio Janso, I am of the people. Of culture and art. I watched with my own eyes the birth of civilization. I will not let the person who will cause the end of it loose on the Earth. I cannot let you live."

Mel tried not to listen to his ravings. Instead, she plotted quickly. What to do? Where to go? The man blocked her way back down, and the stone entrance stretched all the way across the top of the pyramid, blocking her way forward.

Or did it? The stone entrance didn't quite block her way—on either side of it was a tiny bit of space. A ledge no wider than half the length of her foot.

A fall would mean her death. But there was no choice.

Dodging his next attack, she ran to the ledge on one side and stepped out onto it, balancing on the balls of her feet. The wind was tugging at her, doing its best to pull her off the edge. She grabbed at the stone face for whatever purchase she could find. She refused to look down at the forest below.

Where was Janso? He had to be right behind. Or coming around the other side?

She sidestepped as quickly as she could. Finally, she was at the other side of the pyramid. There was another set of stairs here, just like the first. She hurried down them as fast as she could.

She was halfway down the pyramid, trying not to stumble on the steep steps, when with a great whoosh *a giant eagle landed directly in her path. Its plumes were silver and white, and fiery blue eyes observed her over a hooked beak.*

An instant later the eagle was gone and Janso was in its place, naked in the moonlight.

"You cannot run," he said. "Wherever you go, I will find you."

Mel breathed heavily as she studied the man. It was only through sheer will that she had managed to stay out of his hands thus far. She could not keep running. She would have to fight him. And she didn't know how she would fare in a fight against an Original. She had a feeling it would not go well.

"I didn't come here to fight or argue," she said, trying her best not to sound as afraid as she was. "I came for peace. For answers."

"You will find no answers here, Kale. But if it is peace you desire, I will grant it to you."

A blur of motion and Janso was in front of her. He caught her by the arm, crushing the bones, but she felt the pain in her soul.

Mel screamed. It flowed up her throat like scalding water.

Burning, burning, burning…

And far, far away, she could sense Isis's and Quint's fear as they tried to pull her safely out of Inter Spatium Caelum.

"I promise to make your death quick," said Janso, pulling her face so close that she could see the sable in his blue eyes.

She kicked at his groin, and he bent as men do. And I promise to make it hard, *she thought as she clutched her arm and ran as fast as she could down the pyramid.*

Get me out of here! *she thought at the two healers.* Janso is going to peck my eyes out if you two don't do something!

She reached the bottom of the steps. Ahead of her was the forest, thick and lush. Hope bloomed. In the trees, she could hide. Find a crevice to hole up in and wait for the healers to pull her out. She just needed to hide.

… hide?

Run and hide?

She stopped, holding her injured arm, staring at the path ahead. The path to safety.

"Have you seen sense, Kale?" asked Janso from behind her. "Do you know the madness of which I speak? Have you felt it? Do you feel it now? You do, don't you?"

Yes, I feel it, *Mel thought.* I feel it blazing in the back of my head. Is it me? Or the Kale beast?

I feel it. I *feel* it. But…

"I don't want death," Mel said, firmly, decisively. "But I don't want to run either. I'm not a coward."

She turned to face Janso. He still stood naked, as perfect as those statues Mel had seen before. "If it's a fight you want, then I'll give you one. But why? Why kill me in this world? This is our heaven. I would just end up right back here with you."

"You know why. I've said so already. You will cause destruction and death. You will turn evil."

"Evil?" Mel repeated angrily. "You can't punish someone for something they have not yet done. And what harm have I caused? What crimes have I committed? You follow The Ways, as do I. You know very well you cannot just sentence someone to death without a trial. Your honor demands it. Has Consilio Janso forgotten what that is? Has he been dead too long? So long that he's decided he's above the rules? Or maybe you just behave differently when no eyes are upon you. Operating in the *darkness without judgment. Is that what it is?"*

Anger appeared abruptly on his face. "You dare question me? My motives, my intentions? I am Consilio Janso."

"We are all equal under the sun," Mel said. "And if you lay a hand on me again, I swear—on everything I love and hold dear—I will burn you."

Janso stepped back in alarm.

Mel didn't know if she could. Didn't know if she had the power or the strength. But she would die trying.

"This is the reason. This is why you—"

"This is what you sow," Mel said.

She let the fire take her. Let it course through her. It was so different here. Here, it burned in her soul. She felt luminous.

Janso moved, blurring in front of her, and his hands wrapped around her throat.

He was powerful. She had known that when she first laid eyes on him. But nothing had prepared her for the power he now unleashed. It was like an avalanche, the force of an entire mountain, crushing her neck, suffocating her. And with it came an agonizing cutting—a slice that went soul-deep. A relentless removal.

With each passing second, the other side was growing further and further away.

Tick-tock, Mel.

The one thing she did have was time—for it always seemed too slow. Death was never quick. Not for her. It always seemed to take too long. To drag on exponentially. And in that time the blaze erupted so brightly, so uncontrollably, she felt as though she were a supernova exploding in the heavens. Air pushed through her throat, strong and sure, and her pumping heart flooded her with strength.

Mel touched Janso's chest, digging her fingertips into his flesh. When she felt the warmth and strength of his power, she paused, just to give him time to feel her violation. She grinned when he started to shiver. She knew as well as he did that all she had to do was reach right in and pull out his gift, root and stem, and there would be nothing he could do about it. Not one thing.

Then he'd be just a husk. A shadow of himself.

His hands fell from her throat and he backed away, an eagle once more, fleeing into the sky as though she were a sickness to be avoided.

Mel couldn't help thinking that perhaps she was.

****

Mel awoke as if from a nightmare, shaking and breathing heavily, slick with sweat. *Jesus F. Christ,* she thought as she stared at the wide-eyed faces before her. The First Healer and Quint had been standing with their hands raised in mid-chant, but they crowded her bed when she opened her eyes. Keven remained at the door, but the worry was clear on his face.

Mel raised her right hand and looked at the still-glowing gateway stone in shock. A completely unreasonable part of her yearned to throw the stone as far away as she possibly could, but she smartly put it back in her pocket and took the glass of cold water Quint held out to her.

"I'm guessing that didn't go as we planned," the First Healer said, hands sweeping over Mel's head and shoulders. "Thank goodness we're in the Sun Room, or you'd've brought every Kale in the vicinity." She peered into Mel's eyes. "What happened?"

Mel gulped down the water. Feeling a strangeness in her left hand she pulled it out from under the blanket. "Oh, shit." Her fingertips were spidered with glowing white tendrils.

The First Healer moved to get a better look, but did not touch.

"What is that?" asked Quint.

Mel explained what had happened in *Inter Spatium Caelum.* That she had encountered Consilio Janso. That he'd tried to kill her. And exactly how she'd escaped.

"You touched the soul of an Original," the First Healer said in a quiet voice.

"I thought it was his gift," Mel said.

"It's what is left of it—pure white—tangled with his soul," the First Healer replied. "I'm glad you showed restraint. I don't like to think what would've happened if you'd removed his power."

"Neither do I," Mel said. "It made me feel... *dirty.*"

"I was thinking more that you might've killed yourself in the attempt," the First Healer said drily. "But yes, I'm sure there are your feelings, too."

"Or," said Quint, "perhaps you might've removed Janso's soul, sending him to *Inter Spatium Abyssus,* and thereby creating the most powerful Lost Soul *of all time.*"

Mel and the First Healer both gave him a look—Mel's full of glassy-eyed horror, the First Healer's more skeptical.

"Sorry," Quint said. He gestured to Mel's hand. "So how do we remove it?"

"We don't," said the First Healer, then she turned to Mel. "You're marked. Again. Hopefully it will fade in time."

Isis sent Quint and Keven to get a chest for her from one of the many rooms. When the two women were alone, Mel looked at the First Healer with heaviness.

"I didn't like it, Isis. Any of it."

The First Healer didn't need to ask what Mel was referring to. She handed Mel a warm, damp towel and watched as Mel cleaned the paint off her face and neck. "Remember how it felt," she said. "Remember it always. The power to siphon must be used as a last resort. This power is yours and yours alone. It is not passed to any other descendant. If you use it at a whim, the other clans will start to associate you with the evil we were put on the Earth to vanquish."

"This is why Janso hates me," Mel said. She tossed the towel onto the night table. "He said I would burn the world."

"Do not mind his words. Consilio Janso will always look at Kale and her heir as demons to be slain. He does not understand you and does not wish to." The First Healer's green eyes shone in the candlelight. "You will come across many who feel as he does. That will be your cross to bear. As the heir, you will go through this life constantly misunderstood."

"I supposed it's a good thing I'm not alive to witness it," Mel said with more than a little snark.

The First Healer snorted, but then gave Mel a serious look. "I have faith in you. You won't misuse your gifts."

"Every day I feel as if I'm on a hook, and wave after wave is crashing in on me," Mel said with frustration. "Just hours ago, I ordered my own grandmother to a dangerous trial, and I sit here with no memory of doing it."

The First Healer sat on the bed. "It was you, Mel."

"Was it?" Mel asked. "I don't know. I don't know anything anymore."

"Do you wish to give up?" Isis asked, her tone challenging.

"No. But I'm tired of feeling like a pawn. Who moves me across the board?"

"It's *you*," the First Healer said again. "You move yourself. No one else does."

"I wish I could believe you."

"Then who do you think it is?" the First Healer asked. "The Mistress you encountered in *Inter Spatium Abyssus*? It's not—the Kale beast tore her connection away. You said so. She hasn't touched you once here. I would've sensed that, at least. Believe me."

Mel looked into the older woman's green eyes. "It could be the

Kale beast," she said. "Couldn't it?"

"*Speaking* for you?" The First Healer put a hand on Mel's shoulder. "Listen to me and listen well."

"What?" Mel asked. *What are you going to tell me I don't already know? That I haven't thought about a million times?*

"Your Kale beast is rising to the surface, yes, but it's *you*. In its heart, it is a part of you. You need to wrap your head around that. Accept it. Stop fighting it... and *merge*."

Mel shook her head. "You make it sound easy. Even if I were to merge with the Kale beast and become one with it, what about the loss of memory? What about me making decisions and ordering people around and *not remembering?*"

"Did you think this would be *simple?*" the First Healer snapped, losing her patience. "That you'd just—what? *Poof,* you get your powers, and you experience *no* adjustment? No pain? That you would just ascend without any issues. We are *worlds* away from the strength we carried when Kale walked the Earth, Mel. Our blood has mixed so much with that of humans. Our bodies, our minds, our spirits are different now. Time does that. It has changed us, made us evolve. I believe you are evolving back slowly—and yes, painfully—but it will happen. You will endure. Do you hear me? You will *endure*. And when it's over, you will be whole."

Mel felt both anger and shame. But she spoke quietly. "I didn't think about that. I didn't know what was happening until after it had happened. I just thought it was all... a story we told ourselves to make us feel connected to our ancestors. I didn't think any of it was real."

"Mel," the older woman said, calm and controlled once more, "you are undoubtedly going through some form of PTSD. There will be times when you feel like you're in control and other times when you're not. You just need to let us know when you're feeling out of it so we can help you. Have faith in me, in my skills as a healer, and as a Kale. And believe me when I tell you: you are *not* going crazy. You are the heir, and as the heir you will go through trials no one else will. You are strong enough to overcome them. But it will take time."

Mel let the First Healer's words wash over her. She couldn't help wondering if she *had* that time. Time waited for no one. And certainly not her.

Quint and Keven reappeared carrying the chest that the First Healer had requested. As soon as they had set it down and opened it, Isis started pulling items out.

"Here," she said, handing Mel a glove. "You're going to need to cover that hand." Then she pulled out a fresh tunic and breeches. "Now, do you feel up to going to the challenge? If so, you'd best get dressed."

Mel didn't have to be asked twice. She went behind the partition they'd set aside for dressing and quickly changed into the ornate gold tunic of old, along with breeches and boots. When she stepped out, Keven handed her her swords and veil.

They walked up out of the lower levels and through the house without encountering anyone. It seemed everyone had already left for the challenge. As they stepped outside, Mel saw that night had fallen while she'd been traveling. She also saw that her grandmother had amped up security. There were Kale guards at every entrance and others stationed throughout the property.

They followed a path through the woods, and soon the assembly was visible through the trees. The Kales, all dressed in gold, stood in silence, facing the center of the clearing, where a few torches were lit. As Mel drew nearer, she heard raised voices. She pushed her way through the crowd until she could see the scene.

Blas Nunes and her grandmother stood front and center. Viola Nunez and her son were off to one side, and DeLeon and several other black-clad Kales stood behind Blas Nunez, faces frozen in disapproval.

"You agreed to the terms, Blas," Mel's grandmother was saying. At her feet was the crystal candle, its fluttering flame dancing in a nonexistent wind. "We agreed to do this in the ways of old."

Blas Nunez looked disdainfully at the *Sapienti* of Clan Kale, his beady eyes full of arrogance. "This is a trick," he said. "You mean to make me look a fool. I will not be party to this cheating."

"Are you backing out?" Mel's grandmother asked. "That would be breaking the agreement. You will lose your honor and all that goes with it, including your position among the clan."

"As if *you* could take my position away!" Blas Nunez screamed, pointing a finger. "You! A woman who has lost control of my clan! You bring nothing but dishonor to us! Nothing but weakness! You will have Clan Kale become a disgrace with your incompetent leadership!"

"And you could do better if you were in charge, correct?" *Sapienti* Mendez responded. "Is that not why we are all assembled here today? To see who is fit and who is not? So we can be judged in accordance with *The Ways*. But one look at the flame and now you've changed your mind. Who is the weak one here?"

"I did not agree to this—this … *farce!*" Blas Nunez exploded.

Mel grew cold with anger. *Liar.* She pushed her way forward, the First Healer at her side.

Blas turned to face the assembly. "You are ruled by manipulative women!" he screamed. "They want the men sniveling at their feet, taking orders! Waiting on them hand and foot! Do you not see? Is this what you all want?"

The Kales did not move. But those who wore black nodded in agreement, fire in their eyes.

"Do you not all want change?" Blas Nunez went on. "I can give it to you. Equality for everyone. Including men. We are born leaders, and yet we cannot be considered for positions of influence in our own clan! Do you not see how *wrong* this is?"

"That's enough," the First Healer said, her green eyes sparkling with anger. "You talk and talk and talk, howling about injustices, but you refuse to proceed with the challenge that you placed at our Elder's feet. A challenge she *accepted*—as long as it is done *as it was done in Kale's time*. You agreed to these terms. And now you lie to all! You dishonor yourself twice. Once more and—"

"And *what?*" Blas Nunez screamed in the healer's face. "Do you think I care what *you* think of me? As if you're fit to judge me? To judge us all?"

Once more he addressed the larger assembly. "Are you going to listen to this?" he shouted. "These women have led you straight into the darkness! They will lead you to your deaths!"

"Father," Antonio Nunez said, shame and frustration coloring his voice. "Please, Father, carry on with the challenge or walk away. We can go—"

"Shut up, boy!"

"You will not speak to him like that," Viola Nunez said, her voice uncharacteristically steely. "You will not speak *at all*. You will finish what you agreed to do."

"Or *what,* woman?"

"Or Antonio and I will speak as witnesses against you once we are in Cusco," Viola said firmly. "You have many enemies. They will relish picking you apart for this dishonor."

Mel didn't know where Viola had found this sudden strength, but it pleased her to see her aunt stand sure and steady next to her son, who had to have experienced a lifetime of mental and physical abuse.

Mel's grandmother nodded in approval. "And *I* will make sure she and your son have an adequate guard to accompany them on the way home. Should you or anyone else in your retinue have any ideas about silencing them."

Blas Nunez quickly realized that only those in his retinue were of the same mind as he. Furious at this turn of events, he pushed his son away and shoved his hand in his pocket.

Something sparked Mel's senses. Acting on instinct, she rushed forward and grabbed the candle at her grandmother's feet. She hardly noticed its flame abruptly surge, strong and bright, for at that moment Blas raised the hand that he had thrust into his pocket.

Mel struck him with the crystal candle across the face.

Blas fell, blood spurting from his mouth, howling and screaming about her misconduct.

Mel ignored his outburst. She stepped on his wrist, pulled the stone from his hand, and held it up, eyeing it. Red streaked with black.

"A stone of darkness," she said, her voice trembling with anger.

She looked down at Blas Nunez. He was still full of arrogance and anger, but his expression slipped into wide-eyed fear as he caught her gaze.

"In my house," Mel said. "In my *home*. You bring *evil*." She grabbed him by the tunic and pulled him to her face. "You are of my *blood*. You're my family—my *kin*. And you move against *me*."

"No!" shouted DeLeon. He unsheathed his sword and ran toward her.

Mel turned her gaze on him, and the man stopped mid-stride and fell to his knees, his sword dropping from his hand. He grabbed at his chest, fear and bewilderment on his face. Plumes of smoke rose from his black tunic, and when he opened his mouth to scream, smoke and fire shot forth between his teeth, his tongue twisting as it blackened. His chest then burst into flame, filling the air with the smell of burnt flesh.

A sound from Blas Nunez pulled Mel's attention toward the older man. His eyes rolled to the back of his skull before melting and burning into black holes of ash and cinder. She stepped away as his chest exploded, blackened ribs stabbing outward, smoke pouring forth.

Mel squeezed the stone in her hand so tightly she felt it crack. Then she looked at her grandmother and the First Healer.

Understanding filtered through the assembly. Those in Blas Nunez's retinue fell to their knees. Even they understood.

Kale traitors will burn, burn, burn.

From the inside out.

Chapter Eleven

Victor stared at the giant flames dancing on the mass grave, hoping that his clan had done an adequate job of obscuring the bonfire from wondering eyes. At least forty clanspeople had participated in digging a hole large enough to contain all the fetid livestock. For hours they had worked, stressing over the possibility that someone would come across them. It seemed the nearby road was rarely used, but on the more distant highway, the headlights were nearly constant.

Still, now it was almost over. Soon the fire would die down and Victor and the Wileys could pursue the trail of the *Malum*. Hopefully without Cleo Newberry and the Maymes. But even as the thought crossed his mind, Victor knew it was unlikely.

The woman was talking to her clanspeople like a quarterback in a huddle. She was no doubt scheming and plotting; she might even be thinking about taking off half-cocked without any help from the Kales or even the Ferus, several of whom had arrived a couple of hours ago with Killian O'Shea. Now the Kales and Ferus were even in number, which had made Victor uncomfortable at first, but his uncle and the Wileys convinced him that having more support could only be to everyone's benefit.

"These are our allies," his uncle had said. "If we can't trust them, then there is no hope."

Victor hadn't argued, but he couldn't help thinking: *Hope for what?* Was it their friendship? Their help in beating a foe that was as intangible as smoke? But in the end, he decided that his grandmother had maintained the approach of keeping the clans involved in the investigation for a reason, and Victor trusted his grandmother's instincts. If this was the way, he would follow.

Drew Wiley approached Victor, grime on his veil and tunic, and pushed a canteen at Victor's chest. Victor grabbed it and drank from it, then handed it back.

"Find anything?" Victor asked, looking for Drew's sister. He had to keep an eye on Justine, as she had a way of rubbing the Maymes the wrong way. The Maymes weren't the sort to get goaded into a fight, but they sure weren't disciplined enough not to take part in an argument when one presented itself. Twice Victor had seen her in heated exchanges with Maymes about the *Malum*. Heated because the Maymes took offense at the events *and* at Justine's devil-may-care attitude.

It didn't help that Justine's tongue was as sharp as her knives. When the Maymes mentioned for the millionth time how horrible the circumstances were, she'd said, "Sure it's horrible, but nothing is more horrible than how clean you guys look in those *fine* white tunics." When one of them called the situation a disaster, she snapped back with, "Of course it's a disaster, it's a *demon*, you idiots." And when a Mayme once again remarked on the Kale's negligence, Justine hit them with "Oh, you can do better? Maybe in your dreams—your *wet* dreams."

So Victor was relieved when he saw her approach, Smitty at her side, no Maymes around.

"Yeah, we found something," Drew said. "There's a clear path running northwest. The Maymes are already poking around it. I overheard Newberry talking about calling more Maymes to help."

"As if we don't have enough people already," Victor grumbled.

"Well, you don't have to worry about that," Drew said. "I picked this out of her pocket when she wasn't looking." He pulled out a sat phone, and Victor snorted.

Justine laughed outright. "You relieved her of the phone in the midst of all those Maymes?" She sounded impressed. "Looks like all that misspent youth has finally come in handy."

Drew smirked. "And I had the best time watching them searching all over for it." He looked at Victor. "But I'll give it back if it's going to be a problem."

Victor wanted to be the bigger man—but couldn't. "Well, she can always ask to use one of ours if it's really that important to her," he said. But he knew that wouldn't happen. Cleo Newberry would rather fall on a sword than ask him for anything.

Smitty cleared his throat and covered his nose. "I just wish this fire would burn out already. This shit stinks."

Victor wrinkled his nose. The Janso was right. There was something rotten in the livestock that made it smell rancid as it burned.

It took another hour before the fire died down enough for the Kales to bury the remnants. Only then did they set out, slowly picking their way through the brush, with the Ferus and Maymes following. The Maymes were having particular difficulty seeing in the moonlight, and had to turn on flashlights, sending their beams cutting through the darkness.

Let them do as they like, Victor thought.

But when the Maymes moved forward, taking the lead, he grumbled aloud.

Tío Luce, walking at Victor's side, grunted in agreement. "If I've told her once, I've told her a thousand times not to move forward without us," he said. "They may have their own tracker, but these are still our lands."

"I don't think she cares," Victor replied. "I believe she's lost all confidence in us. Lost patience as well."

Tío Luce swept his eyes around the wood, taking account of every Kale's position. "I think I've lost my patience, too."

Drew slowed before them, knelt, and ran his hands along the grass. After a moment he stood and looked at Tío Luce. "Blood," he said. "I think we're getting close."

Shouting went up from nearby. Immediately, all the Kales and Ferus drew their weapons and crouched in the grass, eyes in the direction of the sounds. But as the shouts ratcheted up from startled to terrified, Victor rose from his place and tore through the woods, knowing his clanspeople would be at his back. He couldn't stay in place and ignore those cries, and neither could they.

The group charged through high brush. Trees stood in their path, and Victor drew his axe and hacked away the limbs with powerful swings. Drew appeared at his right, swinging his long knives. They sliced and kicked their way forward, branches scratching at their arms and faces, pulling at their tunics and veils.

More wailing sounded ahead. Fear forced its way, cold and choking, down Victor's throat, so strong he thought bile would rise. He drew a heavy breath and released it, forcing the vise around his windpipe to ease.

"Hurry!" he roared at his clanspeople. "Hurry!"

They scrambled like insects, running, hacking, falling over themselves just to pick up and push, push, push forward. Sweat poured down Victor's back, and he felt electricity in his limbs as he shoved through a thick wall of tangled burrs and branches. As he emerged on the other side, he burst into a tiny clearing illuminated by faint moonlight.

Cradled in that moonlight was Cleo Newberry, bathed in blood. She held in her arms a clansman, his tunic scarlet, his chest destroyed to reveal twisted sinew and tissue and bone. A look of fear remained frozen on his face, his lifeless eyes gazing at the dark skies above.

Newberry's expression held nothing but absolute desolation.

"Cleo!" Victor said, hands clutching his axe. "Where are they?"

The woman did not answer, nor did she look up from her dead clansman.

Victor's frustration boiled into a white noise in his brain. The *Malum* had to be close.

"Cleo! Where the fuck *are they?"*

He was about to reach for her, to shake her out of whatever dark stupor had befallen her, but Drew Wiley drew his attention with a hiss and motioned to a trail that could barely be seen in the gloom. It was an unnatural space. A dark hole of a path that made his eyes narrow, yearning to see past that which he could not see.

"Can you see the way, Drew?" Victor asked, but he was really asking: *Can you see through the oil of darkness? Can you see the dangers before they sprout and tear at us with gnashing teeth and sharp claw?*

"Yes," said Drew, and his eyes glowed a soft yellow. "Yes, I can."

Tío Luce and Killian O'Shea appeared behind them, their tunics torn by the brush, their eyes scanning the scene. Victor's uncle's eyes widened, and he shook his head.

"What's to be done?" Killian asked. "Should we call back to camp and report our findings? This is getting out of hand."

"You don't say, Ferus." Victor ground his molars so hard they almost cracked. "Look to that path," he said, pointing toward where Drew and Justine Wiley now stood with their weapons at the ready as if a *Malum* would come crashing out at any second, "and tell me what you see."

Killian faced the dark hole and blanched.

"That's what I fucking thought," Victor said. "You say this is getting out of hand? I *know* it is. The *Malum* are on our lands. *Ours.*

And they're already making themselves at home, sickening the Earth with that shit right there. So what are we going to do? We're going to follow the path. *You* can call back and report our findings. Then you can join us, or you can go back to camp—the choice is yours. But the Kales will push forward. We'll find what's left of the Maymes, and we'll bring them back. We'll find the *Malum*, and kill them. Because that's what we're *supposed* to do."

Without waiting for a response, he stepped in front of Cleo Newberry, who was still clutching the man in her arms. "Cleo," he said, "I'm giving you two seconds to get on your feet, or I'm sending you back to camp. Decide. Come with us or go back. Those are the choices."

When she still didn't move, Victor shook his head and turned away.

He waited impatiently as his clanspeople readied themselves. Tío Luce ordered two to stay behind with him to carry the dead Mayme back to camp. Finally, Victor turned to Drew.

"Lead the way, fucker."

Drew didn't need to be told twice. He stepped into the gloom, and the darkness greedily swallowing him whole. One by one, the others followed.

*****

It was like walking blind—or at least, how Victor imagined walking would be for a blind man. In pitch darkness with nothing but wits and courage. When his foot caught on a root and he nearly fell, Victor thought that this was not the best idea he'd ever had. What gave him confidence was the knowledge that Mel had gone into *Inter Spatium Abyssus* alone and come out of it in one piece—and she'd nothing but her hands and brains. Victor had ten of his clanspeople with him, all strong and true.

But he was so tired. How long had it been since he'd slept? Two days? Three? He could feel the fatigue in his muscles.

The sat phone rang in the darkness, and the other Kales swore as Victor hurriedly reached for it in his tunic. He answered, and his sister's tired voice came over the line.

"Tío Luce just called," she said. "He says you're hunting *Malum* through a blight. That right?"

The line of Kales had come to a halt while Victor gripped the phone tightly to his ear. He had a feeling they could hear her whispery voice on the call.

"Yeah," he said.

"Describe it to me."

He did. He mentioned the cold and hot feeling on his skin. The thick, claustrophobic darkness. The slickness under his boots. The smell of wet, foul rot. And the ever-pressing discontent pressing into his brain.

"That's bad," Mel said. "It sounds like it's terraforming."

"Making hell on Earth," Victor agreed.

"It's the endgame," Mel said, then: "Listen, don't move. I'm sending help."

"Mel, we can't wait. We're sitting fucking ducks here."

"Light a fire, dummy, and wait. That's an order."

She hung up before Victor could tell her that he didn't take orders from her.

When Victor motioned for Drew to move anyway, Drew whispered, "She said to wait."

Victor sighed but relented. He turned to the others. "We're holding here for reinforcements. Find something dry to burn."

They couldn't find a thing. Every bit of wood they picked up was slimed with a mucous-like substance or fell into dust at their touch. Drew suggested he pick his way out of the gloom to find a dry branch, but Victor nixed that idea quickly. There was no way to tell if the *Malum* were already out there with eyes on them—and perhaps it was only Drew's presence among them that kept the *Malum* at bay. There was definitely *something* out there—high-pitched yowls sounded regularly in the darkness, grating on Victor's eardrums.

It was with great relief when at last a light appeared in the darkness. The flame seemed so bright, so cleansing, it made the blackness collapse. Two figures in gold were picking their way along the trail at a careful pace, and one was spinning a torch that was lit at both ends, creating a perfect circle of fire.

"'Sup, cousin!" said Thrash, with Thomas Thorn at his side. "Good to see you alive in this dark hole."

But Thomas did not seem pleased at all. The older man's eyes were liquid blue heat, and Victor had a sense that under Thorn's veil was a puckered mouth of disapproval. "What are your plans?" he asked coolly.

"To go forward," Victor said simply. "What can you do to make it safer for us?"

"It depends," Thomas said. "What do you need?"

Victor looked at the torch in the man's hands, still spinning. The soft flame lit up the area, revealing an unearthly wet grime beneath their feet, punctuated by infested dirt, limbs, and leaves. It also revealed his clanspeople's gritty faces, stolid and determined.

"We can't fight in this shit," Victor said. "Only Drew can see. The rest of us are blind."

Thomas glanced at Drew. "No, we can't. But we won't have to."

He motioned to Thrash, who slung a backpack off his shoulder and pulled out several small pots. Glyphs were scratched into their aged white casings:

Essence of Reveal.

"Are you sure these will still work?" Victor asked. "They look old."

Thomas raised an eyebrow. "They don't have an expiration date, kid. If anything, they'll be *more* potent. Most magics get stronger as they age." Thomas's eyes stared into the darkness ahead. "Once we find the lair, we'll use the pots for our attack. Drew can be our eyes until then."

"You and Thrash will be joining us then?" Victor asked.

The older man nodded. "This takes precedence over the Eighth. Hurry, let's get this shit over with."

A second torch was lit with a piece of timber from Thrash's backpack, and the group set off at a slow, careful pace. Drew stayed in the lead, his knives at the ready, his body at a crouch, and the other Kales followed his example. Victor gripped his axe in both hands, alternating exposing his left and right side, his toes soft with each step, his breath slow and steady. Quiet. They were all so quiet.

They trekked for hours. A few times Drew directed them to a sudden halt, his quiet voice carrying warning, and they smothered the flames quickly. Each time they sat in the dark, tightly gripping their weapons, pushing their senses outward, hopeful they would at least hear the *Malum* as they approached. Then Drew would rise and direct the torches to be lit, and they'd move on once more.

Thrash walked next to Victor, thrumming with unexpended energy. He was more himself than Victor had seen him in days. He held his sword confidently in his right hand, his brown eyes alert through the veil.

"No luck with finding the Eighth?" Victor asked quietly.

His cousin's eyes didn't leave the darkness as he answered. "We tracked them deep into the woods a few miles from here, but then the trail just ended. Thomas thinks they must've met up with someone gifted who hid their trail."

A shiver went down Victor's back. "The Lost Soul?"

Those soft brown eyes met Victor's. "I hope to hell not."

After that they didn't speak, each lost in their thoughts. The idea of the damn Eighth meeting up with the Lost Soul and colluding would just be the cherry on this shit sundae.

Again, Victor thought about how fortunate it was that his wife and kids were safe, ensconced at home and nowhere near the danger that his life had become. But he knew that very, very soon, he would have to bring them back into the fold. There was no changing that. The quicker his wife realized what was at stake, the better. He hoped that she would come to her senses and see that salvation was through *The Ways*. External and internal. It was the only path to follow.

A clansman near the back of the line called for a halt, and Victor picked his way back to investigate. He arrived to find Cleo Newberry, her progress being blocked by a wall of Kales. Her tunic was still dark with blood, but she had cleaned her face, and her hazel eyes clear of anguish.

"Cleo," Victor said, making a quick decision. "I'm glad you've joined us."

The Kales stepped aside, letting the woman through.

"I'm not alone," she said, and Killian O'Shea and several Ferus appeared at her back as if emerging from black smoke. "We followed as soon as we regrouped."

Killian O'Shea looked apologetic. "I—"

Victor cut him off. "You're a Friend of Kale," he said. "Offering your assistance?"

The Ferus nodded. "Yes."

"Then that's all that matters."

Nothing else was said, and nothing needed to be.

They continued ahead a bit more quickly. Victor felt somewhat buoyed by the help of Clans Ferus and Mayme, and was already strategizing how they might use the extra hands.

They'd walked another ten minutes when Drew motioned for

them to smother the flames again. Everyone froze, and after a long moment, Drew crept back to report on what he had seen.

There was a quarry just ahead. Ridges of stone and whitewashed rock, and a darkness opening below, like a mouth burrowed into the quarry floor. He had seen no Maymes, but there were a few *Malum* milling about. The bodies they'd infected had cracks through the skin, bone and tissue disfiguring their shapes, and that slimy residue all over their bodies. Some were feasting on animal carcasses that they must have dragged into the quarry.

"We need to kill them," said Thomas flatly, blindly pushing one of the small pots into Drew's hand. "Set it off so the wind will carry it through. Then come back here, quickly, without giving yourself away."

When Drew left, Victor asked, "Killian, how many in your number can see through the blight?"

Killian O'Shea was quiet, then said after a moment, "Two."

Thomas grunted as if amused. "So four to six then."

"That's good," Victor said, ignoring the implication. "The smoke of the essence may not reveal the entire quarry. Clan Kale will descend into the cave, find the Maymes, and kill all the *Malum* in sight. It would be best if Clan Ferus surrounded the area to make sure that none escape."

"Surrounding it will be difficult," Killian replied. "Based on Drew's description, the quarry is massive, and we do not know its secrets. There's a chance that some *Malum* may be missed."

"I can help with that," said Thomas, then looked at Victor. "We will also need blood to draw any stragglers that are off hunting."

"You will need more than that," said Cleo Newberry. "I know just the thing…"

But before either could explain, the scene ahead of Victor became clear. Drew must have deployed the essence of reveal, because the quarry began to appear before them, gradually, as if being puffed into existence like smoke from a fire.

Within moments Victor could see everything Drew had described. The carnage littering the rock. The malevolent demons stalking around with jerky motions, many crawling on all fours. Some were nude, while others were clothed in strips and rags. It was a gruesome sight, and one that would haunt Victor's dreams until his dying day.

Newberry ran off to do whatever she had planned. Victor just hoped she wasn't going to go all kamikaze and sacrifice herself as bait, since she was more than likely the only Mayme who would live through this, and they would need her testimony on the other side of all this.

Thomas handed several small scarlet pots to Killian O'Shea. "These will burn anything in their path," he said. "Handle them with great care, and make sure you're downwind when they ignite."

Killian cradled the many little pots like they were eggs. "I'll get these sorted and my clansmen in place." With that he left, sneaking sure-footed into the grey darkness that seemed impossibly bright compared to the enveloping blight that had just passed through.

"These gifts are not very consistent," Victor said quietly to Thomas. "I can see into the darkness, but I can't see into the blight. That's some bullshit."

Thomas sat on his haunches. "It'll come as it comes."

Victor frowned. He was frustrated and hot, his tunic sticking to his back. He wasn't in the mood for Thomas's riddles. "What the fuck does that mean?"

"It means," Thomas said, "that some of us have a seed inside, but it does not grow without nourishment. Nourishment that has not been provided in several millennia. But now the heir walks the Earth, and with every moment, with every breath since she was born, she's been pulling power from the Earth. Minuscule amounts. A drop in the ocean. But it adds up, and it multiplies. And she does not keep it all to herself. She *filters* it—she filters all the negative shit out of it—so that we do not have to go through the same."

"Are you saying…?"

"I'm saying we'll all get stronger and it'll be a relatively painless experience," Thomas said. "But Mel will suffer until the day she dies."

Victor gripped his axe, shaking his head. "No."

"It's the way," Thomas said, sadness in his eyes. "The only way."

"Life is pain? That what you're saying? That's fucking bullshit." Victor gritted his teeth. "I don't accept it. And I know Mel won't accept it. And what do you know anyway? You don't know everything. You can't know. You can't give evidence that a life of pain is all there is."

Thomas opened his mouth to reply, but just then Cleo Newberry reappeared, her face alight with satisfaction. "They come," she said. "I heard them. Ready yourselves."

And then there was no time. *Malum* swarmed into the quarry, pushing their heads side to side, attempting to identify what power had drawn them in. They looked to be in a daze.

"Good job, Cleo," Victor said.

"*Malum* are stupid," she replied. "I've read they are lost without a mind to guide them. No such mind exists here."

"Not yet anyway. Let's kill the fuckers before that damn Lost Soul gets any ideas."

****

"Are we doing this hard and fast or slow and quiet?" asked Thrash.

The Kales were huddled close. Drew Wiley had his knives out at the ready, a glint in his eye. His sister was glaring down at the quarry, a short sword in her right, a dagger in her left. And Thomas held that godawful war club.

"Fucking hard," Victor said.

"Reading my mind, cuz," said Thrash, unsheathing his sword. "After you."

They moved swiftly down the steep sides of the quarry, sliding down loose rock. One misstep could cause a broken ankle or a broken neck. But the thought didn't cross their minds. There was only one purpose here. One goal.

As Victor's feet touched the bottom of the quarry, he zeroed in on a *Malum* squirming on the ground. He raised his axe and let loose with a heavy swing. *Thwack!* The foul thing ceased its movement, and Victor moved on to the next, and the next, and the next. His axe cleaved them all, leaving only lifeless appendages, blood, and slime. His clansmen were about their business in the same way. Quiet in the onslaught, sure in their striking. Cutting and carving their way through the demons.

They'd managed to cut down quite a few before one caught on to their assault and let out an awful screech. Justine flung a dagger at the screaming demon. The gold blade landed deep in its gullet, and the scream turned into a wet hacking. Tendrils slithered out past the blade, but then Thomas was there, cleaving the *Malum*'s throat. Thomas fell upon another in a frenzied assault, his war club dancing to a terrible, brutal song. He was a goddamn machine that would not stop, leading the way into the dark cave that Victor hoped held the Maymes.

He knew they were dead. He hadn't wanted to say so in front of Newberry. But even she had to have known. All they could hope for was to recover the bodies. To afford the dead some peace. A place to rest, far away from this degraded nest.

"Hold up, Thomas," Victor said, breathing heavily. All the Kales were still with him. Drew and Justine Wiley were hardly winded, waiting with barely contained energy. Thrash was wiping the slickness off his blade with his tunic-covered arm. The rest ignored their cuts and scrapes, though Victor saw one woman was clearly favoring her right arm, holding it close to her body.

"Can you fight?" he asked her.

The woman nodded. Victor wasn't so sure, but one look at her face told him there was no way she would leave. Her place, just like his—just like that of all the Kales—was here, in this moment.

"It's time," he said, leading the way into the cave.

Behind, he heard Thomas whispering, a prayer almost. *"For the Chieftress."*

****

They slipped in like thieves. Soft-footed, plumbing the darkness and that unholy infestation that slicked the walls and floors. The deeper they went, the more fetid it grew.

And then, like an adversary that would not be beaten down, the blight fought back.

The inky darkness bloomed around them, and with it came a sound. Not the screeching they were accustomed to, but an incessant clicking, like bugs singing. It sent shivers down their backs.

Thomas lit another of the white pots and threw it into the darkness. The pot went off, and its smoke revealed hundreds if not thousands of white-eyed creatures crawling along the cave walls, their legs chittering along the rock, their quivering mouths splitting open unevenly, tendrils slithering out in mad rhythm.

Thomas fumbled for another pot, this one red, lit it, and threw it in the dead center of the *Malum*. It didn't go off right away, its fuse burning sluggishly. He threw several more pots next to the first, and when it still didn't ignite, Victor swore, dropped his axe, and unsheathed the long knife at his waist. He moved into position as the wave of creatures grew nearer.

And then the swarm was upon them, white-eyed fire spitting hate.

"Keep them back!" Victor yelled, hacking at the *Malum* with his knife, blood and grey matter splattering his face. "Do not let *any* of them past!"

At his back was Thrash, his sword moving with lightning-quick stabs and swipes, slicing through with amazing dexterity and minimal effort. Thomas was simply grabbing the demons with his hands, throwing them on the ground, and clubbing them to death. And Justine and Drew were working together, cutting away at the swarm with mechanical ease and thoroughness. Behind them, many of the others were just doing what they could to stay alive. The injured clanswoman was on the ground, a fresh wound on her chest, but even she cut down what she could, even from that position.

The Kales fought valiantly, but the enemy were too many, the Kales too few. The swarm pushed forward with a hunger for blood and death.

Just when Victor thought they were going to be overrun, the red pot went off. At first it was merely a little burp of fire that hit the rock like an accidental spill, as if it were merely waving *hello*. An instant later its cheerful introduction morphed into a grand *Fuck you!* as it unleashed hell on Earth. All the pots ignited in a chain reaction, putting out heat and rage that could not be matched by the demons. The fire grew and churned, billowing out through the heart of the swarm, burning them to ash.

The Kales stood back in shock, then leaning tiredly against the walls.

"Jesus fucking Christ," said Thrash. "That was *amazing!*"

"Shut up, Thrash."

"It just," he made an exploding motion with his hands, "poof!

And just like that they're all gone. Amazing."

"Thrash," said Victor, looking his cousin in the eye. "Not the time."

"Right, right."

Victor took stock of himself. Some cuts, some blood. Nothing major. Other than the weariness. "Everyone okay?" he asked, sliding his knife back in its sheath and picking up his axe.

"We lost one," said Drew quietly. He stood over the injured clanswoman, who lay motionless.

Victor didn't even know her name. Didn't know if she had family back at camp. God, she had to be younger than Gabe. She could've been mistaken for resting if not for the gaping wound in her chest. *"Goddammit."*

"We can't leave her here," Justine said.

"We have to," said Victor. "We'll get her on the way back."

We will be back, he vowed. *We will not let you rest here, my clanswoman. No, we will not.*

He signaled them all to continue, and they went. Down to where the *Malum* had come from, vigilant for any others that might appear. The rock was hot and steaming, melting the rubber in their boots.

"Careful," Victor warned when Justine lost her balance. He had to grab her by the arm to keep her from falling and burning herself.

They descended deeper, their footsteps crunching on the loose grey gravel. When the cave finally came to an end—in a dark cavern of slick, grimy rock and rubble—the smell was ripe and ghastly. Victor clutched his axe, understanding the implication. His clanspeople reacted the same, eyes searching for the source.

Something was *wrong* here.

Thomas directed the others forward, using the hand-talk the clan rarely employed. The Kales moved as instructed, spreading out and staying on guard as they slipped further into the dark space.

A soft scratching reached Victor's ears, subtle and slow. He immediately cut toward the sound, his axe held firmly in one hand, crouched and stalking. He felt Drew come up alongside him as he drew nearer to the cave wall.

And there, in the muck, was a woman. She was filthy, her skin oozing with something pink. She was scratching glyphs, strange and foreign, into the wall, in the shape of a large arch. She seemed unaware of their presence.

Victor lifted his axe and tightened his jaw. He could end this. Cut her in fucking two. Leave her ruined on the cave floor. Then they could burn this fucking place to the ground and rid themselves of the blight.

But before he could reach her, she spoke.

"You've come a lot sooner than I thought you would."

Victor froze. None of the other possessed had spoken. The *Malum* inside them had turned them into mindless demons.

She continued. "I'd hoped to have finished before anyone was aware."

Victor put one foot in front of the other. He could still do it. Could still cut her in half before she turned around. He could.

She did not cease her work as he approached.

That was when he saw the hasty burial site. On the ground beside her was a pile of gravel, and a sliver of white tunic was peeking through.

Victor felt anger spread through him, and forgetting his caution, he lunged forward, grabbed the woman by her slick hair, and threw her on the floor.

"Who are you?" he demanded.

His clanspeople immediately surrounded them.

"You don't know?" she replied, sneering, her face pale and ugly. "Oh, *tell me* you know. This would be so much more fun if you knew. But then, I heard the ones in white are the smart ones. Your kind—not so much."

Victor shot a look at Justine, who nodded, then slapped the woman in the face.

"Who are you?" Victor asked again.

"Can't do your own dirty work, Kale?" the woman said, spitting blood. "I heard you Kales were *yellow*. Or is this some misplaced chivalry?"

This time Justine sent a blow to her solar plexus.

"Who are you?" Victor asked for the third time.

The woman coughed up blood and phlegm.

Victor knelt before her, looking into her muddy grey eyes that were turning from the blight. But deep in that black hole, he saw something he recognized... and he latched on to it.

"I smell *fear* in you, Eighth."

She froze, and her snide expression fell.

"You know what I think? I think your clan abandoned you. I think you are in *way* over your head, and now you're dying, leaving your husk to be inhabited by a fucking demon. That's what I think."

She glared at him in confusion and rage. Then she pressed her lips together and looked away.

"What happened to the Maymes?" Victor asked.

The woman blew out a deep, furious breath. "The *Malum* tried to turn them, but they just... died. They spoke some words that made their hearts stop."

She sounded jealous of their deaths.

Victor frowned. He had expected they were dead, but was sorry to hear of the manner in which it had happened.

"When were you turned?" Thomas asked.

The woman looked up at him, her eyes fiery again. "Why? Going to save me?"

"Maybe," said Thomas. He nodded to Thrash, who pulled a tube of translucent blue liquid from his pack. "You come with us—no fuss and no bullshit—and I'll give you the cure that will stop the turn."

The woman looked suspiciously at Thomas, her face waxy with sweat. "You're lying to me," she said angrily. "There's no cure for what I have."

"We don't lie," said Thrash. He tossed her the tube. "Go ahead, take it. It's the first of many you will have to take."

The woman eyed the tube suspiciously. "You could be trying to poison me."

"Believe me," said Thrash, "if we wanted to kill you, poison wouldn't be our choice."

"He's right about that," said Victor. "If I had it my way my axe would be coated in your traitor blood, you little bitch. Now drink the fucking potion. I know someone who's got questions for you. Better get a move on, 'cause she's fucking waiting."

The woman looked at Victor wearily, then popped the top off the tube and swallowed its contents.

Moments passed as they all waited. Drew grew antsy and moved away to examine the spot where the Maymes were buried.

After a few minutes, the Eighth woman spoke. "I think it's working."

"Oh, really, Sherlock?" said Thrash. "You can tell? That's nice."

"Yes, I can tell," she said, and her voice held a hint of fear. "Because I can tell you now that these walls have ears."

And then the cave ceiling shook and fell upon their heads.

Chapter Twelve

Base instincts took over. Electricity fired synapses in the brain, adrenaline pumped through blood vessels, and blood and oxygen fought their way from heart and lungs. Victor leaped out of the way of the falling rocks, pulling the damned Eighth woman with him.

And then he looked up.

Above them lurked a demon beast that appeared to consist of only muscles, veins, and blood. A foul, decrepit, heinous mass.

"It's the fucking *Thing*, Victor!" screamed Thrash. And then he pointed up at it as if Victor couldn't see the goddamn thing with his own eyes.

"Got any more of those pots?" Victor shouted to Thomas.

The older man revealed one single pot in his meaty hand.

"Fuck!"

Victor pressed himself against the wall to dodge more falling rock. The demon mass pooled down, twisting and turning, shifting fluidly from one misshapen body to another.

And then the woman spoke at Victor's side.

"*The Earth will break, the sky will fall, the lands will be washed in blood. What is dead will rise. What is evil will walk. What is living will tremble and quake with fear. It is then the Chosen will regain their strength and power. It is then they shall have their revenge.* That's what they always told us."

Victor snarled. "I think the *Chosen* is up for fucking interpretation." He signaled to the other Kales using hand-talk. *Surround. Attack.* Then to the woman: "Just stay here out of the way."

The creature unfurled. Its head, a knot of black and grey muscle possessing opaque white eyes, rose up on a thin neck that stretched grotesquely from its body. A crack opened between the muscles, creating a sort of mouth, and a cluster of tendrils wriggled forth as it emitted a roar that sounded like it would bring down the mountain on top of them. And indeed, the ceiling shook and more rock tumbled down.

Several tendrils shot out of the beast's mouth right at the stunned Kales. The tendrils penetrated their chests before shooting back toward the beast. The Kales stood for an instant longer, suspended like puppets, before falling to the ground, dead.

Victor charged.

He swung his axe at the beast. Black blood spurted forth, and the creature screamed in pain. But at the same time it counterattacked, its head darting down at Victor like a scorpion's tail. Victor leapt to the side, barely dodging the creature's deadly tendrils, before rolling on the broken rock and pushing back to his feet.

The awful head had followed, and by the look in its hate-filled eyes, it was about to attack once more. But just then another scream of pain tore from its horrible mouth. The other Kales had attacked, driving their weapons into the demon's sides, cutting and slicing at every bit of its rotten meat.

They quickly worked out a strategy: surround it, attack in quick succession, take turns flaying its massive body. It squirmed and hissed, readying those ugly tendrils to counterattack, but whenever it reared to do so, another Kale would dive in, diverting its attention.

Little by little the Kales cleaved off bits and pieces of the beast. Black blood pooled beneath it, smelling rank and spoiled. Victor felt proud to be fighting alongside these men and women. They battled with poise, with readiness, with duty in the face of the ugliest thing he'd ever seen in his life. And not one of them had run to piss their pants. No, they'd all stood there as one, protective of one another.

All in.

The demon was clearly tiring, weakened by their blades. It slowed, its attempts to attack increasingly lethargic. And then it began to collapse in on itself, shuddering, and emitted a gruesome death rattle.

The Kales stopped and watched its death, but they remained vigilant, weapons in hand.

And it was a good thing. For in a last burst of desperation, the creature charged.

It went for the closest Kale, but instead of attacking with its tendrils, it attempted to simply smother him under its massive weight. The others descended on it instantly, trying to drive it away from the fallen man, but the demon would not be moved. It just sat like a hen on an egg, its tendrils lolling out of its mouth. It seemed to know it was dying and just wanted to take one of the enemy with it.

"Thomas!" Victor shouted. "Use the pot!"

The older man lit the fuse and threw the pot at the demon. It went off as it struck, and the demon's ghastly form was set alight. The *Malum* recoiled in pain, its monstrous head flailing high in the air, and Victor, seeing an opportunity, threw his axe. It found its mark, and the head was cleaved from the beast's body.

The mass of the demon quieted and fell still. But the head continued to move, trying to squirm away. Drew put an end to that, driving his knife right through its fluttering wormed tendrils.

The demon was dead.

****

The quarry was a hive of activity, with scores of Kales moving about, climbing up and down the rope ladders that had been installed everywhere. They had arrived in the early morning hours and immediately set to work cleaning—which meant dumping all the *Malum* bodies in a pile and then burning them, cleansing their evil from the grounds. The Ferus were still here as well—some helping, some just observing. Their tunics were dirty and soiled, their hands still clutching weapons as if they had seen too much in the night to ever sheathe them again. Shellshocked, yet not willing to leave until it was truly over.

"I thank you for your help," Victor said to Killian O'Shea. "We appreciate it and count you a true Friend of Kale."

The son of *Sapienti* O'Shea had an ease about him that was not there the day before. "The honor was mine," he said. He looked toward the small bundle of white-clad bodies that had been laid out carefully. Cleo Newberry was delicately washing the faces of her fallen clanspeople. "I needed to be here. I needed to witness this."

Victor nodded. "You don't know until you know."

"This *is* war," the Ferus said. "This will get worse before it gets better."

"It's already bad. We lost several good clanspeople tonight." He looked into the mouth of the cave, which still smoldered from the fires set there the night before. "This for fucking sure will not stand."

Several of his clansmen were setting C-4 throughout the cave's entranceway. They'd already placed plenty of it around the quarry, avoiding only those sections were piles of *Malum* still burned. None had wanted to wait until the fires were out, so ready were they to close this awful chapter.

"What of the Eighth woman?" Killian asked.

"She will be questioned."

There had been moments where the woman was unaccounted for,

shortly after the battle with the *Malum* in the cave. She must've slipped out while their attention was diverted—but they'd quickly found her sitting just inside the mouth of the cave, waiting. Thomas and Thrash had shoved a bag over her head and bundled her up without a word. With just a nod to Victor, they'd left, taking her back to camp. That had been hours ago.

"Good," said Killian. "I'd appreciate if you'd let me know if anything worthwhile comes out of the interrogation."

Victor agreed, shaking his hand. It had been a long night, and he was ambivalent about the outcome. The blight had been vanquished, and just the normal night surrounded them now. Most importantly, he'd survived. But several of his clansmen hadn't. Nine Maymes had also fallen. But the *Malum* were dead, killed and burning in the rubble. Soon the entire area would be rubble, and every evidence of the darkness that had inhabited this place would be a distant memory.

Victor was still ruminating about it when a call came over his sat phone from one of the rangers, scouting several miles away. His grip almost crushed the phone as he listened to the man's report, and immediately he relayed the news to the others.

"We have incoming!" he said tersely. "Clear the area. We have to go!" He pointed at the Kale who was wiring the detonator. "I want that cave sealed in thirty seconds! Make it happen!"

They all scrambled to grab items and containers from the ground. The Ferus left, Killian giving them a parting look that implied they were on their own. Victor didn't blame them, but he surely wished he had the extra hands to help with the trek up and out of the quarry. His clanspeople dragged and pulled everything they could handle at a steady pace. Victor watched them from below as they cleared the last wall and disappeared.

Only the fallen Maymes were left. Several Kales had bunched

them together to carry them, but Cleo Newberry was making that difficult. She was pushing them away angrily, growling at anyone who got close.

"Cleo, we have to go!" Victor screamed. "Quit your shit and let us take them."

"Fuck off!" she bellowed. "These are *Maymes*. You have no right to touch them!"

Frustration and anger flooded through Victor. "I indulged you when we removed them from within, but this I can't allow. We have to *go*, Cleo!"

"I'm not going anywhere!" the woman screamed right back. "I will wait for my clanspeople. They will be here soon, and *then* we will remove our lost ones. Not a moment before."

Victor wanted to flog the older woman for her stubbornness—wanted to wrap his meaty hands around her neck until her eyes bulged out of her head. When he spoke again, his voice was low and cold.

"Listen to me. If you stay here, you risk exposing my clan. I will not let you do that, Cleo. Do you understand? I will not let you cause more scrutiny to be placed on us!"

"You know the rites!" the woman yelled back. "You know the respect that needs to be paid to our dead! I will not allow such an offense!"

"You *can!* The circumstances *demand* it!"

Victor signaled the Kales to take the fallen Maymes. But as soon as one knelt to grab a Mayme's shoulder, a knife glimmered sharp and quick, and blood dripped off the back of the Kale's hand. He looked terribly affronted at Newberry as he rose to his full height, hand reaching for his sword.

"Hold," Victor ordered, then looked at Newberry, his face stone. "You make your own bed, Cleo. I wish you'd allow me the courtesy of helping you, but now that I see that that is *not* going to happen, I'll leave you here to it. I suggest you get out of the way of the blast radius." He turned to his clanspeople. "Let's go!"

They all gave the Mayme a hard, ugly look as they passed, and then they scrambled up the quarry walls.

Victor was out of breath, sweat dripping, drenching his tunic and breeches by the time he lifted himself over the edge at the top. From here he could see a line of cars and trucks making their way down the dirt road, blue and red lights blinking in the darkness. They were going slow, careful of the darkness and uneven road. He could just make out the sirens.

The Kale with the detonator raised it at the ready. "Give the word."

Victor looked at him, then down at the quarry where they'd left the Mayme woman. He sighed in frustration, giving his axe to a Kale and taking off his veil.

"You're going back?" asked Drew.

Victor nodded, wiping the sweat and weariness off his face before sliding the veil back on.

"Vic," said Justine. "You're sure about this?"

He nodded again. It was against his better judgment, but he couldn't just leave the woman there—as much as he wanted to. He didn't know if it was because of everything that was happening or if it was the ton of shit they would get from the Maymes for abandoning one of their clanswomen. Or maybe it was just male chivalry. At this point he supposed it didn't matter.

"Hold here," he said. "Await my order."

"We're coming with you," said Justine. She and Drew handed their weapons to other Kales, but those Kales just handed them off to others and followed Victor and the Wileys.

They set off back down the steep side of the quarry, back toward where they'd left the Mayme woman. She was exactly where they'd left her, and looked up at them as they came upon her.

"Thought you'd be halfway back to camp by now." Her voice was quiet, spent.

"I thought about it," Victor said. "Thought I'd give you one more opportunity to change your mind and let us help you."

Newberry reached out a hand and made shapes in the air over the bodies. Glyphs, Victor realized. When she was done, she cupped each face with her hands, her eyes closed, murmuring under her breath.

"I don't need help from you," she said finally. "I need help from my own. Only a Mayme can touch a Mayme. Only a Mayme can proceed with the rites of a Mayme—just as only a Kale can proceed for a Kale. I'd think you'd understand, since you just lost your sister."

Victor felt a moment's guilt for the lie. But it couldn't be helped.

"You've got maybe five, ten minutes tops before the state police arrive," Victor said. "At that point you're spending at least the next few days in jail. After that—who knows? Maybe they'll throw away the key." Victor knelt down beside Cleo. "If you're in jail or prison you can't help get justice for these men and women."

"Justice?" Newberry scoffed. "We had our *justice*." She pointed at the cave. "What do you think last night was all about?"

This Victor could handle. This he knew the answer to. "Last night was damage control." Then at Newberry's disbelieving face he added, "Don't get me wrong—we got them. All of them. And we prevented the blight from festering in our lands. But don't be mistaken. This isn't the only battle to be won. The Eighth Clan will continue to attack us. We can't even be sure that there aren't more out there. And," here he moved closer to her, lowering his voice as if afraid there were unwanted ears nearby, "there is a Lost Soul loose."

The Mayme drew up, her eyes drilling into Victor as if attempting to judge the truth of his words.

"It's true," Victor said. "It's what my grandmother was to hold the gathering for."

"H—How?" the Mayme stammered. "Who—when?"

Victor bit down hard. "Come with me now, Cleo. Come with me, and give me your blood oath. And I will tell you everything. *Everything.* But you need to come with me now. There's still so much to fight for."

Victor knew he had her, and so did the Kales. They were already moving forward toward the fallen Maymes, and Cleo had hardly nodded before they were lifting them up and setting off.

It was a difficult climb to the top, hefting the Maymes' bodies, and a frantic rush. At the top, the trucks had already arrived, but were stopped at the quarry's entrance gates. It wouldn't slow them long— Victor already saw men with bolt cutters. Others wore flak jackets, with revolvers and rifles at the ready.

Victor turned to the man with the detonator—and nodded.

The ground shook. A massive cloud of dust burst forth from the quarry pit, burning eyes and throats.

The Kales used its cover as they sped swiftly away through the woods.

Chapter Thirteen

"I didn't expect you to do that," Gabe said again, rubbing his face tiredly. *Tío Jorge is going to fucking kill me.*

A body lay spread-eagle on the ground before him, eyes closed as if in slumber. But this was death, and an ugly one. The man's face was horrifically mutilated and still bled through crusting rust-colored scabs.

Micos cleaned her blade with elephant leaves. "He was touched. Every moment he lived was torture. This was mercy."

Gabe raised a brow, remembering the quickness of her blade. The look in her eyes as she watched him clutching the wound she'd opened in his throat. As if she'd just been waiting for the perfect time to finish him.

She and Gabe had dragged the man along while they searched the premises, always on the lookout for him to wander away, have some sort of emotional breakdown, or worse, attack them. Hours of this had worn on the both of them, but it had not occurred to Gabe to just… end it.

"Mercy, huh? I'll need to remember not to bring you anywhere near Charlotte."

Micos sat on the grass and sheathed her knife. They had settled themselves in the backyard of a vacant house. All the houses were vacant as far as Gabe could tell. Just empty little boxes. Some still had dinner on the table. Cold and stale. Lukewarm drinks, ice having melted hours before. But no blood. No carnage. Just this one man, as empty as the houses, driven to draw on his face with anything sharp he could get his hands on.

"Your cousin is probably in agony as well," Micos said. "It would be best if she left this world. But not before she is free of the Darkness."

Gabe sat down next to her, resting his hands on his knees. "You know much about these things, do you?"

The woman pulled two protein bars from her bag and handed one to Gabe. "I've made it my purpose in life to study that which can hurt me. I've dedicated myself to learning how to protect myself from those dangers." She bit into her bar with a daintiness Gabe didn't think she possessed. "What do you do with your time, Gabriel Mendez?"

"I fuck off," Gabe said, tearing into his bar heartily. "A lot."

The woman made a soft sound of derision. "I suggest you change that."

"I suggest you *mind your business.*" Gabe polished off his bar and rolled the wrapper in his hands. "Besides, I got a sword and a staff. I'll be just fine."

"I suppose you were just fine when the Lost Soul nearly killed you." Micos lay back on the grass. The perfectly cut grass that looked like it was fertilized and watered five times a week. "Tell me what it was like facing death in the eye."

"And walking away alive?" He threw the wrapper at a trash can that was leaning up against the side of the house. He missed by a mile. "It was splendid, my dear. *Splendid.*"

He pushed to his feet, grabbed his miss off the ground, and put it in the bin. When he sat back down, a seriousness came over him.

"It really was amazing though. All I had were my hands and two tiny blades against his fucking long sword. I looked him in his fucking blood-red eyes. His cracked fucking face. He treated me like I was his plaything. But I wasn't, Micos. I'm a fucking Kale. I wasn't going to go down like some punk. I wasn't going to just let him kill me with that fucking demon blade.

"And then he got through my guard—cut my neck." He slid his hand like a blade over his scar. "I thought I was going to die. I really fucking did. But you know what?" He looked at the older woman, could see he had her attention. "If he came strolling in here right this second, I'd fight him again. Just for the chance to rip that fucking shit-eating grin off his fucking face. And if I die trying—well, burn my body at sunrise and let the winds take my ashes. To the earth, to the skies, to the seas. I'll find my way to the other side *just fine.*"

Micos's laughter was loud and full. It reminded Gabe of Siva's. Boy, he missed the Mayme woman. He'd had hardly a minute to talk to her, or touch her, or hold her. He really needed to find some time alone with the Mayme when he got back.

He was still going through the mental list of things he planned to do with Siva once they were alone when his clanspeople arrived. Tío Jorge looked at the dead stranger, then at the two of them with barely contained fury.

"*This* is what you've been up to?" He knelt on the ground and placed a hand on the man's chest. "This is why you called me?"

"Hey now," Gabe said, trying for levity. "We're only responsible for the slit throat. Everything else he did on his own."

"Gabe…" It was said with such disappointment. Gabe at once felt like a wet-behind-the-ears Novice.

"Tío. He was tainted. He couldn't speak. He wouldn't eat, nor would he sit still." Gabe pulled a screw from his pocket. "He found this screw, and it was the only thing that could capture his attention.

As soon as he held it, he mutilated himself with it. He had to go. We couldn't take him with us, nor could we leave him here."

"We could've called someone to pick him up."

"And wait for them to drive out here? Take him back to the house and question him? He couldn't string two words together."

"That wasn't for you to decide, Gabe." Tío Jorge looked once again at the dead stranger. "Now we will never know what he saw that made him do this to himself."

"It was I who did it," Micos confessed. "Not Gabe."

"I don't care who it was," Tío Jorge snapped. "Gabe should've been paying attention and stopped you. But he *wasn't*. Was he?"

Gabe sighed heavily, rubbing his face. "No. I wasn't."

"What were you doing, then? If not watching your charge like I asked."

"I was napping," Gabe said. "Just a power nap. Just a moment to catch my breath."

"Really," Tío Jorge replied. "Really? You were sleeping? You, who I have pushed and pushed for days on end—since you were a boy— was sleeping?"

Gabe felt his face flush. Felt the eyes of the other Kales. He did not look at them. "Yes."

"You—" And then his uncle's eyes narrowed. He looked at Micos, who had grown more interested in the grass, the trees, the white picket fences. "What happened?"

Gabe powered through. "It doesn't matter. I found something. You need to see it. If I'm to be disciplined for this man's death, I will take whatever disciplinary action you give me. But first, come with me."

He led the others through a gate that opened into a greenbelt. Gabe slipped smoothly through the high grass, careful of his steps. The darkness surrounded them as they moved further from the artificial lights of the houses. The land grew wilder, full of the smells of the earth and animals. Gabe held his short sword in his hand and pulled the face sleeve over his nose as they approached his destination.

Spread over two acres were burn marks of different glyph shapes, still smoldering. The one Gabe stood before sparked some recognition in him, but the others were strange and indecipherable. Micos crouched beside the next one over and placed her hand inches from the smoldering shape. She had done the same when she first saw it. Gabe wondered if she sensed something or if it was just something to do when there was nothing to be done.

Tío Jorge looked around with wide eyes. "How many?"

Gabe shook his head; he hadn't bothered to count. His head hurt just from being in their proximity. He could feel the ache now, throbbing, blurring his vision, making him dizzy. He wondered if his eyes were crossing. It sure felt like they were.

"Gabe, how many are there?" Tío Jorge asked again, but this time Gabe didn't even hear it. The Earth was starting to spin, the ground moving roughly, and Gabe lost his footing. He fell hard on his back, eyes rolling to the back of his head.

"Tío," he said, as images poured into his brain, flitting by so quickly he could hardly make sense of them. Some showed a dark, dry, dead land with an orange sun and grey soil. A horde of *Malum*, screeching and skittering, were kept at bay by a waterfall of bright light. The light held a pureness that kept away the hate and anger, the desire for blood and pain. Other images were of a grotesque woman with pale, black-veined skin. Her face was mutilated on one side, and on the other side she had a glowing, hate-filled red eye. She opened her mouth wide and cavernous, and out spewed evil, dark things that slivered and squirmed along the ground.

The images finally released him, and Gabe found himself looking up into Tío Jorge's concerned eyes.

"I'm okay."

Tío Jorge's brow furrowed. "I don't think you are."

"I am," Gabe replied, pushing himself to his elbows. "It's those damn glyphs. They give me the heebie-jeebies."

"He had a similar reaction when we came upon them earlier," Micos said. Gabe looked at her with betrayal in his eyes, but the woman just shrugged. "I couldn't take care of both him and the human, so I slit the human's throat while Gabe got his bearings."

Gabe supposed he should feel relief that the woman had not seen fit to slit his own throat while he was reeling from the effects of the glyphs. He had been taken utterly by surprise and left completely helpless. *Was this what Mel felt like?* he wondered.

Paul and Coudrou pulled him to his feet, and Gabe allowed it. But he insisted, "I'm not a liability."

"No one said you were, man," said Coudrou, smacking Gabe's shoulder. "You survived a *Lost Soul*."

Goddamn right I did, Gabe thought.

His uncle turned his attention to the glyphs. Stepping carefully between the smoldering shapes, he studied them critically. His face grew darker as he proceeded through the acreage. Finally, he turned to his clanspeople.

"This is a mystery," he said, sounding frustrated. "All the people who lived in this subdivision have disappeared."

"All but one," said Paul, pointing a thumb back the way they came. He continued even though Micos was looking at him with hooded eyes. "I mean he's dead now, but he was technically still alive."

"Even so," Gabe's uncle continued. "That's still hundreds of people unaccounted for. And it looks like they all just got up and left their homes without their belongings, their wallets, or their cars."

"Yeah, it's weird," Gabe agreed. "But what do the glyphs mean?"

Tío Jorge's eyes hardened above his face sleeve. "I have my suspicions, but I don't want to share them until I have more information."

Gabe didn't push, even though he really wanted to. Instead he sat on his haunches as Flores and Puma took pictures of the glyphs. Logan tried to offer Gabe some assistance, but he waved her off. The healer was well-intentioned, but Gabe had already decided that if the sudden urge to puke came upon him, he'd make sure to puke right on Micos.

"What's our next move?" asked Paul. He and Coudrou had taken a turn around the area in an attempt to discover other disturbances. "Should we pull the map out? Try to find where the Lost Soul has gone?"

Gabe fiddled with the hilt of his sword before stabbing it into the ground. "Maybe." His eyes flitted back toward the homes. "We know it ain't here. We would've felt it if it was. It's probably moved on, spreading its evil elsewhere."

Paul and Coudrou fell silent, their eyes dark. Swords still in their hands, they knelt down beside Gabe. Micos just stood quietly beside them, her arms crossed, her face expressionless.

"This place—it's so strange," said Coudrou. "I don't know *exactly* what happened here... but I *know* something awful happened."

"Yeah," Paul agreed. "They're dead. Or worse."

"I hope they're dead," said Gabe.

Micos nodded. "Death is mercy."

The three Kales looked at her and grudgingly agreed. For these people, death *was* mercy.

Gabe shook his head. He felt like a child, like they were all children, stumbling in the dark, trying to find their way through. How were they to know which direction to go when they couldn't see what was right in front of them? There was no light, no path.

They had to forge their own way. But how? How were they going to prevent more people from getting hurt? This supernatural being was several steps ahead of them. And it was fearless, dauntless, and had a thirst only for blood and chaos.

Gabe pulled his sword from the ground, sheathed it in frustration, and stood. He wasn't the type to brood. Never had been and wasn't about to start now. He was a goddamn Kale, for God's sake. He wasn't some whiny little shit.

A phone rang in the quiet morning air. Coudrou's. He pulled it from his pocket and answered it. His face furrowed as he listened without speaking. Then he passed the phone to Gabe.

"Yeah?" Gabe said.

"Where are you?" asked Mel.

Gabe moved a short distance away, not wanting the others to hear who he was talking to. With the exception of his uncle, Coudrou, and Paul, the others were still unaware that his sister was alive.

"We're in residential hell," he said. "Nice to hear from you though, so early in the morning."

Mel snorted. "That good, huh?"

"Worse."

"What do you mean? I thought you all were on the trail?"

Gabe updated her on the recent events. She stayed quiet while he talked, but hissed when he mentioned the empty houses and burning glyphs.

"I want to see those photos," she said. "And Tío Jorge—I wonder what he's thinking?"

"You and me both," Gabe replied. "I'm just… we're kinda at a dead end. The damn Lost Soul isn't here."

"Are you sure?"

"We searched every inch of this place. It's *not* here."

"Goddamnit," Mel said, then after a moment: "It could be miles away. *Fuck!*"

"Hey," said Gabe. "The spell worked once. We can do it again as soon as we're done here."

Mel blew out a frustrated breath. Gabe could hear her shifting on the other end. She spoke to someone for a few minutes, her tired, quiet voice explaining to someone what Gabe had explained to her. He waited patiently, walking further from the others. He stopped at a copse of trees and leaned up against one. He was there for only moments when he felt Micos standing near. The older woman had her sword out and was watching the surroundings with a discerning eye. Behind him his clanspeople had started a controlled fire. It burned quickly through the glyphs, giving Gabe relief. The grip on his throat loosened as each glyph was broken and reduced to ash.

Mel came back on the line. "Gabe, you still there?"

"I'm here."

"Those glyphs sound pretty fresh by your description. I don't know what Tío Jorge is thinking, but if I had to guess, that damn Lost Soul sensed the locating spell y'all performed and did something to disrupt it. I hate to say it, but the spell probably won't work again."

Gabe raised his eyebrows. "I may not have been a good student during *Hae* classes, but I'm pretty sure the amount of power to disrupt a spell like this would be felt."

"Not if it did something to suppress the effects. Like the way Isis carved suppression spells around the house. It would need something of substance to hold it all together. It's not as simple as carving a glyph on a surface."

"A totem, maybe?" said another voice on the other end of the line. It sounded like Quint.

"Suppress? Totems?" Gabe asked.

Micos looked over at him, her attention piqued by his words. Then she took off, charging toward the cookie-cutter homes.

Gabe ignored her. "Okay, let's say you're right. Maybe it used the people here as fodder for the spell." Blood magic was *disgusting*. "Where are the bodies? Where are the bones? There was evidence in Larson's home of the blood magic. Here there isn't anything. And why so many people? It wouldn't need so many people to break the location spell."

"It would in order to to break the location spell *and* the boundary spell," Mel said decisively. "I don't think it was the same kind of blood magic you encountered at Larson's." Her voice grew more contemplative. "I'd need to see the glyphs and do some research… but I'm thinking each glyph marked a person."

Gabe felt a coldness in his chest. It wasn't fear—it was disappointment and anger. He looked toward the field that Tío Jorge was now blessing with oils while chanting in *Old Tongue,* and gritted his teeth. One glyph per person. *One* glyph *per* person. There had to have been hundreds of them—all different sizes. Some as small as…

Gabe seethed.

"Mel…" he said quietly.

"I know, Gabe," Mel said sadly. "I know."

"I'm going to *kill* this fucking thing."

"I hope you do. We just gotta figure out how to do it without killing York." Again he heard her moving, maybe shuffling papers. "We'll figure out a way to draw it out. It'll have a weakness. These things always do. In the meantime, search for its suppression spells and destroy them before leaving the suburb. For all you know it could still be there watching you guys, so be careful. Call me if anything comes up. Oh! Isis says to take the potion she left with Coudrou if you're feeling off. It should help with any side effects of the healing spell performed on you."

"Yeah," Gabe said, a little heated. "Tell Isis I've got words for her. I want to know exactly what she did to me. I've been—"

"Can't be that bad," Mel interrupted. "You're walking around, aren't you?"

With that she hung up, leaving Gabe to stare at the phone. *Way to put things in perspective,* he thought. He imagined his sister was not liking being cooped up at the house while he and Victor were on these hunts. *Oh, well, nothing to be done for that.* All he could do was move forward and get the job done.

At Gabe's request, Coudrou gave him Isis's potion, and Gabe knocked it back in one gulp. It tasted like vinegar and piss, but it made him feel a lot more clear-headed and present.

"Gabe," Micos said, walking toward him. The sun was now coming up, the gloom gradually clearing to a murky blue and grey. "Come." She motioned back the way she'd come.

Gabe looked at his uncle, who was putting away the oils and looking over the field with muted disappointment. Gabe motioned for him to follow before striding alongside Micos toward the homes.

Tío Jorge caught up to them at the gate, and they filed in. Micos led them to a totem that was obscured by the trashcans. Carved on a thick stump was an ugly mark: a skull with a swirl spanning the entirety of its gaping mouth.

Tío Jorge quickly scratched away the image, ruining it.

"I've seen this mark before," Gabe said. "It was at Larson's house." It had been scrawled on the door that shut him away from his clanspeople. He had felt like its ugly eyes and mouth were laughing at him.

"It's mocking us," Tío Jorge said. "There is no purpose to have it here other than to rub in our faces."

It wants to play, Gabe thought, remembering the Lost Soul's broken grin. Well, Gabe wanted to play too. This time with his staff, or a sword. *A more even match.*

"I spoke to our *friend*," Gabe said. "She believes the demon used a suppression spell to hide all of this. The location spell is probably broken. The boundary spell might be, too."

Tío Jorge stabbed his sword into the ground and unfolded the map onto the grass. He perused it, then looked toward the sky and exhaled. Gabe thought the game was wearing on his uncle. *Maybe he's too old for this?* But as soon as he thought it, his uncle folded up the map and looked to the gathering Kales with determination.

"The boundary spell holds by a thread," he announced. "We have work to do. I want this whole area searched again. We obviously missed this"—he motioned to the mark of the Lost Soul—"and there must be something more holding the suppression spell. Look for totems, objects, anything and everything. Leave no stone unturned. I want every dark glyph, mark, or fucking scrawling scratch destroyed."

Then Tío Jorge pulled his sat phone out of his pocket and started dialing. Gabe figured he knew why.

They were going to need far more Kales.

Gabe just hoped they showed up quickly.

****

Gabe carefully pushed aside a rosebush, mindful of the thorns, then let the branches fall back after seeing no signs of molestation. "Nothing here," he said to Micos.

The woman was standing a few feet away watching the happenings on the road. She looked back at Gabe and shrugged, unconcerned. Gabe didn't blame her; they'd been at it for hours now with nothing to show for the effort. Others had had better luck, finding four totems surrounding the subdivision and its greenway. All four had broken the glyphs and sent them back to camp.

"What do you think they're going to do?" Micos asked, motioning to the SUVs parked along the drive.

Tío Jorge had not only called for more reinforcements, he'd also called Sheriff Sam Cosby. From where Gabe stood, he could see the older man's tan, weathered face and greying brown hair. He was talking to Tío Jorge, while several of his deputies loitered around.

"Let's go see," Gabe said. He and Micos walked across the street to join the two men huddled together around a map.

"—the boundary spell still holds, but the location spell is broken," Tío Jorge was saying. "We'd need to search any populated areas—it could be anywhere within the radius."

"How big is that there radius?" the sheriff asked, his voice a slow drawl, his steel-blue eyes on the map.

Tío Jorge indicated the area, and the sheriff whistled between his teeth.

"That there's a lot of ground to cover, Jorge. We ain't got that kind of manpower, what with some of my men dealing with that quarry business. You're welcome, by the way, for sending those Staties on a wild goose chase. Maybe next time get your boys and girls to find other options other than those there pots. They can be heard for miles."

Tío Jorge shook his head. "There weren't other options. As for the manpower, I have it—what I need is interference. This place, Larson's, and any other place that the Lost Soul comes across... any loss of life, I need your help keeping the humans away."

Sheriff Cosby chewed a wad of tobacco thoughtfully before turning and spitting in the grass. "Well, I'll do what I can, but you got a lot of missing folks here. It's gonna be hard to cover this up. As a matter of fact, I don't think it *can* be covered up. This here is a damn mess. A damn mess, I say."

"I know it, Sam. I'll appreciate anything you can do."

"Well, if you got any ideas on how to explain hundreds of people vanishing, you gotta let me know. And for God's sake, kill the damn thing before more people die."

Gabe shook his head. Nothing new to report, nothing new to

find. They were going in circles without new leads. He fiddled with the sword hidden under his coat, wishing he had an adversary to use it upon. Or better yet, he could use his staff.

"*Seniorem*," said a Kale to Tío Jorge. The Kale looked so bright-eyed and bushy-tailed that Gabe wanted to smack the freshness off his face. "We've searched the entire area. Nothing else has been observed."

Tío Jorge nodded. "Get everyone ready to leave. It's time we got out of here."

"That I agree with," said Sheriff Cosby. "The quicker y'all vacate the premises, the better."

The Kale left to make preparations, leaving Gabe and Micos rooted to their spots. Tío Jorge looked at them pointedly. "Don't you two have something to do?" he asked.

"Not really," said Gabe. "You, Micos?"

The older woman didn't answer, just looked intensely at the sheriff, who eyed her with the same level of interest.

"No," said Gabe. "No, we don't have anything."

Tío Jorge's eyebrows rose off his forehead. "What about that unfortunate soul that maimed himself? The one Micos killed out of *mercy*? I'm sure he needs to be prepared for removal. Grab a stretcher and load him into one of the trucks."

Gabe sighed and turned to do as bid. "Quit eye-fucking the sheriff, Micos. We've got work to do."

Micos waited until they were a reasonable distance away from the sheriff and Tío Jorge before saying, "He's a very good-looking man for his age."

"Oh, yes. He's just strapping," Gabe said lightly.

"He is," she agreed. "Very fit. Is he married?"

Gabe snorted. "Are you serious right now? I can't tell if you're serious."

"He's got a lovely accent. Nice deep voice. He sounds as a man should."

She *was* serious. And Gabe didn't know what to say to that, so he kept quiet.

They grabbed a stretcher and hauled it to the dead man, his throat now crusted over with blood, his pale skin grey and pasty. The mutilated face was a sobering reminder of the darkness that had inhabited him.

"Do you think he's at peace now?" Gabe asked.

Micos looked at Gabe, not at the man. "One can hope. If there had been a way to alleviate his pain, I would not have ended his life."

Something grabbed Gabe's attention. Something poking out of the man's sleeve. "Hold on. What's that on his arm?"

Micos pulled up the man's sleeve further, revealing a tattoo of a vulture on his forearm.

"He's Eighth Clan."

Gabe stood, stiff with anger. His mind on all those people that had lived in these boxlike homes—the men, the women, the *children.* It could not be a coincidence that there was an Eighth clansman here. It could not be. So many lives... gone senselessly. And this man...

Gabe couldn't help it. The fury took him. He now had someone he could cast blame on, someone on whom he could unleash the full weight of his wrath. He fell on his knees, drew his fist back, and punched and punched. Eyes blazing, he swore and cursed as blow after blow landed on the Eighth's dead face.

"That's enough," Micos said. She grabbed him and hauled him away. It wasn't easy to do. "Enough, Gabe."

"He fucking killed them, Micos!" Gabe roared. "He fucking led that demon to them. Then he slaughtered them like they were fucking animals."

"You don't know that," Micos said. "Not for sure."

"I do!" Gabe said. "I *know* he did. That fucking traitor. That fucking piece of shit. I wish I could kill him again for what he's done. I wish I could."

"Gabe. Stop," Micos said loudly. *"Stop."*

Gabe gritted his teeth, the anger making his heart pound like a piston as he looked up at the older woman.

"I know your anger," she said softly. "I feel it too. But you cannot spend it here. This man is dead and gone. You cannot hurt him. You only hurt yourself now."

"I want to stick my knife in him," Gabe snarled.

Micos looked like she was going to slap him. *"Él está muerto."* She rubbed her face tiredly. "Save your anger for the traitors that are *living.*"

She moved the stretcher beside the body, grabbed the Eighth's shoulders, and looked pointedly at Gabe. After a moment he got up and positioned himself at the Eighth's feet. Together they placed him on the stretcher. They carried the body to a pickup, set him in the bed, then slammed the tailgate shut.

Soon all the Kales had packed up and set off back to camp. Everyone but Gabe. The sheriff and his deputies cleared off too, leaving Gabe alone, standing in the perfect green grass of a pretty white house, on a street that should have been completely ordinary, completely safe.

Gabe knew no one was ever safe. And so he turned, trudging toward the field of burned, destroyed glyphs, where hundreds had died in the name of Darkness and Evil. He pulled the case from his shoulder, took out the two ends of his staff, and connected them. Then he removed his coat and pulled up the face sleeve before loping off into the wilderness.

Chapter Fourteen

Mel ventured to the kitchen to find something to eat. This was the perfect time to go, she figured, seeing as the house was almost empty. It seemed her nosy clansmen were all off seeking news about the events of the night before.

Sure enough, she had the huge, opulent kitchen all to herself. Granite countertops, stainless steel appliances, and a massive island in whites and grays.

Of course, she wasn't actually alone. She was never alone anymore, not now that Keven and Quint had become her shadows, the proverbial angel and devil on her shoulders.

"I can go get you food," Quint had said earlier, when Mel started upstairs. "I'll be back in a flash."

But Keven had taken Mel's side. "I think a stretching of legs is in order. A quick trip upstairs won't hurt."

"But the Peruvian Kales…" Quint had argued. "They're… you know…"

Mel smiled as she put on a glove to cover her glowing fingers. "I can't wait till you finish that sentence, Quint. I know it's going to be the epitome of communication. An economy of words."

"Oh, shut up," Quint said. "You know what I'm trying to say."

Mel looked at the healer. His pale yellow tunic was wrinkled, and his messy hair made Mel wonder if he was allergic to hairbrushes. But his skills as a healer were more than she could've hoped for, and she'd grown fond of his company the last few days. He was good people.

"Yes, I do," she replied. "And you don't have to mince words with me. I know they're not taking Blas's death well. And even though the little man was a beady little shit, I'm trying to give them space. But this is my *home*. If they don't wish to see me, then it isn't me who must go."

"I know that," Quint said quickly. "I'm not trying to tell you to sequester yourself in the Sun Room every second of every day. Truly, I'm not. I just—well, I sense something in them that makes me uneasy, and you're not at full health."

Mel studied him. "You think they'll turn on me."

"Anything is possible," Quint said with a frown. "It looked like you cursed them. I know you didn't," he added, when it looked like Mel was about to let loose a retort, "but from the outside looking in, it looked like you just... burned them both. So they're undoubtedly thinking things about you—"

"I can't control that."

"I know—and I'm not saying you can. But we don't know much about the spell that killed Blas Nunez or the other guy."

"DeLeon," Keven said.

"Yeah, that guy," said Quint. "It's just—it would be really convenient of us to just assume that there's something that's keeping us honest and preventing us from betraying the clan, but really? Can we just go on without investigating it? Should we just operate on assumption?"

Mel sighed and rubbed her face. She was exhausted. She'd had very little sleep the past few days, and she was so brain-dead that at times she felt like she was having an out-of-body experience. "Ahh, Quint. Why do you have to talk so much sense? Okay. We'll look into it."

"Yeah?" Quint said.

"Yeah. After breakfast."

"Breakfast that we're getting upstairs?" Keven asked hopefully.

"*Oh* yeah," said Mel.

Now, a few minutes later, Keven was peering into the huge fridge. "We got leftovers from last night," he said. "You want picadillo?"

"It'll probably help with your iron deficiency," said Quint.

Mel raised her eyebrows. "You know what will also help with my iron deficiency? Steak."

Quint snorted. "Steak?"

"And eggs." Mel pulled the items from the fridge.

"And *pancakes*," Keven added. He pulled out a few more things from the fridge and cupboards, including a large mixing bowl, then took everything to the island and set to work with flour, milk, and eggs.

"From scratch, Keven?" Mel said with surprise as she grabbed some potatoes from the pantry. "I knew there was a reason I kept you around."

He smiled, but didn't respond.

The two made breakfast, and Quint grabbed silverware and plates. They'd just forked the steaks and spooned the eggs and potatoes onto a platter when Victor and the Wileys stumbled in, covered from head to toe in some disgusting substance Mel didn't care to look at. They stopped in the entrance and stared at the food longingly.

"Y'all can join us, but not until you've cleaned up," Mel said, spooning herself a large portion of potatoes.

Victor and his group walked out of the kitchen with a humph.

Mel, Quint, and Keven had finished eating and were sipping coffee when the three came back, clean and reinvigorated. As they sat and ate healthy portions of everything, they filled Mel in on the night's events, laughing about it as if it were all a dream, as if they hadn't all come *this* close to death. Mel listened with a keen ear, asking a question here or there, and wishing she had been there.

"I found this," Drew Wiley said, placing his hand on a cloth-wrapped object by his plate. "Things got a little crazy before I could question the Eighth woman about it."

He uncovered it, and everyone pushed away from the object in revulsion. It was a large ring made of a peculiar black metal. It looked crudely put together, but it glowed slightly. Sections of it shimmered with gold.

"Whoa," said Drew. "It wasn't glowing that brightly before. When I found it, it was just a slight glint that I didn't even see until I got close."

The sight of the glyphs made Mel's chest rumble in anger. She hesitated for a moment before touching the ring. Instantly, scratched glyphs began to glow in scarlet.

"Do you think you should do that, Mel?" asked Justine. "We don't even know what it is."

"I have a feeling." Mel picked up the ring and studied it closely. She remembered the conversation between her and Cori about Daniels's mutiny. "I think this is used to cut off a descendant from their gift."

Victor slapped the ring out of Mel's hands. "Jesus Christ, Mel! Stop touching that thing—it's not fucking jewelry! Drew, get it out of here!"

Drew quickly covered it with the cloth, but Mel put a hand on his arm.

"It would have to be placed around my neck," she said to her brother. "And that's not something I plan on doing. So let's just relax before we do anything hasty?" She got up and washed her cup in the sink. "We probably should show it to the First Healer and Grandma.

Let them decide what they'd like to do with it."

"There's also the question of who it's for," said another voice.

Thomas stood just inside the kitchen, looking resplendent in Kale gold. He didn't look like he'd just spent all day and night out hunting Eighth Clan or battling *Malum*. He strode to the table, uncovered the ring, and looked at it for moments.

"I'll take this and keep it safe until *Sapienti* Mendez and the First Healer have a moment to inspect it." He looked at Victor, waiting for his nod. Victor assented, and Thomas picked up the dark object and tucked it away in a pocket.

"Now," he said. "We're about to question the Eighth woman. Mel, I thought you'd like to be there."

"I'd like to be there too," Victor said quickly.

Mel waved him off. "You've had a long night. Finish up and relax. Then get some sleep."

She could tell Drew and Victor were itching to question the woman, but Justine was looking at Mel with relief.

"Actually," Thomas said, looking at Victor, "there's been a call a few miles from the quarry. I sent a few clanspeople to look for any signs of Eighth—we needed to know how they traveled there, and how long they'd been there—and they reported that they've found something. I know you three have been up all night, but…"

Victor looked at the Wileys. Drew was already putting his plate away while Justine just sipped her coffee. Victor took that as agreement from both.

"We'll get back out there," he said, pushing away from the table. "Come on, let's see what they found."

"All I wanted was food and sleep," Justine said, throwing her napkin on the table. "I guess one out of two isn't bad."

As Mel watched them go, she felt envious of the mission—and of the freedom to leave the house. But at least she'd be here for the questioning of the Eighth. She and Thomas, followed by Quint and Keven, set off back down to the sub-level.

"So what's with this woman?" Mel asked. "Victor only gave me a few details—he was more focused on the *Malum* and the fighting."

"She was carving into the stone, intending to create a door into *Inter Spatium Abyssus*," Thomas said. "She was in the late stages of turning and was already communing with the *Malum*. We've given her three doses of the antidote, and she's well on her way to recovery."

"And the door?" Mel asked.

"Underneath tons of rubble."

"But how close were they?" Mel pressed. Something twitched beneath the skin of her face. "Would the door have opened for her?"

"I don't know."

"You don't know?"

Thomas didn't answer, leaving Mel to work through it on her own.

"Well," she said. "Let's go find out."

When they reached the cells, they found Thrash with *Sapienti* Mendez and the First Healer. An incessant thumping could be heard from one of the prisoners. *Jonah*, Mel thought.

"*Someone* is active early in the morning," she said.

"Hey, cuz," said Thrash. "He's been throwing himself at the door all night. For all the good it'll do."

"He'll ruin himself if he keeps at it," Mel replied.

"He already has," the First Healer responded archly.

Thomas unlocked the door to the Eighth woman's cell, and numerous clasps and locks retracted from the stone walls. Before pushing back the last lock, he veiled his face, and the others followed suit. Only then did he open the door.

Thomas and Thrash entered first, followed by the First Healer and Mel's grandmother. Mel looked back at Quint, who looked uncomfortable under his veil. He was probably uncomfortable with what was going to happen beyond this door.

"Quint, why don't you start on that research we talked about?" she suggested.

Quint immediately perked up. "That's a good idea. Keven, you wanna come?"

The young man looked longingly toward the door, but Mel gave him a look that he couldn't refuse. "Sure," he said, and he and the healer started back the way they had come.

"Lost Soul first, then the Kale spell," Mel said to their retreating backs.

Quint put up a hand in acknowledgment.

Mel entered the cell. At its center was a long table of cold steel. On one side sat Mel's grandmother; on the other was a mousy-looking woman with a red, freshly scrubbed face. Thomas and Thrash stood behind her like sentinels.

"Why must you cover your faces?" the Eighth asked. "Are you afraid? Do you fear me?" She moved her hands on the table, revealing the chains around her wrists, which were attached to the floor. "What's there to fear? It's not like I've ever killed any of *your* kind." She made an ugly noise in her throat. "The *Great* Seven."

Mel's grandmother gave the woman a steely look. "I'm told you were found carving a door into the quarry wall—festering and sick, turning into *Malum*."

The woman pressed her lips together, her eyes scanning the walls. Moments passed, but she did not speak.

"Who ordered you to carve the wall?" *Sapienti* Mendez asked.

The woman still didn't respond. She pulled her hands away from the table and turned her face away.

"Was it your Master?" *Sapienti* Mendez asked.

The woman shuddered, and curled into herself.

Sapienti Mendez sighed with frustration. "Why do you protect them? They left you to a fate worse than death. To turn, to bleed and twist into a foul, evil creature. They care not for you. At least Wershall was a *thrall*. He still held his own thoughts—his own body. *You* were chattel."

The woman shut her eyes tightly. A long moment of silence followed before her eyes fluttered open again. She shifted her gaze from the Elder of Clan Kale to the First Healer standing behind her.

Mel, growing impatient, stepped forward and sat on the edge of the table so she could look directly down at the mousy woman. She met her grandmother's eyes, and received a nod in response.

Mel waited until the Eighth looked up at her, then spoke.

"Every time I've come face to face with the Eighth it's always been… aggravating," she began. "Whether it's descendants from the Great Seven that have fallen, or those like yourself who were born into the Eighth, you all seem so… *selfish*." She folded her hands in her lap. "I ask myself: why? Why is it so important to sacrifice the world as we know it for power? To unleash evil upon the world for— *what?* Your gifts? Abilities none of you *truly* understand. Not *one* of you. Because let me tell you—if you knew, if you truly *knew* the cross it is to bear, you wouldn't want anything to do with it."

The woman didn't move, didn't blink, didn't look away from Mel's dark eyes. But Mel waited, and finally the Eighth blew out a frustrated breath and spoke.

"What makes you think this world is so good?" she said. "Maybe for all of you, sitting here in your splendid gold tunics, hiding under your fine gold veils, but for many, the world as we know it is a world that needs to change."

Mel was nodding along as the woman spoke, and perhaps something in the woman's tone got under her skin, because she removed her veil and wrapped it around her hand, giving her something to turn her agitated energy toward. "I see," she said. "So that means it needs to be *destroyed* to be remade anew? *Billions* will die if that's what your plan is."

"No," the woman said. "They don't have to die. They will have our protection."

"How?" Mel said. "How would you protect them? You can't even protect yourself."

"With our gifts which have been denied to us."

"Denied..." A soft noise escaped Mel's lips, and she shared a look with her grandmother and the First Healer. A look that spoke of exasperation and annoyance.

Mel sniffed, then cleared her throat. "Look. Your gifts have not been *denied* to you. They were sacrificed in exchange for banishing evil upon the earth. I happen to think that it was a good exchange, but then I've come face to face with *Malum* and Lost Souls and thralls, so I know the damage they can do. I would think after the night you had that you would feel the same way, but then again, you're Eighth. And my experience with the Eighth is that they're not the most reasonable of people."

The woman looked away in what might be shame. "Not all of us are like that."

"Show me then," Mel said.

She got up and gestured for Thomas to give her the dark ring. When he did, she pulled it from its cloth wrapping and placed it in front of the woman.

"Who was this for?" Mel asked.

The woman looked at the ring with wide eyes. It still glowed from Mel's touch, but the glyphs were already fading, leaving it to shimmer gold. "They didn't tell us," she said, then looked up at Mel. "But it was obviously for *you*."

"What do you mean?" Mel asked.

The woman's hands closed into fists and she pulled away from the ring. "We were told there was a Kale woman among you that held her gift. We were to capture her and take her back to the Circle."

Mel's anger simmered. *Capture? Take me?*

"And what were their plans after?" she asked. "Once they took me from my home and family." Mel bit off the words, leaning in so close to the woman's face that she could see the grey eyes dilate, could feel the cold sweat of fear. If she breathed deep enough, Mel was sure she would smell the stink of it on the woman's skin. *"What were their plans?"*

"I believe you've scared her to silence," *Sapienti* Mendez said, and Mel drew back, seeing the rigid fear in the Eighth woman.

"I don't think we will be getting more from her today," the First Healer said, picking up the ring with cloth-covered hands and inspecting it with sharp eyes. It glowed softly in her grasp. "Besides, I think we can guess at what they would've done."

Sapienti Mendez rose from her seat and left the room. Mel and the First Healer followed. They shut the door behind them, leaving Thomas and Thrash to keep an eye on the prisoner for now.

Mel turned to her grandmother. "How did they know I was still alive?"

Sapienti Mendez shook her head. "They don't. More than likely they didn't have a name or description of the woman. They were going off the dark object's behavior. This ring, like the one Cori described the other night, disconnects a descendant from their gift. Like you saw, it glows when in proximity, but only when that person touches it do the glyphs activate." She looked to the First Healer. "As plans go, this one has to be one of the worst of the Eighth. It's lazy, lacking in good intel and direction."

"I agree," said the First Healer. "It's flimsy. They sent a bunch of Eighth clansmen to find one Kale woman with the gift? What do they think we are? Livestock? Gonna rustle one of us that shies away from the herd, hoping she has the gift? Dumbest plan I've ever heard."

"This is the second ring we've found in their possession," *Sapienti* Mendez said, frowning in thought. "The first was in the group that you, Mel, handled the other night. The more I think about it, the more I'm certain that Cortez's exposure was to set us off balance in the hopes that we would be distracted enough for the Eighth to make their way to camp to abduct a woman who activated the ring."

"If they had infiltrated all the way to camp…" the First Healer said.

"They wouldn't have even gotten past our boundary without Browning's help," *Sapienti* Mendez said. "I know there are questions about what happened to Blas Nunez and DeLeon, but Browning's death makes it more of a certainty that there is some sort of spell that keeps Kales from betraying the clan."

Mel was nodding. "A *curse*, you mean. I was thinking the same— but I didn't see any harm in looking into it and finding more information. If only to appease some folks who are afraid that one bad word against the clan will curse them to a horrible death. But back to my original question: what would the Eighth have done when they found someone? If they found *me*?"

"More than likely, they wished to root out the seed," *Sapienti* Mendez said.

"They would've tried to root my gift out? Is that possible?"

"No," the First Healer responded. "But that wouldn't have stopped them from trying."

"It's *never* stopped them from trying," said *Sapienti* Mendez. "Mel, there's so much of the Eighth that you don't know, and I haven't had the chance to tell you—but the most heinous of Eighth Clan practices was the abduction and testing of descendants in an attempt to siphon their gift. They were never successful, and as far as I'm concerned will never *be* successful. The knowledge, strength, and practice that goes into a Kale's gift of siphoning is complex and dangerous, and the Eighth never got close. But the practice of torture and experimentation was a gateway that led toward the evils of *Malum* and Lost Souls."

Mel closed her eyes, trying to remember everything she'd seen in Wershall's memories. "I don't think Wershall had knowledge of this."

"No. His focus was to bleed the heir and break the Orb of Lasade. Which is the number one goal of the Eighth. Secondary is to steal the gift from those who still have it."

"The past is riddled with the dead bodies of descendants, and humans, that the Eighth perceived had power," the First Healer spat. "They are the epitome of evil."

Sapienti Mendez nodded. "I have no doubt that if Wershall had been successful in his plot, the next step would've been to kill him. The Eighth is above all secretive, and they would never share all their plans or secrets with someone born of the Great Seven, nor would they keep them alive. Especially someone like Wershall, who seemed to have gained a Lost Soul's favor. This *Mistress* that you came across in *Inter Spatium Abyssus* is powerful. The Eighth could not take the chance of her bestowing more dark gifts upon him."

"Remember," the First Healer added, "the Eighth are arrogant enough to believe evil can be used for their purposes—and like you just heard from our guest, some are foolish enough to believe it can be used for good."

Mel unfurled the veil wrapped around her hand. "I need to know more about them. Where they came from, how the clan was created." She placed her veil around her neck, fisting it with both hands. "Wershall's memories only give me a portion of the story. I need to understand it all."

Sapienti Mendez placed a hand on Mel's arm. "Mel, I'm in agreement that you need to understand your enemy, but I don't want this knowledge to make things more complicated."

Mel smiled grimly, understanding what her grandmother was hinting at. "I won't soften my stance toward them. I promise you that. I judge people by their actions, Grandma. Only their actions."

"That's exactly what I mean," *Sapienti* Mendez said. She gestured toward the closed door of the cell. "That woman is not innocent. She's committed crimes against humanity, crimes that cannot be forgiven. You will encounter more like her. The only reason she is here, alive, is because we needed someone of the Eighth to question. But when that is not needed... I don't want you to hesitate. I don't want you to think. I want you to *vanquish* them."

"In battle, I assure you, I *will* do that," Mel said firmly. "But what is to come of the prisoner? She cannot harm anyone locked behind that door, but she can't be let go."

"What do you want to become of her?" *Sapienti* Mendez asked doggedly, staring up at Mel with keen eyes. "What shall we do with the traitor?"

Mel pressed her lips together, knowing what her grandmother was attempting to do. It hadn't been that long ago that the older woman would often challenge Mel with moral questions such as these. Hard choices that had the power to change the landscape before them in ways no one could predict.

"There are only two choices," Mel replied. "We keep her alive... or we don't."

The First Healer shifted, the ring in her hands held away from her body as if it could burn her. "Our clan is not known for its leniency," she said.

Mel leaned against the wall, feeling the hard stone against her back. She didn't want to kill the woman. She knew that was what her grandmother wanted—and what her grandmother wanted *her* to want, too—but there was a foul taste in her mouth at the thought of it. It was so different from killing in battle. It presented a complexity that could not be simplified or rationalized. Not to Mel. And definitely not here, on the spot.

"She attempted to open a door into another world," Mel reasoned. "That cannot be excused."

"No," her grandmother agreed. "It cannot."

Mel looked at the First Healer. "And you? What does the healer have to say?"

The older woman's eyes softened with regret. "The Eighth's fate was sealed the moment she saw your face."

A sharp pain filled Mel. A tightness that made it difficult to breathe. *So. It's decided.*

And, in the end, it was Mel who had put the final nail in. There was no way her grandmother would let the woman go now, not after she'd seen Mel's face. Too much was on the line.

Mel nodded and opened the door to the cell. Thrash and Thomas were still standing in their places, and the woman was still in her seat, though she had placed her head on the table. As the three women entered, the prisoner lifted her head and looked up with tired eyes.

"What is your name, Eighth?" *Sapienti* Mendez asked.

The woman did not speak. Did not move except for the eyes that flicked from one Kale to the next.

"You should tell me your name," Mel's grandmother said again, her voice weary. "I can sentence you with or without it, but I'd much prefer to know your name."

The woman snorted, her eyes filling with angry tears. "Why? Going to record it in some book? Or are you going to say it so *stately* when you burn me at the stake?" Tears fell, the woman's lips shook, and her nostrils flared. "I've heard about the brutality and callousness of the Great Seven, and now I get to die and see it firsthand."

Mel glanced at the First Healer, but the woman looked away.

"Fine," *Sapienti* Mendez said. "I'll sentence you without it, then. In three days' time, your sentence will take place. All the clan will stand as witnesses."

With that, the *Sapienti* of Clan Kale turned and left the cell, the First Healer following her.

Mel spoke to Thomas. "Move her to a more comfortable cell. Take the chains off and give her something to eat."

"Should we stop the doses?" Thrash asked, eying the woman who now had her head in her hands and was shaking with sobs.

"And have my grandmother sentence a *Malum*?" Mel asked. "No. Continue the doses."

With one final look at the broken woman, Mel was gone.

Chapter Fifteen

While Mel was with the Eighth prisoner, Quint gathered just about every book in existence regarding Lost Souls in the library. Mel found him and his collection of books at a corner table next to a large window that provided plenty of natural light. Keven sat next to him looking bored out of his mind. He looked up at Mel hopefully when she arrived, but was disappointed when she sat down across from Quint and immediately tucked into one of the larger volumes.

"Find anything useful?" she asked as she skimmed the open page. It was a horrible account of an attempted summoning of a Lost Soul in France during the seventeenth century, including descriptions of the mutilated bodies, the botched investigation from the authorities, the uncouth and aggressive fallout between Clans Ferus and Janso as they quarreled over which clan's territory spanned France—*for the millionth time,* Mel thought—and the debacle of a trial for the accused, who was just some local merchant who had stumbled on the spell and decided to kill his enemies. All in all, it was a hot mess.

"No," Quint said. He motioned toward the book in front of Mel. "But that one is interesting."

"I think the word you're looking for is sickening," Mel replied with a grimace.

"No, seriously. It proves that although Kale drained the world of power, there were still small echoes left behind. The summoning was destined to fail—there was really no chance of pulling a Lost Soul into Earth—but there was evidence that a clear effect was left on the people and the place where it occurred for years after."

He pointed to the bottom of the page, where a passage described the madness that took over the area after the failed summoning. "Good, bad, it still leaves an imprint," he said. "The echo branched out like tendrils."

"Yeah, infecting people," said Mel. "So you're saying there will be negative effects from the summoning on Larson's property?"

Quint bit his lip and nodded.

"And this time it wasn't a failed summoning. This time a Lost Soul was *actually* summoned," Mel said. She turned the page, and her gaze fell on an awful picture of a darkness with eerie red eyes. A naked human was in its clutches, his eyes dulled. "That's got to make it worse, right?"

"Not necessarily." Quint held up another book. "This has an account of a successful summoning, and the only thing that happened after was a number of cases of *barrenness*. But that was after a thorough cleansing of the area."

Mel frowned. *Barrenness* was no small thing. The earth in a *barren* area would die, plants and trees would stop bearing fruit, the air would grow rank, and the living would only rarely be able to bear children—and those babies that managed to be carried to term would be born disfigured and grotesque.

"I know," Quint said, reading her look. "But *Sapienti* already had Larson's property cleansed. And if I had to choose between spots of *barrenness* and something unimaginably worse, well…"

Mel sighed in agreement. She looked at the book in Quint's hand. "So, how did they exorcise the Lost Soul?"

Quint moved next to Mel and placed the book on top of the

other. "Yeah, well that's the bad news. I haven't found anything in here about expelling the demon from the possessed. In this instance, the Lost Soul was lured into a trap and then drawn and quartered. Its split body was wrapped in a lace of *sanctus,* and each piece was buried where no eyes could see. I hate to say it, but it looks like killing a Lost Soul, at the expense of the possessed, was the normal course of action."

Mel had hoped there was a way to save York by banishing the Lost Soul from the Kale's body. She'd heard that his family was doing their best to keep strong and hopeful. They would come almost every hour for an update, crowding the front hall, awaiting their *Sapienti* with barely concealed urgency. Mel's grandmother had assured them that York would be brought home, but she was careful not to state in what manner the man would return, and the family had not pressed for clarification.

Mel rubbed her eyes tiredly. "There must be other accounts." She looked at the stack of books on the table.

"Oh, I'm sure there are," Quint said. "There are probably older accounts downstairs. But it'll take us a long time just to get through these."

Mel grabbed a scrap of paper and scribbled some names on it. "Keven, I want you to find these clanspeople and bring them here."

Keven looked at the paper. "Some of these are just Advance students."

Mel stood up and stretched her back. "They're not much for fighting, but they've all shown a keen interest in *Hae.*"

"All right," Keven said. "I'll find them. You won't go anywhere while I'm gone, right?"

Mel looked at his wide, sincere eyes and sighed inwardly; her plans of taking a short stroll outside evaporated into thin air. Thomas had been a goddamn genius when he recruited his nephew to be part of her guard. Mel couldn't break the kid's heart, nor give him something to worry about.

"I'll be downstairs by the time you get back," Mel said. "Quint, come find me when you get them all sorted. Oh, and bring Pilar and Memo with you."

She went back downstairs at a slow pace, frustrated at her self-imposed isolation. *Faking my own death?* she thought. *Could I be more dramatic?*

On the lower level, she paused in the atrium that featured the seven grand alcoves, each with carvings depicting one of the seven clans. The circular room was so tall that the light from the torches could not penetrate all the way to the ceiling. One of the alcoves glowed, incandescent, its carvings dancing with golden ribbons, and as Mel watched it, she was filled with angst. She'd opened the door when she came back from *Inter Spatium Abyssus,* but for the life of her, she couldn't figure out how to close the damn thing. And now anyone could step right through it, if they so chose.

The First Healer and Mel's grandmother had tried to convince Mel that the chance the Eighth would come through that door was slim. That everyone who had been a part of Wershall's plot was dead or in a cell. And though Mel knew this to be true, it was only the assurance of round-the-clock guards that kept her from panicking all the same.

They stood here now, like sentinels, armed with swords and large rectangular shields, ready for anything. Thomas had handpicked them himself. *Good, hard Kales,* he'd said. *None of that fancy Agora shit here.* Mel had smiled at that, and when Thomas had mentioned that they'd all done well at the trials, it had given her additional comfort.

And the guards here were just the beginning. Thomas planned to have the first legion established before the end of summer. Under the circumstances, it seemed only natural to begin implementing the traditional command structure.

"It's a wonder, isn't it?"

Mel looked at the guard who had spoken. Gerald Cade was tall and slender, with cobalt blue eyes. His dark hair was always meticulously combed.

"I didn't think I would see such a thing in my lifetime," he continued, gazing at the gate.

Mel noticed the subtle pin on the collar of his tunic. *Great, now he's ranked.* Mel had never been fond of Gerald Cade. He was notoriously contrary and opinionated, born to question and challenge Mel's every movement, every word, every thought.

She stayed stubbornly silent, focusing on the other guards, who were standing at attention like statues.

"You didn't either, did you?" Cade said, amusement coloring his voice. "No. Of course you didn't." He stepped up to the alcove, admiring it like one observes a painting at an art display. "You probably lacked the imagination."

The man sure was enjoying his one-way conversation.

"Well, we can't all have your sense of the fantastical," Mel said, one eyebrow rising as she turned to look into his face. "Must we have this conversation, Cade? Why are you so obsessed with the fact that I questioned our ways? Any rational person would've done so. What with the lack of proof."

Cade cocked his head, inspecting Mel like one might inspect an insect. "I never had an issue with your questioning—just your failure to accurately describe *why* you questioned. Were you being rebellious, pushing against the authority of your Elders and their traditions? Was it just to be ornery? Was it ethically driven? It seemed it was a bit of everything, just depending on your mood at any given time. If I didn't know any better, I would say that you just like the sound of your own voice."

"Hmm," Mel said, narrowing her eyes. "*That's* not condescending."

"Why is it condescending? I'm being honest."

"And you can't be condescending if you're being honest?" Mel asked.

"You don't want me to answer that question," Cade replied as if he were shooing away a fly. "You've already made up your mind."

"Yeah," Mel said lightly. "Yeah, I have. The fact is, you're projecting. If there's anyone who loves the sound of their own voice, it's you."

Cade looked down his nose at her. He was so goddamn tall. "You've always been such a sensitive person."

And you've always been an asshole, Mel thought. She rolled her eyes as she turned and headed down the long hallway. Unfortunately, Cade fell into step behind her, following with his straight posture, hands clasped behind his back.

"What do you want, Cade?" Mel asked as she found the door she wanted and pushed through it into the dimness beyond. As her eyes adjusted, she knelt beside one of the large chests along the wall and proceeded to pull out tome after tome.

Realizing she hadn't gotten a reply, she stopped and turned back to Cade. He looked befuddled as he stood in the doorway. "Well, are you just going to stand there all day?"

"How can you—?" He seemed to think twice before shaking his head. "Thomas alerted me that you're always to have a guard. That is why I'm here."

"Ah," Mel said, stamping down her annoyance. She *had* agreed to protection, so there was no reason to get upset. If only it were someone other than Cade.

She studied the older man, his serious face, the way his eyebrows always formed a 'V' on his forehead. She'd have to speak to Thomas about never including Cade in her honor guard.

"Okay," she said. "Well, this might take a while, Cade. You're free to do your duty how you see fit."

Mel carefully opened one of the books. They were older and in a delicate state, not like the hardy books in the library. Their pages were brittle, the writing faint, the covers weathered and worn. It made for slow going. But soon she was consumed in her work, concentrating hard to translate the *Old Tongue* to common English. She barely noticed when Cade went around the room lighting lamps, then summoned someone to bring a table with chairs, among other things.

After a time, Mel rose to her feet and set one of her books on the table. "This book records several accounts of summoning, but it doesn't make sense…"

She grabbed a sheet of paper and copied the text. Maybe if she wrote it out herself it would be more comprehensible? But it didn't help. She plopped down in a chair and leaned tiredly on the table. She needed to figure this out. There was so much at stake.

She suddenly remembered she was not alone in the room. Cade still stood at the door, eyeing Mel's work with interest.

"Well, come on then," Mel said. "Take a look."

She pushed away from the table, and Cade took her seat to review the book. Mel's grandmother had always preached the importance of fresh eyes, after all. Even Gerald Cade's.

Mel was relieved when Quint showed up a short while later with two other Kales. He took one look at Mel and Cade, and all the open books on the floor, and grinned.

"Excellent!" he proclaimed. He was totally in his element. "Looks like you've gotten a good start. Come on Pilar, Memo—let's join in."

But Memo was not nearly so enthused. "Dammit, Mel!" he cried, rubbing his short grey hair with both hands. "You can't just leave these books on the floor! They're valuable!"

He began gingerly picking up the books, and Pilar joined in.

"I agree," Pilar said, her dyed blond hair falling in haphazard curls around her heart-shaped face. "This is *not* how you treat clan treasures."

"Sorry," Mel said, and she meant it.

"We're happy you're alive, by the way," Memo said. "You gave us such a scare! Poor Pilar was crying and crying for *days!* And I couldn't focus on *The Life and Death of Florence Villa.* But these…" He caressed one of the books. "*These* make up for all the hardship."

"*Sí,*" Pilar agreed. "All is forgiven."

Quint gave Mel a look that seemed to say: *You chose them.*

And she had. Memo and Pilar were definitely not fighters. They were both in their fifties, and even when they were younger, they had never been chosen to represent the clan in the Agora. But they were intelligent, they had an abiding love for history and *Hae,* and they were both analytical and thorough. *That* was what Mel needed.

Pilar sat down in a chair and drummed her fingers on the table in anticipation. "*Bueno.* Let's hunt ourselves a Lost Soul."

****

Hours passed as the group pored over the texts. Pilar and Memo proved immensely useful, each interpreting several accounts in the time it took Mel, Quint, and Cade to struggle over only one. Eventually Mel asked the older Kales to take a look at the passage that had confused her. Pilar looked at what Mel had scribbled down, and immediately spotted the problem.

"Ah! See, this account wasn't done chronologically," Pilar said, numbering the paragraphs. "The scribe probably didn't have all the information at one time, so wrote as it was provided."

"That happens sometimes with the older texts," Memo said, looking over Pilar's shoulder. "In the early days, Clan Kale put more of their energy into defeating evil, not so much in documenting how it was done. Some of the accounts Pilar and I have been looking at have been a dry reporting of bare-minimum details, whereas others are dramatic, as if the scribe was writing a work of fiction. Neither is helpful. But our procedures were immature, and scribes were few and far between until Kale's consort revamped the whole thing."

Memo handed her a report that he'd been preparing on their translations, and she saw what he meant. There were plenty of dates and times, but details were sporadic and, in some places, downright cryptic. She scanned a few of the passages.

> *A Damned is begun in ~~night~~ shadow, born from blood of the ~~dull~~ human. Dark and cold will come from its ~~feel~~ touch. Beware. Death will come.*

> *It ~~has~~ clutches the soul of the captive until it ~~of~~ is ~~gone~~ spent. Worn to the quick. The Darkness spreading like sickness.*

> *Hatred is its purpose. A grudge once formed is eternal. It will seek its prey through worlds. One to die—one to live.*

There was one passage that made the hair on the back of Mel's neck stand up:

> *They gather and pray to die. ~~Fire~~ Burned to ash. To Summon the Evil. To bring upon the end of days.*

Quint was looking over Mel's shoulder. "This section that speaks about the grudge," he said. "Could we use that? To draw it in? Maybe we can use Gabe?"

Pilar was shaking her head before he'd finished. "Those grudges are sparked from more than just fighting the Lost Soul. They have more to do with what was done to it to bruise its pride and ego. As far as I know, that didn't happen when Gabe fought it. Besides, we would've heard if it had zeroed in on Gabe already, as he's been outside our borders for hours without issue."

Memo shook his head. "We're going to have to use the power of deduction," he said. "There's really nothing else for it."

Mel turned over all the information they'd learned in her head. "Well, this last passage sounds very much like what Gabe mentioned this morning. People were burned. Glyphs were left in their place. Is there anywhere else where this is mentioned?"

Pilar shuffled some documents. "Yes," she said, handing a page to Mel. "There are several accounts that mention *gathering* and *burning*, as well as *Summon the Evil*."

"So people attract the Lost Soul," Quint said. He leaned on the table as he attempted to follow the paper trail Pilar was laying out. "It could be anywhere then."

"No," Mel said. "It would be within the boundary set by Tío Jorge."

"There aren't very many populated areas within that area," Cade said. "We need a map to help us find the most likely places it might go next."

"I'll get it," Quint said.

But as he turned to go, he ran into Thomas, who was blocking the doorway. His eyes were dark and his jaw tense. Something was very wrong.

****

"What do you mean Gabe is *missing*?" Mel demanded, two seconds from losing her temper entirely.

She was in the atrium with Thomas, Tío Jorge, *Sapienti* Mendez, and the First Healer. Cade and Quint had come along as well, but Memo and Pilar had stayed behind to continue work on the ancient texts.

"He was not among the Kales that returned," Tío Jorge said. He looked angry, upset, and disappointed—though whether at Gabe or himself, Mel couldn't tell. "We've attempted to call him on the sat phone, but he's not picking up."

"Of course he's not picking up!" Mel snapped. "He's Gabe! He's gone off half-cocked to hunt down a goddamn demon that nearly *killed* him!" She shook her head in disgust. "I'm going after him."

"You *cannot*," *Sapienti* Mendez said. "You *know* you can't."

"I have to!" Mel replied, pacing the floor. "He's my *brother*. I'm not going to stay here while he goes strutting off into danger... the *idiot!*"

"You know you can't, Mel," *Sapienti* Mendez repeated. "There's already talk of strange surges of power along the grounds."

Mel stopped pacing and looked at her grandmother.

"Yes," her grandmother said. "Some have detected you using your gifts. If you leave these grounds and use your powers, they will follow, and they will *never* stop until they find out what or who is the cause."

"Well then, station guards!" Mel yelled. "We've got enough clanspeople now! Keep everyone on the campgrounds!"

"We can do that," the First Healer replied. She stood to Mel's left, watching Mel keenly through narrowed eyes. "But what of the Kale beast? It comes and goes, making you strong or weak at its whim. You cannot leave without resolving this."

Mel was just about to respond in a rude fashion, but just then Thrash and Tío Luce walked in. Mel could tell her uncle was in a mood; the tension was etched in the lines on his face.

"We'll bring him back," Tío Luce said, red-eyed and harried. He inclined his head toward Tío Jorge, who nodded in confirmation, then continued. "I'm taking Thrash with me. We'll alert Victor as well. We're leaving immediately."

"Take whomever you like," *Sapienti* Mendez said, then looked sternly at Mel. "*You* will *stay*."

Mel acquiesced with a heavy sigh. "Fine," she huffed.

Chapter Sixteen

Victor closed his weary eyes and took a deep breath. He was exhausted. He didn't even know how many days he'd been awake for now, and it wasn't like he'd been getting good sleep beforehand either.

God, what I wouldn't give to be home with Liz and the kids.

But no, he was on a mission to find signs of the Eighth.

He and the Wileys had rendezvoused with the Rangers who'd reported to Thomas, and the Rangers showed the new arrivals what they'd found. It was decidedly strange.

They stood in the trees and looked out at the tall grass. A man stood there, still, looking like he was listening for something. Then he ran his hands through the grass and strode some distance away.

"He's done that several times," said the Ranger who'd been keeping watch. She was veiled, but the hair poking out from her veil was blond, and her eyes were blue. "He's been walking around in circles."

Victor shared a look with the Wileys. "Seen anyone else?"

"No," said the Ranger, keeping her eyes on the man. "But that doesn't mean he's alone."

"You think he's Eighth?" Justine asked Victor.

"Let's find out."

Victor set his axe on his back and whistled once. Thirty-some-odd Kales appeared from their hiding places and started forward.

They stepped quietly, using the cover of the trees. They followed for half an hour, always staying in shadow. At times the man stopped, his back to them, hands spread to his sides, palms down, and the Kales would stop as well. Then the man would resume, and so would they.

It went on for miles and miles. Victor wondered where they were heading. He knew of nothing in this direction, not a structure nor campground.

He signaled to Drew and Justine to scout forward. The Wileys unsheathed their long knives and swept quickly away from the group, disappearing in the brush, their gold tunics blending with the dried foliage.

Another few slow miles passed before he heard their call. Victor made the signal to halt, and he let the man move on ahead, just out of their view, before giving the signal to move again.

They met up with the Wileys, who had chosen a well-covered area to hide in. Justine passed Victor a scope and pointed. A few miles away stood a large cabin that clung to darkness even in the light of day. The windows were filmed with dirt and debris, the walls weathered and beaten. A large group of men and women was gathered around it, many of them lying down and holding themselves as if cold.

A scream sounded from inside the cabin—and was quickly smothered to silence.

Victor passed the scope back. "Well?"

"I want to get in that fucking cabin," Justine said, glaring. "Just give me the okay. I'm ready."

"There may be innocents," said Drew to his sister. "If we barge in there, they could be harmed."

"Look," Justine said, frustration in her voice. "These fine Rangers followed a path from the quarry that led to this cabin. Those people are fucking Eighth. They've unleashed fucking mayhem all over our territory. If I have to sacrifice a few innocents to cleanse them of this place, so be it."

"I'm not arguing with you, just pointing out that innocent lives may be lost," Drew replied. "We should move carefully. Wait until nightfall."

Victor didn't want to wait until nightfall, but it seemed the smart choice. He turned to the Ranger that was waiting attentively behind him. "What's your name again?"

"Wendel," she said.

"You're York's sister," said Justine, making Victor do a double-take.

Wendel York nodded, her blue eyes looking warily at Victor. "You're not going to send me back, are you?"

Victor didn't know anything about the woman. He looked at Drew and Justine in question.

Justine picked up on his hesitation. "You're more of a scholar than a fighter, Wendel. You sure you want to do this? How'd you even get this Ranger assignment?"

"I think it's best to stay busy in times like these," Wendel replied. "I think you can understand that, Victor."

Victor tilted his head as he deliberated. "That doesn't answer the question. How *did* you get the Ranger assignment?"

The woman looked abashed, shifting from one foot to the other. "I'd rather not say."

Justine snorted. "Sounds like subterfuge, Victor. She might fit in after all."

"But can she fight?" asked Drew.

"I can fight," Wendel York said firmly. She had one of those quiet, assertive voices that seemed to carry the weight of the world.

"Okay," Victor said. "You're with us. Tell the others to surround the area and observe. *Only observe.* I don't want anyone doing fucking *anything* that will get us exposed. Give that cabin a wide perimeter and stay out of sight."

****

Hours passed before nightfall, and idle time made for idle thoughts. Victor couldn't help but think of things he ought not to. Especially not now, when he had to be on his guard. But he couldn't help it. His wife, his kids. How was he going to bring them close? How was he going to fix things when he couldn't even pick up a phone to call? *Jesus, what's wrong with me?*

At one point he actually did pull out his phone and dial the number he knew by heart, but when one of the men from camp looked over at him, Victor quickly put the phone back in his pocket.

It was late afternoon when shots rang out, echoing through the woods. Victor immediately sprinted toward the noise—not just the shots, but now shouts as well.

When Wendel York appeared in front of him, Victor slid to a stop.

"Some of us have been spotted!" she said. "They saw our tunics and started shooting. This way!"

"Was anyone hurt?" Victor asked as he raced after his clanswoman.

"I don't know."

As they ran, the shouts grew louder—and panicked. Victor didn't know what he would see when he arrived, but he would never have imagined what he actually came upon when he reached the site.

Several of his clanspeople were on their knees with their hands in the air—and one was flat on his back, clutching his side, stemming the blood that leaked out—while a group of men stood over them with guns trained on them.

Before stepping into view, Victor handed Wendel his axe and whispered, "Find Drew. He knows what to do. Go!"

Victor waited until she was out of sight, then took off his veil and stepped out into the open.

"What's going on here?" he yelled.

The guns were immediately turned on him.

Victor tried a conciliatory approach, sputtering out the excuses they had been told to spit out since they were children. "What the hell? What's all this for?" *Distract, distract, distract.* "We were just hiking and saw you guys at the cabin and wanted to see what was going on." *Lie, lie, lie.* "That's not cause to shoot anyone. We didn't do anything—"

"Shut the fuck up! Hands up! Hands up!" one of the men yelled.

"Okay, okay," Victor said.

He was just about to kneel, but the man hurried toward him. "I said put your fucking hands up! *Now!*" The man rested the barrel of his gun on Victor's forehead. "Just give me a reason, Kale, and I'll fucking pull this trigger."

Now, what you gotta do that for? Victor thought.

His hands fisting at his sides, Victor eyed the man coldly, wanting to put one of those fists through the man's face. He had a ruddy complexion, with a shaved head and eyes so dark they were almost black. And like all the men with guns, he looked angry—angrier than Victor could understand given the circumstance.

It's not like we snuck into your home and killed your people.

"Victor, just do as he says," said Justine. Victor looked over and saw her on her knees with the others. "We don't want anyone else getting hurt. Stokes is hurt pretty bad."

"Yeah, *Victor,*" said the man. "Do as I fucking say, and get on the fucking ground. Put your fucking hands in the air before I put a bullet in your head."

"What are you waiting for, Carl?" asked another man. "Let's just shoot them now. Get rid of them."

"No!" said Carl, manic and sweaty. "We can bring them to the Master. He might forgive us for failing."

"Will he forgive us these?" The other shook his hands, motioning to the gun. "Will he forgive us our abandonment? Our loss of faith when we refused the gift? We took an oath and broke it. Chose to keep our bodies and minds. Nothing is gonna save us, Carl. You know what they do to those who fail. We should just leave."

"And go where? There's nowhere to run!" Carl yelled. His wide, frantic eyes met Victor's. "We can take them to *him*."

The other man groaned and shook his head.

Carl ignored him. "How would you like that, Kale? You can be a plaything for a *demon*." He pressed the barrel forward, pushing Victor's head down. "I won't say it again. Get on your fucking knees."

Victor was seeing so much fucking red, he couldn't think straight. He could feel heat surging up from somewhere deep within him. Red hot, and wanting, yearning, spiraling outward...

"Victor!"

Justine's voice cut through the fog in his head, and he grudgingly fell to his knees, hands up over his head.

"That's right, *boy*. You do what I say."

Victor smiled at him grimly. "Maybe one day soon, you do what *I* say."

The butt of the gun met his temple. *Hard.*

That was the wrong thing to do, Victor thought groggily.

He shut his eyes against the pain that exploded in his head, the sun bright behind his eyelids.

That was when he felt something roll up against his leg. He cracked open one eye and saw a pot. A little mustard-yellow one.

Oh! I know what these ones do!

He looked up at Carl with amusement, gave a quick hand signal to his clanspeople, then made a huge show of holding his breath and closing his eyes.

The pot went off. Yellow smoke burst forth, thick and oppressive, quickly smothering the entire area. The Eighth began hacking and screaming, and the Kales seized the opportunity.

Victor rose up, batted Carl's gun away, and headbutted him right in the face. Blood and saliva spurted forth as Carl's head snapped backward. And then Drew was there, grabbing Carl's head from behind and sliding his knife across the man's neck. Carl fell to the ground, dead.

Victor turned to see that his clanspeople had taken similarly violent action, clearing out the debilitated Eighth.

"Head back to the cabin," Victor said as the smoke abated. "We take out the rest—no fucking around anymore."

"There's only a handful of them besides these," said Drew. "They're boarded up inside."

"Good," Victor replied, feeling hollow and tired. "Burn it down."

Several Kales took off to do the deed. Victor found a place in the shade, took out a cloth, and cleaned the blood from his face.

Drew followed, sheathing his knife. "The trail ends here. This was good work, Victor. We found those responsible for the quarry. We've put them to justice. The Maymes will be pleased."

"There's still the ones who escaped Larson's," Victor said, pulling his canteen out and taking a swig before handing it to Drew.

Drew took the canteen and drank. "How do you know there were survivors?"

Victor sat back, leaning on the wide tree behind him. He wished he were in bed. "They mentioned the Lost Soul."

Drew sucked in a breath. "They wouldn't have mentioned it if there hadn't been survivors to tell the story."

"Exactly."

The smell of burning wood met Victor's nostrils. He pushed to his feet to watch the cabin go up in flames. He felt no pity or remorse.

"Victor!" Justine shouted.

She was leading two other Kales, who were dragging a man between them. The man they'd followed through the woods. The Kales stopped before Victor and dropped the man roughly on the ground.

"Should we kill him?" Justine said.

"Please don't!" the man cried, red-faced and afraid. "I've done nothing wrong!"

"You are Eighth," Justine said. "Don't lie to us."

"I'm not! I don't know what that is!" he pleaded. "I was—I was just taking a walk."

"Funny," said Victor, sharing a look with Justine. "So were we."

"Just taking a stroll…" Drew said.

"Heard the commotion…" Justine continued.

"And wanted to check it out," Drew finished, looking at Victor. "I think I've heard this before."

Victor nodded at Justine, then looked at the man. "My patience is done for the day, and I don't like loose ends."

Justine unsheathed her knife.

"Please no! No!" the man begged.

But when Justine grabbed his hair and placed the blade at his neck, his entire demeanor changed. His face and eyes shifted, and his mouth twisted. "The Nephilim will burn in the black fire of Hell," he intoned darkly. "God commands it."

He put a fist over his heart and smiled even as the blood spilled from his neck.

"Run!" Wendel screamed suddenly. Victor didn't even know where she'd come from. "Take cover!"

Victor didn't bother to ask why. He ran, then dove for cover, with Justine and Drew right on top of him.

The explosion was deafening, leaving a ringing in Victor's ears. When he stood again on shaky legs, there was a small crater in the Earth where the man had been, and around it was a spatter of blood and bone and sinew that formed a star on the dirt.

"Is everyone okay?" Wendel asked, going around to help Kales onto their feet, checking them over. "Come on, we gotta get moving."

"What *was* that?" Victor asked.

Wendel York looked at him with wide eyes. "I'm not sure—I've only read stories." She bit her lip. "There are people—humans—outside of the Eighth that know we exist. And they believe we are an abomination and need to be exterminated."

What the fuck?

"Are you telling me there's some Knights of the Templar shit we have to deal with?"

"The Knights Templar were actually allies and very amenable to our existence. They worked with us by helping identify dark objects in which we—"

"York!"

Wendel put her hands out in a placating manner. "Yes. I think there are zealots out there that we're going to have to deal with. If memory serves, there was a couple loitering around the house the other day, said they were God-fearing folk. I'm guessing they were probably with this guy, sniffing around, getting intel. The zealot might've thought the Eighth were us, and followed them, intending to attack them away from the camp."

"Fuck!" Victor yelled. He remembered the harmless-looking man and woman who had knocked on their door. *I just let them off without a care.* "Fuck! Fuck! Fuck!"

He turned to look for his axe. Where the fuck was his axe? He needed his axe.

But then his sat phone rang, and the zealot, the Eighth, and everything that had occurred in the woods didn't matter.

Gabe was missing.

Chapter Seventeen

The waiting was the worst.

Mel couldn't focus. Not on the research. Not on anything. Every bit of room in her head was dedicated to updates on Gabe.

She paced the floors with a nervous energy that affected everyone around her. Even the unflappable Thomas seemed to feel its effects. He urged Mel to work out some energy by training with another Kale—a Kale who earned a broken arm and a busted nose for his trouble. After that, Thomas merely shadowed Mel as she prowled the halls.

The sun was already low in the sky. The day had nearly passed, and still they had no word on Gabe. Keven took over as guard, relieving Thomas, and suggested an early dinner, but Mel had no appetite. She took small sips of the drink he provided her, but otherwise she sat listless at the kitchen table, looking blankly at the wall, thinking about the infinite possibilities...

Quint shuffled in and stuffed some food in his mouth, then gave Mel a side-eyed glance as he piled more food on a tray—"for the researchers"—and headed right back out.

Mel shot up from her chair and resumed her stalking of the halls. She passed the front door once, twice. The third time she paused in front of it, as if she could will Gabe—or anyone with news—to walk through.

No one did.

"Please," Keven said behind her. He sounded scared. "Mel... please don't. Can we just sit down? Just for a second."

As she turned to glare at him, she felt a buzzing in her head, growing steadily. Her thoughts became disjointed, and her vision blackened, as if she were looking through a darkened lens. Her heart thumped heavily. *Just like those times I—*

Then the pain hit her. Hot and sharp, cutting through her chest. She fell to her knees, hands outstretched.

No, no, no, no, no!

"Quint!" Keven screamed in alarm. He held his hands inches from Mel, not sure if he should touch her. "I'm here, Mel. Tell me what to do."

But Mel couldn't speak. It took all her energy just to keep from screaming.

Keven watched her, wide-eyed and unsure. "I'm getting help," he said finally.

Mel heard his feet slapping the floor as he ran through the house.

Don't black out... don't black out... she thought as she lay frozen on the floor. She drew breath painfully through her teeth, her heart pumping suffering through her veins, white-hot fire that shot through muscle and bone. For long moments, it was all she could do to stay conscious.

Then, slowly, she pushed herself back to her feet, leaning heavily on the wall for support. Her mouth grew wet, saliva thick on her tongue, jaw aching. She tasted blood, sharp and tangy. It dripped over her lips. *I'm changing,* she thought, feeling the sickness bone-deep. The Kale beast was shifting under her skin. Slithering like a serpent.

Mel pushed herself away from the wall and staggered toward the library. *Sun Room*, she thought. *I need to get...I need to...I need... I need...outside! I need to get outside!* She passed the doorway that led to the library and instead stumbled toward the rear door, leaning on the walls and stumbling through furniture. She turned the knob and staggered out of the safety of the house.

She didn't know where she was going. Only that the sun's warmth felt good on her face and skin, and the further she went into the woods, the *freer* she felt.

No, a part of her thought. *Stop.* She'd made a promise. One she meant to keep. She'd given her word she'd stay within the protection of the house. *Control,* she thought as she took another staggering step. *Control yourself. It's the Kale beast that wants to be free.*

She took another step. The pain maintained its hold on her, molding her, shaping her, manipulating her like a puppet on strings. But Mel was not a puppet. She reached deep, deep within herself.

I will have control. I will.

The stone that was always in her possession grew warm in her pocket. Calling her. Neither beast nor woman could fail to answer. Mel pulled it out of her pocket...

... and fell into *Inter Spatium Callum.*

****

Night, just as it was back on Earth. The twilight brushing the sky in purple and blue. Mel found herself atop the large stone pyramid. The braziers smoldered, and black smoke plumed above in thick sheets.

She quickly turned, fearing Consilio Janso would be there, watching her from some hidden corner. Mel stretched her sight to its limits, attempting to decipher every shape in the darkness, but she was alone.

She frowned. Why here? What was so special about this place that the stone sought to bring her back?

That white noise started up again, buzzing in her ears. Mel looked into the dark passageway atop the pyramid, but her eyes could not penetrate the blackness. She stepped closer, and the buzzing increased as the wind whipped at her hair.

"I see you've found your way back, Melanie Mendez."

Mel gasped, her heart nearly leaping out of her chest. She knew that voice. Had heard it several times in her dreams.

Mel turned to find that Lasade Kale looked just as she remembered. Feral and untamed. Tanned skin with dark wavy hair and shimmering gold eyes. Each eyelid had a black line that stretched to her temple.

"I've come before, and you were nowhere to be found," Mel said, her frustration bubbling up. "I have so many questions."

A small part of Mel's brain realized she and Kale were speaking in Old Tongue. It was an odd thing, but something to deliberate upon at another time.

"I can't come every time you call, Melanie Mendez."

Mel gritted her teeth. "So you pass this curse to me, and I'm just supposed to figure it out by myself?"

"Curse?" the golden-eyed woman asked. "You think I've given you a curse?"

"What else would it be?" Mel replied, feeling years of frustration and indignation crawl to the surface.

She remembered the fear she'd felt the first time she'd lost control and nearly killed a boy her age. The time she quit the clan for good. And then, just when things were looking up, just when she'd felt her life was in order... that awful scene in the woods, pulling her back to the clan.

"I've got a goddamn ticking bomb inside me," she snapped. "Do you know what it's like walking through life feeling like you're going to unleash pain and destruction at a moment's notice if someone so much as says the wrong thing to you on the wrong day?"

"Yes," the woman said simply. She crossed her arms, and Mel noticed for the first time her thick nails. Sharp, sable edges glittering in the night. She wondered what those glinting weapons had been used for.

"How do I control it?" Mel asked. "How do I keep the Kale beast from taking over whenever it wants?"

Kale smirked, those glowing eyes shifting. "Why would you want to control it?"

"Why would I—?" Mel felt like her head was going to explode. "Why would I want to control the Kale beast? Well, let's see. There's the fact that I'd like to live my life in a way that will cause the least harm to others. The fact that I would like to breathe and feel my chest loosen in relief."

"You speak as if you've got an insatiable yearning for the blood of others. I have seen many like this before. They love the feeling of holding life in their hands, and find excitement in watching it slip away. They find happiness in being the cause of death. Do you find happiness like this?"

"No," Mel said, offended. "That's not what I mean."

"You claim you are destructive," Kale responded, frowning. "What is more destructive than killing for the sake of killing?"

Mel eyed Kale shrewdly, pausing to think on the woman's words. "You're trying to make a point... that I'm not a monster."

"No, you are a monster," Kale replied harshly. "Just as I am." She stepped past Mel and stood by the dark doorway that led into the pyramid. "We are two-sided, you and I. Although even our civilized side is not that civilized." She grinned that feral grin of hers. "Which means there is much overlap between the person and the monster. But the monsters—yours and mine—serve a purpose. And more importantly, they serve us. Because they are us."

"That's what I've been told," Mel said. "But I can't hold it in."

"Nothing can hold it in, Melanie Mendez," Kale responded. "Nothing can stop it. Only you."

"I've tried," Mel insisted. "But I keep falling short. It comes and goes when it wants. It takes all my strength just to keep a lid on it. And I fear *it'll take me in the most inopportune moment, and then I'll be compromised. Or worse, I'll fail someone I love."*

Kale paused. "This is very worrisome. I see why you want answers... but the answers are too complicated for your human brain."

Mel didn't know whether to be offended by that or not.

Kale continued. "I will give you a point from which to start. To cease your worry, you must accept who you are. Fully. Reconcile the past with the present. Then the answers will come more easily. To do this, you must travel to Luna del Sol."

Mel grew frustrated. Of all the places...

"Your time here grows short," Kale said. "I have heard you were accosted by Consilio Janso." Her gaze moved to Mel's hand. "May I?"

Mel raised the hand that had touched Janso's power. Its white tendrils glowed brightly in this world.

"Ah, yes," Kale said with an air of approval. "He will not like this. I will need to settle things with him. For good."

"What does that mean?" Mel asked. Was Kale going to fight Consilio Janso to the death? Again? Could they do that? And more importantly...

"How do I fix my hand?"

"Oh, Melanie Mendez," Kale said with that smile of hers. "This is not a time for fixing. This is a time for gloating. *"*

****

When Mel awoke, the sun had set. She was pleased to find that the pain had abated, that the piston in her chest had slowed and calmed. Some heat still flowed, but it was a slow stream and not the raging river from before. Her breath, too, came easier now.

She was lying next to a tree, and for a time she didn't bother to move, just allowed the last of the energy that had consumed her to leak away. She watched as tendrils of light slipped from her body and into the grass, where they disappeared into the soil. She ran her tongue across her teeth and was relieved when they felt as they always did: blunt but with a grungy feel. There had been one sick moment where she'd feared they'd grown, elongated into the terrible fangs that had torn into Wershall's throat.

She moved to sit up against the tree, but before she could do so much as take a breath, she slipped right back down onto the forest floor. It seemed that although the pain had receded, her strength was slow to recover. So once again she lay still, in the middle of nowhere, watching the cloudless sky. The stars and moon were bright, bathing everything in a soft glow.

I guess I'll just wait here until I can get back on my feet, Mel thought. She closed her eyes, letting the exhaustion have its way. Sleep beckoned—a slow, soft, comfortable call. *I'll just rest a while. Then I'll go back to the house.*

Mel was just about to slip into unconsciousness when she heard it. The footsteps of someone attempting to stay quiet—and failing.

Four figures loomed out of the darkness. She knew before she saw them that they were not friends; they'd come from the wrong direction, wearing dark clothing, their faces cold and hard, like the faces of all the Eighth she had come across. One of them held a ring that glowed in muted gold. It brightened as they drew closer, and when they were on top of her, the ring glowing with a blinding glare.

Cold fear spread through Mel. She opened her mouth to yell, to call for help, but no sound came forth.

One of the Eighth knelt down, holding the ring in shaky hands. He didn't say a word as he put the crude thing around Mel's neck. Mel clenched her teeth as the ring tightened like a noose, biting into her skin.

The severing was immediate. It cut her connection to her beast. To *herself.*

Then they gagged her and bound her feet.

And Mel felt utterly, utterly alone.

****

The Eighth pulled Mel through the wood, handling her roughly. She was dragged along the ground, roots grabbing at her tunic and breeches, her head lolling from side to side, the ring tight around her neck.

Still, she managed to get a look at her captors. There were four of them, all short, with slight statures. The two at her feet were a woman with unkempt dark hair, fair skin, and a heart-shaped birthmark on her cheek, and a man with short brown hair and a perpetual frown. The two at her head were both men, dark-haired, with sun-kissed skin. One of these was the one who had put the ring on Mel. He struck her as a nervous, creepy fellow, with shifty eyes that kept flitting over her body. Twice he lost hold of Mel's arm and shoulder, earning him affronted looks from the others.

The third time it happened, the woman scolded him. "We have to hurry, Bateman. They might already know she's missing. I don't want Kales coming down on top of us."

"Don't talk to him," snapped the other man at Mel's head. "If you're in such a hurry, then shut your fucking mouth and keep moving." He pulled Mel roughly forward, forcing the others to move at a quicker pace.

"Really, Hershal?" the woman whispered angrily. "How about you get your lackey to pull his weight."

They stopped sharply, Hershal practically yanking Mel back. "Hold her, Bateman," he said, releasing Mel's shoulder.

Bateman obediently moved so that he was holding both of Mel's shoulders.

Hershal then picked up Mel's head by her hair, and she felt the cold, sharp edge of a knife against her neck.

"Don't," said the woman.

"Don't what, Griggs?" growled Hershal. "Don't kill this little girl? Y'all paid me and Bateman here to get you through this well-protected property. *That's* what was in the bargain. *This part* ain't my responsibility. I got y'all here. What happens next don't matter. I still get paid."

The woman, Griggs, dropped Mel's feet angrily. The man beside her did the same.

"You'd be signing us all up for death, you vindictive, sociopathic piece of shit," Griggs said. "Who the hell do you think you're dealing with? Some fucking low-level organization? That's not the Eighth Clan. If we fail, we *all* die."

The man at her side stayed silent, but he pulled a knife of black metal with a serrated edge.

Two different parties of origination, Mel thought. *This should be interesting.*

"Oh yeah?" Hershal said. "Is *that* how it works?"

"I told you how it works," Griggs growled. "You've done jobs for us before without complaints. You were all for it then. Now you pull this shit? Why? What's the point?"

Hershal's hold on Mel's hair tightened. "Because I don't like the way you speak to me. I don't like the way you look at me. I don't like the way you all treat me and Bateman like we're fucking slaves and pay us like we're fucking servants. I do good work for your *Masters.* I don't ask questions. I don't ask why you've got glowing *rings* that you like to put on little girls. I don't ask why you want me and Bateman to be the ones to hold the goddamn thing and put it around her neck. We do what we're told. But y'all don't—"

"We don't have time for this shit, Hershal," said Griggs, cutting him off. "We have to fucking go. *Now.* Put the knife away."

Hershal tensed, and Mel felt as if the man was going to spring into action, but before he could move or speak, an owl swooped down, and the noisy flutter of its wings made everyone jump. The owl seemed like it was coming right at them, but edged up toward the sky at the last moment. The event seemed to jar the four out of their argument. They put away their weapons and, with one last resentful look, they lifted Mel up once more and continued on their way.

The gag in Mel's mouth prevented her from calling for help. She had tried, but her voice was so muffled it was lost in the night sounds. So instead she focused on working through the possibilities. *Where are they taking me? Are we nearing the border yet? Shouldn't a Ranger catch sight of us?* And finally, *Where is my strength? Why has it not come back?*

She knew she wouldn't be able to feel the fire in her chest—the beast beneath her skin—but she should have at least recovered physically, especially since the very thing that sucked away all her energy had now been severed from her. And yet, even had she not been bound and held, she was certain she would barely be able to move her arms and legs. She was being led to the Eighth like a lamb to slaughter, and she couldn't even fight back.

Mel closed her eyes and willed herself to stay calm, even as the fear filled her chest.

And then a call went up—a shrill whistle that was music to Mel's ears. They must have been spotted. She heard them, her clanspeople, their urgent shouts, the *shink!* of weapons being unsheathed.

Her captors began to run, handling her with even less care.

"Over there! Hurry!" Cade's voice, strained and urgent.

The four pushed even harder. Mel turned her head to look for her clanspeople, but saw only trees.

And then they broke out into the open, and Mel heard the roar of an engine and the grinding of tires on hard dirt. A blue van stopped abruptly in front of them, and the door slid open. Mel was tossed in like a sack, and Hershal and Bateman climbed on board with her. Bateman held her tightly as if he feared she would flee.

Griggs jumped in after them, and her clansman was just about to follow—his hand already on the door—when he gasped and reached for his thigh, where the hilt of a dagger now protruded. He tried to stumble into the van, and Griggs reached to pull him aboard, but another knife flew through the air and plunged right through her hand.

"Fuck!" she shouted, clutching her hand.

Mel looked out the open door to see Keven running full-tilt through the trees, a look of intense concentration on his face as he flung another knife. This one struck Griggs in her throat, and she fell to the floor of the van, looking at Mel in shock.

Hershal kicked aside the Eighth clansman, still trying to get in the van, and slammed the door shut. "Go! Go! Go!" he yelled.

The van's young driver looked back, hesitant. He was already half off of his seat as if he wanted to come back to help Griggs.

He's not with Hershal, then, Mel decided.

Something struck the driver's window. The glass shattered, and the driver was yanked harshly through the opening.

"Fuck!" said Bateman, shaking. Mel wondered if he was holding her to assuage his own fear. "We're not getting out of this alive! I knew as soon as I held that ring that this job would go south!"

"Shut the fuck up, Bateman!" Hershal yelled.

He clambered into the driver's seat, and the instant he was in place he slammed on the gas and tore off. Mel heard the alarmed yells of her clansmen, no doubt throwing themselves out of the way.

"That's right, motherfuckers!" Hershal whooped as he pounded the steering wheel. "See that, Bateman? Those dumbasses are chasing us on foot! Fucking idiots! We're home free!"

He drove at breakneck speed, and Mel felt each minute taking them further from her home. She closed her eyes and sought the fire. She kept her breaths even, just as the First Healer had coached her. But there was nothing. Nothing there. Not even a spark.

After a while, Bateman let her go, climbed into the front passenger seat, and started joking with Hershal. Which even Mel thought was disrespectful, seeing as Griggs still lay dead on the floor right behind them. But Mel supposed the farther Bateman moved from Mel's clan, the more confident he felt.

That was a mistake.

What a bunch of rubes, she thought, as the two men laughed and joked. As if it was already *over.*

This was far from over.

Even if Mel died, this wasn't over. Her brothers, her uncles, her cousins, her grandmother… they'd find these two. They would hunt them down and bring them back.

Then they would tie them to a stake and burn them as the sun rose.

Dead men walking, these two.

"What are you doing, Hershal?" Bateman asked. "Why the fuck are you slowing down?"

"I'm not!" Hershal said as the car came to a rolling stop. "Fuck!"

They opened their doors and stepped out. Mel heard their footsteps on loose gravel.

"Fuck those fucking Kales!" Hershal shouted. There was banging at the rear of the van. Something striking the metal body.

"What are we going to do?" Bateman asked. The tremor in his voice was back.

"Get her," Hershal said. "We carry her the rest of the way."

The side door opened, and Bateman looked at Mel with

uncertainty. "But it's so fucking far. Why don't we just leave her here and run off?"

"And live the rest of our lives looking over our shoulders?" Hershal said. "I hated Griggs's fucking guts, but she was right about that."

"But there's nothing *special* about her," Bateman said. "She's quiet as a mouse and hasn't fought an inch. That seem right to you? Don't you think she'd've fought us?"

Hershal appeared beside Bateman. He looked at Mel with narrowed eyes, then pulled off one of her boots. "You got a pen?"

"Why would I have a pen?"

"Jesus Christ." Hershal looked around on the ground, then bent to pick something up. It was a thin twig. He ran it down Mel's foot. Once. Twice. Then a third time.

"Whatcha doing?" Bateman asked.

"Checking to see if she's paralyzed."

Mel narrowed her eyes. She was *not* paralyzed. *Can't you see the goddamn Babinksi reflex, you fucking rubes?*

"She's what?" Bateman said. His eyebrows lifted toward his hairline. "You mean… she can't move? We can… do what we want to her?" He looked at Hershal with growing expectation.

Hershal quit his testing and sighed. "We don't got time for that. Let's get her up. We're already running late."

"What are we going to tell them about the others?" Bateman asked as he started pulling Mel out of the van by her sore arms. "Won't they be mad about Griggs?"

"They weren't last time," Hershal said with a shrug. "As long as the Master gets what they want we'll be fine." He grabbed Mel's feet and the two of them lifted her up. "Jesus Christ she's heavy for a little thing."

"Yeah," Bateman agreed. "You'd think she'd weigh a feather from the look of her."

Mel looked back inside the van at the dead Eighth woman, Griggs. Her eyes were lifeless and cold, her heart-shaped birthmark even more striking now that her face had gone pale from blood loss. A knife still stuck out of her throat, but the knife that had embedded itself in her hand—the one Mel had nicked—was missing.

Mel had to suppress a smile as the van door slid shut.

Chapter Eighteen

Gabe ran through the woods not even knowing where he was going. He just needed to find something, *anything*, that would give him direction as to where the Eighth were. He *knew* there had to be more of them around. He knew they had to have somehow identified the Lost Soul's whereabouts and prostrated themselves like the sycophants they were. He knew they had assisted with the spell that had killed all those people in that small idyllic subdivision.

As far as I'm concerned, Gabe thought, *they're just as fucking guilty.*

He picked up his pace, lungs burning, his staff secure in his hand. He liked to imagine that he could smell them, their desperation, their thirst for power. It was as if their stink was souring everything good in the world. Pulling the pieces apart and throwing them into the void so there was no hope of putting things back together. Annihilation at its most basic and dangerous. They had to be stopped. They had to be brought to their knees. But how? How was he going to that? Was he even the man to do it? He was just one person.

Are you man or clan?

That was the question. It burned in Gabe's ears and made him slow to a stop. He stabbed his staff into the ground and stared off at the setting sun, eyes stinging from the brightness. The anger that had pressed him into action fizzled into nothing, leaving him with only the despair that was the root of all his anger and hate.

Are you man or clan?

His breath came heavy from his lips as he closed his eyes, remembering the empty homes, the lifelessness. He imagined the moment when time stopped for those innocents. A parent putting their child to bed for what was the last time. A husband and wife sharing their last kiss. It was all *over*, in one terrible, sinful moment.

Are you man or clan?

This was too much for one man to handle. Too much.

Gabe pulled out the sat phone and wondered again why no one had called him. Did they not know he was gone? Did they not care?

It didn't make any sense. Mel was all over him only a few hours ago, and now, what? Hands off? It didn't make any sense.

He dialed her number, but there was no ring, no answer, just a strange white noise.

What the fuck?

He called Tío Jorge and Tío Luce, with the same result.

"What's the point of having a sat phone if it doesn't fucking work!" he screamed into the trees. He pressed it in between his hands, wanting so much to rip the plastic apart. "Fuck!"

He took several moments to regain his composure before he put the phone away. He might need it later. There might just be a glitch in the satellite system. He would try again later... when he was calmer.

"You don't look so good, Gabriel Mendez."

Gabe grabbed his staff and whipped it into a defensive position before realizing the voice belonged to Micos. She stood with Paul, Coudrou, Puma, and surprisingly, Ana Flores and Reese Logan.

"What are you all doing here?" he asked in surprise and relief.

Coudrou gave him a wide, gap-toothed grin. "Micos noticed you didn't get in the truck when we were leaving… so we came after you."

"Figured you were going to continue hunting," Paul said. He was slightly out of breath and red in the face, but in good spirits. He put a hand on Puma's shoulder. "We're all about the hunt."

"Got that right," Puma said with a nod.

Gabe looked at Logan and Flores. "What about you two?"

Logan smiled and shrugged. "Can't leave you all without a healer."

Flores, on the other hand, rolled her eyes, "I just didn't want you four to overrule Micos with your idiocy."

"Hey now!" Coudrou exclaimed. "We would never!"

"Not on purpose anyway," said Paul. "We're always open to hearing what you ladies have to say."

"If that's the case," Flores said assertively, "then you won't mind if I take charge of this mission."

"Well, uh, wha—" said Coudrou, looking at Gabe. "We could—"

"Kale rule depicts that when no one is formally assigned to lead, the most senior clansperson is the de facto leader," Logan said, giving the men a gentle smile.

"Most senior clans*woman* you mean," said Gabe with a knowing smirk.

The healer just shrugged. With none of the male members being close to Flores's age, it was a moot point.

"Then that would mean it would be Micos that would be in charge," said Coudrou with a frown. "But I don't know how I feel about that, what with her being a Peruvian Kale." He looked at Micos. "No offense."

"None taken," said Micos with a wave of her hand. "I would not feel comfortable with it either." She looked agreeably at Flores. "I will follow your lead."

"Wait," said Paul. "That rule has an exception. When one is related to—"

"We'll follow your lead, Flores," Gabe said roughly, cutting Paul off. He grabbed his staff and urged the rest to prepare to move. He hadn't a clue where, he just wanted to *go*. Anywhere would do.

"Gabe," Paul said, "this isn't the time for secrets. Everyone here should know."

"Know what?" asked Flores, her hazel eyes narrowing. "What aren't you telling us, Gabe?"

Gabe gave Paul a hard look. This wasn't the time. In fact, this was probably the most *inconvenient* time. But now Flores, Puma, Logan, and Micos were all looking at him expectantly.

"You should tell them," Coudrou said. "They should know."

"What is it?" Flores demanded, eyes glittering in anger and frustration. "I swear, Gabe, if it's something that could've helped us save those people—"

"It's not," Gabe said. "It wouldn't have changed the situation. It won't help us right now, either."

"I doubt that," said Paul. "She could just come meet us and take care of business."

"Shut up, Paul," Gabe said, frustrated all to hell with the young Kale. "It doesn't work like that." He looked at the others and shook his head. Finally, he just blurted it out. "Mel is alive. She survived *Inter Spatium Abyssus*."

"No, Gabe," Flores said, terribly calm. "That would mean that *Sapienti* Mendez is lying to all of us, and she wouldn't do that."

"She did," Gabe said. "She had to." How did he say the rest? It was so incredible. So inconceivable.

Flores reeled back as if her world was coming down around her. She moved away from the others, pacing, before coming back and pointing an accusatory finger at Gabe. "No!"

"That's not our way," said Logan, slowly and patiently—the voice of reason. "It's unheard of to be lied to by your clan Elder. They're chosen specifically because of their honor. To lie so phenomenally, so *carelessly*, to all… Unless…" Logan looked at Gabe with wide eyes. "Mel is the heir, isn't she?"

Flores looked at Logan in astonishment, as did Micos, but Puma looked unsurprised.

Logan continued in full investigative mode. "It's the only thing that makes sense. To survive *Inter Spatium Abyssus*, she had to have her gifts. I mean, I—I always *suspected*, since her Journeyman trials, when those two other Kales died and she'd survived… but I wasn't there."

"I wasn't either," Gabe said with a frown. By tradition, none of the family were allowed during the trials; the only exception was his grandmother, and that was only because she was the clan Elder. And even she could not be truly present, and had to rely heavily on the Journeymen overseeing the trials to make sure everything was up to par.

"You were there, weren't you, Puma?" Logan asked, looking at the tracker with curious eyes.

Puma looked furtively at Gabe, who had turned toward him, frowning. "We were told not to speak of it—not to anyone. Not to you or your brother or your cousins. *Sapienti* was very clear about that." He waited until Gabe nodded before continuing. "To be honest, the truth is a lot more dire than what was on the record. The two clanspeople that died—it was their own fault. They'd done something incredibly stupid and dis—" He stopped, perhaps realizing he was saying too much. But he left the rest of them hanging, waiting for his next words, so he cleared his throat and continued. "After… none who were there could go a day further with anyone questioning her honor," he said with flinty eyes. "We handled anyone who did. *Hard.*"

"That's why the clan's opinion of her shifted," Flores said. She crossed her arms, facing the tracker. "I was never one to judge Mel for her choices; I'd had plenty of experience training with her to know better. But I remember rumors started a bit after her trials, and clanspeople who had false opinions of her started to sing a different tune."

Puma nodded. "Cade started a rumor that had *just* enough information about the trials, but didn't break our word to *Sapienti.* It really smoothed the way."

Gabe remembered hearing it weeks after the trials. He and Victor had been attending a training exercise and were paired up with several other Kales who'd already heard the rumor and were asking Mel's brothers for confirmation. They'd heard that Mel's heart had stopped, that she'd been pronounced dead, that she was already wrapped in gauze and silk when her heart started beating again. She'd been given a reprieve. Kales were a superstitious sort, and a woman coming back to life... well, there had to be a very good reason for that.

An *honorable* reason.

Poor Victor, he'd been struck dumb, unable to say a word. But Gabe had smiled right through their telling, and, afterward, he had totally fed the rumor. *Why yes,* his sister's heart stopped! *Of course* she was brought back to life! Kale herself sent her soul back into her body! Told her she had shit to do! He had a joyous time with it.

But when he asked Mel about it, she had no recollection of it. She was just surprised that she'd woken up a Journeyman.

"There were still a few that questioned her, though," Puma said. "They just got better at staying quiet about it. I don't think her presumed death has changed their opinion of her either—and, by association, *Sapienti* for raising someone they perceive as weak." Puma rolled his eyes, showing how he felt about those Kales. "But Cade knows who they are, and so does Thomas. And Nico Solis—

Jesus, that guy! If there was ever a clansperson I'm glad is on our side, it's him. That man is fucking scary."

Paul and Coudrou nodded in agreement, and Gabe almost snorted. Nico was good people.

"What was it like?" Flores asked. When Puma looked at her, she clarified: "When Mel… presented?"

Puma frowned, his eyes distant. "It was wonderful… and terrifying at the same time. I couldn't imagine being that full of power and not melting from it. And after—she was so drained. So sick."

Reese gave Gabe a look of concern, and he hated it—because she *knew*. She was a healer; she had to know. "She's struggling, isn't she?" Reese said.

Gabe nodded and leaned on his staff. "Her gifts are… unpredictable and dangerous." It felt good to finally be able to speak of it to someone who wasn't as close to it as he was. "Her powers are so strange, Reese. She's still my sister, but she's also something else, something just under her skin, just waiting to take over. It's always been there, honestly, but now it's *right there*. Just a breath away from manifesting. If you saw her, you would understand; there's no explaining the experience. The *heat* of it." He looked at them all, voicing the words he couldn't say to his family. "I think it's killing her."

Logan stepped in front of him and put a hand on his shoulder. "I'm so sorry, Gabe. But it's best to have hope. Hope that everything will be as it should. I don't think we would be blessed with having an heir just for her to die from her own powers. That's not Kale-like."

"I agree, Gabriel Mendez," said Micos. "The heir's path will be tumultuous and grave indeed, and the power within is a blessing and a curse, but as long as she has the will and desire, she will survive and live. That is our way."

Gabe felt embarrassed at his display. "Well, she has plenty of that. More than everyone here."

"Then do not fear," said Micos soothingly. "That is the first step. The rest shall be taken one day at a time." She clapped her hands together and looked at the others. "Come! We've got a Lost Soul to kill. Let us continue. Time enough to talk after, yes?"

It took only a moment to prepare to move again. Everything they had they carried on their backs. The only issue was the destination, which Puma readily supplied, directing them to a path he'd discovered while they'd chased Gabe through the forest. It was an accident, really, the short man had said. A curious thing he'd noticed when he slipped on a stone and nearly fell. In the moment it took him to regain his balance, he'd sensed something odd and unnatural about the ground.

Gabe didn't understand what Puma meant until they returned to the spot and Gabe felt electricity snap at his skin, making the hairs on his arms rise.

"Wait!" he called, but it was too late. Puma had already led the way onto this other path, and immediately fell to his knees in pain and let out an excruciating howl.

"Pull him back, hurry!"

The others grabbed him by his feet and dragged him back. The yelling stopped, but Puma was still in obvious pain. Logan quickly checked him over, her hands moving quickly over his body as she chanted quietly. The others could only look on worriedly.

"You'll be okay," Logan finally said to Puma. "Whatever it was shocked your system, but it's quickly making its way out of your body. Just give yourself a moment." She looked back at the others. "We need to find what caused it."

"I already know," Gabe said, lowering himself to his knees and checking the ground near where Puma collapsed. "There's a boundary here. Look around, see if you can find a totem or object."

Logan and Puma sat quietly observing while the others searched. It took a while, as they were being careful not to venture too far, afraid of triggering the same response as Puma. It was dusk when Coudrou finally called out and pointed high into a tree. A fresh carving of a strange glyph was on the trunk facing inward, hiding it from the south. It looked sharp and forbidding, with a darkness to it.

"I don't recognize that glyph," Coudrou said. "Should we break it?"

"We should *definitely* break it," said Gabe, looking at Flores, who nodded in agreement. "Then we'll press on. I have a feeling this is the Eighth's doing."

"I have a feeling you're right," said Flores. "Go on, Coudrou."

As Coudrou climbed the tree to mar the glyph, Flores pulled out a map, and Gabe stepped up beside her. "We're here," she said, pointing to a spot in the middle of the wilderness. "If we continue through the boundary, there are only a few areas that have shelter, but they're spread out pretty far. It's a lot of ground to cover." She surveyed the area. "I wish we could know how far this boundary goes."

Coudrou had now scaled the tree, being careful to stay on the side that didn't have the glyph. Before destroying the glyph, he pulled out his phone and snapped a picture. Then he used his knife to cut the bark next to the glyph. As a thin piece cracked and pulled away from the symbol, a flash of light sparked brightly, just for a moment. The glyph was broken. Paul proved the point by stepping gamely across the spot where there had once been a barrier.

"All good," he called up to Coudrou.

Coudrou climbed down and sidled up beside Puma and Logan, who were now getting to their feet. Micos had already joined Paul on the other side of the barrier.

"Is it too much to hope that the damn boundary is down along the whole perimeter?" Gabe asked.

"If I had to guess," said Flores, "and I do fucking hate to guess, I'd say the barrier is only broken here."

"I have to agree with you," said Logan. "Coudrou showed me the pic he took of the glyph, and it's a sophisticated one. I believe it was designed to keep anyone armed from entering—which means the boundary was triggered because of Puma's sword. There's more to it as well, stuff that I'm not familiar with, but the point is, they took great care in its design. So it seems unlikely that destroying just the one glyph would open up the whole perimeter."

Flores looked at her map. "We still have all this ground to cover," she said with a sigh.

"Not necessarily." Gabe pointed toward a lake a few hours from where they stood. "We should focus here. It's far enough from civilization that they wouldn't grab attention, but close enough for them to venture out for supplies."

"I think there are some hunting cabins there, too, if I remember correctly," said Logan. "I agree, we should start there."

"Good plan," Flores said, folding up the map. "Let's go."

****

Night fell upon them with a thick heaviness. Gabe let Puma lead the way, the man having recovered from his earlier episode. Flores stalked just behind, her sword gripped in her hand. Paul followed with Coudrou, and Logan and Micos brought up the rear. No one spoke as they traveled, and Gabe wished they would. The silence made him edgy and paranoid, and he expected the Eighth to jump out from between the trees at any moment.

So he was relieved when Flores said to him quietly, "Can I ask you a question?"

Gabe looked over his shoulder. Flores had pulled up her face sleeve, just as the others had, except for Coudrou and Paul, who were wearing those ridiculous pig masks Coudrou had brought.

"I guess," he said.

"What was it like?"

Gabe raised an eyebrow, knowing without a doubt what she was talking about. Fighting the Lost Soul. "You know, I asked Mel the same thing when she got back," he said with a grin. "What's it like to be in *Inter Spatium Abyssus*? To fight a Lost Soul? To be around that much danger and darkness? What's it *feel* like? I wanted to know *everything*."

"And? What did she say?"

Gabe looked her dead in the eye. "There aren't words. There's nothing to prepare you. All our training, all the *Hae*, it didn't matter. When it happens, you'll know what to do... or you won't."

Flores was quiet for a long moment before speaking again. "I thought you would say something like that. I'd hoped you'd say something more helpful."

Gabe smirked. "If you're looking for encouragement, I'm not your guy."

"So I've gathered."

"But," Gabe continued with a smile, "you can be sure I won't run when I see the fucking thing. *That* you can count on."

That seemed to settle Flores, and she lapsed back into silence.

The Kales continued through the woods in their soft, deliberate way. At last they came across the lake, which meant the cabins were now just a few miles away. Flores signaled for Coudrou and Paul to scout forward while the others drew back, finding cover.

Gabe settled himself behind a thick bush that hid him from view. He watched his surroundings with careful eyes, keeping his staff at the ready, gripping it with both hands. Micos sat next to him, quietly arranging her weapons in a meticulous manner as if she were going through a mental list, checking each item off one by one. When she was done, she pulled out a canteen and took a swig before offering it to Gabe. He declined, focused instead on the direction Paul and Coudrou had taken. It had been over half an hour, and Gabe was getting antsy.

He rose to a kneeling position and looked over at Flores, who was poking her head around a tree. Something had happened; Gabe was sure of it. And sure, from Flores's expression, that she was aware of it too.

Gabe gave a signal, and they all began to rise—but Micos grabbed his arm and yanked him down hard. She jutted her chin out toward the lake, where several boats were sliding stealthily through the water just offshore, their oars silent, searchlights canvassing the woods.

Gabe ducked back down quickly, holding his breath as one of the lights passed over him and Micos and continued on. He hoped the others had found decent places to hide. He and Micos shared a look and gripped their weapons tightly.

One of the boats came ashore. Four men jumped out, armed with bronze swords.

Bronze weapons? What is that about? Gabe wondered.

Two of the men came uncomfortably close, peering into the woods as if they could see through the darkness. Gabe squinted his eyes to try to get a better look at the men, but the searchlight behind them prevented him from seeing their features.

The men moved slowly along the shore, never straying too far from the water. One of the men passed mere feet from Gabe's hiding place, and it took all of Gabe's willpower not to cut the man's Achilles. He could taste it rising in the back of his throat, the heat and violence that he so wished to cut loose. He felt his control beginning to unravel. And then with one slow, quiet, tightly regulated breath, he let the anger go.

He looked over at Micos, who lay next to him on her stomach, looking as calm as a summer breeze. He envied her. So detached. So heedless of the situation.

It seemed the men in the other boats felt their search was over, for they turned and went slowly back the way they had come, leaving behind only the one boat that had come ashore. And shortly thereafter, the four men from that boat appeared ready to retreat as well. One got in and while two others started to push the boat out into the water. But the fourth man hesitated at the water's edge.

"Come on, Sam," said one of the men pushing the boat. "There's no one out here. Blake is just being paranoid."

Gabe's heart skipped a beat. Maybe Coudrou and Paul were okay.

"I ain't fucking paranoid," said the other man pushing the boat. Blake, apparently. "I saw what I saw—a man in a pig mask. Scared the bejesus out of me."

"Sure, sure, a man in a pig mask was just standing there in the doorway."

"Ronson believes me. Right, Ronson?"

"Don't bring me into this," said the man in the boat. "If I had it my way, I'd be in bed catching some sleep. None of y'all had to stay up for forty hours straight keeping watch."

"Maybe if you weren't such a lick-ass trying to impress—"

"Fuck you, Jacob," said Ronson, but there was no heat in his words, just fatigue.

"Yeah, yeah," said Jacob, shaking the boat with both hands, then throwing a rude gesture at Ronson. He looked back at Sam, who hadn't moved. "Sam, get your ass in the boat already! We need to get back. We should be hearing from Griggs soon."

"I think there's someone out there," said Sam in a quiet voice. "I can feel them."

"Really?" Jacob snorted, and stomped noisily in the water. "Do you think they're hearing us right now? Like, right now, *now?*"

"I'm being serious, Jake," said Sam.

"Hello! Is somebody out there!" Jacob yelled. He walked over to Sam and quickly pulled him into a headlock. "My little brother says you're out there! Come out and surrender yourselves! And we will spare your lives!"

"Come on, Jake! Get off of me!"

"Aw, come on! You're such a pussy!"

"I saved your life, didn't I? You nearly shit your pants when you saw the red-eyed demon and the spell it cast."

"I didn't sign up for that shit, Sam," said Jacob, letting Sam go. "Killing babies and kids. That's fucked up."

Ronson spoke up, tiredly. "You two should be honored."

"Yeah," Blake agreed. "The Master only chooses—"

"Shut the fuck up, both of you," said Sam, showing anger for the first time. Then he said quietly to Jacob, "I know it's not what we signed up for, but until Lilly gets back, we've got to play nice."

At that moment, Gabe's phone rang. It sounded ear-splitting in the quiet of the night. He hurriedly cut off the ring, but it was already too late—all four men were now watching the woods with unease.

Well, nothing for it now, Gabe thought.

He rose from his hiding place. He must've looked like a madman to them—his face covered, a golden staff in his hand. He pointed his staff at them, hoping they would understand the challenge.

"He's the one," Sam said, voice trembling. "He's the one I felt. He's touched."

Before he could say another word, Coudrou rose like a sea monster out of the lake, grabbed Blake around the neck, and dragged him into the water.

After that it was chaos. Micos charged ahead to engage with Jacob and Sam. Gabe threw his staff at Ronson, and the bladed edge impaled him in his sternum. It was all over quickly.

"You killed them all," said Logan, with a deep sadness.

The others looked at her in bemusement. Healers had such bleeding hearts. Something to do with *Spiritus*, Gabe thought.

"We're at war, Reese," Gabe replied quietly. He was doing his best to clean the blood off his staff's blade. "They're Eighth. They're the same people who tried to kill my sister and cousin. Who tried to end the world."

"I know that," Logan said, still troubled. "But those two"—she pointed at Jacob and Sam—"didn't want to be here. They didn't want to be a part of this."

"And yet they did nothing to stop the killing of those innocent people," Gabe said, with more patience than he thought he held. "They're still guilty. We can't just keep them around 'cause they were…" *Happy? Fun? Playful?* Gabe didn't finish his sentence. At the end of the day, there was nothing he could say to make the healer feel better. Especially since he felt no remorse. He'd kill them all. Men, women, maybe even some evil children. He'd kill *all* of the Eighth if he could.

While Gabe and Logan spoke, the other Kales had pulled the men and their boat into the woods, hiding both under the thick brush. Now Coudrou shouted in surprise.

"Hey! Two of these fuckers are still breathing!"

Gabe went over to look. Sure enough, Jacob and Sam were still alive. Barely.

Logan quickly took charge. "I'm saving them," she announced with finality. "Put your goddamn sword away, Paul. I'll take the responsibility for any fallout."

Gabe shared a look with Flores and shrugged.

"Suit yourself, Logan," Flores said. "I'm going to hold you to that."

Gabe turned away from Logan and grabbed the phone from his pocket and dialed the number that had called him moments before.

"Hey, asshole," said Victor. "You can't answer your goddamn phone? Where the fuck are you? I'm coming to get you. Tell me where you are."

"Brotha!" Gabe said, relieved. "I'm so glad to hear your voice! Tell you what, I'll send you the coordinates. I hope you have many, many Kales with you. We're going to need help—as much as we can get."

"What for?"

"Why, to kill Eighth, brotha," Gabe said, a smile breaking across his face. "To *kill* Eighth."

Gabe didn't have to hear the assent from Victor. He knew his brother well enough to know he was always ready for a fight.

Chapter Nineteen

As Hershal and Bateman dragged Mel through the darkness, the night—a grey transparency—grudgingly allowed Mel to see into it, to discern its secrets with a remarkable clarity that never ceased to surprise her, in spite of her predicament.

Perhaps there is hope, she thought. She searched for that fire in her chest again, but found only a wall, firm and unyielding. And painful. Like the barrier the Eighth used in *Inter Spatium Abyssus* to keep Charlotte captive.

Interesting.

The two men were struggling. Hershal had gotten turned around twice, trying and failing to identify the North Star through the canopy of trees, and Bateman was hopeless. They'd stopped and called someone on a cell phone multiple times, and grew more irritated each time. Mel had to presume whoever they were speaking to was just as irritated, for it was clear they had sent the two men coordinates, yet the two rubes were having a difficult time using their GPS to find the location.

"It's not working!" Hershal groused. "I'm trying to use this fucking app and it won't—hello? Hello?"

He threw the phone on the ground in disgust, then turned toward Bateman. "The goddamn thing just died on me! It had half a fucking battery—I've barely used the fucking thing! Where's yours?"

Bateman pulled his phone out of his pocket and handed it over. "Mine has some juice left. Not much though."

Hershal turned on Bateman's phone. "Not *much*? It's got *five percent*, Bateman! Didn't you fucking charge it beforehand?"

"Yeah," Bateman said. He scrunched his face into a frown. "At least, I think I did."

Mel tried to keep herself from scoffing. The more time these two wasted, the more time there was for her clanspeople to find her. Maybe they could get these two to spill what they knew about the Eighth and where they were holding up.

"Fuck!" said Hershal, throwing Bateman's phone back at him. "We're just gonna have to wait here for them. Better to stay in one place. Build a fire or something so they can track us down, will you?"

"It could take ages for them to find us," said Bateman, but he started gathering branches for a fire. He shook his head. "I knew this job was a bad idea from the start."

While Bateman worked and Hershal seethed, Mel surreptitiously pulled out the knife she had stashed in her sleeve and started to very, very quietly cut her bindings. She was done by the time Bateman had finished with the fire. She shifted her legs, which were still heavy with numbness, stinging with pins and needles. But she knew if the opportunity arose, she had to try to run. She just needed to bide her time. With these two idiots, an opportunity was bound to come.

A roar went up in the woods around them, a dull rumble that made the hair on the back of Mel's neck stand up, and a strange energy pulled at her. Heart racing, she tilted her head in an attempt to locate where it was coming from. Bateman and Hershal seemed not to have heard the roar or felt the energy.

What is that? she thought. *I have to see—I have to know.*

Instead of biding her time, she threw off her ropes and pushed herself to her feet, her legs trembling.

"Hey! She's loose!" Hershal shouted, lunging at her.

Mel sliced the knife across his hand, and he jumped away with a yelp.

Mel stood her ground, the knife in front of her threateningly, her eyes flitting from Hershal to Bateman.

"Listen here, girl," said Hershal, holding his bleeding hand. "You're coming with us. We mean to get paid."

Bateman charged at her, but Mel dodged, threw her fist out at the last moment, and caught him on the side of the head. He fell to the ground in a tumble.

"Ow! Fuck!" he screamed. "She hit my fucking ear!"

Mel turned and ran—or tried to. Her legs were lazy and uncoordinated, and the best she could manage was a stagger. *Fucking fuck, fuck, fuck!*

It took only seconds for Hershal to catch her, wrapping his arms around her in a bear hug from behind.

Mel flung the back of her head into his face. *Hard.*

"Motherfuck!" he yelled as blood squirted from his mouth and nose. "You fucking bitch! My tooth!"

But he still kept his hold on her, so Mel stabbed the knife into his right arm, creating an ugly, deep gash. That got him to let go—with a scream—and Mel pulled away.

But Bateman was there, his face contorted in rage and hate. He threw himself at her, grabbing at her arms, knocking her to the ground. "The things I'm going to do to you!" he growled.

Mel brought the knife up and savagely stabbed over and over, the softness of his throat giving like paper. He choked, his mouth opening and closing like a fish, the whites of his eyes turning red. Blood sprayed as Mel pushed him off her. He fell on his face, his movements slowing by the second.

She lay on the ground, spent. That thing inside her, it was growing now. *But it's not enough.*

Hershal stood, seething in anger, holding on to his arm, which bled terribly all over his shirt and pants. As he pulled his own knife and stalked toward her, Mel tried to wriggle away, but her limbs were still heavy and uncoordinated.

He stood over her and grabbed her by her tunic. "You're gonna fucking p—"

A blur appeared behind him, striking him savagely across his head. He fell, his head split open, grey matter and bone on display.

And Mel looked up in horror.

Above her was the Lost Soul, his eyes glowing red, a terrible, broken smile stretched across his face, Hershal's blood dripping from the red blade of his sword.

Mel tried to flee, driven by raw self-preservation. The thing inside her pushed, but the collar dug into her throat, and every breath hurt.

"So we meet again, Kale," the Lost Soul said.

Something stirred in Mel's brain. Pushing through her weakness and pain. It rose up like a flood as she looked into the Lost Soul's eyes, the malice radiating off him in waves.

"Mordred," she said.

His smile widened, and his laughter rang out through the woods.

****

Victor held his axe in his hand as he stood in the darkness, eyes flitting around, catching the fires that lit the campground where some of the Eighth had shared quiet moments before retreating to bed. The Kales had walked tiredly toward the cabins that were scattered by the edge of the lake. From sixty yards away they had watched as the Eighth disappeared one by one, leaving the campfires smoldering and several braziers still burning. They were placid, these

Eighth. Not detecting what was to come.

Victor looked over at Gabe, who was back in Kale gold with his face veiled. "I want them to know I'm a Kale," Gabe had said as he changed back into a tunic and breeches. Victor had just nodded in agreement and held his brother's staff as he stood guard over the two Eighth prisoners who had been gagged and tied to a tree. They were brothers too, he'd been told, and one might have the sight… or something. There had been some disagreement as to what to do with them. Kill them or keep them. Either way, it wasn't his business, wasn't his problem.

What he was most concerned with was the plan of attack.

"What we gonna do?" he'd asked Gabe, who had surprisingly deferred to Ana Flores.

The older woman's keen hazel eyes were cold. "Kill 'em," she'd said, and proceeded to give the instructions. "We'll surround them— they don't even have anyone on watch. It will be easy to sneak into the cabins. We'll wait till they've all gone to bed."

The Kales numbered almost thirty, and though the Eighth had more, it just wouldn't matter. With all the disorder Victor observed, they could've had quadruple the numbers and it still would have been over before it had begun.

Now a call went up from Flores, and Victor crept forward toward the Eighth man standing alone, a cigarette between his lips. He stopped just inside the cover of trees before breaking into a full sprint, holding his axe in one hand. As he drew nearer, he brought it up in both hands… only to feel something hit him hard on the shoulder, sending him crashing to the ground. An arrow had sunk into his flesh.

Victor rolled painfully to his feet as a roar exploded from the camp. The Eighth streamed forth from underground, where they'd hidden under camouflaged sheets. Others attacked from the cabins and their rooftops, even from the lake.

Victor pulled the arrow out and drew back, dodging more arrows as they flew. They whizzed past, missing by inches.

The Eighth screamed their war cries, and scores of them came running at him, armed with steel and bronze swords.

"Archers on the rooftop! In the trees!" Drew screamed. "Fall back! Fall back!"

The Kales retreated into the woods, but the Eighth came in droves, attacking with their strange swords. Victor met one man's sword with his axe, and the bronze weapon shattered in the man's hand. Victor didn't hesitate; he swept his axe into the man's chest, nearly cleaving him in two. Blood spurted thick and hot on his face as he pulled his axe out of the man and turned his attention to his next opponent, who met the same end.

Another signal went up from Flores, and Victor rushed to meet the directive: *Defensive Formation.* He looked to his left and right, where the Wileys had moved closer as well, forming their end of the perimeter around Flores, who would direct them from her position. Victor cut down any Eighth that came near him, keeping them from getting past. He saw two of his clanspeople fall, but their sections were quickly filled by other Kales, striving to keep the enemy at a distance. Victor swung his axe from one opponent to the next.

But the Eighth kept coming. They would not stop, would not slow down, so set were they in their purpose. The sun was starting to rise, allowing him to see the true force of their enemy, surrounding them, smothering and unyielding. Their numbers were staggering.

How did they get so many here? Victor thought.

Drew stepped back within the perimeter, and Victor and the Kale on the other side of Drew filled his area.

"What are you doing, Drew?" Victor yelled as he parried with two Eighth, managing to strike them both down, only to have others take their place.

Drew didn't answer, but after a few moments Victor saw yellow pots being thrown into the thick of the Eighth forces. They exploded seconds later, giving the Kales some reprieve, but not enough. The Eighth quickly moved back out of the cloud of gas, but within seconds they'd regrouped and charged again.

One by one, the Kales fell, until there were only a handful left. Justine took a nasty wound to her side, and Victor's shoulder was throbbing from the arrow wound. The swing of his axe grew more sluggish. Flores had joined the circle, and now the last of the Kales stood almost back-to-back, fighting tooth and nail to keep the Eighth from overwhelming them.

Victor looked for Gabe, who was holding his position beside that Micos woman, his staff moving in swift circles, slicing down any Eighth who came within range. Nearby, Wendel York took a wound to her thigh, and Gabe pushed her back into the circle, where she knelt with Hector Puma and Alec Paul. Reese Logan was doing her best to treat the injured Kales, but she looked sallow and weak, and her patients the same.

We're going to die here, Victor thought angrily. *I'm never going to see—*

A horn sounded through the woods. At the noise, the Eighth drew back a small distance, their weapons held aloft as they looked toward each other. Again the horn sounded, and with it came a roar that grew like a wave. Louder and louder it rolled, until finally it was upon them.

They came screaming from the trees, Victor's clanspeople, in heavy numbers, running with their swords in hand. They crashed into the Eighth with abandon, tearing through their numbers with ferocity and savagery.

Victor saw Tío Luce and Thrash among them, and Thomas and Keven. Hope exploded within him. With adrenaline pumping through his body, he ran, heedless of the downpour of arrows coming down around him. Many of his clanspeople were not so lucky. But he ignored their screams as he sprinted toward his adversary.

With a mighty roar, he tackled an Eighth clanswoman to the ground. Her head was shaved, and she had a tattoo of a bird on her face. *No—a vulture.* The woman swung her sword at Victor's head, but he blocked the attack, catching the woman's sword arm with his own. With a violent twist, he snapped her arm, leaving the woman howling on the ground.

Drew appeared at his side and finished the woman with a quick swing of his knives.

"No mercy!" Drew shouted. "No one leaves alive!"

Victor savagely agreed, cleaving another Eighth nearly in half. He looked for his brother but couldn't spot him in the mayhem. Last he had seen, Gabe had been fighting alongside Micos and Flores, the three pushing forward with driving intent. He wasn't worried; Gabe would handle himself.

Another enemy came at Victor—same hate, same dark clothes, but a different tattoo, this one a condor of some kind. Victor killed him with a nasty wound to his leg, cutting through the artery and bone. Another came, then another and another. All met his axe. None were left standing.

The battle raged all around the campsite. Men and women screamed in anger and agony. The Kales cut down the enemy coldly. They charged into the cabins, crashing through windows and kicking open doors. The enemy were struck down where they stood. When the Kales managed to take out the remaining archers, Victor sensed the battle was nearing its conclusion, his clan heading for victory.

He knew it was truly over when the Eighth turned and fled, some even plunging into the lake. But the Kales pursued, striking them down without mercy.

****

Mel sat on the ground, leaning forward with her hands splayed on the grass. Her breath came in short, shallow gasps, and blood dripped from her mouth and nose. She hadn't said a word to Mordred since she'd identified him, which angered the Lost Soul. He was one for spectacle and games, and she was a fan of neither.

She looked longingly again at where the small knife had been batted away. *If only...* If only she'd stuck the knife in the Lost Soul's eye, or chest, or neck. Anywhere, really. But Mordred had carelessly flicked it away.

Mel had heard a horn in the distance earlier. Her clanspeople were close. But Mordred seemed unconcerned, if not pleased that Mel's clan was so near.

So near, yet so far away.

"You will tell me your name, Kale," he said. His teeth were a runny, rust red, his once-gold tunic filthy. "I will have that power over you before you leave this world. You will be my slave, sniveling at my feet like the weak little worm you are."

Yes, yes—so you've said, Mel thought, leaning away from him and his foul breath. She wouldn't give him a thing. If it was her time to die, then so be it—but her soul would rest in peace with her ancestors, not locked in *Inter Spatium Abyssus* with this psychopath.

Come on, come on, she urged the beast inside her. *I know you're there. I know you want out.* And it did. It was pressing against the strength of the collar. Bumping up against it, attempting to shove it out of the way.

"From the second I first laid eyes on you, I knew it would end like this. You were the first descendant I'd seen in so, so long. The others—the ones who betray the Great Seven—are too easily twisted and molded for our purposes. They're no fun, no challenge. But you... you're a Kale, and I *hate* Kales." He drew closer to Mel. "I stalked the lands close to your home, playing with the humans under your charge. I knew you would venture forth. Knew you would hunt me. You Kales can't help it. You're always so meddlesome."

The Lost Soul fingered the collar on Mel's throat, and she jerked away.

"Oh ho! Don't like the feel of my touch?"

He wrapped his hands around her throat, squeezing. Mel gasped, sucking for air.

"I'm hurt, Kale. After all we've been through, you would treat me so harshly?"

Mel pushed against his hands, but she was so *weak*. So *disgustingly* weak. His face was inches from hers, taunting. His malice was seeping through her skin. It didn't hurt the same way as when he'd touched her with his true body—that was a different kind of pain. This was an icy cold that burned bone-deep.

"Do you not have anything to say?" He released one of his hands and pulled a knife from his belt, its blade blood red. "Hmm… maybe you won't tell me your name. I'll just have to… get my pleasure in other ways."

He smiled and pressed the knife into Mel's chest, angling for her heart, stabbing slowly. The pain flooded through her—and like a trapped animal, the thing inside her pressed desperately, fiercely against the constraining power of the ring, its power going from cold to hot, spilling into her vision. She felt the ring around her throat give, ever so slightly, but enough for her to draw a breath.

She screamed, the roar tearing from her throat and echoing through the trees.

The Lost Soul pressed the blade deeper, and her warm blood spurted forth. The pain was sharp and intense, and she gritted her teeth against it, perspiration breaking out everywhere.

And then Mordred paused. She looked up to see his smile gone, his eyes serious. For a long, charged moment, the two stared at each other. And in that moment, Mel knew.

He knows. He knows I'm the heir.

Mordred's action was sudden. He yanked the knife roughly from her body, and even as she screamed in agony, he unsheathed his sword, raised it over his head, and swung it down toward her neck.

Mel twisted toward him, and the sword landed in the dirt. Frenzied, he grabbed her by her tunic, shoved her onto her back, and pressed the blade of his sword with both hands toward her neck once more.

Mel caught the sharp blade in both hands. In one hand she felt the meat being sliced right to the bone, but her other hand—the *marked* one—held the blade securely, keeping it from her neck. And as that hand began to glow, it dulled the malice—the *evil*—of Mordred's blade.

"No!" Mordred shouted. He pulled the blade back, grabbed the wrist of her marked hand, and pinned it to the ground. Holding his knee on her arm to keep it in place, he again raised his sword and pushed it toward her neck.

Now Mel could do no more than try to stop it with the bloodied flesh of her ordinary hand. It was useless. Mordred was relentless, and so strong, while she was still so weak. He smirked as the blade touched her throat.

"I killed your clansman. Slit his throat like a *pig!*" he spat in triumph. "And now I get to kill the *Chieftress*. My Mistress will be so pleased."

Mordred pushed with all his might. Mel turned her head, her hand still grasping the blade, her eyes tearing from the effort…

And then Mordred screamed, and his weight shifted, sending the blade sliding to one side, across her neck, cutting flesh and gliding along the ring, sending sparks flying. Mel looked up to see the Lost Soul pulling a throwing knife out of his shoulder.

He rose to his feet, and that was when Mel saw Keven. He stood tall, veiled, his tunic bloodied, his long, thin sword in his hands.

He didn't pause for a moment before attacking Mordred with all the fervor and skill he possessed.

Mordred tossed the knife to the ground, raised his blood-red blade, and met Keven's charge, laughing maliciously. The two fought ferociously, but Mel could tell that Mordred was merely toying with Keven, giving him wounds here and there, along his arms and legs, laughing and insulting him along the way.

And then a nasty exchange ensued that resulted in a deep wound to Keven's leg. He fell to one knee, and Mordred towered over him.

"You did decently, Kale," the Lost Soul said loftily. "Not as good as your ancestors, but *decent*. Still, enough is enough. It's time to die. Then I will move on to killing your Chieftress." He looked back toward Mel, right where he left her, bleeding from her wounds. "You can see she's nearly dead already."

Keven looked up at the Lost Soul, tiredly, then over to Mel. "I'm sorry."

Mel shook her head, trying to stand, trying to do *something*. But she couldn't. She could do nothing to stop the inevitable.

Mordred stabbed his sword at Keven's chest, impaling him on it. The blood-red sword glowed as it sank through Keven's flesh, and when he pulled it out, Keven fell face-first to the ground.

Mel drags herself over to him, pulling him to her. He's still breathing, but he's losing so much blood. *No, no, no, no...don't die.* She presses her hands, even the ravaged one, to his chest to stem the bleeding, then quietly chants, putting her heart into the healing spell.

"This is touching," Mordred chortles several paces away. "This is why your side was *always* so weak. You care *so much*." He strides forward, raising his sword. "Nothing but death awaits you now, Chieftress. Come now. I shall give you over to the darkness."

"No you fucking won't," says a voice from the trees.

Mel looks up to see Gabe walk calmly forward, his eyes glowing like chain fire, his staff securely in his hands.

"How 'bout a fucking rematch?" he says. "I think we're more evenly matched now."

And then he attacks.

****

Gabe didn't know what to expect when he caught up with Keven, but this wasn't it. It was like Christmas and his worst nightmare come to life. Why did life have to be so shitty? Well, there was nothing to do about it now. He'd worry about that after he stuck the blade of his staff into this fucking Lost Soul. He just needed to get him away from Mel so Thomas and Cade could swoop in and get her ass out of here.

He charged, swinging his staff around his head and body, meeting the Lost Soul's bloodied blade with nothing but justice urging him on. *Kill my fucking sister and clansman? Hell to the no!* The Lost Soul swung his bloodied blade in terrible arcs and swings that narrowly missed Gabe, grazing his tunic and breeches.

Their weapons clashed together, sparking the air, each striking with strength and purpose. When Gabe's blade caught the Lost Soul on his shoulder, spraying black blood, the demon pulled back, his blood-red eyes glaring in shock and indignation. *Yeeeah, motherfucker!* Gabe charged again, switching to *Mist and Arrow,* a form he favored when going in for the kill. And if there was anything he wanted to kill more than this fucking demon, well, he'd never seen it. He swung his staff in quick circles around his body, attacking the Lost Soul from different angles.

The Lost Soul dodged and rolled away from Gabe's attack, on his heels and reeling, swinging his sword in shallow defensive postures. Gabe could smell it: the victory—the kill. It was on his tongue... he just needed to clench his teeth and *bite*.

His opponent's blade came out of nowhere, slicing Gabe's side. He bent down and groaned; he knew the cut was deep. Blood, thick and hot, spurted out onto his tunic and breeches.

The Lost Soul laughed. "You have much to learn, Kale. Much, much to learn. You are no match for me."

Gabe winced behind his veil. He saw his clanspeople now, surrounding the area, Victor and Thrash among them. Cade and Thomas were already pulling Mel and Keven to safety.

"I may be young and stupid," he replied from his crouched position, "and you're old and fucking decrepit. So yeah, you're bound to have the advantage when it comes to experience." With great effort, he straightened to his full height and pointed his staff at the Lost Soul. "But what I've learned today, is nothing beats fucking numbers."

The Lost Soul frowned, barely bringing his sword up to defend as the Kales attacked, coordinated and disciplined. The Lost Soul was good—Gabe would give him that—and even if there were times when he did seem to anticipate their attacks, he wasn't all-powerful or all-knowing. Many attacks found their marks, and he suffered numerous wounds on his body, growling in frustration each time a Kale blade met his flesh. He managed to fight two, three, even four Kales at a time, but even he, with all his knowledge and power, was only one. One against the clan.

They surrounded him, spinning around him in a frenzy, taking turns thrusting at him with their blades. Some of the Kales took serious wounds but they kept on fighting as if unscathed, and those who did fall were quickly replaced by another Kale taking their place as healers pulled the wounded away.

Then Thrash took his turn, driving the Lost Soul back with clear and precise strikes, his eyes narrowed in concentration, his blade swinging in swift arcs and stabs. He moved with discipline and ferocity, parrying the Lost Soul with ease. *He's like a goddamn machine,* Gabe thought, watching his cousin as he drilled into the Lost Soul with murderous intent.

When Thrash's blade met the meat of his enemy's torso, the Lost Soul fell to his knees.

"Cheat!" the Lost Soul yelled at Gabe. "You couldn't beat me in a fair fight, Kale!"

Gabe shrugged as Thrash knocked the blood-red blade out of the Lost Soul's hand. "I probably could've. But why chance it? I'd rather take the sure win, you evil son of a bitch, and wipe you off the face of the goddamn Earth."

Gabe stepped forward and kicked the Lost Soul onto his back. His clanspeople fell upon the Lost Soul's arms and legs, holding him in place.

"Time to die, motherfucker," Gabe said. He lifted up his staff as if it were a spear, and brought it down for the killing blow.

"Stop!"

It was Mel, yelling in *Old Tongue.* She was making her way back toward them, being helped by Cade and Thomas. She looked dreadful. Her tunic was blooded, one hand looked gored, a wound on her throat was seeping with blood, and a collar around her neck glowed brightly. *How the fuck is she still alive?*

At least someone had had the good sense to put a veil on her.

Cade and Thomas lowered her down gently by the Lost Soul's head, but they might as well have dropped her with all the heaviness with which she fell. Gabe could see the glow in her eyes, but it was very dim and dull compared to the other times he'd witnessed it.

"Ah," the Lost Soul sneered, also in *Old Tongue. "The Chieftress finally decides to speak. Care to tell me that name, now?"*

"You know I won't, Mordred De Cantu."

Mordred narrowed his eyes. *"So, the knowledge comes, and you know my full name. But will you be able to harness all that power in you, Chieftress? Or will you burn bright and short like so many of your predecessors?"*

Gabe's heartbeat accelerated. What did that mean? Thrash came up beside him and put a hand on his forearm to keep his staff lowered.

Mel frowned in consideration. *"It doesn't matter how bright or how short my life is—as long as I've lived to fill my purpose."*

"And what is your purpose? Do you even know? I would wager that you do not. You would not be so calm if you did. There is nothing but darkness in your future. Darkness and death and uncertainty."

Mel laughed at him—*laughed*—and moved closer. *"Life is uncertainty, Mordred De Cantu. But perhaps you're right. Perhaps I won't realize my full potential. Perhaps I'll wake up tomorrow and have no recollection of you or this conversation. So it goes. So it comes. My body will not give in to these wounds you've given me—that I'm sure of. This ring that wraps around my neck—it will be removed. The sun will rise and set, and a new day will be born. And I will try again, and again, and again, and* again. *Like the sun, I will always be there, a new day on the horizon. Can you say the same?"*

"Empty words, Chieftress," Mordred said ruefully. *"Your enemies surround you. They will throttle you. And when it happens—and it* will *happen—you will not know if it came from friend or foe."*

Mel shrugged and took off the torn glove from her good hand. The skin beneath shone with a bright, white light. *"Such is the life of the heir and a Chieftress of Clan Kale. You know that, as you were once one of us. But now... now I'll draw you out like the sickness you are. What I do next will send you to the deepest recesses of Hell. I'm sure you will crawl out of there in a millennium or two. By then, I'll be a distant memory."*

"No!" he screamed, squirming, and more Kales had to fall on him to keep him in place. *"No! No!"*

Mel placed her glowing hand on Mordred's head. The smell of burnt flesh and hair filled the air, and Gabe had to look away when the Lost Soul screeched in horror. The sound made his skin crawl.

Finally, it ended. And when Gabe looked back, it was York's eyes that stared upward.

York. Alive.

Mel motioned for the others to turn him onto his side. They did so, and York purged all the darkness into the grass in the form of disgusting black vomit. Then the healers fell on him with the same fervor Gabe had just fought the Lost Soul with—and York's sister, Wendel, trembling, took her brother's hand.

Gabe knelt next to Mel, and Victor, Thrash, and Thomas also converged. "Are you okay?" Gabe asked.

Mel looked at him with those dull eyes. *"I will be. Remind me later that it's a weapon or item forged or touched by one of the Originals that will expel a Lost Soul,"* she said. *"Perhaps one day I'll be strong enough to expel one on my own, but until then…"*

She collapsed then, planting herself headfirst in the grass.

Gabe pulled her toward him, letting her rest awhile in his arms.

It was the least he could do.

Chapter Twenty

Gabe stood along one wall in the atrium, watching his grandmother hold court while the other clans listened to her explanation of the Battle of the Red Lake, as the Kales had so dubbed it. Everyone was listening closely, no snide remarks, all rapt attention.

But Gabe knew all this already, so he only heard bits and pieces of what his grandmother said.

"... most of the Eighth were killed in the fighting, but a very small contingent got away through the woods... There are efforts to track them down as we speak... The Lost Soul was killed, vanquished from the Earth... Many Kale lives were lost... In the spirit of friendship and unity we will invite you all to pay your respects to the Kales that lost their lives... The Burning Rites will be held tomorrow at daybreak..."

Mel was safely ensconced in the Sun Room, the collar removed, her wounds tended to. She was still unconscious, but the First Healer was sure that she was in no danger. Gabe had stayed for a little while, sitting with her while Victor helped Tío Luce and Jorge transfer the many wounded to the infirmary—or as close to it as they could get. There were so many wounded, they were spilling out on the grounds just outside.

Gabe would never forget the looks on the faces of the other clans when they saw the impact of the events for the first time. Clans Mayme, Tam, and Ferus had volunteered their healers immediately, and the others volunteered hands to help with carrying the wounded and dead back to camp—a choice that would no doubt let them witness the devastation of the battle and provide a bit of reconnaissance to their leaders.

But that was fine. The Kales had already protected the secrets they wished to keep.

Gabe felt a hand wrap around his, and he turned to see Siva, who graced him with a wide smile.

"Hey, stranger," she said. "It's nice to see you on your feet."

Gabe pulled her to him and gave her a quick peck on the cheek. "Nice to *be* on my feet," he whispered into her ear. "I've missed you."

"I've been here," she said with a raise of her eyebrows. "Just sitting at camp waiting to hear from you."

Gabe pulled back and looked in her eyes. Sensing her dismay, he motioned for her to follow him out of the room. Once the door was closed behind them, he circled to face her once more.

"I didn't mean to leave without a word."

"But you did," Siva said, crossing her arms.

"Whoa, whoa, that's not what happened. I was sick! I was a weakling! And then the First Healer—" He looked around to see if anyone was near. "The First Healer did some weird shit to me that gave me my strength back…"

He could tell from her eyes that he wasn't reaching her. So he made a last-ditch effort.

"I was kidnapped!" he said.

"Kidnapped?" she repeated with a frown.

"Yes," Gabe said, putting his hands on her arms and rubbing them briskly as if to warm her. "After the First Healer did her thing, I conked out, and when I woke up, I was in a truck with Roy

Coudrou. I swear, I didn't leave without telling you on purpose."

Siva squinted doubtfully, then thawed right in front of him. "Okay. I really am glad you're okay. When I'd heard what happened…"

"I know—but I'm here." He pulled back a little and motioned to his side. "I got sliced pretty wicked, but it wasn't as bad as the first time. Something about the moon and stars and sky? Don't ask me to explain it—it confused the heck out of me."

"It's okay." She smiled, wrapping her arms around him. "I know all about Wyland's Theory on Degrees of Placement."

"What?" Gabe said, pulling back. "It's got a name?"

Siva nodded. "It's just a theory, but it's the only thing that comes close to explaining why some clanspeople die from a small nick of a Lost Soul's blade, yet others live through mortal wounds."

"Tell me about it," Gabe said, holding her close as if she'd fly away. "We lost so many that just had minor cuts, and yet Keven Thorn is still hanging on. It doesn't make sense."

"Don't try to make sense of it," Siva said, her head on his chest. "Just be grateful to be alive and that we're here together."

"I can do that," Gabe said, pressing his nose into her hair. "I can definitely do that."

"Gabe…" Siva said. "There's something I need—"

The door opened and a Kale pushed through. "We need you back in here, Gabe."

Gabe released Siva and followed the Kale back into the atrium. Cleo Newberry and Lovel were now standing in the center of the room. Gabe shot a questioning look at his grandmother and the First Healer, and their looks in return suggested they wanted him to *listen*.

"The last few days have proven to be an educational experience for my clan," Cleo Newberry said. She looked the worse for wear, if Gabe was being honest. Which was no wonder—Gabe was aware of the clanspeople she'd lost. "Hunting down *Malum*, the Eighth Clan's part in it all, and the darkness and death that was the result of the Lost Soul. Being a witness to most of these events has led me to believe that Clan Kale has responded the best they could under the circumstances. I think we can all agree to that now."

She paused to look around the room, silently asking if there was any dissent. Many of the clans shifted uncomfortably.

"That may be," said a Moors who looked like he'd swallowed something sour. "But that's only for the events of the past few days. There is still the question of the Agora and who is responsible for the death of our *Sapienti*."

Cleo Newberry nodded in agreement. "I understand, Elias Verease. If the last few days have shown us anything, it's how important it is to have the facts of the situation. And you are correct: there is still one question to put to rest." She pulled a stone out of her pocket, a crystal of grey and bronze. "Clan Mayme has called for a tribunal to be held at Sage Estate. We will get to the bottom of these events. We will hold those responsible and charge them as *traitors*."

Gabe wondered if this was bad or good. Mel, obviously, couldn't speak as witness.

The other clans spoke among themselves for a few moments. Then Elias Verease stepped forward. "Clan Moors approves of this tribunal."

"As does Clan Ferus," said *Sapienti* O'Shea, nodding at Cleo Newberry.

"Clan Ivor as well."

"Clan Tam agrees."

Sapienti Mendez nodded her assent, which left one clan left.

Sapienti Reddy looked as if he was being backed into a corner. Gabe realized that the man probably didn't want his brother's part in the event to be on the record, but that was no reason to stall a tribunal, and refusing would only prove that the Janso Elder had something to hide. *Sapienti* Reddy must've realized this as well.

"Of course Clan Janso agrees," he said with a hard look at *Sapienti* Mendez. "We look forward to hearing the truth."

The meeting ended and everyone dispersed to make the needed arrangements. Cleo Newberry gave *Sapienti* Mendez a slight bow as she departed.

Once the Kales were alone, Gabe approached his grandmother and the First Healer. "So…" he said with a clap of his hands. "I'm gathering we've made an impression on that old bird."

Sapienti Mendez nodded. "That's your brother's doing. Unfortunately, we're going to have to introduce Mel to her before she leaves."

"What?" Gabe shook his head. "He *told* her?"

"Apparently there were agreements made during battle," the First Healer said drily. "He told her earlier today. She wanted to see Mel immediately for proof, but at least your brother had the good sense to say that wasn't possible—at least not right then at that moment. Though it was only Siva Reddy stepping in that led to Newberry agreeing to wait. A blood oath has been extracted."

"She's dead-set on standing before her and seeing with her own eyes," *Sapienti* Mendez said with a sigh. "But there's nothing for that now." She waved her hand, then looked at Gabe with serious eyes. "You will go to Sage Estate and give your testimony. You will share what you witnessed in the most damning light possible. You will do everything in your power to clear the clan of any wrongdoing."

Gabe raised his eyebrows. "That will involve sullying a good man." The late *Sapienti,* Hermanth Reddy—*Sapienti* Sandeep Reddy's brother and Siva's uncle.

Sapienti Mendez's slight frame was uncompromising. "Do what needs to be done, Gabe. When the tribunal is over, I don't want to hear another negative thing about Clan Kale. Understood?"

Gabe looked at his grandmother grimly and gave his assent. There wasn't anything else to do. The clan came first. Gabe would do what was required. He just hoped that Siva would understand.

****

Victor pressed himself to the wall, letting the two Ferus clansmen through. They carried a Kale on a stretcher, writhing in agony as he held one arm. It had become obvious within a few hours of the battle that some of the Eighth had laced their blades with poison, with the result that many Kales who had suffered what had seemed to be minor wounds were now fighting for their lives.

The Ferus placed the Kale on the very crowded floor of the infirmary and stepped away as Mayme healers moved in to do their work. When one of the Maymes pulled out a silver-bladed knife and cut into the Kale's wound, Victor quickly moved away as well—but the screams followed him as he left the infirmary and stepped outside into the dark, warm night.

There were still more wounded out here, in varying conditions, being worked on by Ferus, Tam, and Kale healers. Braziers smoldered with fires throughout. The moans of the pained were constant, and yet this scene was better than the one inside the infirmary, where the sicker patients were taken.

When he spotted Drew Wiley sitting alongside his sister, who was lying on the ground while Logan worked on her injuries, he started in their direction.

"Looks like hell, huh?" said Thrash, coming over and falling into step beside him.

Victor nodded. "This is what war looks like."

"I suppose it could be worse."

Victor agreed.

They reached the Wileys, and he saw that Justine was unconscious "How's she doing?" he asked Logan and Drew.

Logan tossed some bandages of pus and blood into a small fire that burned nearby. "I've gotten most of the poison out. She's comfortable now, and is finally getting some rest."

"But she's going to be okay, right?" Drew asked quietly from the other side of Justine.

"Yes, I believe so," Logan said, rising to her feet. "She's handled the poison better than most. I really think she's out of the woods. I'll check in later tonight—but call me if you need me." With that, she moved on to another patient.

Victor knelt down next to Justine. She looked like she was getting her color back.

"I think I'm going back to the house," Thrash said. "I need to check in on my sister. You coming, cousin?"

Victor shook his head. "Nah, I'm going to stay for a bit."

As Thrash left, Drew said, "You don't have to stay, Vic. I know you got people you're worried about, too, that you wanna check in on."

Victor shrugged, shifting so he could stretch his legs out in front of him. "Well, Gabe is fine, and the only one I really wanna check on at the moment is out like a light. I'm of more use out here."

Drew frowned, opened his mouth, then shut it and looked away.

"What?" Victor said. "You got something to say, say it."

Drew eyed him seriously. "You know you got more to look out for, Vic. Don't you think it's time you reached out?"

Victor felt a rush of anger. He almost unloaded on Drew right there in front of everyone. Instead he took a few steadying breaths until he calmed. And once he'd let go of the anger, he realized... Drew was right. Victor had been working up the courage to reach out to his wife for days. He'd given himself this reason or that as to why he shouldn't... but he'd be damned if he kept being a coward about it for one more minute.

He got up without another word and moved away from the infirmary, attempting to find someplace where he could have a bit of privacy. When he was alone, he pulled out the sat phone and dialed the familiar number, urging his wife over hundreds of miles to answer.

"Hello?"

Victor gripped the phone so tightly, he was afraid it would crack in his grasp. "Liz... it's me." His voice trembled with emotion. "It's Victor..."

He waited, hoping she wouldn't hang up.

"Finally," she said. She sounded relieved. "I've been calling your cell for days with no answer. I've been worried. Are you okay?"

Victor laughed and covered his eyes. He felt like crying. "I need you. Can you come here? With the kids? Please?"

It was so unsafe. It was probably the dumbest thing he'd ever done in his life, asking them to walk into *this*... but he couldn't do it anymore. He needed his family. He needed his wife close to him— the kids, too. They were the only thing that would keep him level-headed through the days ahead. And the house was the safest place to be now, with the wards and protections.

That was what he kept saying to himself. Long after his wife said yes. Long after she agreed to be there soon.

It's the safest place to be. It's safe. It's safe. It's safe.

It was a mantra. A hope. Born of nothing but his will and desire.

****

"Jesus Christ! You look so..." the words petered out. "I mean... you're alive... and it could be a lot worse..." A sigh of frustration, then the rest of the words came out in a rush: "I can't fucking believe they lost you! They had *one* fucking job! *One!* I leave you alone for a day—*a day*—and they fucking *lose* you! *You!*"

"You can't be there for me all the time, Cori," Mel responded softly.

She moved slowly out of bed, careful not to jostle the arm in the sling. Mordred had done some damage to her shoulder when he was playing his games, and it turned out that wounds from a Lost Soul's blade could be anywhere from *ridiculously easy* to *impossibly hard* to deal with depending on the day of the injury, the week, the year, the moon, the sun, the stars… As far as Mel could see, there was no method to it at all. She looked down at the black spider web near her collarbone. There was nothing for her to do now but trust the healers.

When she started to pull on one of her boots, Cori immediately pulled it out of her hand and forced Mel's foot in. She was a little rough about it, but Mel forgave her. She knew the Ferus had been through quite an ordeal. It had started with her feeling that Mel was in trouble—yet being able to do nothing but sit on her hands, ordered by her father to abide by the lockdown the Kales had enacted on the campgrounds. And waiting, Cori had said, was the worst kind of hell. Then, when Mel finally did show up again, she was a bloody, unconscious mess.

"I can damn well try," the Ferus bit out quietly, grabbing Mel's second boot and shoving it on. "If I'd been there…"

Mel put a hand on the woman's shoulder and waited until Cori looked her in the eye. "We're not going to do that. We're not going to put blame on ourselves when something bad happens to the other when we're not around. That's too much to put on anyone."

Cori sighed. She sat down next to Mel and—gingerly—put an arm around her. For a long moment she said nothing. Then: "You're right."

Mel smothered her smile. "I'm glad we agree. Because I need to tell you something." She paused. "I have to go to Villa Del Sol."

Cori snapped to her feet. "To fucking *Peru?*"

Mel put a hand on her again, trying to calm her, but Cori wasn't having it.

"They're fucking vipers, Mel! I've been there before—they are not made of the same stuff you and your family are."

"Cori—"

"No, listen to me, please." Cori got on her knees before Mel. "I went once, five years ago. They invited my father and brother, but my father wanted to show solidarity with your grandmother, so he refused the invitation and sent me instead." She moved a hand on top of Mel's. "There's this movement there, Mel. It was uncomfortable to watch and be around. They tried to impose it on me, but I... well, I ended up putting one of their strongest in the infirmary, and after that, they treated me as if I was male. The fact that I was gay only seemed to feed into it for some weird reason. But understand this: they only allowed it because I was not of their clan. Kale women who show that strength are *not* celebrated. They are cursed and beaten."

Mel closed her eyes and sighed. Her anger was a cold burn, not the uncontrolled rage she was used to. "Well, looks like I have three objectives in Villa de Sol. One, to figure out if what killed Blas Nunez is a curse or a protection. Two, to bring the Kale beast to heel. And three, do the same with my unruly clanspeople."

She tightened her hold on Cori's hand, but that didn't soothe the look on the Ferus's face. So Mel touched her forehead to Cori's.

"I'll be careful," she said. "I promise."

Cori blinked slowly, a softness in her eyes. "I want to kiss you—I mean *really* kiss you—but you're hurt and you've got a split lip..."

Mel tilted her head and smiled. And when she moved forward,

just an increment, Cori covered the rest of the distance. The kiss was gentle, and warm, and patient. So, so patient. And Mel couldn't get enough.

****

Mel and Cori walked together in the early morning before dawn. Mel did not take the path that the rest of her clanspeople took, instead choosing a wide path away from the crowd. Thomas followed discreetly behind. When they reached the clearing, they saw the funeral pyres—more than a hundred of them.

Mel's clan—men, women, and children—stood quietly, waiting for the beginning of the Death Rites. Mel marveled at their numbers. Many more must have arrived in the past day. She spotted her brothers, cousin, and uncles standing next to her grandmother. All in shiny gold tunics, veiled out of respect for the occasion.

Not far away were the other clans, segregated into small groups, standing just as quietly, just as respectfully.

A horn blew, and the ceremony began.

Mel's grandmother gave the last rites as the pyres were lit. Mel couldn't hear the words—she was too far away—but she'd heard them before, and knew them by heart.

> *The wind take your ashes*
> *To the earth, to the skies, to the seas*
> *May you find your way to the Otherworld*
> *May you find your way to peace*
> *Because Kale has you now*
> *And we will move forward indeed*
> *So fret nor fight no more*
> *May you find your way to peace*

The pyres burned. The smoke rose in plumes, reaching toward the sky. Mel felt the heat on her face and the burning in her eyes. Beside her, Cori took her hand, strong and sure, grounding her firmly in place. It was exactly what Mel needed. It was what kept her going long into the day, even after the pyres had burned down.

She, Cori, and Thomas were the last to leave. Only after the last of the pyres had completely burned out did they depart. And Mel and Cori walked, hand in hand, back toward the house.

Epilogue

It was mid-morning chaos in London's Underground. Commuters hurried to trains, desperate to get to work, bags were held overhead to avoid colliding with bodies—although often that just meant only briefcases and satchels struck faces and heads instead—and everyone was drenched. An hour before sunrise, the clouds had opened, the kind of downpour that soaks straight through clothing even on a short sprint to the Underground.

One man squeezed through a narrow space in the crush of bodies. He aimed for an opening and passed into the train tunnel itself, walking into a darkness where he knew no one would follow. He had dirty blond hair and hazel eyes, and his face had high, carved cheekbones and a square jaw. In a jacket slick with rain, he moved with purpose.

The train was coming—he could hear it approaching, squealing its presence. He looked at it only once before jumping toward a door along the wall, pushing the door open, and stepping through just as the train passed behind him.

"Close the door, Anton."

The speaker was an older gentleman. English. Clean-cut, in an expensive black suit.

Anton did as he was told, cutting off the noise of the train.

"I didn't think you would make it," said the older man. "I've heard disturbing news about you for the past few days."

"Lies," said Anton.

"I can see that," said the man, smirking. "You're obviously here. Very much not in chains."

Anton let his hazel eyes roam the room. It was desolate, just a maintenance room, with pipes running along the walls and a grey concrete floor. The fluorescent light overhead buzzed and flickered.

"I'm sorry about the Mendez girl," said the older man. "I'm sure you've heard by now that your plan was unsuccessful."

Anton furrowed his brow. The older man was taunting.

"It's unfortunate that things didn't turn out as planned. It seems we lost the entire southern US network," the older man said. "No one knows exactly what happened. We were hoping maybe you could shed some light."

Anton shook his head and looked away.

"Ah, that's unfortunate," said the older man. "Well, situations change."

The light buzzed and flickered.

"Well?" said the older man.

Anton met the man's eye.

"The stone, Anton. Give it to me."

Anton said nothing. Hazel eyes staring. A long moment passed.

"The fuck?" said the older man. "Are you hard of hearing? Give me the fucking stone."

"I don't have it."

"You don't fucking *have* it?" The older man's voice rose. "You don't fucking have the gateway stone?"

"No," Anton replied. He walked past the man to the door on the other side of the room. He opened it and looked out, seeing a long hallway. There was no one outside. "Excellent," he said.

"What the fuck is so excellent, you stupid fuck? You had one job—to bring the stone."

Anton closed the door and turned back around.

"Your name is Jamie Murphy," he said. "You're Warren Daniels's second."

"Yes, you fucking idiot," said Murphy, pulling out a knife. "And *you're* fucking dead."

Anton smiled, and his hazel eyes turned a shimmering gold.

Murphy paused, his hand squeezing his knife. "What the fuck are you?" he asked, slowly moving toward the door.

"What you always wanted to be," said Anton. But his voice had changed. It now had a subtle twang that didn't belong to someone from Greece.

If Murphy planned to flee, that plan was shattered when the door behind him opened, and two more figures stepped through. They had matching faces with short hair, brown eyes, and olive skin. They looked like teenage boys, but they could be girls as well. It was difficult to tell. They pulled thin steel daggers from their sleeves.

"Who are you? What do you want?" asked Murphy.

"To destroy the Eighth Clan," said Anton… or the man who *looked* like Anton. "But I need something from you first." The light flickered off then, plunging them into darkness. All but the glowing eyes. "For the Chieftress."

Then the three attacked.

Later, after the morning rush hour had passed, an older man walked out of a door into the London Underground. He was English, clean-cut, and in an expensive black suit. And he whistled as he walked the clear, wide-open halls.

Glossary

Aenigma—the puzzle; a competition within the Agora

Ambulant Laboriosum—the laborious walk; a competition within the Agora

Assurgere—to achieve honor above others

Decerto—to fight (to fight to the finish); a competition within the Agora for both weapons and hand-to-hand combat

Eligendo—the choosing ceremony

Exhaustus—the draining of celestial powers

Hae—the history of the seven Originals and their clans; also considered a teaching of *The Ways Impedimentum*—the obstacle course; a competition within the Agora

Inter Spatium Abyssus—the world between hell

Inter Spatium Caelum—the world between heaven

Libero—lifting; a competition within the Agora

Malum—demons

Sapienti—wise one, Elder of a clan

Seniorem—a senior Journeyman; officer in charge

Supervivere—a teaching of *The Ways* that instructs clanspeople how to survive any situation

Tenebrae Transeunt—the gate between *Inter Spatium Abyssus* and the world of the living

Author's Note

Thank you so much for reading *Dead Woman's Curse*. I hope you enjoyed reading about the new adventures of Mel and her brothers as much as I enjoyed writing about them.

If you enjoyed reading this novel, please leave a review. As a self-published author, reviews are essential and will help this novel reach other readers.

Also, if you'd like to stay up-to-date with what I'm working on, please follow me using the below links:

Website: kmmartinezauthor.com

Twitter: twitter.com/kmmartinezauth

Instagram: instagram.com/kmmartinezauthor/

Facebook: facebook.com/kmmartinezauthor/

About the Author

K.M. Martinez was born and raised in San Antonio, Texas. She spends most of her days with friends and family. She is also an avid baker, enjoys undertaking home improvement projects, and cheering on her favorite sports teams.

Ingram Content Group UK Ltd.
Milton Keynes UK
UKHW040946010623
422707UK00004B/122